VIRGO

CORONA
BOREALIS

THE LAW
OF SIMILARS

a novel by

Chris Bohjalian

HERCULES

DRACO

LITTLE DIPPER

POLARIS

PUBLISHER'S NOTE: This is a work of fiction. The names, characters, places, and incidents either are the product of the author's imagination or are used fictitiously, and any resemblance to actual persons, living or dead, events, or locales is entirely coincidental.

Acknowledgment is gratefully made to Cooper Publishing for use of the Samuel Hahnemann quotes from the sixth edition of his *Organon of Medicine*.

Copyright © 1999 by Chris Bohjalian

Published by Harmony Books, a division of Crown Publishers, Inc., 201 East 50th Street, New York, New York 10022. Member of the Crown Publishing Group.

Random House, Inc. New York, Toronto, London, Sydney, Auckland
www.randomhouse.com

HARMONY and colophon are trademarks of Crown Publishers, Inc.

Printed in the United States of America

Design by LYNNE AMFT

Library of Congress Cataloging-in-Publication Data

Bohjalian, Christopher A.
    The law of similars / by Chris Bohjalian. — 1st ed.
    I. Title.
  PS3552.0495L39   1999
  813'.54—dc21   98–15807

ISBN 0-517-70586-9

10 9 8 7 6 5

FOR SHAYE AREHEART

Has it not got down as thin as the homeopathic soup that was made by boiling the shadow of a pigeon that had starved to death?

ABRAHAM LINCOLN
OCTOBER 13, 1858

✧

A merry heart doeth good like a medicine: but a broken spirit drieth the bones.

PROVERBS 17:22

THE LAW
OF SIMILARS

PROLOGUE

For almost two full years after my wife died, I slept with my daughter. Obviously, this wasn't Abby's idea (and I think, even if it were, as her father I'd insist now on taking responsibility). After all, she was only two when the dairy delivery truck slammed into her mother's Subaru wagon and drove the mass of chrome and rubber and glass down the embankment and into the shallow river that ran along the side of the road.

In all fairness, of course, it wasn't my idea either. At least the two years part. I'd never have done it once if I'd realized it would go on for so long.

But about a week after Elizabeth's funeral, when Abby and I were just starting to settle into the routine that would become our life, I think the concept that Mommy really and truly wasn't coming back became a tangible reality in my little girl's mind—more real, perhaps, than the lunch box I packed every night for day care, or the stuffed animals that lined the side of her bed against the wall. It happened after midnight. She awoke and called for Mommy and I came instead, and I believe that's exactly when something clicked inside her head: *There is no Mommy. Not tonight, not tomorrow, not ever again.*

And so she had started to howl.

Forty-five minutes later, she was still sobbing, and my arms had become lead wings from holding her and rocking her and pacing the room with her head on my shoulder. I think that's when I paced out the door of her room and into mine. Into what had been my wife's and my room. There I placed her upon Elizabeth's side of the bed, pulled the quilt up to her chin, and wrapped one pajamaed arm around her small, heaving back. And there, almost abruptly, she fell asleep. Sound asleep. Boom, out like a light.

Later I decided it was the simple smell of her mother on the pillowcase that had done the trick. I hadn't changed the sheets on the bed in the week and a half since Elizabeth had died.

Of course, it might also have been the mere change of venue. Maybe Abby understood that she wasn't going to be left alone that night in that bed; she knew I wasn't going to kiss her once on her forehead and then go someplace else to doze.

The next night it all happened again, and it happened almost exactly the same way. I awoke when I heard her cries in the dark and went to her room, and once again I murmured "Shhhhh" by her ear until the single syllable sounded like the sea in my head, while Abby just sobbed and sobbed through the waves. Finally I navigated the hallway of the house like a sleepwalker, my little girl in my arms, and placed her upon what had been Elizabeth's side of the bed, her head atop what had been Elizabeth's pillow.

This time as I lay down beside her I realized that I was tearing, too, and I was relieved that she'd fallen instantly asleep. The very last thing she needed was the knowledge that Daddy was crying with her.

Was the third night an exact replica of nights one and two? Probably. But there my memory grows fuzzy. Had Abby asked me at dinner that evening if she could sleep yet again in Mommy and Daddy's room? In my room, perhaps? Or had I just carried her upstairs one evening at eight o'clock—after dinner and her bath, after we'd watched one of her videos together in the den, Abby curled up in my lap—and decided to read to her in my room instead of hers? I haven't a clue. All I know is that at some point our routine changed, and I was putting Abby to sleep in my bed before coming back downstairs to wash the dinner dishes and make sure her knapsack was packed for day care the next day: Her lunch, a juice box, two sets of snacks. Extra underpants in case of an accident, as well as an extra pair of pants. A sweater eight or nine months of the year. The doll of the moment. Tissues. Lip balm when she turned three and developed a taste for cherry Chap Stick.

I rarely came upstairs before eleven-thirty at night because I had my own work to tend to after I'd put Abby's life in order—depositions and motions and arguments, the legal desiderata that was my life—but once I was in bed, invariably I would quickly doze off. The bed was big, big enough for me and my daughter and the stuffed animals and trolls and children's books that migrated one by one from her room to mine. And I reasoned that after all Abby had been through and would yet have to endure, it was only fair for me to give her whatever it took to make her feel safe and sleep soundly.

Occasionally, I'd wake in the middle of the night to find Abby sitting up in bed with her legs crossed. She'd be staring at me in the glow of the nightlight and smiling, and often she'd giggle when she'd see my eyes open.

"Let's play Barbie," she'd say. Or, "Can we do puzzles?"

"It's the middle of the night, punkin," I'd say.

"I'm not sleepy."

"Well, I am."

"Pleeeeeeeease?"

"Okay, you can. But you can't turn on the light."

In the morning, I'd see she'd fallen back to sleep at the foot of the bed with a Barbie in one hand and a plastic troll in the other. Or she'd fallen asleep while looking at the pictures in one of her books, the book open upon her chest as if she were really quite adult.

I learned early that she would sleep through my music alarm in the morning. And so I would usually get up at five-thirty to shower and shave, so that I could devote from six-thirty to seven-thirty to getting her dressed and fed, her teeth brushed, and a good number (though never all) of the snarls dislodged from her fine, hay-colored hair. I usually had her at the day care in the village by twenty to eight, and so most days I was at my desk between eight-fifteen and eight-thirty.

I think it was a few weeks after Abby's fourth birthday, when she was taking a bath and I was on the floor beside the tub skimming the newspaper as she pushed a small menagerie of toy sharks and sea lions and killer whales around in the water, that I looked up and saw she was standing. She was placing one of the whales in the soap dish along the wall, and I realized all of her baby fat was gone. At some point she had ceased to be a toddler, and in my head I heard the words, *It's time to move out, kid. We're getting into a weird area here.*

The next morning at breakfast I broached the notion that she return to the bedroom in which she'd once slept, and which still housed her clothes and all of the toys that weren't residing at that moment on my bed. Our bed. The bigger bed. And she'd been fine. At first I'd feared on some level her feelings were hurt, or she was afraid she had done something wrong. But then I understood she was simply digesting the idea, envisioning herself in a bed by herself.

"And you'll still be in your room?" she asked me.

"Of course."

That night she slept alone for the first time in almost twenty-three months, and the next morning it seemed to me that she had done just fine. When I went to her room at six-thirty, she was already wide awake. She was sitting up in bed with the light on, and it was clear she'd been reading her picture books for at least half an hour. The pile of books beside her was huge.

I, on the other hand, wasn't sure how well I had done. I'd woken up in the night with a cold—what I have since come to call *the* cold. A runny nose, watery eyes. A sore throat. The predictable symptoms of a profoundly common ailment, the manifestations of a disease that decades of bad ad copy have made us believe is wholly benign. Unpleasant but treatable, if you just know what to buy.

There was, in my mind, no literal connection between evicting my daughter and getting sick, no cause and effect. But it was indeed a demarcation of sorts. The cold came on in the middle of that night, the cold that—unlike every cold I'd ever had before—would not respond to the prescription-strength, over-the-counter tablets and capsules and pills that filled my medicine chest.

The cold that oozy gel caps couldn't smother, and nighttime liquids couldn't drown.

Indeed, things began spiraling around me right about then. Not that night, of course, and not even the next day. It actually took months. But when I look back on all that I did and all that I risked—when I look back on the litany of bad decisions I made—it seems to me that everything started that night with that cold: the very night my daughter slept alone in her room for the first time in two years.

✧

People who meet me now would be astonished to know there was a point in my life when I was wary of what I once called alternative medicine.

My mind, to them, must seem open and tolerant and wide. After all, I have a small vial of peppermint oil for headaches. When Abby and I fly, we take ginger instead of Dramamine. And when others tell me they have regained the lost parts of their health with Reiki or reflexology, with kinesiology or craniosacral therapy—with color therapy, music therapy, myotherapy, or hypnotherapy—I no longer nod warily, secretly relieved that we're not a part of the same HMO.

And I know well that the bridge between body and mind is sturdy. Sometimes I'm more convinced that we can worry ourselves ill than that we can will ourselves well, but for better or worse, I understand that the link between what we think is going on inside us and the daily battles that occur in our bones and bladders and spleens is more pronounced than we understand. We know a lot more than we realize.

Carissa Lake, my first homeopath, taught me that.

When what would prove to be the longest week of my life was over—longer by far than even the week after my wife died, since most of that week I spent in a fog—my sister, Diana, said I should have seen it coming. She said the walls and the ceiling of Carissa Lake's office should have tipped me off the moment I stepped through the door.

Maybe. But Carissa had had a lot of patients before me, and none of them did what I did. Most of them, I know, would simply have given Carissa testimonials that ranged from glowing to benign. And I've yet to find a homeopath who would quibble with the remedy she prescribed for me. The fact is, it worked.

Nevertheless, those walls of hers were controversial. They still are. Even now no one has rented the space she was using, and the building's owner hasn't bothered to paint over the walls. (I understand there was some talk that the family was going to roll gallons of primer and sealer across the murals, but I think that talk was just rumor. Apparently, it was even suggested at a selectmen's meeting that the town pay the landlord to have the walls repainted, but that idea smacked of salting the rubble of Frankenstein's castle, and the discussion didn't last very long.)

There is, as far as I know, no room like it in all of Vermont. There are other ceilings with paintings, of course, though not very many. But certainly there are no other replicas of the night sky over Paris. Over Le Cimetière du Père Lachaise.

Actually, *replica* is inaccurate. The constellations are perfectly aligned, and the view of Paris that fills the northern and eastern walls is essentially what one would have seen from the highest point in the twentieth arrondissement in 1843—the year homeopathy founder Samuel Hahnemann died. But the real vault of heaven is never the eddies of purple and black and gray that the painter chose in consultation with her for the sky. Had the night sky been authentically dark, the room would have been depressing and dim—especially since she had one of the three large windows in the room walled up, so the spire of Sainte-Chapelle would not be conspicuously absent from the vista.

Apparently, the French-Canadian painter had known nothing about homeopathy when they met, but before he started to work, he dutifully skimmed the books she had given him about Hahnemann, and the one specifically about Hahnemann's much younger wife, Melanie. She, too, was a homeopath. And it was clear that the painter also read the books she loaned him by renegade Jungians about something they called the soul, some of which had been bubbling along on best-seller lists for years.

She said that they talked all the time as he labored, and he'd asked her all kinds of questions about homeopathy and her work. He knew she was a psychologist as well as a homeopath.

"Why," she remembered him asking one evening, his voice heavily accented from his childhood in eastern Quebec, "do you want the view to be from a cemetery? This Père Lachaise? You're a healer. It seems to me you'd want the view to be from someplace about life."

"Hahnemann is buried at Père Lachaise," she told him.

"If this is about Hahnemann, then why not pick a view from a place where he lived? The book said he lived near Montmartre for a while. The views of Paris from Montmartre are spectacular."

"You've never been to Père Lachaise?"

"No."

And so she said she'd described for him the small city of aboveground monuments: a hundred thousand tombstones and sepulchers—well over a million bodies—crowded into a mere one-hundred-plus acres. She told him about the thin cobblestone avenues and pathways between the plots, and the fact that there is almost no grass. No space. No fields. Just rows and rows of marble and stone ascending a hill, a series of seemingly endless ranges of magnificent memorials and crypts and mausoleums, some twenty and thirty and forty feet high.

"Balzac is buried there," she told him. "And Proust and Piaf and Richard Wright." As well as, she could have added, Jim Morrison and Frédéric Chopin. Isadora Duncan and Simone Signoret.

Now and then the room would scare one of her patients, and it would take her a moment to calm him. For a time she even feared that she'd made a colossal mistake, and the room was doing exactly the opposite of what it was meant to: Instead of offering the sick who had come to her for help a place so surreal and unexpected that they could open their minds to the possibilities of homeopathy, it was jarring them. Alarming them. It didn't matter that only the tips of tombstones or statuary were visible on the walls, and only then in two lower corners. The fact remained, few of her patients had ever seen a ceiling with stars, and fewer still had ever seen a wall that was a painting—in this case, two walls. A trompe l'oeil of spires, towers, and the crosses that stood atop distant churches. Waves of small buildings with roofs of gray slate.

She thought it was lovely; they—some, not all—thought it was downright disconcerting.

Over time, however, word of Carissa's room spread, and eventually most people just viewed it as the local homeopath's eccentricity. Everyone had one; this was hers. And so when people came to see her, they knew what to expect. A chance for healing. A room with a view.

Carissa's office was on the westernmost quarter of the top floor of the old school building in Bartlett. But the clapboard octagon hadn't schooled children in almost three generations, and for many of those years had been absolutely vacant inside. Had it not been situated between the village's thriving Catholic church and the post office, it probably would have fallen into complete disrepair. It might have become the hangout in which the town's teens experimented with illegal substances and tried to discover the difference between short, furtive wrestling matches and intercourse.

At some point in the mid-1980s, however, as more and more New Yorkers and Bostonians began taking pride in their downward mobility and migrated north to Vermont, even Bartlett developed the need for an office building of sorts, and the three-story octagon was converted into the closest thing the village had to a white-collar skyscraper. Lawyers and a CPA on the first floor. A little insurance company on the second. A massage therapist, a travel agent, and a homeopath on the third.

I had never met Carissa Lake before I called and we spoke on the phone about my cold. I was vaguely aware that there was a woman in town who was involved in some esoteric form of healing, and I'd heard about the walls of the Octagon. The ones on the highest floor. In hindsight, I'm not even sure that I knew the woman and the walls were related until her niece made the connection clear to me in—and the irony is inescapable—the health-food store.

When I did make the connection, I don't believe I was any less interested in seeing her. To the contrary, I probably wanted to meet her even more.

✧

This is not just my story, of course. Nor is it simply Carissa's.

In many ways, it's Richard Emmons's story, though I said barely more than a word to the man in his life, and he never, that I can recall, said a single word to me. But I know his wife and I've met his children.

And now Jennifer Emmons knows the peculiar bond that Richard and I share, the strange ways we are linked. Hubris and hypochondria. Homeopathy and hope. Carissa, of course.

Carissa is what makes our link tangible.

In that short period in which Jennifer and I had the chance to be friends— that brief window before she heard the rumors of what I had done—she shared her memories with me.

After all, she thought I was an ally.

She told me, for example, about that time she was in bed with Richard at the very end of the fall, and she felt him suddenly sit up beside her and wheeze. She remembered how she had opened her eyes and seen darkness.

The sun had not yet begun to lighten the sky; they were still in the darkest part of the night. She was careful not to allow her eyes to roam toward the foot of the bed, because if they had, she would have seen the digital clock on the bureau near the door, and she would have known exactly what time it was. She would have learned whether she had a mere ninety minutes left to sleep or a languid three or four hours.

Long ago she had discovered that she fell back to sleep more quickly if she didn't know the time, if she didn't know her place in the night. The alarm would wake her when it was time to get up.

Her mind formed the words, *Honey, are you all right? Richard? Are you okay?* But she knew the answer. He was, more or less. Not completely fine, not completely okay—he'd needed his inhaler a lot lately, he'd been extremely short of breath—but, for the moment, he was all right. This wouldn't become a full-blown attack, she had thought. They almost never did. And so she'd remained silent. This, too, would help ensure that she'd fall back to sleep.

She recalled listening to him opening the drawer of the night table beside him and reaching inside for the inhaler. She heard the click when he popped off the plastic tip that covered the mouthpiece. The half-second-long whistle of the medicine as it was propelled in a spray into his lungs, an initial burst of air that sounded a bit like her son Timmy's air hockey game when he first turned it on. Richard had used his inhaler twice that night; he'd given himself two blasts. With each one he'd taken a deep breath and held it for what must have felt to him like a long while.

Jennifer remembered wondering that night if Richard was ever scared. She knew she would be. That night she couldn't imagine anything scarier than not being able to breathe.

"I can now," she said when she related this memory to me.

She'd hoped that night that he would call the doctor in the morning. They'd discussed it earlier in the evening, and he'd said he would if his breathing didn't improve. After all, this had been going on for a couple of days. God, the poor thing, she had thought. But then she had reassured herself that this, too, would be fine in the end, because Richard was reasonable and Richard would call his doctor, and his doctor would give him some prednisone.

And maybe something for his hands—for that skin thing that had come back. It was, she knew, the eczema that seemed to tag along with the asthma that really disturbed Richard. He was sure it repulsed other people, because he himself found it so disgusting. And, of course, it itched. It could itch like chicken pox.

Maybe the doctor would have something better this time than Eucerin cream. Sometimes the Eucerin worked. But sometimes it didn't.

At the very least, however, the doctor would give Richard some prednisone. That's what had worked the last time. Last year. A few days on prednisone, and he'd been as good as new.

Prednisone. Theophylline. The white inhaler. The blue inhaler. That thing that looked like a pistol, with a barrel he put in his mouth. An Aero-Chamber.

Sometimes, Jennifer told me, she would come home from the animal hospital aware that she might be making his asthma worse. After all, he was allergic to cats. And so she never wore in the house the fleece sweatshirts and sweaters and turtleneck shirts that she donned the few days a week she was neutering kittens or giving adult cats their annual vaccinations. She had, essentially, two completely separate wardrobes: one covered with dander she stored in a closet at the animal hospital and wore Thursdays and Saturdays, and one she kept at home and wore the rest of the week.

Still, she knew well that feeling of worry: *I'm making it worse.*

That night when he'd finally lain back in bed, his face toward the nightstand, she'd rolled over and pulled him close and then drawn the quilt over them both.

She was unsure whether he called Carissa the very next morning, or whether it was a day or two later. She was certain it was within a week or ten days. But only the very basics of the chronology will ever be fully clear: A half hour after she pulled the quilt over their shoulders, she was driving as fast as she could to the hospital. To the emergency room. There he was given steroids and oxygen, and the attack subsided.

And Richard indeed called his physician the next morning, and he in fact saw him that afternoon.

But had he already phoned the homeopath as well? Or would he make that call days later? Perhaps when he was, once more, off prednisone?

Jennifer told me that she wished she knew exactly when the end had begun. She said she wished she hadn't thought to herself that night after he'd used his inhaler and she'd snuggled against him, At least people don't die of asthma.

Because of course they did. Especially, in her opinion, if they were in the wrong hands.

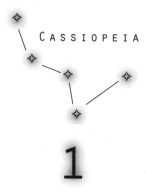

CASSIOPEIA

1

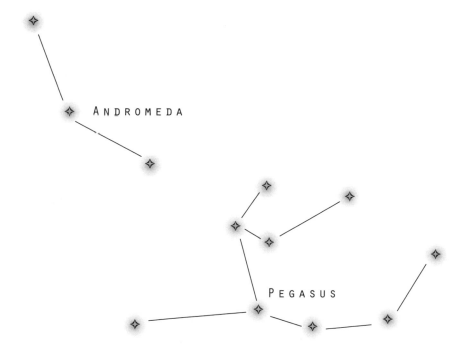

ANDROMEDA

PEGASUS

1

N U M B E R 7

A single symptom is no more the whole disease than a single foot a whole man.

D R . S A M U E L H A H N E M A N N ,
O r g a n o n o f M e d i c i n e , 1 8 4 2

W h e n I a w o k e a f t e r s l e e p i n g a l o n e f o r the first time in almost two years, I hoped I was wrong about the cold. I was pretty sure it had made itself right at home behind my eyes and deep in my throat, but I still wanted to fight it. I was too busy for a cold, it was just that simple.

Wasn't it hard enough just getting Abby out the door in the morning, and then keeping up with the endless pageant of wife beaters, drunk drivers, and petty thieves who paraded through the Chittenden County court system every day?

And wasn't my house alone sufficiently burdensome? I was determined to raise Abby in the only home she'd ever known, a century-old farmhouse I'd purchased with Elizabeth in East Bartlett—a small collection of houses, a church, and a general store in the hills six miles east of the main village itself. It was on a paved road and it had a paved driveway, but otherwise a realtor would have been hard put to call it convenient—especially for a single father working almost twenty miles away.

Often it was a nightmare just leaving Burlington in time to be back in Bartlett by six-thirty at night so I could retrieve my daughter from the various homes around the day-care center where she would stay between five P.M.—

when the day care closed its doors for the day—and the moment I arrived in the village. Some months, Abby would spend that hour and a half at the home of the neighbors to the north of the center, with a nice, playful sixteen-year-old with the inappropriately elderly name of Mildred. But Mildred played field hockey in the fall and softball in the spring, and so other months Abby would wind up in the house just to the south, spending those ninety minutes with the legitimately elderly—and aptly named—Henrietta Cousino.

No, I told myself, I could not cope with a cold. At least not a bad one. And so that night I went to bed early. With Abby's help, I whipped up a batch of Kraft macaroni and cheese, allowing my four-year-old to pour the packet of neon powder into the pot and onto the counter, and then add the milk—slopping no more than a quarter-cup onto the floor. I remember it was Abby's turn to pick the vegetable ("Can mayonnaise be our vegetable tonight?") and say grace ("Thank you, God, for the food and the stars and my new Barbie Dream House. Amen."), but it was my turn to choose the movie we'd watch after dinner, and so I picked the shortest tape in my child's ever-swelling collection: three antique Gumby stories her aunt—my sister—in New Hampshire had recorded.

I managed to get Abby upstairs in her room by eight, and I was done reading to her by eight-thirty. I left the downstairs a shambles—the macaroni-and-cheese pot in the sink, the plates on the counter, Abby's Barbies and trolls and plastic dwarfs scattered like confetti across the den floor—and was in my own bed by quarter past nine. The last thing I did before going upstairs was pop a cold reliever rich with chemicals I still can't pronounce, and chase the tablet with a big glass of orange juice.

I hoped that the pill would, as the box warned, cause drowsiness. Sleep was exactly what I wanted that night.

When I awoke in the morning, the cold was worse. I ached and my eyes were two spheres of itch. The back of my throat was raw from the waterfall that had begun cascading behind my nose as I'd slept.

Of course, the idea of calling my doctor didn't even cross my mind. This was, after all, a cold. The important thing was to wash my hands and face like a madman around Abby. Pour Lucky Charms and Kix, wash hands. Pour milk. Wash hands again.

Eventually, over the next day or two, my nose did stop running. The nasal glacier in the back of my head receded, and my eyes no longer yearned to be rubbed and pressed and scratched.

The problem was that I still felt…out of sorts. Out of kilter. Out of whack. I just didn't feel great. As the summer slowly gave way to the fall, I told myself that I was simply exhausted, beaten down by the demands of the way I had chosen to live my life. I decided that sometime that winter, perhaps in January, Abby and I would take a vacation. I'd find a Caribbean resort with the hemisphere's most creative and nurturing children's program, and the two of us would go someplace warm and fun.

On that island I might even meet a woman, and the two of us would have monster amounts of sex. Maybe, in addition to being the author of a best-selling handbook on sex, she'd be the perfect new mother for Abby.

That summer I seemed to be fantasizing often about finding the perfect woman for both father and daughter. But I also thought frequently of Elizabeth. Sometimes it would be the desperate way that I'd loved the small of her back—the river of spine that disappeared abruptly into the land just below her waist—and sometimes it would be the astonishingly quick and clever way she could make Abby's lunch those nights it was her turn. Juice box, pieces of apple or apple sauce, pretzels, cookies, a small tangle of spaghetti and sauce in a dish that could be zapped in the center's microwave oven. Maybe a banana and some goldfish-shaped crackers.

She'd worked in Burlington, too, and some days we'd have lunch together, a luxurious treat in the middle of our harried, gray-suited lives. She was a commercial loan officer in the main branch of a bank only two blocks from the courthouse where I spent most of my days.

Somehow, she was always back in Bartlett by five.

To this day, I have no idea how she did it. Just no idea.

✧

In an effort to feel better, I started to make small changes in my life that seemed, at first, easy to implement. I cut back from seven or eight cups of coffee a day to a mere five or six, and I made some of those cups decaf. Then I threw my old toothbrush away, even though I knew that my body had already built an immunity to any germ on those pathetic, curlicue bristles.

For a while, I even had fruit for breakfast—and nothing but fruit—instead of the doughnuts or bear claws that I usually bought on my way into work.

And yet while I discovered that Abby loved melon, it was hard to find the time to split a honeydew each morning, or pull the seeds from a watermelon slice. It was difficult to finish getting dressed with banana peel slime on my hands. A doughnut at my desk was just so much easier.

But no one said good health was going to be easy, and so for a time I went to the health club I'd joined before Elizabeth died. Clearly it was going to be impossible to go there before or after work, and so I tried working out during lunch. But then what seemed to be my annual murder trial began, and this one would take some effort because there was no witness or weapon. The defendant, an auto dealer whose affluence stemmed from the enormous amounts of hashish he was floating into the country via Lake Champlain and not from the cars that he sold, had shot a fisherman who'd stumbled upon his operation in a cove just south of the border.

I'd probably gone to the health club next to the courthouse a dozen times before the trial began. Once it was under way, though, I had to begin relying instead on isometrics in the car and in meetings and while sitting through testimony that was particularly irritating because it was perjurious.

And then the cold came back in full force, just about the time that the trial ended and the dealer was sent to prison for whole generations. In all likelihood, I decided, I'd never kicked the disease. It had been lurking inside me all along, resting, rallying, and now it was back. I really never had gotten better.

This time I didn't expect to defeat it with mere OTC cold relievers or big glasses of juice. I decided to get a physical. It had been, after all, years.

"What's wrong?" my doctor asked, and I told him that I hadn't been feeling well for months, and I had a cold that seemed to want to stick around.

He nodded. My doctor was tall and trim and muscular. He was probably fifty, but it was clear he could bench-press 240 pounds and run two miles without breaking a sweat.

I, on the other hand, was pretty sure I couldn't walk two miles without needing cardiopulmonary resuscitation.

And so the physical began. I squatted and breathed, I gave up blood and blood pressure. I lay flat on my back for the EKG, I rolled on my side and curled my knees up to my chest for the glove. I grew embarrassed about the ten or fifteen too many pounds I couldn't hide on the scale.

And then I listened as my doctor told me that I really must start getting some exercise. I really must drop ten pounds. I really must start eating right.

The lab results would be back in a few days.

"My cholesterol might be a little high," I heard myself saying, and then I thought: A little high? Oh, please. It's going to be interplanetary.

A week later, I got a letter that said my blood work was indeed normal and my cholesterol was indeed high—though, actually, it wasn't as high as I'd feared. That week without bear claws might really have helped.

Overall verdict? Healthy.

Perhaps as a consequence, for a week or two my cold symptoms seemed less severe, and my throat felt less raw. I rarely felt woozy or light-headed; I slept through most nights. I told myself I was on the mend.

Eventually, however, it grew clear to me that I wasn't. The cold was still inside me somewhere; I still felt out of sync.

Some days, I'd wonder if I was a hypochondriac. *Maybe that's it,* I'd tell myself. *You're a wimp. It's your head that's screwed up, not your body.*

Of course I'd take some pleasure in this possibility. Not only did it suggest that my body was doing, more or less, what it was supposed to, it meant I was still growing as a person: Thirty-five years old, and I was still gaining new insights into what it meant to be Leland Fowler, even if Leland's nose happened to be running like a snow-swollen river in March.

Yet it was difficult to see a bright side to all this in the middle of the night. In the middle of the night, I woke up really and truly frightened. When I'd been sick and Elizabeth had been alive, there was always her reassuring presence at three in the morning. Often, her nearness alone would remind me that there was more to my world than my cold or my flu or my twenty-four-hour bug.

I hope I'm not keeping her awake, I would think, as I tossed and turned. I hope I'm not so restless she, too, is losing sleep.

I began to wonder if I had allowed Abby to stay so long in my room because I had needed someone else there. I thought I'd been doing it for my little girl, but perhaps I'd been doing it for myself instead. Perhaps I'd needed a focus away from my own sadness and grief and fear.

Now alone in my bed in the night, I could only look inward and speculate: Just what did that occasional dizziness mean when I'd bend over to pick up a dime or a pen or a section of the newspaper? What about those headaches? They were always in the same spot. And sometimes, it seemed, it had gotten hard to swallow. My throat would grow sore for days at a time, and I'd wonder if I was becoming addicted to Halls Mentho-Lyptus.

Had Elizabeth been alive, she would have stopped me from going quite so squirrelly. She would have reminded me that I was being ridiculous, she would have told me—either at breakfast or, for all I know, at three A.M.—that it was highly unlikely I was dying.

But I didn't have her. And the pictures of her by the bed didn't speak.

✧

By day, of course, things seemed better. In the morning, I'd see how silly I'd been. Still: Those nights alone were scary and long.

When almost another whole season had gone by, marked more in my mind by Halloween and Abby's macabre desire that the two of us trick-or-treat together as skeletons ("You be the daddy skeleton and I'll be the little girl skeleton, and we'll make everyone so scared they'll give us their candy!") than by the fact that my baby was suddenly in preschool four days a week, I finally decided it was time for the heavy artillery. The big guns.

And so on my way home from the courthouse one evening, before turning onto the street of houses in the village in which my daughter was waiting for me with Henrietta Cousino, I stopped by the health-food store and bought a little bottle of echinacea. The tincture was dark, the bottle as well as the fluid, and it came with an eyedropper. I bought it upon the advice of a woman in sandals with fantastic toes—just the tiniest sickle-moon of white on each nail. She probably knew what was good for you, I decided: It was almost mid-November, for God's sake, and she looked healthy and fit. Even her feet looked good, and I had never been into feet. She must have been ten years older than I was, maybe fifteen, but her skin was smooth, her eyes were bright—as bright as the blue on the Actifed box—and I loved the metal shine to her swirls and swirls of gray hair.

"What exactly is echinacea?" I asked.

"An herb," she said, and the word *herb* had never sounded so sexy. From this woman it sounded like a purr; it was a gentle, cooing, polysyllabic moan: heeerrrrrrrrbb. "That's all. An herbal extract, to be precise. Do you know what coneflowers look like?"

"My wife grew them."

"Well, the roots of that beautiful plant are the source. The tincture you have in your hands also has burdock in it. And gentian. Wood betony. And goldenseal. We also carry an echinacea without goldenseal, but from what you tell me, I'd recommend your trying some with it."

"Is goldenseal also an…herb?" I asked, hoping I, too, could make the word sound like foreplay. (I couldn't. From my lips, a drawn-out *herb* sounded more like a stutter than a verbal aphrodisiac.)

"It is. It's an antibacterial. Sometimes it helps clear the sinuses."

"I am pretty sniffly, aren't I?"

"Oh, no. Not at all."

"How much should I take?"

"A couple eyedroppers a day."

"In water?"

"You can. I prefer it in herbal tea."

"I'll bet I would, too," I told her, knowing how much I despised herbal tea. I told myself I was lying to make this woman feel good about her suggestion, and therefore about herself. I appalled myself by looking at her left hand to see if there was a ring.

"Do you need any?"

"Any…"

"Tea?"

"Tea. Yes, sure." And I bought a box of caffeine-free, wild-cherry black-berry tea, exactly the one she recommended. There was a vaguely Nordic, vaguely Grimm-like painting on the top of the box of two little children in lederhosen gathering berries the size of footballs. They were surrounded by birch trees.

That night I tried both the echinacea (an abomination that was acidic and bitter at once) and the tea (less abominable, but only because it was boring and watery instead of acidic and bitter). The next morning, I dropped the precious echinacea into my orange juice, and I discovered that a big glass could mask the taste. At lunch I buried the stuff in my coffee, aware on some level that the coffee was probably neutralizing the benefits of the miracle herb extract, and at dinner I simply swilled it as fast as I could in a glass of tap water.

"What's that?" Abby asked, looking skeptically at the tumbler with swirls of brown. Marsh water, I thought: I'm drinking marsh water.

"I think it's ground-up flowers," I said.

"Yuck! Why are you drinking *that*?"

I tossed back my head and emptied the glass. "It's supposed to be good for you. Want some?"

"No. I like grape juice."

"Good choice."

For a week and a day I took my echinacea, and suddenly the bottle was empty. I wasn't sure if I was feeling better, but I knew I wanted to return to the health-food store. I wanted to hear that woman say *herb* again, I wanted to see her toes and her feet and (just maybe) her slender ankles in November.

And so all the way home I thought about what I would say to her. I imagined telling her how much better I felt, how I was so glad—so grateful—that she'd suggested an herb called echinacea.

By the time I arrived in the health-food store's parking lot the sky was dark, but the lights were on in the clapboard building that had once been a home. I didn't see the woman I wanted, and so I told myself she must be someplace in the back.

Once inside, I scanned the aisles, my eyes bouncing over the organic fruits and vegetables trucked in from someplace far to the south, darting between the teas and bulgur and hummus. She was nowhere to be seen.

"Can I help you?"

I turned, hoping against hope that the voice belonged to the lady with the drapes of soft silver hair, but it didn't. I knew that the moment I'd heard it, but still I hoped I was wrong.

"Yes. Sure."

The voice belonged to a woman a decade my junior. Mid-twenties. For all I knew, she was even younger than that. She may have still been in college. Maybe she worked here after class. But in some way she reminded me of the older woman I had met the week before. She, too, was wearing sandals despite the approach of another New England winter, and she, too, was wearing a flouncy peasant skirt. (I tried not to think of it as the shade of red on the Actifed box, but the vividness of the dye was unmistakable.) The top two buttons of her white blouse were undone, just enough that I could glimpse the hint of an ivory bra. I looked away fast. A reflex.

"What do you need?" She smiled. Perfect white teeth. A headband pulling back blond hair that fell just below her ears. Incandescent green eyes.

"I need echinacea."

She nodded and started toward the aisle of dark little bottles. I followed her, my eyes (unavoidably) on her hips. Before I knew it, I was telling her about my months and months of physical unease, vague discomfort, premonitions in the night of profoundly ill health.

"Have you ever thought of seeing Carissa?"

"Carissa?"

"She's a homeopath. Her office is on the green."

"In the Octagon?"

"Yup. She's the one with the painted room."

"Paris?"

"Right."

"Usually I only think of the other lawyers in that building."

"Are you a lawyer, too?"

"I am."

"Cool," she said, and I shivered at the realization that this attractive young woman was clearly a college student. What was I thinking, giving her an extra five years? She couldn't be more than twenty! I'd been staring at the breasts and hips of a child! I'd been sharing my midlife night terrors with someone who was not merely fifteen years younger than I was, but who probably drank keg beer and slept happily in a bed the width of a desk blotter.

I told myself I had to get out more.

"I have her number," she said when I remained quiet, when I was still standing there absorbing the word *cool*.

"I'd like that," I said, and I watched her rip a small scrap from a brown paper bag and scribble a name and a phone number upon it. She handed the paper to me as solemnly as if it were a business card.

"Carissa Lake," I said, murmuring the woman's name aloud.

"Yup. Ol' Carissa."

"How old is ol' Carissa?"

"Oh, I don't know. I guess she's about your age. You know, mid-thirties. She's my aunt."

"Your aunt."

"Yup." After I had paid for the echinacea—as I was dropping the little bottle in one of the front pockets of my suit jacket—this much younger woman extended her hand and said, "My name is Whitney."

"I'm Leland."

"Say hi to Aunt Carissa for me."

"I will. For sure."

The next day I called Aunt Carissa, and I made an appointment for a consultation. And I was off, crossing the boundaries of conventional medicine.

Is this how it happens for everyone, is this how everyone finds their first homeopath? I couldn't say.

But it was clear that Carissa and I were destined to meet, it was clear our paths were going to cross. And it wasn't simply because Bartlett and East

Bartlett are small towns in rural Vermont. I wish it were that simple. Almost three thousand people live in the village, and another eight hundred in the hills to the east. Like me, some of them work in Burlington, one of the few settlements in the state to grow into a city. I am never going to meet even a sixth of the people in the two Bartletts if I spend the entire rest of my life here.

No, if I had not met Carissa Lake because of some malaise or disease or real or imagined unease, I would have met her through the Chittenden County State's Attorneys Office. Had I not already met her—had there not been a somewhat obvious conflict of interest—I might have been the one assigned to her case. Expected to prosecute her.

It easily could have happened that way.

Imagine. Leland Fowler, chief deputy state's attorney, cross-examining Carissa Lake, Bartlett homeopath.

No, I can't imagine that. Even now. Even when I am awake in the middle of the night. Even when I think about what she did and what I did and the things I must someday explain to my daughter. Even then, I cannot imagine the path to Carissa unfolding before me in any manner but the way that it did: Sniffles. Echinacea. A phone number on the scrap of a brown paper bag.

2

NUMBER 84

The patient tells the history of his complaints...
The physician sees, hears, and observes with his other
senses what is altered and peculiar in the patient.
He writes everything down exactly.

DR. SAMUEL HAHNEMANN,
Organon of Medicine, 1842

Of the five senses, only smell goes
first to the limbic system, the part of the brain, including the hippocampus,
that seems to be involved with memory and emotion and self-preservation.

And so here are the aromas that conjure for me the beginning of the end:
Lavender, because that was the oil she put into the diffuser. A match at the
moment it's lit. And vanilla, because that was the fragrance of her body lotion,
and we made love that morning when we were through burning the original
notes.

Of these three, of course, it is the smell of a match that comes back to me
most often. From late September through April, I am likely to have a fire
burning in the woodstove throughout the weekend, and many weeknights
when I return home from work.

Nevertheless, at least once a month I find myself wandering down to the
Burlington waterfront and visiting a store there that sells essential oils. The
proprietor knows me now, and the moment I walk in the door, she will pre-
pare a small glass vial of peppermint oil for headache relief. It's all I ever buy
from her.

But she is aware that I am drawn to the smell of lavender, too, though of course she doesn't know why. And so while we are chatting, she will pour a small puddle of lavender oil into a clay bowl that sits in a wrought-iron holder on a glass counter, and then light the burner beneath it.

And I will lose sight of this woman's face as she speaks, and the sound of her voice—more soothing than a massage—will become an ambient hum, curtained from me by the invisible mist made from hot oil.

I am still not sure whether the aroma is a punishment or a blessing. It probably doesn't matter. I am drawn to it, and to the memories that it triggers.

❖

Sometimes, Carissa viewed her mural as a litmus test for new patients, a way of seeing how receptive they'd be to her work. Men, she knew, were more likely than women to have trouble with it when they'd first come to see her, and businessmen were especially likely to be dubious.

In her experience, if the mural made the patient a little edgy or uncomfortable, it usually meant that he was suspicious of the very premise of homeopathy, and unsure as to why he was there. Perhaps it was too great a leap from what he was used to. Perhaps it demanded too vast a willingness to accept the idea that everything he knew about medicine and healing might be wrong—or, at least, inappropriate. Clumsy. Unsuitable for some kinds of disease.

Often, she said, those doubters became believers. Like the CPA in the Octagon two floors below her. Or the Burlington developer, the fellow responsible for bringing chain stores the size of airplane hangars to the cow fields six and seven miles southeast of the city. And, certainly, Richard Emmons: advertising executive, asthmatic, and father of two.

But, equally often, Carissa saw people—frequently men who had come to her at the insistence of wives or lovers or friends—who remained absolutely unwilling to give what she did half a chance.

And that usually meant that even if they took the remedy, it didn't work. Or, if it did, they'd attribute their recovery or the abatement of their symptoms to something else. A conventional remedy, perhaps, or a change in their diet. Sometimes, they'd simply assume their bodies had healed themselves because the time was right.

When Carissa became wearied by the most profound skeptics, she'd wonder why she was even bothering to practice in Vermont at all, and she'd imagine how different her life would have been had she hung out her shingle in Paris.

After all, France—most of Europe, in fact—regards homeopathy as a commonplace alternative method for treating a disease. You walk down almost any street in Paris, and there's the perfectly square, blinking neon cross: the word *Homéopathie* above it, *Herboristerie* below it. There's the butcher, the baker, that store full of chocolates. There's the *homéopathie*.

They're just drugstores, of course, everyday pharmacies. But that's the beauty of it. They look just like any drugstore in America, except the packaging for the products we use all the time seems more elegant. Prettier. Especially the skin creams and lotions.

But then there is always that small cabinet beside the pharmacy counter where the homeopathic remedies are stored. The belladonna and the chamomile, the Rhus tox and the Ignatia. A few dozen little drawers, each one no more than two or three inches high, filled with the cures.

In France, you can even get them in the form of suppositories.

But Carissa didn't believe that she could have settled in Paris when she first started her practice. Her family lived in Vermont, the man she assumed she would marry lived in Vermont. All of her life she herself had lived in Vermont.

And she liked the state. She liked hiking the small hills in the summer and skiing the larger ones in the winter. And once her mural had been completed, she found that she liked the celebrity that went along with being a bit of an oddball in a small town: Mysterious. Esoteric. Exotic. But still, in the eyes of her neighbors who knew her, very talented.

That was, after all, what had drawn most of her friends and lovers and patients to her. She was good at what she did. And she was unique.

She was a native plant with some strangely foreign flowers.

✧

I had no foreshadowings of upheaval when I met Carissa Lake the next to last day in November, no inklings that our relationship would become controversial. Problematic. Insane. If I felt anything when I first walked into Carissa's office and looked down from the stars on her ceiling to find her sitting comfortably before her computer, it was relief that I wasn't going to have to exchange my clothes for one of those open-backed little gowns that barely stretched to mid-thigh.

Briefly, when we'd first spoken on the phone to schedule an appointment, I'd feared that I would. "No gown?" I had asked, not at all pleased that this New Ager was going to expect me to sit around some examining room in the buff, but not exactly surprised. In my experience, people trekking down alternate paths had always been way too comfortable with their bodies, even when they had bodies like mine.

"Of course not. Why would I give you a gown?"

"Modesty, maybe?"

"You won't be taking your clothes off, Leland."

"Oh."

"I mean, I guess you could if it's important to you. But based on what you've told me so far, there doesn't seem to be any reason."

"Will you examine me?"

"Yes, absolutely."

Carissa had a professional woman's short hair—manageable and fast in the morning—just a shade closer to blond than brown. A round, girlish face. Eyeglasses that she'd slid to the top of her head like a hair band. She was wearing a V-neck sweater the night that we met, and when she swiveled in her chair to face me, I was immediately drawn to the creamy triangle of skin above the black cotton—no shirt between fabric and flesh. A thin gold chain hung like a smile against her collarbone.

With the mural of buildings behind her, it looked for a brief moment as if she was working on the balcony or the roof of a brownstone.

"Well," she said when she saw me. "Right on time."

I smiled, regretting that my recent enthusiasm for the health club had lasted at best a dozen visits. I wasn't fat as that winter approached, but I'd noticed when I shaved that my extra ten pounds were particularly gelatinous, and had a tendency to shimmy across my midsection whenever I swung my arm toward the sink to rinse my razor.

Carissa stood to greet me, and I realized she was almost as tall as I was, and I am close to six feet. Unlike my sister, Diana, however, there was nothing spindly or awkward about Carissa. She moved like water on slickrock.

"Welcome," she said. "It's nice to meet you."

"Likewise."

She offered me herbal tea, and I declined, and then she suggested that I sit down on the couch beside one of the two large windows that faced west. The sun had long set—I'd come here after work, after a long day that included almost six hours in court—but I had a sense that she enjoyed wonderful sunsets.

"You know," I said as I sat, "I'd heard this room was a big painting of a cemetery."

"And you came anyway? You're a brave fellow."

"It isn't a cemetery, is it?"

"Nope. Paris. It's just a view of Paris I happen to like."

"I don't see the Eiffel Tower."

She smiled. "It's Paris circa 1843."

"Ah."

She had a strangely, wondrously cherubic face: Put a long face on a tall woman and you have either a disaster or a supermodel. Put a round face on a tall woman and you have Carissa Lake.

"Your niece says hi," I said when she did nothing to fill the quiet between us.

"Are you and Whitney friends?"

"Whitney can't be half my age. Maybe half. Maybe even sixty percent. But she's much younger than I am."

"I guess that means no."

"I'm sure she's a terrific person, but I really just know her from the health-food store."

"Oh, she's a delight. She's more like a younger sister than a niece. She goes to college in upstate New York, but she's home for a while."

"Taking a year off?"

"A semester," she said, as she sat in the chair across a mirrored glass table from the couch. "Now, I'm going to take my shoes off and relax. You're welcome to do the same," she went on, as she slipped off her loafers to expose a pair of thin pearl-colored socks dotted with tiny red flowers. She then curled one leg beneath her, and I noticed that her blue jeans were almost white at the knees.

I looked down at my wingtips. I couldn't imagine taking them off at that moment, because I had a pretty good idea of the smells that might emerge after almost a full day in Courtroom 3A. Felony status conferences. Arraignments. A public defender's appalling motion to suppress, coupled with a cop who couldn't keep his facts straight.

"I think I'm a shoes-on kind of guy," I said.

"Your jacket?"

"I can do my jacket, sure."

"Maybe even loosen your tie?"

"Maybe."

"Wish I had gowns?" Her tone was light, just this side of flirtatious.

"I've just never been to a female doctor before," I said, hoping this explained my unease.

"You still haven't. At least technically. But I am a licensed psychologist. I don't know if that matters to you."

"Should it?"

"It matters to some patients. It's how I backed into homeopathy."

I shrugged. "Doesn't matter."

I looked around and noticed that only two of her walls were actually a part of the skyline of Paris: Another was lined floor to ceiling with books, and the fourth—the one with the westerly windows—had small prints of wildflowers hung in an arc.

"Usually I like to begin by asking if there's anything you'd like to know about homeopathy. Or the process," she said, massaging the spot on her nose where her eyeglasses usually rested, before lowering those eyeglasses into place. Tortoiseshell ovals with just a hint of black. "Have you done any home-work since Whitney suggested we visit?"

"A little. I read some magazines at a bookstore in Burlington."

She wrapped her hands around her knee and let a pad of paper rest in her lap. "Good for you. What do you think?"

"I haven't read that much. I learned belladonna has a cameo in *Little Women*. That's about it."

Carissa smiled. "Louisa May Alcott had a homeopath."

"Yeah, but I probably wouldn't advertise that. I think the article said she died of mercury poisoning."

"Administered by a physician. Traditionally. Not homeopathically."

"Oh."

"It was during the Civil War. She didn't die for another two decades."

"I see."

"You're a lawyer, Leland. I'm sure you took the time to learn more about homeopathy than the fact that Louisa May Alcott had a homeopath. Why don't you tell me a little about what drew you here?"

Although the notion passed through my mind to begin with a pair of women I had found erotic, one who was older than I was and one who was younger, I wanted to make a good impression, and decided almost instantly that lust probably wasn't a particularly savvy way to curry favor with my homeopath—especially since one of those two women was Carissa Lake's niece.

And so I started to tell her about the cold that never went away, and about the days and days I would have to carry a handkerchief with me into court. I described my sore throat and I brought up my watery eyes. I told her my doctor didn't seem to be able to help me, and how at three in the morning I could vacillate wildly between the profound belief that I was a hypochondriac and the desperate fear that I was dying. At some point she started to write, and I watched her hand move across the pad in her lap as I spoke; I tried not to imagine which were the key words she was choosing to save.

"You live with your little daughter, right? It's just the two of you?" she asked.

"It is."

"Are you involved with someone?"

"No. I've had very few dates since my wife died," I said, emphasizing the word *died*. I never said "passed away" when I talked about Elizabeth's death. "Passed away" suggested disease and expiration, a death that took time. Elizabeth didn't die instantly, but she never regained consciousness in the few hours she lived after the accident.

"How come?"

"I don't know. I think it's mostly because I'm away from Abby—my four-year-old—five days a week from seven-thirty, quarter to eight in the morning until six or six-thirty at night. The idea of deserting her on top of that to go out to dinner or a movie seems a little unfair."

"Selfish?"

"I guess."

"What else? What else keeps you from dating?"

"Let's see, what else," I said as her voice echoed inside my head. I liked her voice, I liked it a lot. It was a competent voice, a fast voice—the sort of voice I always associated with the female prosecutors with whom I worked. And so I told her about a beautiful summer afternoon—not a cloud in the sky, not a drop of water or a wet leaf on the pavement—and what an accident reconstructionist would tell me later had occurred on a road by a river.

Elizabeth had been running late for a two P.M. appointment with a young entrepreneur at the site (*factory* was too grandiose a word) where he was manufacturing disposable toothbrushes. The fellow had a loan from the Small

Business Administration, and he wanted one from Elizabeth's bank as well. She was driving fast, but she was on her side of the two-lane state highway.

The driver of the dairy delivery truck had been trying to get something from the glove compartment of his vehicle, reaching all the way across the front seat—stretching his arm into the drawer under the dashboard, craning his neck to see what his fingers were failing to find. He must have taken his eyes off the road just long enough to miss the fact that the road was curving to his right and he needed to turn the truck accordingly. He didn't, and thus plowed into the Subaru driven by the thirty-two-year-old loan officer for a Burlington bank, the front end of the truck slamming into the driver's side of the car at about forty-five miles an hour. Entangled, the two vehicles careened off the road, through the guardrail, and over the bank into the shallow waters of the Lamoille River.

Much of the milk and cream and half-and-half poured out onto the river-bank and briefly turned a stretch of shore white. It was soon after the accident that I developed a distaste for dairy products and began drinking my coffee black.

The driver of the truck, a twenty-three-year-old fellow from Enosburg Falls, died instantly, while Elizabeth hung on, unconscious, for close to four hours. She never opened her eyes or awoke while the rescue squad was cutting her from the car, or while they rushed her in the back of their ambulance to the hospital in Burlington. Had the fellow driving the dairy delivery truck been wearing a seat belt, he might have lived: He ended up underneath the crinkled metal sculpture that had once been a truck and a car.

And though Elizabeth had been wearing a seat belt, it hadn't made any difference in her case. She had been impaled upon metal shards from the door by her side, gored through lung and spleen and the very back of her neck. The roof of the car had been driven hard into her head.

"What do they think he was trying to get?" I had asked the reconstructionist a few days later, referring to the twenty-three-year-old. "Sunglasses?" I was aware that the truck driver had been heading west.

"That's a good guess, but he didn't seem to have any sunglasses in the truck, and we never found a pair by the river."

I remember nodding, waiting for him to continue. Finally the reconstructionist offered the two syllables that I had been unwilling to share with anyone until that moment in Carissa Lake's office, because they seemed to lessen the horror of both the young man's and my wife's deaths.

"Tic Tacs," the reconstructionist had said. "He was probably trying to reach for his Tic Tacs."

I even told Carissa how angry I'd gotten inside whenever anyone had told me to take comfort in the notion that Elizabeth had not suffered long: She may have been aware of the accident a split second before it occurred, people said, but no more than that. No more than a second or two.

But that comfort held little value for the toddler whom I'd now be raising alone. She was a month beyond two when well-meaning people told me that sort of thing, and the only suffering she really understood was her own.

"You and Abby aren't all that alone, are you? I don't get up to East Bartlett very often, but I've always envisioned it as a very close-knit community," Carissa said.

"There are lots of people who help. Really, lots. And I need every single one of them. Her godparents only live a few houses away—though that's about half a mile, given where we live. And the church has been remarkable. I don't think I cooked a meal for three months after Elizabeth died. And now I have the preschool network to help, too. But the fact is, it's still just Abby and me in the mornings and evenings. I'm the one who's tickling her awake, or ironing her dresses, or helping her pour her cereal in the morning. I'm the one who's making sure she has a glass of water by her bed every night, as well as her beloved trolls and her Chapstick and whatever plastic monstrosity happened to fall out of her cereal box that day."

"You sound angry."

"Not at all: I love her madly. I have no idea what I would have done after Elizabeth's death without her. Just no idea. I'd probably have gone completely to pieces. Right now I'm just tired...."

"And?"

"And, I guess, feeling guilty because I didn't pick her up tonight at her usual time."

"Where is she now?"

"Having dinner with the family of her sixteen-year-old baby-sitter. She's about three blocks from here."

"And you're really feeling guilty?"

"I am."

"What about grandparents, or aunts and uncles?"

"Both of my parents have passed away," I said. "Cancer in my mother's case. Alzheimer's in my father's."

"Your mother went first?"

"She did."

"And Elizabeth's parents?"

"They live in Florida. I have a sister two hours away. In New Hampshire, near Dartmouth. That's where Abby and I spend most of our holidays."

"Ever consider a nanny or housekeeper?"

"I have, but it's complicated. There's no day care in East Bartlett, and I want Abby to be around other kids, so that means she has to be in the village of Bartlett during the day—where there is day care. And that, in turn, means a nanny would just be filling in around breakfast and dinnertime. And I want to have breakfast with Abby, so that just leaves the gap before dinner, and I've got that covered right here in the village: I've found people in town who'll look after her from the moment the day care closes until I get here from Burlington."

"What about friends?"

"Oh, she has plenty of friends. She has friends from day care, and Sunday school, and now preschool. The Sunday-school kids and preschool kids are pretty much the same batch. The East Bartlett batch. But then there's also this whole other batch from here in the village. In Bartlett. The day-care batch. But between Greta and Chloe and Cole and—"

"I meant you."

"You mean, do I have friends?"

"Yes. You."

"Of course I do. I just never see them. Sometimes I talk to them on the phone. Mostly I send them E-mail."

"But isn't there someone you, I don't know, play squash with during lunch?"

"When I actually have a free lunch hour, it's usually spent buying Pocahontas underpants and little tiny socks. Or grocery shopping for nonperishables so Abby and I don't have to ruin a Saturday stocking up on cereal and toilet paper for the week. Recently I tried squeezing in visits to the health club, but it didn't last. And that really wasn't about bonding, anyway. It was about not dying any sooner than I have to."

"Who do you talk to—or E-mail—most?"

"Probably Steve Wagner."

"I know that name."

"He's the Chief Medical Examiner for the state of Vermont."

"And he's your best friend...."

"It's not as ghoulish as it sounds," I said, but I nevertheless found myself thinking back on what I'd told her so far. I wondered if I sounded pathetic.

"You said you don't date much because of Abby. If Elizabeth had died before you two had any children, do you think you'd be dating now?"

"Meaning?"

She shrugged. "Do you think your libido survived Elizabeth's death?"

Well, I thought, there's my answer: I do sound pathetic. And ridiculous. Downright ridiculous.

And yet, usually, I didn't view myself as either pathetic or ridiculous. Just overweight. Just a slightly overweight guy with a cold.

"Oh, God," I asked, "must I do this?"

"It helps me," she said, her voice even. "But no, you don't have to." She stared at me and then scribbled another note.

"Oh, what the heck. I've never been to a therapist."

"Even after the accident?"

"Even then."

"So my professional advice is to go for it. You've already shared a very great deal with me."

And so I was off and running once more, telling her that my libido—a word I wasn't sure I'd ever verbalized in my life until then—was just fine. Teenage boys, I heard myself saying, spent less time surfing the Internet for smut than I did, and were certainly less creative about it. After all, how many fifteen-year-olds would think to search linking the words *female* and *ejaculation*?

"But you have so little time to begin with," she said.

"Oh, you know, just the morning routine: Shave, shower. See what the Web has to say about *cunnilingus* while sipping my coffee."

I watched Carissa think for a brief moment, then jot a quick note. Abruptly I became aware of the sorts of things she might or might not read into my body language, and so I spread my arms like an eagle's wings across the back of the couch and uncrossed my legs.

"Let's talk a little bit about your digestion," she said.

"My digestion."

"How is it?"

"It works. Given the five—okay, ten—pounds I should drop, my appetite seems fine."

"Do you lean toward constipation? Or diarrhea?'

"I don't have a preference. Neither, in my experience, is especially pleasant."

"You know what I mean. 'Fess up."

"I think I tend toward the…the solid end of the spectrum. I guess I get a lot of iron in my diet."

"Once a day? Twice a day?"

"Every other day."

She reached for the hardcover book without a dust jacket on the table beside her chair and glanced at a page. The cloth cover reminded me of her jeans: once entirely blue, now faded in parts to white.

"Any aversions?"

"Aside from talking about my stools?"

"Right."

"Let's see. Dates—the food, not the male-female go-to-a-movie thing. There's another attorney in my office who must live on them. She's eating them constantly, and they've always looked to me like big Palmetto bugs. Roaches. Once she insisted I try one, and it only reinforced my disgust. It was exactly like eating a bug—or what I've always imagined eating a bug would be like."

"Do all bugs make you a little squeamish?"

"I hope not."

"How do you feel about spiders?"

"Oh, I guess I hate them. Especially mother spiders, late summer and early fall. They hang out like gigantic marbles with legs in exactly the spots outside the house where I'm scraping and painting. It's inevitable. I'll be at the top of a thirty-two-foot ladder, underneath the eaves maybe, a scraper in one hand and a brush in the other, and there's Charlotte, staring right at me. Big and fat and about to unleash into the world a gazillion little Charlottes. I'm amazed I haven't stared up at one and fallen to my death."

"What do you do?"

"Well, I kill them. Sometimes I try to sort of bat them intact to the ground. I've always figured spiders don't mind falling thirty-two feet. And it's probably better than being squashed. I really don't want to kill them, because I know it's supposed to be bad luck to kill a spider, and the last thing I need at the top of a thirty-two-foot ladder is bad luck."

She laughed, and I took more pleasure from that than I thought was appropriate. It made me want to flirt. Seriously flirt. Tell her how much I liked her socks. The fact that the fabric was thin. And flowery. I wondered if socks were like lingerie.

"Do you have other superstitions?" she asked.

"Yeah, probably. But most of the time I'm not sure if they're superstitions or part of an undiagnosed obsessive-compulsive personality disorder."

"Such as?"

"Well, whenever I leave my office, I have to tap the light switch four times. Whenever I leave my house, I tend to check the stove a zillion times to make sure it's off. And whenever I'm in Courtroom 3A—like I was a big part of this morning and afternoon—I have to sit in the chair with the small white stain on the cushion. That's my stain, I put it there. It's from this cinnamon bun I was eating one morning before a trial began."

"Why do you have to have that specific chair? Did you win that case?"

"I did. But it wasn't just that we sent the guy away for a long time— though we did. It's that I was good. I mean really good. Clarence Darrow good."

"What else? What other aversions do you have?"

I thought for a moment, returning to the image of spiders with egg sacs the size of my eyeballs, and began an eclectic litany that included mushrooms and flying and finding my shaving stubble in the sink. I told her I was afraid of singing in public—even in church if I wasn't in the very first pew—and of dying. Death scared the hell out of me. Prostate cancer and pancreatic cancer really terrified me, the former because it might leave me impotent, my bottom bagged, before I finally withered away, and the latter because it was just so horrifically incurable.

"What about cravings?" she asked when it seemed I was through.

"Are you thirsty?" I asked. I knew I was.

"Ah, right now you crave water." She got up for the first time, stretched the leg that had been underneath her—toes pressing against the thin cotton sock, and in my mind I saw the smooth sole of her foot, her arch, her ankle— and went to a water cooler on the far side of her desk.

"Yeah, I really am thirsty. I'm not used to...to talking about myself so much. I feel like a bore—like a guy in a bar who meets a woman for the first time and just spends hours talking about himself. I'm really sorry, Carissa."

"You're very entertaining," she said.

"I know this is your job and all, but...but still."

She handed me a coffee mug filled with water and returned to her chair. "Want to tell me about your cravings?"

You, I thought as I took a long swallow. Right now I really crave you.

◇

The consultation lasted almost two hours. It was past eight o'clock by the time we left the Octagon and discovered how cold it had become while we'd been talking inside. There were no stars in the sky, and I saw the first flakes of snow were starting to fall.

"Your house is on the Huntington Road?" she asked as she turned up the collar on her parka.

"It is," I said. "I thought long and hard about selling the place after Elizabeth died, and moving into Burlington. It would have saved more than an hour of driving each day—which would have given me more time for Abby. And any place I bought in the city would have been easier to maintain than the money-and-time sucker we live in right now. But Abby loved her day care and her friends, and I just didn't want to drop another big change into her life."

"Or into yours."

"I guess. I have a lot of wonderful memories tied up in that house."

Carissa opened the back door of her station wagon and tossed the good-sized shoulder bag she carried with her onto the seat. "You said you'd lived in Burlington before moving to East Bartlett. Is there anything you miss?"

I opened the front door of her car for her, and for a moment we stood with the metal shielding our legs from the crisp November wind.

"The view, maybe. Elizabeth and I had an apartment that was right on the lake. It had a really amazing view of the Adirondacks."

"Anything else?"

"Oh, I don't know. Maybe being able to walk to restaurants and movies. Who knows? Perhaps I wouldn't be able to count my dates on one hand if Abby and I had moved to the city."

"I think you know that would be a good thing."

"Moving to Burlington?"

"No, not at all. Dating. That's all I meant. Dating."

I nodded, and waited for her to slide into her car. When she was settled behind the wheel with her key in her hand, I asked, "Want to join me some night, then? For dinner?"

She smiled, but she was shaking her head with what looked like great resolve. "It's very sweet of you to ask, but you know that's completely impossible. It would be wildly inappropriate."

"Wildly," I repeated.

"Yes. Wildly. But thank you for asking."

"Are you seeing someone?"

"I'm not even going to answer that, Leland."

"Wildly inappropriate?"

"Wildly." She started the car and reached for the door handle. "I'll call you in a day or two—probably two—with a remedy," she said, then pulled shut the door. She mouthed good night through the glass, and then that foot with the thin cotton sock was pressing down on the brake as she shifted her car into reverse and backed it into the street bordering the green.

I waved, and she waved back. In my other hand I was holding the little paperback book on homeopathy she had loaned me. A more thorough introduction, she had called it. I dropped the book into my wide overcoat pocket to protect it from the snow and then burrowed my hands under my arms. The pizza parlor in town was still open. I'd get a calzone I could reheat once I'd put Abby to bed, and then I'd read all about arsenic, tarantula, and belladonna.

Please don't prescribe tarantula, I thought to myself. Spiders really do repulse me.

✧

I would not be present when Carissa gave her statement to the police three days after Christmas, but my boss, Philip Hood, would wait in the very next room.

He was not in the same room, because he didn't want to risk being called as a witness in a trial. But he was a presence during her statement nevertheless, making absolutely certain that the questions that mattered to him as State's Attorney were asked.

Sometimes I envision that meeting; I see Carissa and her attorney in her lawyer's Burlington office.

She used the counsel I recommended, a woman named Becky McNeil who had beaten Phil and me and at least one or two other prosecutors at some point in her career.

In my imagination, Carissa is sitting beside Becky, the two of them on the same side of the massive cherry table in the meeting room in her firm that overlooks College Street. The detectives from our office are sitting across from them, and because they both happen to be male, it looks a little bit like a settlement conference for a divorce: the men on one side of the divide, the women on the other.

But of course the stakes are considerably higher. Richard Emmons has not yet been declared brain-dead, but there is little doubt in anyone's mind that brain-dead is where the body in the ICU bed is going.

Three times, one of the detectives excuses himself from the table and leaves the room, and tells Phil exactly what Carissa has said. He tells Phil about the pages and pages of handwritten notes the homeopath wants to turn over to our office. Then, with instructions from Phil, the detective returns to the conference room and closes the door behind him.

And as the spools in the tape recorder twirl in their place in their box, Carissa resumes speaking, her hands in her lap, repeating exactly the lies I've concocted.

3

NUMBERS 9 AND 11

In the state of health the spirit-like vital force (dynamis)
*animating the . . . human organism reigns in supreme sov-
ereignty.*

   *It is only this vital force thus untuned which brings
about in the organism the disagreeable sensations and
abnormal functions that we call disease.*

DR. SAMUEL HAHNEMANN,
Organon of Medicine, 1842

In that period before it became clear
to Jennifer Emmons that friendship with me would be intolerable, she told me
doctors would come into the ICU room in which Richard was lying, and they
would talk to her with the complete confidence that her husband couldn't hear
a word they said. "The surgery won't relieve the intracranial pressure," one
physician informed her, her husband so close that either could touch him.
"But that's not its purpose. What the procedure will do is allow us to implant
a switch over his brain so we can monitor the pressure."

   "A switch?" she had whispered. The nurses, unlike the doctors, all
behaved as if Richard could hear them. They'd talk to him as they worked over
him, as if he had merely broken his leg. Or had just had a gallstone removed.
An appendectomy, maybe. When the nurses wanted to share something with
Jennifer that might have upset the patient, they would motion her into the
corridor, or they would whisper.

   Jennifer appreciated the nurses' hopefulness and their faith, and so she always whispered, too, when she had a question for a physician. Just in case. Likewise, she recalled, she had explained to the children that although their father was in a coma and was unable to speak, he probably heard them when they told him they loved him.

Some moments, she said, she believed this herself, but those moments grew less and less frequent as the days passed by after Christmas.

"An electrode monitoring device," the doctor had continued. "The surgeon will drill a small hole through the front of Richard's skull and lower the device in place. It really doesn't take very long. And to you, or anyone who comes here to see Richard, it will just look like there's a little watch battery in his forehead."

She had probably nodded, she told me, if only because she recalled nodding all the time. She either asked questions or she nodded. That's all that a person who knows nothing really can do.

Jennifer, I would learn, was the sort who would nod with the doctors but ask lots of questions of lawyers.

✧

I was lying beside Abby in the bed in her room, our noses within inches of each other. I watched her eyes close for a second longer than a blink, then abruptly open wide. She was fighting sleep as long as she could, determined to make it to the end of the story. She was adorable.

"And even though the trolls were only four and five inches tall," I murmured, making the story up as I went along, "they stood on each other's shoulders so that they could reach the handle on Abby's door...."

She looked so comfortable and content, I grew envious of the fact that she was already in her pajamas and under the covers. I hadn't even taken my necktie off yet. And because I'd spent so much time with Carissa, I'd decided to allow Abby to stay up with me until ten o'clock, which meant I wouldn't be in bed before midnight.

"The troll on the top of the living troll ladder had to use both of his incredibly pudgy hands to turn the knob, and it took all of his strength...."

I thought to myself that I might not even bother to reheat that calzone.

"God's really strong, isn't he?" Abby asked. The question seemed sudden, but I knew there was a natural connection somewhere in my four-year-old's brain. The word *strength*, maybe. The fact that I'd told Abby earlier that night that I'd been to a lady who was sort of like a doctor.

"I think so," I answered. "Why?"

She took a deep breath in through her nose and then wiped a strand of hair that had fallen across her eyes. She reached over and began to toy with my tie, her thumb disappearing momentarily behind the silk.

"Welllllll," she said, drawing the word out the way she did whenever she was figuring something out, "my mommy died. And your mommy and daddy died. And God had to carry them all up to heaven."

I kissed her once on her nose. "He sure did," I said, ignoring the literalist inside me who had started to murmur, *Well, they all died a few years apart, Abby, so God didn't have to carry them up to heaven at exactly the same time. He probably took a couple of trips.*

"Yeah, I thought so," she said. She released my necktie and sat up for a moment in bed, and turned her pillow over so the cotton pillowcase felt cool once again. Then she lay back down upon it and curled her hands up beside her head.

"Should I go on with the story of the night the trolls came to life?"

"Please," she said, and I resumed with the moment the trolls escaped from her room and started down the stairs of the house. She was sound asleep by the time they'd gotten to the kitchen and had started to raid the refrigerator.

I must admit, I was disappointed when Carissa said she wanted to think about my case for a few days before suggesting a remedy. I'd hoped she would simply open a cabinet that I imagined was filled with homeopathic potions, and give me a first dose of something that would magically restore me to what I'd begun to think was as close as one gets to perfect health. There had been a time, I'd begun to realize, when I really had felt so good that I'd never even thought about my health—a time when the pockets of my jackets and pants weren't constantly filled with the tiny scraps of paper that surrounded each cough drop.

The first thing I did once I'd put Abby to bed was to pick those wrappers out of my pockets and throw them away. I even thought that the next morning, when I stopped at the gas station outside of Burlington for my newspaper and coffee, I might start weaning myself from the cough drops: I would not allow myself to buy one of those inviting little square tubes. *Good-bye, Mentho-Lyptus. I'm going cold turkey.*

I decided I should eat something after all, and so I zapped the calzone for a few minutes in the microwave while I changed into my pajamas, hanging up my suit and putting wooden shoe trees into my wingtips, and then I listened to the pair of messages on my answering machine. The professor of the criminal justice course at UVM had called to thank me for speaking to her class the other day, although it was clear she thought my view of the system was a tad one-sided. "You took a group of aspiring public defenders and turned them into a lynch mob," she'd said, more than a trace of an edge in her voice. And Howard Lansing, a friend of mine and a church trustee, had phoned, wondering if the rails I had volunteered to build for the church's handicapped-access ramp back in April would be up in time for the Christmas tea in December.

The Christmas tea was on the tenth this year. I figured I'd have a chance to take care of the railing if the weather was decent over the weekend, especially since Abby would be at a friend's birthday party most of Saturday afternoon. Of course, I also figured there was a chance that between the wife beaters and drunks who peppered a state's attorney's view of Vermont, I might be tied up for some part of Saturday or Sunday, since it was my turn to be on call.

I scribbled the words *hardware store* on a yellow Post-it note and pressed the sticky strip against the inside of my front door. I was pretty sure I didn't have a lunch scheduled the next day, and so I'd try and use that time to pick up the materials for the railing.

When I finally sat down with Carissa's book and my dinner at the kitchen counter, I realized I was exhausted. Carissa had, as Abby would put it, tuckered me. I'd never in my life talked about myself for anywhere near as long as I had with the homeopath; I'd never examined my past with such purpose. I'd recalled things I hadn't thought about in years—some, perhaps, I hadn't thought about since they'd actually occurred.

I realized I'd told Carissa about the hour I'd spent staring into Elizabeth's closet the day after she'd died, when I was supposed to be picking out a dress for her to wear inside the coffin. Although the casket was going to be closed, what she was wearing still mattered greatly to me. Yet when I'd wandered upstairs to our bedroom and stood before the walk-in closet, I froze. Was I supposed to bury Elizabeth in one of the business suits and skirts she might wear during the week, or the sort of casual dress she might wear to a cocktail party on somebody's porch in July?

I still don't know what would have happened if Elizabeth's friend Lorraine hadn't shown up. Who knows if I would ever have made a decision. I might still be standing in that bedroom, a catatonic attorney more mannequin than man, while Abby was being raised by her grandparents in Florida, or my sister in New Hampshire.

But Lorraine had shown up, calling up the stairs to me when she'd found the front door open.

"You know she loved blue," Lorraine had said, choosing a white pleated jumper that was covered with tiny irises.

"It's sleeveless," I remembered telling her, disturbed on some level because even in June the Vermont ground could be cold. But Lorraine had been a step ahead of me: She was already pulling Elizabeth's favorite cardigan sweater from a bureau drawer.

"These always looked nice together," she had said.

And tonight, for the first time in my life, I'd verbalized the fact that I'd never been wild about the teddy bears my father's company had made. They cost a small fortune in upscale toy stores around the country, in part because they were made in Vermont (which mattered to people for reasons I just couldn't fathom—after all, it wasn't like the teddies were made of maple syrup), and in part because they were always eccentrically dressed. Over the years, Green Mountain Grizzlies had dressed its bears in girl group sequins, disco king leisure suits, and some extremely punk leather. In the seventies, there'd been a teddy dressed like a jelly-doughnut-filled Elvis Presley, and another that had looked more than a bit like Henry Kissinger.

No one suspected that my father's big idea of Desert Storm Grizzly was probably a sign of his oncoming Alzheimer's. After all, the camouflage-clad grizzly had been a huge success—due at least in part to my father's suggestion that the teddy come equipped with a toy gas mask.

But I had never cared for the bears, even when I was a boy. I didn't like the way the arms had joints at the shoulders, and the way the paws had claws made of a rubber that felt like a pencil's eraser. I'd just never found the bears very cuddly.

Yet my sister and I owned one or two of almost every single grizzly ever made. Abby must have had a dozen of the things in her room, and at least a dozen more in a sealed moving box in the attic.

With Carissa, I'd gone into the childhood embarrassments that were an inevitable part of what my parents would refer to eventually as their weird midlife hippie phase. There was my father standing beside the tiny bleachers at the Little League field in Burlington in the summer of 1971, his hair in a ponytail. There was my mother picking me up from the school nurse's office one morning in second grade when I had a fever that reached triple digits. My mother was wearing an Indian sari, and what I believe were called "granny glasses," with deep purple lenses.

"We were meditating," she'd explained to the nurse when the other woman had actually had the audacity to ask.

And I'd told Carissa what it had been like to witness my mother die slowly from lung cancer—although it was the treatment, I thought, that had made it so painful to watch. Especially the radiation. The esophageal radiation. My mother couldn't eat because she couldn't swallow, and sometimes after struggling through one of those tiny cans of high-protein shake, the pain in her throat would become too much, and she'd end up vomiting all she'd consumed.

Finally, I had recalled—whether for Carissa or for myself, I hadn't a clue—a few predictably painful teen memories, including the afternoons I would rifle through my older sister's underwear drawer to find bras I could practice unsnapping. And that April morning when I was seventeen, and Laurel Palmore's septic tank had overflowed, and all of the condoms Laurel and I had used our last year of high school had floated onto the stone terrace in the Palmores' backyard. ("I guess I should have carried them home with me," I'd said when she called me, sobbing, the night her mother found them. I knew it would cost me my girlfriend.)

"You really do have a healthy libido," Carissa had said, and while I hoped it was meant as a compliment, I was pretty sure that the homeopath was just trying to be gracious. She must have seen I was on the verge of tears.

❖

That night as I was starting to drift off to sleep, I realized my throat was growing sore. Burning, once more. I tried not to swallow, afraid swallowing would cause pain and that pain would cause me to wake up. But it took an effort not to swallow, and that effort pulled me back from the brink. I opened my eyes, I stretched my neck. I was awake.

Carissa, I decided, was going to prescribe arsenic. And it was going to kill me. I was sure of it. The little book I'd skimmed at dinner had said something about arsenic being a good remedy for people whose symptoms included restlessness. Anxiety. Fear.

A sore throat.

Well, that's me, I thought. I'm going to get arsenic, and I'm going to tank.

In the morning, I knew, arsenic would stop scaring me. After all, there really wasn't any arsenic at all in the remedy. Just like there was no tarantula in tarantula. Or gold in gold. Or belladonna in belladonna. That was the beauty of homeopathy. (Or, I thought, why it was such incredible quackery. I wondered if instead of seeing this woman for help, I should be prosecuting her for fraud.) Unlike conventional medicine or naturopathic medicine or even that seemingly wholesome New Age standby herbalism, homeopathic medicine was completely safe. It might not do a bloody thing to heal me...but it sure as heck couldn't hurt me.

The book had even said the whole essence of a homeopathic remedy was dilution. You took a substance and kept diluting it and shaking it, diluting and shaking, until there was virtually nothing left of the original ingredient. The dilution might go from one part arsenic and ninety-nine parts water to one part arsenic and a million parts water. Maybe the ratio would become one to one hundred million.

Homeopaths believed, of course, that even at that infinitesimal a level, the remedy retained a memory of the original substance—just enough to set the body on its path to recovery.

But from a chemist's perspective, it was certainly harmless. And most likely quackery.

No, it was the other way around: Certainly quackery. Most likely harmless.

It couldn't possibly be absolutely, positively—*certainly*—harmless. After all, who the hell knew how that stuff was made? The fact is, the remedy began with arsenic. Arsenic! Poison! And just as it was possible that there could be a bad batch of a prescription drug—Amoxil or Claritin or Seldane gone wrong—it was certainly conceivable that there could be a bad batch of arsenic.

I imagined a homeopathic chemist—a barefoot blonde in a white lab coat, Carissa Lake in a lab filled with ferns—and saw her holding a pair of beakers, wondering, Let's see, which one is one to one hundred and which one is one to one thousand?

Carissa had said the remedy was usually diluted beyond something called Avogadro's number—beyond a detectable trace. Well, it seemed to me that was fine if this Avogadro fellow was a NASA scientist with a NASA scientist's toys, the tools for a proper, twenty-first-century chemical analysis. But what if Avogadro were some eighteenth- or nineteenth-century alchemist? A guy in a hood who lacked even the tools to weigh himself properly? I decided I'd have to ask Carissa about Avogadro the next time I spoke with her, or look him up on the Web in the morning.

I reached into my nightstand drawer, hoping to find a tube of cough drops. No luck. I'd have to go downstairs for a spray of Chloraseptic. Elizabeth and I had always talked about putting a bathroom on the second floor of the old farmhouse we'd bought, but we had never gotten around to it. And so the only bathroom in the whole place—on the first floor, on the far side of the kitchen—seemed about an acre away in the middle of the night, especially on cold nights in January and February.

For a moment I watched it snow from my bedroom window, the larger flakes rafting in the occasional gusts like leaves in a stream, before settling finally in the grass. I'd suspected the snow had resumed when I'd turned out the light, because the world had seemed so quiet.

Downstairs I passed through the kitchen. There were my dishes in the sink, and there on the counter was the little book Carissa had lent me. And there on the cover was the picture of that old bald guy with a beard. Hahnemann. Samuel Hahnemann. Mr. Homeopath. Dr. Like-Cures-Like.

Carissa had said that Hahnemann had begun his "provings" in the late 1700s and continued them into the nineteenth century.

Provings, of course, sounded scientific, at least in a vaguely mad-doctor-with-a-monocle sort of way. But Hahnemann was also a bark eater. His exploration of what would become homeopathy had begun when he'd started eating Peruvian bark in 1790 in order to try and replicate the symptoms of malaria.

That, in turn, probably meant that Avogadro had lived in the nineteenth century, too. Perhaps even earlier.

Shit. Carissa, I realized, was going to give me arsenic. And I was going to get sicker for sure.

4

N U M B E R   7 4

Among chronic diseases we must unfortunately include all those widespread illnesses artificially created by allopathic treatments, by the prolonged use of violent, heroic drugs in strong, increasing doses.

DR. SAMUEL HAHNEMANN,
Organon of Medicine, 1842

Jennifer realized her husband was serious about homeopathy while she was watching him shave one morning late in November. It wasn't long after their race to the emergency room in the middle of the night, and he may still have been taking prednisone.

She remembered sitting on a small bar stool in the corner of the bathroom off their bedroom, watching his reflection in the mirror as the razor cleared the white foam from his face like a snowplow.

"And you could get a cat," Richard was saying, his eyes on his chin.

"Is that what all this is about?" she'd asked. "You want me to have a cat?"

"You love cats. And the kids could have a dog."

"Timmy talks a good game, but I don't think he really cares one way or the other."

"What about Kate?" he had asked, referring to their daughter. "She brought it up again just the other night."

"She starts high school in a year. Ten months. Trust me, pretty soon boys will matter to her a whole lot more than a dog. She won't even remember she'd wanted a dog."

"Ah, but you'll still want a cat."

"I'm fine, sweetheart. I really am. I see more than my share of cats and dogs at the animal hospital. I get my fix twice a week. Don't feel you need to do this because your family wants pets."

She'd watched him start on his neck, tilting his head back as far as he could, and she'd wondered how men managed to shave there. It didn't just look like it hurt: It looked downright deadly.

"There are other reasons."

She thought she had probably smiled. She knew exactly what he was going to say next. "Such as?"

"No inhalers. I have this great fantasy that someday I won't have an inhaler with me wherever I go. I won't see one every time I open my desk drawer at work. There won't be one taking up space in my attaché case. I won't have to sleep with one next to our bed."

"It's not like you're an invalid," she had said. Because, after all, he wasn't. Not at all.

"And I'd love to go off theophylline. You have to wonder what I'm doing to my body long-term with that stuff. Every time I look at the warning about side effects, my stomach gets a little queasy."

"You'd be much worse without it."

"Right now I would be." He'd rinsed the razor, and the Eucerin ointment on the back of his hand glistened like vegetable shortening. The eczema had flared up the other day with the asthma, and even through the skin cream she could see the scabs and patches of red flaky skin.

"But you know what scares me the most?" he'd said. "The prednisone, that's what. I hate the whole idea of pumping my body full of steroids."

"I don't think you've been on prednisone more than six or seven weeks in all the years we've been married."

"Well, it's been more often than that. And two weeks in the last year alone, counting last Tuesday's little debacle."

"It wasn't a debacle."

"A three A.M. race to the emergency room? Waking up Kate in the middle of the night so she knows we're gone in case the house catches on fire?" He'd shaken his head before rolling the razor over a thin strip of white at the edge of his neck nearest his ear. "I don't like being in the hospital, and I don't like being unable to breathe. Trust me: It was a debacle. A complete and utter debacle."

"Have you talked to your allergist about this?"

"About seeing a homeopath? No way. Dawson would never approve. He'd feel much too threatened."

"So you're doing it anyway?"

"Dawson's a drug dealer, for God's sake. The man's a pusher. You know what his response was to Tuesday's attack? New drugs. More drugs. Accolate. Zyflo. Things called pathway interrupters. Well, I don't want new drugs. I want no drugs."

She'd sighed. "Have you checked this woman's credentials?"

"She comes highly recommended."

"Oh, does she now?"

"You betcha. She saw Christine through menopause—"

"Go on! Christine's been through menopause?"

He'd shrugged. "She's forty-eight, forty-nine years old."

"I knew she was older than us. But not six or seven years older than us."

"Yup—"

"She told you she was in menopause?"

"She was having hot flashes in meetings." He'd said it so matter-of-factly that she'd thought to herself, My body would have to be in the midst of a jet-engine flame-out before I'd announce in a meeting, Yikes! Hot flash!

"And she helped Dan go a whole winter without a cold," he'd continued.

Downstairs she heard a replicated explosion—a car crash, perhaps—from one of Timmy's video games. He knew he wasn't supposed to play on the computer before school.

"Maybe you should start by seeing if she has anything for the dermatitis," she'd suggested. After all, it often seemed that the skin thing bothered him more than the asthma. On days when his ad agency had a new business presentation, he'd be miserable. Absolutely miserable. He'd find himself beginning the pitch by apologizing for refusing to shake people's hands.

It had been so bad lately that they hadn't made love since before his attack, because he couldn't bring himself to touch her.

"The dermatitis goes with the asthma," he'd said.

"Well, does she at least have a license or something?"

He'd paused, then put the cap on the shaving cream and the can in the small cabinet by the sink. "Do you think homeopaths need licenses?"

"Oh, God, I hope so."

"Who'd license them? The State Medical Board?"

"I have no idea. But I'd look into it before I put my trust in some holistic hippie."

He'd splashed cold water on his face and then dried himself with the hand towel by the sink. "I'll look into it," he'd said, and his words had made her feel better. He'd sounded so serious.

"Good. After all, most of the time your asthma's completely under control. But this homeopathy thing? Who knows what that could do."

Anyone who's lived in Vermont for any time at all knows the old joke about Burlington: It's a great place to live because it's so close to Vermont.

I had heard the joke all my life. My family had moved to Burlington from a Connecticut suburb of Manhattan when I was a toddler, and it was very soon after settling there that my father founded Green Mountain Grizzlies. My parents, like so many other flatlanders who migrated north to the city on the lake, fell in love with Burlington exactly because they could say that they lived in Vermont without having to endure rural poverty, roads that smelled of manure, and the isolation that was a natural by-product of the mountains of snow and rivers of mud that arrived between November and May.

Burlington sits on a hill that slopes gently into Lake Champlain. At the top of the hill are the rows of stately Victorian homes and Gothic Revival cottages built by lumber and potash barons throughout the nineteenth century, as well as the greens and quadrangles dotting the campus of the state's two-century-old university. The downtown itself has evolved into a lakefront of boathouses and bike paths, with perhaps a half-dozen blocks, all told, of expensive specialty shops, coffee bars, and small office buildings—none taller than seven stories.

The place is constantly cited by magazines and newspapers as one of America's most livable cities, which was probably why Elizabeth and I bought a farmhouse in the mountains twenty miles to the south as soon as we could. The neighborhoods in the city where we were likely to live were just getting too damn mannered.

And while our jobs might demand that we work in the town, we sure as hell didn't have to join the throngs who were drawn there from around the country by the high-tech giants that were employing literally thousands of aspirational Vermonters by the end of the 1980s. After all, if we had stayed in the city long enough, we might have wound up joining a Kiwanis Club, like fully two-thirds of the bankers in Elizabeth's department. Worse, we might have ended up volunteering for the Chamber of Commerce, like Philip Hood.

Hood, the State's Attorney for Chittenden County, had the sole corner office, and the only one that faced Lake Champlain and the Adirondacks. That was, in my mind, a perfectly reasonable perk, given the fact that Phil actually spent more time at his desk and less time in court than any of the other lawyers.

As Phil's chief deputy, I knew I had the best office of the dozen other state prosecutors in Burlington—the best view of the city, the most light, the shortest walk to the copier and the printer and the coffee machine—but it was Margaret Turnbull who had the best toys. That made sense, of course, because she handled easily eighty percent of the child-abuse cases that came our way. And so whenever she wanted to discuss whether a case should go to trial or what sort of sentence to offer the accused—that human litany of fathers and uncles and new boyfriends of Mom, that group of men who were despicable, unrepentant, and (in Margaret's and my minds) patently guilty, even if the evidence wasn't there—I'd go to her office. I liked beaching the plastic whales beside the glass snow globes (one of which was filled with a real starfish and actual sand), and walking her Barbies and Kens around the edge of the desk. I liked the small cubes and puzzles and blocks.

Sometimes the toys would remind me of Abby, and in the back of my mind I'd be thinking of new games I could invent to entertain my daughter. Other days, however, I'd see the dolls and lose complete sight of the fact that I was a father: I'd view them instead as profoundly erotic little models of people—men with washboards for stomachs, and women with fetish-thin waists— and I'd forget the fact that these were the very same sorts of dolls around which my four-year-old crafted whole worlds.

I remember I met with Margaret in her office the morning after my very first consultation with Carissa. The clouds that had dusted the ground with snow were well to the east, and the sky was the neon blue that comes only in winter. It was freezing out, but with the sky that crisp, I lost all fear that the homeopath would make me down arsenic. She'd give me something that sounded vaguely magic, like belladonna. Or Gelsemium. Or Ignatia.

Ignatia, I decided, that's what I'd like. Sounds just like a saint.

There were three cases Margaret wanted to discuss: an attempted sexual assault, an "L and L" with a minor—a lewd and lascivious act—and a possible murder.

"Let's start with the murder," I suggested, sitting archaeologist Barbie on the arm of the chair I'd taken opposite her desk, and resting the chocolate doughnut I'd bought in my lap. I'd never seen this Barbie before; she was new. Dark, dark hair. A wide-brimmed hat to protect her plastic shell from that searing hot desert sun, a fossil hunter's fatigues. A colorful map in one hand, a tiny magnifying glass in the other. I made a note in my mind to be sure this particular doll would be among Abby's new Christmas Barbies.

Margaret dove right in. "Remember that guy in Underhill who died in a hunting accident on Sunday? When he shot a deer, his gun blew up in his face?"

"I do." How could anyone forget? The poor son of a bitch had ended up bleeding to death in the woods, but his younger brother—a guy in his twenties—was one hell of a hero nevertheless. He'd carried his older sibling on his back close to three miles in the bitter cold that comes after Thanksgiving.

"The gunsmith who repaired the gun might have rigged it to burst."

"What makes you think so?" I wondered what a homeopath would do for a guy who'd had most of his face blown away by a defective gun. It began in my mind as a snide little inquiry but then grew merely curious: Maybe Ferrum phosphoricum stopped bleeding. For all I knew, nux vomica—now, there was a remedy that needed public relations help—was a coagulant.

"The victim was sleeping with his wife."

"Oh, that's clever," I said, "using one buck to bring down another," but I knew Margaret wouldn't smile. Margaret was profoundly earnest about her work, perhaps because she was still, technically, a newlywed. I imagined she was so happy with her older, wiser psychologist husband—Margaret was twenty-eight, but Dr. Strangelove was somewhere in his late forties or early fifties—that she was all business in the office. In the ten months she'd been married, she'd arrived promptly at eight every morning and left like clockwork at five. Even those weeks when she was in the midst of a trial, she'd managed the seemingly impossible feat of going home almost the moment court recessed for the day.

"But the gunsmith's record is clean," Margaret said, ignoring me. "Not even a parking ticket."

"And the widow's?"

"We haven't checked."

"Do it. Any kids?"

"Nope. Thank God."

I placed archaeologist Barbie on Margaret's desk, and started my dough-nut. "Does the gunsmith know he's under investigation?"

"Yup. Already has counsel. Oren Candon."

"He's a very successful gunsmith."

"Guess so."

"Where's the gun?"

"What's left of it? At the crime lab. It's a muzzle-loader."

The regular deer season when rifles were allowed had been over for almost a week, and so the victim had been one of the small group of Vermont-ers who took to the woods with "primitive weapons"—antiques or replicas of antiques—like muzzle-loaders.

"Since he has a lawyer, he's probably not doing much talking himself," I said. "So make sure the detectives are talking to his friends. Maybe he said something."

"Customers, too?"

"Customers, too. And see if there's a history of these guns blowing up. I think we'll both be very interested in what the ballistics report says."

I knew it sounded like busywork to Margaret; I could see she wanted to start laying the groundwork for a charge of first-degree murder. But first we had to rule out other causes. Then we might see if we could show deliberate-ness.

"And see if gunsmiths are regulated," I added.

Margaret's hair was black as licorice, and for some reason I thought she looked a bit like the doll on the desk. It might have been the nose. Margaret's nose was tiny, too. When she looked down at the notepad on the blotter, as she did that moment, it disappeared completely behind a curtain of bangs.

"Okay, we will," she said. "Can we do the sexual assault next?"

"Sure." I saw that beside her notes was the little Ziploc bag of dates she munched through the morning.

"Attempted, actually. Burlington firefighter, thirty-four years old—"

"A firefighter? I never expect untoward behavior from firefighters."

"And he's a father. Three kids. But his wife and children were in Boston visiting family, and Dad hired an exotic dancer to come to their house on North Winooski. 'Adult dancing,' it said he was getting on the MasterCard slip."

"Married father of three was putting it on a credit card?"

"I'm sure the monthly statement would be discreet."

"Nevertheless, talk about leaving a paper trail..." I looked down at the napkin in my lap and was astonished to see I'd already managed to scarf down my entire doughnut. And still I was hungry. Worse, I wanted a cup of coffee. Desperately.

But Carissa had said the coffee bean sometimes interfered with a remedy. That little book on homeopathy had said the same thing. Consequently, I'd made the spontaneous decision that morning not to purchase a cup on my way into work, so that when Carissa called I could say, *Look at me: crisp and clean and no caffeine. Make me well, you sexy healer, you.*

Well, I wouldn't say that second thing. But that crisp-and-clean line wasn't an abomination.

"The firefighter had agreed to a hundred-and-sixty-dollar dance. Apparently that's about five minutes of stripping to lingerie, five minutes in lingerie, and five minutes in the buff."

"He got a little overexcited?"

"So it would seem. He asked her to—as the French say—clean his pipe. And she said no."

"That's what I like: a stripper with morals."

"He said he'd pay her whatever she wanted, and still she said no. So then he asked how much it would cost if she just climbed on top of him on the couch for a minute—no penetration."

"And she said no."

"No, she said yes."

"Oh, Lord."

"She says the minute she straddled him, he grabbed her and started trying to slip inside her. And so she slapped him hard on the face."

"Good for her."

"Based on the mug shot, it was a really good whack. Then she says she jumped off the couch and grabbed her things. And though she did call her driver, it's clear she wasn't all that frightened: She also took the time to call her boss to get approval for an extra three hundred dollars in charges."

"And there went the grocery money for the month," I said.

"You haven't heard the best part. When the driver arrived, the guy flashed some firefighter badge and said he was a cop! He said they could either tear up the credit-card slips or he'd arrest them. For a minute the driver believed him, but then the dancer asked to see more I.D."

"And it got nasty?"

"Yup. He took a swing at the driver, missed, and then grabbed the girl. Who knows what he had in mind. The driver—who, I hear, is one very large animal—pulled the firefighter's arms apart and extricated the dancer. Then, as they were leaving the house, a police cruiser pulled up."

"Who called the cops? A neighbor?"

"Nope. Dancer's boss. He didn't like how she sounded on the phone, and he got worried."

I wondered, suddenly, if there were homeopathic aphrodisiacs. Or anti-aphrodisiacs. Something to suggest to that firefighter, maybe, the next time his wife was away. After all, there were certainly a great many conventional drugs that diminished a person's sex drive.

"When's the arraignment?"

"Three-thirty."

"See if you can get some conditions. No alcohol. A curfew. No contact with the victim."

"You don't approve of this firefighter."

"I don't. In fact, let's not be content with attempted sexual assault. Let's also get him for assaulting the bodyguard. And impersonating a police officer."

I looked at my watch and saw I was due in court in ten minutes, and we still had to address the lewd and lascivious.

And somehow I absolutely had to find a moment to grab a quick cup of coffee or pop an Advil. If I didn't, I was going to have one doozie of a caffeine-withdrawal headache.

From the package insert that comes with the Ventolin brand of albuterol, one of the prescription drugs Richard Emmons would breathe into his lungs by means of an inhaler: "Ventolin Inhalation Aerosol can produce paradoxical bronchospasms that can be life-threatening."

Then: "Fatalities have been reported in association with excessive use of inhaled sympathomimetic drugs. The exact cause of death is unknown...."

And this, under the bold subhead, "Carcinogenesis, Mutagenesis, Impairment of Fertility: Albuterol sulfate caused a significant dose-related increase in the incidence of benign leiomyomas of the mesovarium in a two-year study in the rat...."

Most of the Ventolin insert is written like this: The language is incomprehensible, vague, and relentlessly ominous. The words are scary and long.

The language on the insert that comes with the Aerobid Inhaler System is better. The downsides of its active ingredient, flunisolide, are spelled out in prose that is precise. In clinical trials with flunisolide, there was a:

- 20 percent incidence of sore throats;
- 10 percent incidence of diarrhea, nausea, and vomiting;
- 3 to 9 percent incidence of heart palpitations, abdominal pain, edema, fever, and decreased appetite;
- 1 to 3 percent incidence of capillary fragility, enlarged lymph nodes, hypertension, tachycardia, and good old-fashioned constipation.

Meanwhile, beclomethasone dipropionate, known commonly by asthmatics as Vanceril, is warning its users that patients have died as a result of "adrenal insufficiency" while transitioning to it from systemic corticosteroids. Fluticasone propionate can cause rhinitis, dermatitis, and pains in the joints. Theophylline—that pharmacological workhorse in the battle against asthma—can lead to "caffeine-like adverse effects," "cardiac arrhythmias," and "intractable seizures which can be lethal."

And almost every anti-asthma drug insert admits somewhere that "the long-term effects on human subjects are not completely known."

Or—I can imagine Richard Emmons surmising—at all.

5

NUMBER 94

While taking a case of chronic disease one should carefully examine and weigh the particular conditions of the patient's day-to-day activities, living habits, diet, domestic situation, and so on.

DR. SAMUEL HAHNEMANN,
Organon of Medicine, 1842

While I was discussing with Margaret how best to go after a married firefighter with an inordinate interest in strippers, Carissa was at her kitchen table, contemplating possible remedies for her anxiety-rich new patient.

I know now that Carissa did much of her thinking at home over breakfast, before leaving for her office in the Octagon.

And so I have a vision in my mind of Carissa at work at that moment: She has her *Materia Medica* open before her, with a mug of herbal tea to her side. She is still in her nightgown, and she has wool socks on her feet because the hardwood that is her kitchen floor is so cold in the winter.

She has to lift Sepia, her cat, off the book, because without fail the cat will try and plant herself exactly upon whatever magazine or book Carissa is reading. Anything to get her attention.

Gently she places the animal onto the floor and then sips her tea. She bookmarks the page and writes down a note on one of the charts she has made about me or my constitution. Perhaps it has to do with the way she believes I have suppressed my grief. Or the fact that I tend to awake in the night and grow anxious. My fear of spiders. And cancer. And death.

Then, maybe, she returns to the notes she took during our session and rereads what I said about food and sleep and sex. She looks at the medical history I offered and then reviews the chart she has made that lists my symptoms by intensity and depth. My sore throats and my sneezing. My wooziness. My headaches. My ongoing unease.

Sometimes, I'm told, the cure is clear-cut, but sometimes it demands a great deal of thought and exploration. Sometimes you get the cure right the very first time, and sometimes you don't.

Perhaps what will help her finally decide my remedy will be one of my memories of Elizabeth. How some of the smallest ways we would manifest our love were my favorites: the hours we would spend chatting in a bath together before Abby was born, or the summer evenings we would spend in our vegetable garden, happily pulling weeds from the beets and the carrots and the corn until nine or nine-thirty at night. Then there were those long walks we would take together after Abby arrived. We'd put our little daughter in the stroller on a Saturday or a Sunday afternoon and follow the road to the top of the hill to see Mount Abraham and Mount Ellen, or we'd wander without purpose through the old and the new cemeteries in East Bartlett.

Elizabeth and I imagined that someday we would be buried there, but it hadn't seriously crossed either of our minds that in one of our cases that day would come soon.

Eventually, Carissa has to shower and get dressed. Her first patient that day is due at nine-thirty. And so I see her inspecting her notes and her charts one last time, and then writing down the name of a remedy in my file. She will think about it some more, but not for very long. After all, her deliberative choice matches her instinctive one.

I am, she will tease me later, the sort who wears his disease on his sleeve.

I realized while driving home from work that night just how badly I wanted to see Carissa. I'd thought of her often that day. I'd thought of her whenever I'd sniffed or sneezed, whenever I'd walked past the coffeepot without pouring myself a cup. I'd thought of her whenever I'd seen a woman in eyeglasses, and the two times I'd seen one who'd taken her shoes off: One was in a booth at the restaurant where I was grabbing a take-out sandwich for lunch, and the other—clearly a law student—was in the front row of the courtroom when I was arguing a motion mid-afternoon.

I'd even been reminded of Carissa that morning when Margaret had chomped into a date—slicing the wrinkled, rust-red roach into halves, one chunk in her mouth and one in her hand—because from now on dates would remind me of confession, and confession would remind me of Carissa Lake.

But I knew I couldn't see her and I knew I shouldn't call her. I had to wait for her to call me. And so I decided if I couldn't see Carissa, I'd do the next best thing: I'd try and bump into a relative. I'd try and bump into her niece. I had time; it was barely ten after six. Mildred and Abby wouldn't expect me for at least another ten minutes.

As I pulled into the parking lot, I could see Whitney at the lone front register, weighing organic tomatoes for a customer before dropping them gently into a brown paper bag. I wasn't sure whether I'd figure out a way to bring up her aunt, but I also wasn't sure that it mattered. The genetic proximity alone was comforting.

The only part of the store I knew at all was the section with herbal tinctures, but Whitney gave me a wave and a smile as I walked in the door, and I felt sufficiently emboldened to explore other aisles. I took off my overcoat as if I actually meant to stay awhile, and wandered toward the alcove with the rice and the beans.

Rice and beans, I knew, were a whole lot better for me than bear claws and doughnuts. And a whole lot less appetizing. In all fairness, of course, I wasn't going to have a bear claw for dinner. I'd probably have another calzone—like the night before—though this time I'd have one with my daughter.

Clearly, my image of rice was simplistic compared to that of the people who shopped here. When I thought of rice, I thought white. Here, however, there were dozens and dozens of kinds of rice, and the distinctions were considerably more varied than color (brown versus white), or the length of the grain. Little markets like this probably didn't make the rice buyer at Grand Union quake in his boots, but it had to affect the guy's self-esteem: In four neat rows of clear plastic buckets, each row eight buckets long, was a universe of rice I'd never imagined existed. I wasn't sure any store really needed five kinds of basmati—white, brown, Indian, organic, and something called Piper and Slim's Hindu Love—but the choice was impressive. And so was the handwriting. Calligraphy on yellow and blue slips of colored paper.

There'd been a time back in the sixth or seventh grade when my parents

had joined a natural-foods co-op. Like their revolutionary reading group—
Soul on Ice, The Greening of America, biographies of Zelda Fitzgerald as femi-
nist martyr—it hadn't lasted very long. Fortunately.

"Hi, Leland."

I turned, thrilled that Whitney had remembered my name.

"Evening, Whitney."

"How are you doing?"

A heavy sweater tonight, instead of a button-down blouse. But still a big
skirt and sandals. It took more than a little snow on the ground to make those
feet grow modest.

"Good. Better, maybe."

"Cool. Back for more echinacea?"

"Can't have too much."

"Oh, I bet you can. Need some help here?"

I turned back to the rice. "Um, yeah. Basmati. I was going to get just plain
basmati, but now I'm not so sure."

"White?"

"I guess that's what I had in mind."

"Try Piper and Slim's instead."

"The Hindu Love?"

"Cooks up perfect. It's Piper's absolute fave."

"Slim's, too?"

"He practically inhales the stuff."

"Okay. I'm sold," I said, grabbing the scoop and a brown paper lunch bag.

"Did you ever go see my aunt?" she asked.

"As a matter of fact, I did. Last night."

"Cool," she said, her head bobbing with approval. "What did you think?"

"Of her? Or homeopathy?" The two questions slipped out reflexively
before I could stop myself.

"Whichever. No, my aunt. Isn't she savage?"

"Awesome."

"Think so?"

"I think so."

"What's the remedy?"

"She hasn't decided."

"The first time she gave me a remedy, I felt like this little baby bird in her
hands. Then, when they were gone, I got all tingly. It was the best."

"They?"

"The remedy. The sugar pills."

"Sugar's a remedy?"

She shook her head. "Doubt it. But some of the remedies are dropped onto small sucrose pellets."

"How many…remedies has your aunt given you?"

"Two."

"For the same thing?"

"Oh, no way!"

"Each worked?"

"Sure did."

"Can I ask why you were seeing her?"

"Sure. I broke my arm playing field hockey when I was sixteen, and it hurt like crazy even after the doctor said it was healed. Aunt Carissa took care of the pain completely. Hasn't hurt a bit in four or five years."

"And the other time?"

"Mondo woman's problems. Cramps, bloating. I become a real pain in the ass twelve or thirteen times a year. And so this summer I asked her if there was a remedy."

"And there was?"

"Pulsatilla. I think it's made from windflower."

"And it worked?"

She smiled and opened her arms. "Am I not one sweet girl this very minute? I'm going to get my period Sunday or Monday. If I hadn't seen Carissa in August—you know, professionally—we wouldn't be talking right now because you'd still be staring at the rice and I'd be fuming at the counter. I'd be, like, screaming at you in my mind to hurry the fuck up."

"Are all her patients so satisfied?"

"You bet."

I nodded, and for a long moment I felt her staring at me.

"So," she said abruptly. "When are you going to see her again?"

"She said she'd call me when she has a remedy."

"And you're going to wait?"

"Shouldn't I?"

"I'd call her."

"Really?" I thought I knew what she was hinting at, but I wasn't completely sure. I decided confirmation was worth the possible embarrassment.

"Is your aunt seeing anyone?"

"You mean, other than patients?"

"Yes."

"Not a soul."

The word appeared from my mouth like magic, and I wondered if there was something transforming in the air of the health-food store: "Cool," I said, and I watched her face—already impossibly radiant—brighten some more.

"We need to decorate the house for Christmas this year," Abby informed me as we drove home to East Bartlett in the pickup.

"Didn't we last year?" I asked, hoping I didn't sound defensive. The fact was, I really hadn't done a whole lot in the two Christmases since Elizabeth had died. A tree had been about it, and even that had always been a last-second addition.

"We need lots of decorations."

"Lots?"

"Stuff on the windows. And stuff on the tables. And stuff in bowls."

"Stuff in bowls?"

"It's a project," she said. *Project* was the word Kelly McDonough, the woman who ran Abby's day care, used for everything the kids did with glue sticks and colored paper. Sometimes the arts-and-crafts efforts were ingenious: puppets made from Popsicle sticks, poker chips, and small scraps of fabric. And sometimes they were simply insane: The pretend stained-glass windows they'd made by pressing grape jelly and lemonade drink mix between thin strips of clear plastic had looked beautiful for a day, but had gone bad pretty fast. And since they'd made the mock windows in July, some parents suspected the "project" was actually a do-it-yourself ant farm. The thing was a magnet for bugs.

"Oh, I see," I said.

"It'll be ready tomorrow."

"Does it have a name?"

"Welllllllll, it's got lots of pinecones and leaves and stuff. And cotton balls."

"For snow?"

"Uh-huh. And Daddy?"

"Yes, sweetheart?"

"Can we have stockings this year?"

"Sure."

She nodded, satisfied, and stretched her leg in her booster seat, using the toe of her snow boot to push an audiocassette into the truck's tape player. I reached over and turned up the volume, and we listened to the story of *Madeline* for the last few minutes of our drive home.

✧

I almost called Carissa the moment I'd put Abby to bed Thursday night, going so far as to stare at her name in the residential part of the phone book. But I couldn't bring myself to bother her at nine o'clock at her house—or, worse, not bother her because she actually had a life and was out for the night.

I considered leaving a message on her machine at her office, but decided against the idea because she'd told me she would call when she was ready, and that might take a couple of days.

And I wondered if she even had an answering machine in the Octagon. Perhaps she had an answering service instead. Maybe her phone clicked over to a live human being who answered calls for a living, and that person beeped Carissa when there was a patient in crisis:

Hi, Carissa, this is your service. The young lady who took foxglove this afternoon says she's having heart palpitations. She thinks she may have taken too much.

Even if there wasn't such a thing as a homeopathic emergency, perhaps she needed a service as a psychologist. Or was it a psychiatrist? I couldn't remember. She'd said she was a licensed something, and so maybe she still saw patients as a shrink.

I could call and find out. I could call and see if I got an answering machine or a service. And then hang up.

No, I couldn't do that. After all, I'd probably get an answering machine, and no single woman wanted to press a button to retrieve her messages and find a hang-up recorded. Not even in Vermont. Especially in Vermont.

And so if I wanted to call her, I'd have to wait till tomorrow. I'd have to wait to call her during the day.

Before changing into my pajamas, I went out to the pickup to unpack the long strips of wood that would form a railing at the church Saturday afternoon. The materials felt good in my hands, and the idea of building something excited me. Especially something for the church: That little congregation had helped me to retain a semblance of sanity in the months after Elizabeth died.

When the screws and brackets and wood were tucked in the barn, I went back inside, unusually tired for nine-thirty at night. As I brushed my teeth, I remembered why: I'd made it through the day without coffee. Whole damn day, nine to five, and all those hours on either side.

Granted, it had taken a couple of Advil mid-morning and a third one just after lunch to silence the giant rotary drill that was pounding through my skull in search of water. But at some point that afternoon, the caffeine-withdrawal ache in my brain had gone away and I'd completely forgotten that I wanted a cup of coffee.

Son of a bitch, I thought, there's hope for me yet. Tonight I am going to sleep like a baby.

✧

I couldn't remember any details of the dream, I just knew it had awakened me. No, I didn't know even that. For all I knew, it was the sore throat that had caused me to open my eyes.

There were no Halls upstairs, that was guaranteed. So, there would be no falling back to sleep without an excursion downstairs. I kicked off the sheets and walked through the house without turning on a light. Past the bedroom in which my daughter was sleeping soundly. Past the guest room still dominated by a cardboard mover's wardrobe full of Elizabeth's clothes, and the smaller boxes with the scarves and purses and shoes I planned to offer Abby as she grew up. Down the stairs that descended sixteen steps, through the thin hallway that led to the kitchen, and then into the old house's lone bathroom.

I smacked my tongue against my teeth after zapping my throat with Chloraseptic.

Sweet.

Not, I imagined, as sweet as a sugar pill—even a sugar pill doused in belladonna or Pulsatilla, or whatever it was that Whitney had said she'd been given.

I decided I wouldn't have minded if Whitney had been in my dream. Of course, if someone was going to intrude upon my sleep, I would have preferred Carissa. But if not the homeopath...I would have forgiven Whitney.

Hell, I would have forgiven that older woman who worked in the store, too, the one with the toes from heaven. I would have been perfectly happy if it had been her in some kind of sexy dream.

The problem was that the dream hadn't been sexy at all. It had been stupid and violent and messy. It had had something to do with a particularly brutish drunk who'd passed through the system that day, a guy who for no apparent reason—other, perhaps, than a four-dollar pint of Canadian Ltd.—had taken a shotgun and blown out the windows of a parked patrol car in Burlington. It was a miracle that no one had been hurt.

I stared at the shadow in the bathroom mirror that was as close as I'd get to a reflection in the dark, and saw myself shaking my head as I sighed. It was three in the morning and I was awake once more with a sore throat, and it was all because of some idiot who'd drunk way too much whiskey. Unbelievable.

And the most frustrating part, I decided, was that I hadn't had a single cup of coffee all day. Not one tiny drop. And still I was awake in the night.

6

NUMBER 27

The curative virtue of medicines thus depends on their symptoms being similar to those of the disease, but stronger.
It follows that ... disease can be destroyed and removed most surely, thoroughly, swiftly, and permanently only by a medicine that can make a human being feel a totality of symptoms most completely similar to it but stronger.

DR. SAMUEL HAHNEMANN,
Organon of Medicine, 1842

Jennifer Emmons would call the state psychology board about Carissa the day after Christmas, probably not long after calling the State's Attorneys Office in Burlington, the physician who was treating her husband for asthma, and the Attorney General's Office in Montpelier.

It was from someone in the Attorney General's Office that she had learned that the state of Vermont does not regulate homeopaths. Naturopaths and hypnotherapists and acupuncturists, yes. Diathermists and hydrotherapists, most certainly.

But not homeopaths.

Nevertheless, at some point she'd recalled that Carissa was also a psychologist. And psychologists were regulated in Vermont.

Jennifer would make her calls from the phone in the waiting room outside the ICU. When she left messages, she would leave the number for the hospital, along with the extension for the nursing station near her husband's room.

And then she would return to the chair beside her husband's bed and wait for people to call her back.

Richard's physician was enraged, though I think a part of his anger stemmed from the fact that his patient had gone behind his back to another healer. Richard had never told the fellow he had gone to a homeopath, and I imagine there was a certain amount of territoriality in the doctor's response.

The lawyer in my office who returned her call, Bob McFarland, only spoke with her for a minute or two, just long enough to determine that she'd already given a statement to a trooper.

Her longest conversation that morning, without a doubt, was with Garrick Turnbull—the head of the state psychology board and the husband of young prosecutor and date-eater Margaret Turnbull. When he called Jennifer back, she told him all that she understood about the Law of Similars, because she knew that it mattered. She wasn't completely sure why, not yet anyway, but never for a moment had she thought that her husband had tried to kill himself. Not for a second.

No, in her mind, he did what he did because of a ludicrous philosophy of healing called homeopathy and a dangerously irresponsible homeopath named Carissa Lake. And so she had related to Garrick the little she knew about homeopathy, and what she said Richard had told her about the Law of Similars.

"The law of what?" she'd asked Richard when he first tried explaining it to her one evening in early December, sipping the eggnog he'd poured.

"Similars," Richard had said, stretching his legs in his chair. Lately he'd complained to her that on top of everything else—on top of his asthma and his eczema—his joints had started to ache in the night. Only when he moved did the aching subside. "She calls it the Law of Similars."

"Meaning?"

"Like cures like. Sort of like immunization. You know, giving someone a little polio in a polio vaccine. Or the way you'll give a cat a trace of feline leukemia."

"She's going to give you asthma? How is she going to give you asthma?"

She hadn't meant for the question to sound antagonistic, but she knew instantly that it had—especially since it was clear Richard himself understood that his grasp of homeopathic basics was pretty shaky. He had only the vaguest idea of what he was talking about, and what, therefore, he was getting himself into.

"Why are you being so skeptical about all this?"

"Well, you have to admit, it sounds pretty kooky," she'd said, trying to make light of her concern. "It sounds a little like some of that New Age hokum you hear about at pricey spas."

"Wouldn't you like to see me off drugs?" he'd asked.

Outside their living-room window, great, puffy dots of white had continued to fall. It had started to snow that day just after lunch, and it hadn't stopped for a moment ever since. There was probably a half-foot on the ground by the time Richard had gotten home. Christmas, then, was still close to three weeks away, but we were all confident it would be white.

"No. I don't care about the drugs. *You* do. I just want to see you well."

"Well, that's why I'm seeing her."

She'd sighed. She'd wanted the conversation behind them before dinner, because she didn't want to be having this discussion in front of the kids. "If she's not going to give you asthma, what exactly is she going to give you?"

"I won't know until I see her again next week."

"But she's going to give you something."

"Yes."

"What will it do?"

"I think it will boost my body's immunity to things that cause asthma— sort of like a shot. Now, does that really sound 'New Agey' to you? It sounds pretty darn normal to me."

"That's the Law of Similars?"

"That's right."

"Why don't they just call it immunization, in that case?"

He'd rolled his eyes, irritated and defensive. "Look, I don't know that much about it. But it's not like this stuff is experimental. It may be 'alternative' in the eyes of a veterinarian or a doctor. But she says it's been around for almost two centuries."

Jennifer told me a thought had passed through her mind at that moment, but she'd kept it to herself: *Medicine isn't like wine. I don't want my pills carefully aged. I want the latest, freshest, newest stuff that they have.*

"So long as it won't make you worse…" was all that she'd said.

Though the time would come soon enough when she would wish to God she'd said more.

✧

"You really should see a doctor," my boss was saying to me. "I know, I know. You have. See one again. Or see another."

"I don't think there's a heck of a lot they can do," I said, swallowing the last of my cough drop so I could sip my coffee. Months ago I'd discovered it was no easy task to sip coffee with a cough drop in my mouth. Actually, the sipping part was easy. It was the enjoying part that was hard.

"Not true. There's always something they can do. And, more important, there's always something you can do."

"Think so?"

"I do."

Phil Hood never seemed to be sick. As far as I knew, the only time the man didn't come in to work was when he was on vacation with his children or, those days, his children and grandchildren. Three years earlier he'd become a grandfather for the first time, and evidently he'd liked the role so much he'd convinced his other two children, both daughters, to have babies as well.

I had met the infants, and they looked nothing at all like Abby had when she'd been a baby: a nearly doll-like round face, a mouth almost always molded into a smile. This kid, Elizabeth had observed soon after Abby was born, just loves this world.

Phil's grandchildren, on the other hand, were gargoyles. All of them. The oldest one, the one who was three, wasn't quite so repulsive anymore, but he still had the potential to grow into the Elephant Lad. Not literally, of course. Thank God. But the child's head was huge, and shaped like a beet.

"First of all, you drink way too much coffee," Phil went on. "I'm sure that's part of the problem. You might just as well be pumping it into your system with an intravenous feed."

When Phil had turned fifty a few years earlier, he'd given the stuff up completely. Gone cold turkey, replaced it with bottled water. It had seemed to me almost preternaturally easy the way Phil had learned to live without java.

"Some of the cups are decaf," I said.

"Poison," Phil said. "Pure and simple." Then he and his wife had gone vegan. No meat. No dairy. No doughnuts.

"Oh, come on."

"Really. The process often involves drenching those little brown buggers—the beans—in an extremely caustic chemical solvent. Your system has to cope with that."

"I'm sure some of the decaf's been made with water."

"It's still acid-forming. It's still putting a nightmarish burden on your kidneys. Your urinary tract." He paused, and I was about to respond, when he added, "Ever think of buying a dialysis machine? They're not cheap, but I'll bet it's the sort of thing you could rent to own."

Behind Phil, in the lake in the window, I could see a ferry moving west across the water toward New York. It was the first of December. Although a warm front was about to arrive, eventually even this part of the lake would freeze solid.

"I'll buy a snowblower first, thank you very much."

"Does that shaman you call your physician know how much coffee you drink?"

"That shaman's the primary-care physician I got with our health plan."

"Oh, great. You're going to put your health in the hands of the state. Wise decision."

"Phil, would you give it a rest?"

"I just think you should take better care of yourself."

"I appreciate that. But ever since you went out and decided to take care of your body and Margaret went out and married Dr. Strangelove, I can't go into either of your offices without getting a lecture about something. I'm afraid to open my mouth around either of you."

"He's not a doctor."

"Who?"

"Margaret's husband. Garrick. He's a psychologist, not a psychiatrist."

"I know that. It's just a nickname."

"Not a very flattering one. I gather you don't like him."

"I like him fine. I just find him a little uptight. Officious."

"Officious…"

"Inflexible. A real rule-maker."

Phil swiveled in his chair and rested his wingtips on the radiator. There was snow on the mountains across the lake.

"You know," Phil said, pressing the fingertips on both hands together. "There are those who would say the same thing about you."

"About me?"

"Absolutely. Leland Fowler, they'd say, shits in rows."

"Nice, Phil." Ever since Phil had discovered natural health, he'd become, in my opinion, way too comfortable with feces.

"See what I mean? You are an extremely uptight fellow. Probably even more uptight than Garrick."

"That's not possible."

"He's on the state board, you know."

"The psychology board?"

"Uh-huh."

"Why am I not surprised?"

"Most people think it's a great honor."

"I'm sure."

He turned back toward me. "Sometimes I think you're a very angry person."

"Margaret's supposed to be telling me that. You're just supposed to criticize my eating habits."

"See? You put everything into these little tiny boxes. Your life is too compartmentalized. Don't get me wrong: It's clear you're doing a great job with Abby. And you do very, very good work here. But you're still incredibly anal."

Someday, I decided, I would find out who had set Phil and Barbara Hood on the road to better health. And then I'd kill him. I realized I'd been in Phil's office for close to half an hour and we still hadn't gotten to the litany of cases I needed to discuss. And now I was due in court to explain why some asshole— now, there was a colorful word I'd be sure to use around Phil the next time we had a chat—who'd blown 2.0 when he was picked up going the wrong way on I-89 shouldn't be allowed near the keys to his car ever again.

"I'll work on that."

"Oh, I know you won't. At least not yet. Sometimes it's hard to change."

I considered informing Phil that I'd actually gone to see a homeopath, but telling him now would sound defensive. Besides, I couldn't bear to give him that much satisfaction; I couldn't imagine giving him the notion that Leland Fowler was now among the converted. He might think he had had something to do with it.

"I have to run, Phil, I'm due in court. Will you be around later this morning?"

"I expect so."

"Can we connect then?"

"Good chance."

When I went to my office to get the files I needed on Derek Linder, the

DWI King of Vermont, I saw a message from Carissa Lake. With any luck, Linder wouldn't keep me more than half an hour. For all I knew, I might have my remedy in forty-five minutes.

Take that, Phil Hood, I thought. I've got myself a homey.

✧

I stopped by the coffee machine on my way back to my office. Most of the time I loved the fact that the state's attorneys worked in the same building with the state courtrooms, but there were occasional moments when I wished I had an excuse to escape the second and third floors of the illustrious Edward J. Costello Courthouse. I would have loved to have been flirting with Carissa Lake while sipping a decent cup of coffee, for example. Instead I was drinking the paludal muck someone had brewed in our office two or three hours ago. Maybe longer. I wondered if I'd have to confess to my homeopath that I'd gone back on the juice.

"How are you feeling?" she asked me. "Still emotionally wrung out?"

"A little less so."

"Good. I have some news for you."

"You have my remedy?"

"I do."

"I've been dying to know. What is it?"

There was a long beat at the other end of the line, and I began to hear in my mind the word *tarantula*. Shit. *I'm going to have to eat a damn spider.*

"Do you have your calendar in front of you?" she asked, instead of answering my question.

"I should be sitting down, shouldn't I? This is going to be one of those 'Are you sitting down?' kind of remedies, isn't it?"

"There's no such thing."

"So I'll like my remedy?"

"That's not why I called. I called because I want to schedule an appointment to give you your remedy."

"Won't you tell me what it is?"

"I'd rather not. Sometimes it's better that way."

"Tell me the truth: Are you going to make me eat a spider?"

"That's not the issue. That's not why I'd prefer not going into the details of your cure."

"Will you promise me that it won't be a spider?"

"No."

"Because it might be?"

"Leland, you're the type who's either done some reading in that book I gave you or would do some once I told you the remedy. You'd look it up."

"You've mistaken me for an informed consumer. Trust me, I'm not."

"You're a lawyer!"

"Sticks and stones…"

She laughed briefly, but then went on, "Sometimes it's for the best that the patient doesn't know. Sometimes patients read more into the cure than is there. It affects their self-esteem."

Even if this wasn't going to be an "Are you sitting down?" kind of remedy, I began to fear that the conversation had the potential to offer an "Are you sitting down?" kind of revelation. And so I sat down.

"Go on," I said.

"Some remedies treat a variety of symptoms. Some cure a variety of maladies. I don't want you to read into my choice something that isn't there."

Impotence, I thought. She thinks I'm impotent.

"What if I promise not to look up the cure?" I asked.

"I want to schedule an appointment," she said, ignoring me. "I want you to come to my office for the remedy, and we can talk about it then."

"The name of the remedy."

"Right."

"How's tonight?"

"It's Friday."

"Ah. Of course."

"I mean, if you don't have plans, you could certainly drop by on your way home from Burlington."

"Do you have plans?"

"I may go to a large, loud party I have little interest in attending. I may not."

"And you wouldn't mind giving me the remedy this evening?"

"No, not at all. You're caffeine-free?"

I paused, balancing my health and my horniness. At that moment, I decided, it was clear my horniness was more important. I could always regain my health when I wasn't drooling over every woman I met in the health-food store.

Yet even as I opened my mouth to boast that I was caffeine-free, I couldn't bring myself to lie. Even when the image of Carissa Lake curled in her chair like a very long cat flashed before my eyes.

"I got through yesterday without any coffee," I said. "But I had to have some this morning."

"Work-related?"

"I guess. And sleep-related. I didn't sleep well last night."

"Any cough drops?"

"Well, my throat has been sore," I said, sounding more like a six-year-old than I would have liked. I hadn't even realized I was supposed to avoid cough drops.

"Let's plan on Monday, in that case. Try and go the weekend without coffee. Sunday may be hard, but at least you won't be at work. And Monday should be a breeze."

I sighed. I'd have to go the weekend without seeing her. I'd have to go the weekend without knowing my cure. I'd have to go the weekend without coffee.

"Okay."

"Avoid cough drops, too—any product with menthol, in fact."

"I'll try."

"Would you like to come in before work? Maybe first thing in the morning, right after you drop off Abby at day care?"

"Monday morning looks like chaos. After work might be better," I said.

"Five-thirty?"

I calculated that that would mean leaving the office by five or ten minutes of five. Doable. Not usually, of course. But for Carissa Lake? One time? Easy.

"Five-thirty's good," I said. "Do you think you might be able to tell me the cure in person?"

"Maybe. But more than likely I won't. At least I won't want to."

"Okay."

"It's supposed to be a lovely weekend, Leland. Treat yourself: Get outside."

"I will."

"And remember: no coffee."

I looked at the Styrofoam cup on my desk. I couldn't wait to dump it down the sink.

✦

East Bartlett had been settled at the very end of the eighteenth century, but—unlike its contemporaries with names like Jericho and Chelsea and Bristol—no one had tried finding a few flat acres for a central green or town commons. They knew a few flat acres didn't exist.

Instead they found three small hills that were somewhat less precipitous than the mountains nearby, and huddled there in their homes, raising sheep—and then cows and then nothing—on the rises around them, which may not have been literal mountains but were nevertheless about as steep as beginner ski slopes.

If East Bartlett had been known for anything in recent memory, it had been known for dairy farming. As recently as 1946, the hill town of barely eight hundred people had forty-five dairy farms. By the time Elizabeth and I had moved there—a half-decade after the federal government's attempt to stabilize the price of milk by buying whole dairy herds from small farmers—there were five, and by the time Elizabeth died, there were none. Zero. The last herd went to auction the winter before the accident.

On one of those three hills sat the closest thing East Bartlett had to an urban skyline: a church steeple, a weathervane atop the brick monolith that served as the town hall, a twelve-by-twelve roof of a gray general store, and a bell tower atop the volunteer fire company's two-bay garage.

Abby and I lived about a third of a mile from the center, our house angled so that the village was visible from the den, a porch, and one of the windows in Abby's bedroom. Like most of East Bartlett, to get to work I drove down a winding, torturously thin road that linked the community with a wider, straighter two-lane state highway that in turn linked us with civilization: Bartlett to the immediate west, and Hinesburg, South Burlington, and—eventually—Burlington to the north. Most of East Bartlett either worked in Bartlett or commuted to Burlington.

My favorite structure in the town was the church, and not just because the congregation that worshiped there had helped me through those months after Elizabeth died. The building itself had merit. It was small, but it had a deceptively high steeple, and the white clapboard additions along the north and south sides made the century-and-a-half-old church look a bit like a seagull with her wings folded underneath her.

Since Elizabeth had died, I had become the congregation's most enthusiastic volunteer who absolutely, positively could *not* be counted upon. This had,

I believe, nothing to do with what I have heard called a crisis of faith. Nevertheless, in the past year alone, I'd failed to get the garland and ribbons for Pentecost, I'd had to ad-lib every single one of my lines as a Capernaum rabbi during Vacation Bible School, and two days before Sunday school was due to begin, I'd bowed out after promising I'd be a teacher. One of the other state's attorneys had resigned, and—budgets being as tight as they were—I knew it was unlikely the position would be filled in the foreseeable future (or, to be realistic, in my lifetime). Which meant there would be more work for the rest of the attorneys, and less time for me to figure out how to explain parables and plagues to a group of dubious seven-year-olds.

And then, of course, there was that railing for the handicapped-access ramp. I'd volunteered to build it in April. It was now December. Human babies became viable in less time than it had taken me to get around to the project.

I couldn't figure out why that was, because Abby was growing into an extremely undemanding little person. And while my job was time-consuming, most of the things I was failing to accomplish weren't that hard. Would it really have been all that difficult to have dropped by the dime store two blocks from my office to pick up the ribbons for Pentecost?

Nor was it simply that my spirit was strong but my flesh was weak: The fact was, for most of my life I'd been excellent at doing what I'd said I would do; for most of my life I'd been the sort of person people could count on.

Not lately, it seemed. As Phil had said, I was still doing a pretty good job as a taxpayer-funded good guy, and at least a reasonable job with my daughter. But everything else?

There was nothing else.

Whenever I tried to layer in anything else, I botched it. Became a complete nincompoop.

And so the Saturday after scheduling my follow-up appointment with Carissa, I was determined to become the vaguely dependable person I'd once been, I was determined to complete the handicapped-access ramp at the church. I hoisted what had once been my father's Delta crosscut miter saw into the back of the pickup, along with all the lumber and brackets I'd purchased that week, and drove a third of a mile to the center of town. It was an absolutely beautiful afternoon, one of the warmest days I'd ever seen in December. The temperature, I'd heard, was supposed to sneak into the mid-fifties, and already much of the snow on the ground had melted. Abby was at a little friend's party until dinner, and so there really wasn't even any pressure to work fast.

Yet here's what I remember most about that afternoon: I am staring briefly at the saw, anchored that moment on the back hatch of the pickup, and I am pressing the yellow foam plugs into my ears to make sure they are snug. I glance once again at the church ramp, switch on the saw, and then run another long, tube-shaped piece of pressure-treated pine through the blade.

And, once more, nearly cut off my thumb.

Normally I am a pretty able guy with a saw; my father taught me well. But that day? That was at least the third time I'd come within a fraction of an inch of losing a sizable part of a finger. If I wasn't careful, I'd end up trick-or-treating as a logger next Halloween.

At the time, I attributed my incompetence entirely to caffeine withdrawal. I was a junkie, I decided, and while I might finish the banister, there would be a price to pay and it wouldn't be pretty: *Good evening,* I imagined myself saying Monday night to Carissa Lake. *I have a new chief complaint. Shooting pains at the edge of my hand where I once had a thumb.*

But while caffeine withdrawal might have been a distraction, it wasn't the only one. It hadn't yet crossed my mind, however, that I just might be falling in love.

✧

Late Sunday night when Abby had long been asleep, I pressed into the VCR one of my tapes of Elizabeth and watched her swimming in the river that ran through the woods along a part of East Bartlett. I watched her telling me to turn off the camera while she was sitting in her bathing suit on one of the tremendous boulders that were virtual islands in the slow current. She was wearing the black maillot with nothing but webbing along the sides, the one she'd bought the January we'd gone to Aruba.

I watched her smile, then pretend to be annoyed, then slip back into the water and swim under the surface until she was out of sight behind the rock.

She reappeared a moment later before the birch that had fallen that winter into the river, the trunk buoyed above the water by another big rock, so the tree was like a bridge that spanned half the stream. She climbed onto the woody overpass, the wet Lycra molding itself to the line of her spine and the thin crevice between her cheeks, and then she turned around and faced me once more.

"Leland," she said, trying to sound exasperated. Using the fingers of both hands to push that long, creosote black hair behind her ears. Pulling the elastic edge of the suit back down over the sharp bones of her hips, over the demarcation line between olive skin and merely tan.

Elizabeth could look tan in December. In the summer, when I would have to smear an SPF 28 on my face and my arms, she could have slathered her body with baby oil and not gotten burned.

"Lord, Leland," she said when I hadn't stopped filming, but by then she had settled onto the wide birch on her knees and gotten into the spirit. Smiling, she offered an impromptu parody of the uncomfortable poses that were demanded of the models in page after page of the swimsuit and lingerie catalogs that seemed to pepper our mail as Valentine's Day approached.

"Note my expression," she said to the camera. "There's a knot digging into my shin right this second, but you don't know that because I'm a professional. Beauty before pain."

We'd just gotten the camera, and it seemed I was taping her constantly. There she was weeding the carrots in the garden, playing croquet with friends, leaving the house in a business suit for the bank. Putting on lipstick. Brushing her hair. One time just sleeping.

The next time she appeared on a tape, that long hair would be cut.

And the time after that, she'd be pregnant, but no one knew but the two of us, and she certainly didn't look pregnant on the tape.

A few tapes later, she would.

The tapes had become small, treasured icons for me, more meaningful than the pearls Elizabeth had worn around her neck that I was saving for Abby, or the deep-green chemise that she had always thought she looked sexiest in.

This silk strap has touched her shoulder, I would think as I'd hold it some nights in my hands.

Those tapes meant more to me than the encyclopedia-length shelf of photo albums that were filled with pictures of Elizabeth, because on the tapes she moved and she talked and in at least two she sang to our daughter.

Abby had no idea that the tapes of her mother existed. In the months immediately after Elizabeth had died, they would just leave me sobbing and angry, and so I'd stopped watching them. But I'd still kept them in my armoire with the few other items in my life that had totemic value: The letters Elizabeth had written to me over the years, the studs I'd worn in my shirt the day we were married. My diploma. My law degree. A pair of my father's wristwatches.

And I'd been in no condition to follow my two-year-old around the house with the video camera after the accident. Before Elizabeth had died, I'd filmed Abby all the time—with little plush dolls, her bath toys, while pushing her play lawn mower across the living-room rug—but not once in the year after.

At some point soon after Abby had turned three, when the first anniversary of Elizabeth's death was behind me, I bought some blank tapes on a whim during my lunch hour in Burlington, and that summer night filmed Abby and her friend Greta while they'd played in my daughter's sea serpent–shaped sandbox. I'd told my daughter the video camera was brand new.

After that, I couldn't bring myself to tell Abby that the tapes of her mother existed. I wasn't even sure if I should. After all, she seemed to be perfectly satisfied meeting her mother in the two-dimensional snapshots that filled easily a dozen photo albums. She knew exactly what her mother looked like, the sorts of things her mother liked to do. She knew what she herself looked like in her mother's arms, in her mother's lap, in a Snugli upon her mother's chest.

What would it mean to Abby, I wondered sometimes, to suddenly hear her mother's voice? To see her mother singing to her when she was a toddler barely a year and a half? To see her mother pregnant one Easter Sunday? Hamming it up on a fallen tree in the river?

I was afraid it would be too much for her; I feared it would anger her in a way she'd never known—make real, once again, the loss, but with the added burden this time of a four-year-old's sense of the world. And so I'd kept the tapes to myself, watching them in the dark when the house and the hills were quiet and I was completely alone.

7

NUMBER 25

Administered properly...this medicine will rapidly, thoroughly, and permanently destroy the totality of the symptoms of the disease, which means the whole disease itself, changing it into health.

DR. SAMUEL HAHNEMANN,
Organon of Medicine, 1842

"Like cures like," Carissa explained to me. "That's essentially what we mean by the Law of Similars."

Her socks were black that night, just like mine, but she was wearing orange flats. I found myself gazing at her shoes so I wouldn't stare at the almost miraculous way her floral leggings (black like her socks, but silhouetted with flowers) were pasted to her calves and her thighs. I hoped whoever had invented Lycra spandex had been awarded some sort of Nobel Prize.

"The remedy you're about to receive begins with a substance—a natural substance—that might cause symptoms in a completely healthy person, but will cure those symptoms in someone who's ill."

"Someone like me."

"Someone with your symptoms. But understand, I'm not treating your symptoms. And I'm not treating the microorganism inside you that's giving you burning sore throats and a runny nose. I'm not giving you an antibiotic. As a matter of fact, I'm not giving you an anti-anything."

"If you're not treating my sore throat and runny nose, what are you treating?"

"I'm treating you."

"You're treating me," I echoed, nodding. I wondered what she saw when she looked at me. Could she see that I needed to lose a few pounds? Probably not. Not in a button-down business shirt. And if she had noticed my feet, she'd noticed my socks were *GQ* perfect. New, as a matter of fact. And surely she'd noticed them, because I'd slathered powder on my feet in the morning so that I could take my wingtips off that night in her office. Cheerfully I wiggled my toes.

"Right. I'm treating you. Your system. There's something going on in your body that's making it the perfect environment for the virus inside you to live. My goal tonight is to give you a remedy that will replicate your symptoms and restore your body's natural ecology. This way, your body can heal itself."

"Since the remedy will imitate—"

"Not imitate. The cure simply begins with a substance that causes symptoms similar to the ones you currently have."

"Does that mean I'll get one heck of a sore throat tonight?"

"That's a wonderful question."

"Thank you."

"You might."

"Oh, good."

"And you might not. In the remedy I'm about to give you, there's only the barest trace of the original substance. Only an infinitesimal genetic template remains. Make no mistake, it's going to be a strong, highly potentized dose… but still only enough to strengthen your body's ability to fight the infection on its own."

When she looked at me, I decided, she probably hadn't even noticed my socks. She took things like socks and bare feet for granted. Sort of like a doctor. But she wasn't a doctor, she was a homeopath. That was the whole point, wasn't it? She treated the patient, not the disease.

And so while she might take things like socks and bare feet for granted, she was likely to think of me as more than a symptom, more than a sore throat and a runny nose. If that was the case, I thought, then perhaps she saw before her a successful lawyer. No, it was better than that. She saw a successful state's attorney. A criminal prosecutor. One of the good guys. Granted, my hair had begun to recede, but whenever my mug appeared in the newspaper in the midst of a trial, I was always surprised to see I had pretty good cheekbones.

"Besides," she added, "the sore throat is only one manifestation of the way your entire body's tipped out of balance." She slipped off her eyeglasses, ran one of her long, elegant fingers across the bridge of her nose and underneath one of her eyes, and then reached down—she's going to slip off her shoes, I thought, and I'm going to moan out loud if I'm not careful—and briefly massaged her ankle.

I realized my mouth was dry. Really dry. Drier even than the last time I'd been here. "So?" I croaked. "My remedy is…"

"Leland, there are just so many reasons why I don't want to tell you that."

"I know, I know. You're worried I'll think less of myself. I promise, I won't. I'm not even sure that's possible."

"And I really fear if I tell you the cure, you'll look it up. And then the symptoms will indeed grow worse for a time."

"I can live with a sore throat a little longer."

"That might be your chief complaint, but it's only one symptom."

"I'm not going to win this argument, am I?"

"That's not the point."

"Okay, then. Let's do it," I said, trying to sound confident and eager and willing at once, but pretty sure I'd sounded only sickly and thirsty and hoarse.

"You're ready?"

"Absolutely."

"Had any coffee this weekend?"

I shook my head no: "Crisp and clean and no caffeine."

"Honestly?"

"I swear it. I mean, I paid the price on Saturday and Sunday. But today's been pretty easy."

"Good. Any cough drops?"

"Nope."

"Excellent. How do you feel?"

"Thirsty."

She smiled and stood, adjusting the monster ski sweater she was wearing. "I'll get you some water."

When she had started toward the water cooler at the other end of her office, I noticed a tiny vial of pellets in the cushion of her chair. It looked a little like a drugstore bottle of prescription pills, right down to the typewriter type on the label, except for the fact that this vial was clear instead of tinted and the contents were...tiny. The white dots inside were even smaller than the Claritin I scarfed down through the late spring and early summer. *Now, those were small pills.*

I was about to sip my water as she was standing beside me—over me—when I suddenly felt the urge to stand, too. She was tall and I was sitting, and it made for a bad combination. It wasn't that I minded feeling small and vulnerable as she towered over me, it was the fact that I was staring right into her stomach. Or her chest, I realized, if I rolled my eyes one way, if I leaned my head back to finish my water. Her groin, I realized, if I rolled my eyes down. It didn't matter that Carissa was wearing a bulky sweater that hung to mid-thigh, it was my simple proximity to paradise. I couldn't stand it, and so I stood beside her to drink.

"Better?" she asked when I finished.

"Better," I said, and she went to her chair for the little vial.

"As I said, at first your symptoms might get worse. Or they might stay the same. Either way, you shouldn't fear that nothing has happened. Give yourself a week or two," she said, and she popped off the little container's top.

"I understand."

"Now. Make like a baby bird," she murmured, and she tilted her own head back as a model.

When I did, I thought immediately of her view of my nose hair, but there wasn't a whole lot I could do.

"This will taste sweet. These are sucrose pellets."

"How many am I getting?"

"Four or five."

"That precise, huh?"

"Downright clinical," she said. "Open wide, and hold the pellets under your tongue. Don't swallow them, and don't chew them. Just let them dissolve."

"Okay."

She tapped the pellets into my mouth, and before I felt the sweet that she'd promised, I felt something burning. It was brief but real. Hot. It was as real as the sugar candy now melting atop my tongue. But of course it wasn't sugar candy. It was a sugar pill hiding tarantula. Or belladonna. Or sulphur.

Perhaps even arsenic. Maybe that was the burning I'd experienced. Maybe the burning was the medicine. Then, not just under my tongue, but every-where, I felt a prickliness rolling inside me.

"I feel a little tingly," I said.

"That's natural."

I swallowed, careful not to swallow the pills in my mouth. "I really do feel strange."

"Good."

"I'm not going to overdose, right?" I asked, smiling, hoping she'd think what I'd said was a joke, but reassure me nonetheless.

"Nope."

"Because I really have the...the creepy-crawlies."

"Why don't you sit down, then?"

I sat down on the couch and she sat down in her chair, and I turned toward the window and sighed. At night, the glass looked like a mirror coated with stovepipe paint, a black hole beside the skyline of Paris.

"How much longer?" I asked without looking at her.

"Till the pills dissolve?"

"Yes."

"It varies. Maybe another two or three minutes. No more."

I nodded. I was thinking that nighttime was the worst time in the world for hypochondriacs, when waves of goose bumps streamed over my arms, and I felt a shiver ripple along the back of my neck. It was as though that prickli-ness on the inside was now on the outside. And then, suddenly, I felt a rush I could only call good. Then great. Then...well, it wasn't just that I no longer felt anything in the back of my throat, it wasn't just that I no longer felt even thirsty. I felt happy. Really happy. Not happy like when I would realize the food I was eating actually tasted pretty good, or happy like when I'd leave a theater thinking a movie had been worth seven-fifty; I was happy, I realized, like that day when I was seven, soon after my family had moved to Vermont, and my parents had gotten my sister and me the puppy we'd wanted so badly. That amazing, perfect, half-springer mutt we'd named Herman. *That* happy. A-little-boy-rolling-in-the-Vermont-grass-with-his-dog happy.

Happy without complication.

This was visceral joy, that elation that must begin at the chromosome. Elemental...rudimentary...fundamental joy.

"How are you doing?" she asked.

"Fine," I said, my voice no more than a whisper.

"Good."

I turned toward her and saw she'd curled one of her legs up beneath her. Her orange shoes against her black pants made me think of Halloween, and that made me think of those marvelous, wondrous nights when I'd come home with whole shopping bags of Mars bars and M&M's, Milky Ways and Mike & Ikes, fireballs and Tootsie Rolls and UNICEF cartons of coins. The litany of costumes passed before my mind's eye: Lion, skeleton, jack-in-the-box. Vampire. Shortstop. Batman, sheik, bum.

And, always, cans and cans of shaving cream. Never used. But always there. Just in case.

"Still with us?" Carissa. Carissa's voice.

"I guess."

Nights that were numinous, more magic than fire. The costume—earthy, commercial, it didn't matter—always transcended the Barbasol and the curfew and the cold.

"Good."

Another masquerade: warlock. With Elizabeth as a witch—an incredibly beautiful, slinky witch. And a little girl we called Demon Baby, sometimes in her arms and sometimes in mine: Abby, fast approaching eighteen months. Black mascara rings around her eyes, and rub-on tattoos on her cheeks. We went trick-or-treating at the homes of the elderly in town, and Abby let us show her off to almost a dozen of our older neighbors before deciding this ritual was for the birds and melting down.

But it had been a luminous forty-five minutes.

"How are you feeling?"

I blinked, and Carissa came back into focus. "Great," I said.

"I'm glad."

Yet *great* did not do the feeling justice. This was more. This was more than serenity or well-being or confidence. This was different.

I sighed, aware that I was smiling. This isn't just contentment, I thought, this isn't just any old joy. This is Elizabeth-back-with-me-in-a-green-silk-chemise sort of bliss.

"When can I see you again?" I asked.

For the first time since I'd taken the cure, I was aware she was watching me. I knew instantly what she was going to say—not the exact words, but certainly the sentiment. *You mean professionally, of course.* That was what she was going to say. Something like that. But it didn't bother me, it didn't matter at all. It wasn't rejection. It was that doctor-patient thing. And once I was better—*Jesus, God in heaven, I think I'm better now!*—that would change.

"Let's see. Today's the fourth. Why don't we plan on a follow-up between Christmas and New Year's?"

"Should we schedule it right now?"

"Would you like that?"

"Very much."

I felt the last of the pellets disappearing, and I took a deep breath when they were completely gone.

"Will I need more?" I asked.

"You sound like you want more."

"I'm a junkie. I have a homey-jones, Carissa."

She grinned. "You might. We'll talk about that at your follow-up."

"I won't need any more tonight? Or tomorrow? It won't be like a prescription?"

She shook her head. "Sorry."

"I wish I'd come to you sooner," I said. "Is it like this for everyone?"

"I can only guess what you're feeling, but—"

"I'm feeling unbelievable, Carissa! Fantastic! Absolutely, unbelievably fantastic!"

"No. It's not like that for everyone. Not even for everyone who receives your remedy."

"And that is?"

"You're just dying to know, aren't you?"

"I am."

"Fine, I give up." She held up the vial in her hands, and while the type was too small to read from where I was sitting, I had a pretty good idea what it said. And I could feel myself starting to smile inside. Here the notion had given me so much anxiety in the middle of the night only the week before; it had terrified, angered, and appalled me at once. And now it made all the sense in the world. Like cures like. The Law of Similars.

"Think you know?" Carissa asked.

"I do."

"Want to venture a guess?"

"It won't be a guess."

She spread wide her arms, the vial disappearing behind her fingers in the palm of her hand. "Go for it."

"Arsenic."

"Bingo."

"It's not just a homey-jones, Carissa. I got me an arsenic-jones."

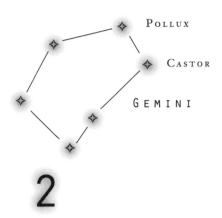

POLLUX

CASTOR

GEMINI

2

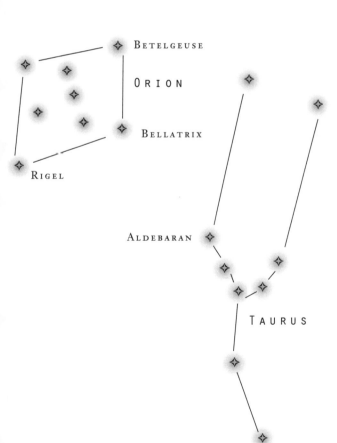

BETELGEUSE

ORION

BELLATRIX

RIGEL

ALDEBARAN

TAURUS

8

N U M B E R   1 1 7

What we call idiosyncracies belong to the last category.

We mean that particular physical disposition, in otherwise healthy persons, to become more or less sick from certain things that do not appear to make any impression or alteration at all on many other people.

DR. SAMUEL HAHNEMANN,
Organon of Medicine, 1842

No two witnesses will recall an event in exactly the same way. This is true even when the witnesses are wholly well-intentioned and interested solely in what they perceive to be truth. No two memories are ever exactly alike.

Moreover, memories change over time. In rare cases they grow more accurate, the details more vivid and real, but most of the time those details turn hazy or become transformed: Colors of cars change. Men grow beards. A woman, suddenly, is wearing slacks instead of a skirt.

Sometimes a witness knows he is changing his story. Sometimes not.

Most prosecutors want the police or state troopers to get statements from witnesses as soon as possible, simply because memories tend to age so badly.

Jennifer Emmons came to my office the day after Christmas. Her recollections there of what had occurred in her home on Christmas Eve differed little—if at all—from the taped statement she'd given a state trooper and his detective sergeant on Christmas Day.

Have some of those details changed for her now? I suppose. The simple act of telling the story to me—that lawyer who, in her mind, went from ally to enemy—must have affected what she remembered. Stories, after all, are merely memories given a certain tangibility with words, and it only takes a few words to subsume a memory completely.

Still, I will always be respectful of Jennifer's memory, and the way, desiring justice, she had pulled from her mind the fresh details of her horror. What she told me in my office would match, more or less, with what I'd hear later from the first responders—the term we use in Vermont for the EMS volunteers scattered throughout our rural communities, including East Bartlett, who will invariably arrive at an accident scene before an ambulance.

Like most first responders in Vermont, they knew the victim. Their patient. They knew Richard Emmons.

All of them, like me, must now have a vision of what preceded the emergency call. Unlike me, however, they probably do not have the advantage of having heard the story directly from Jennifer, and building that vision from her words: Richard sitting up in bed, wheezing. Jennifer opening her eyes in the dark and telling him to use his inhaler. Maybe it comes out like a command. Maybe, by that point, like a plea.

"Fine," he says, and it sounds as if he barely can speak. Which is exactly the case. He is getting so little air by this point, he really is having trouble talking.

But then she hears him using his inhaler, and she assumes he will be somewhat better in a moment. Much better soon after that. And so she is relieved.

But then he surprises her: He climbs out of bed without turning the light on, and he starts for the door. She hears him head down the stairs.

Maybe he's getting something to drink, she thinks. She hopes. At least, even those days just before Christmas, he had been good about fluids.

And maybe—just maybe—he is going to check the presents under the tree. Timmy, after all, will be up in three or four hours. No later than seven o'clock, that's for sure.

But Jennifer told me in my office that she had known in her heart this wasn't his reason for going downstairs, she had known even then this wasn't why he was leaving their bed.

He is getting up because he can't breathe.

How long has he been off his drugs, she wonders, how many days has it been? Five? Six? She calculates in her mind the last time he used his inhaler before tonight, or the last time he took a pill, and as far as she can recall, it was Monday. Monday morning.

Tomorrow will mark a full week. That's how long it has been.

It has in fact been so long that bronchospasms are no longer the problem. Inflammation is. His airways have become irritated, swollen, and congested with mucus. His windpipe, normally the width of his thumb, has been reduced almost to a drinking straw: Imagine a half-inch pipe that is choked with debris. Consequently, his reliever medication for bronchospasms, his albuterol inhaler, has become all but irrelevant. It has no effect on the cascade of thick fluid that has built up inside him.

And so now it is the night before Christmas and he is unable to breathe, his inhaler has failed, and he has gone downstairs to try something else. Take a prednisone, perhaps. Take one of the pills he's been given to help prevent exactly this sort of emergency.

She pushes the quilt off her shoulders and gets out of bed, too, surprised by how cold the floor has become. She always seems to forget. She grabs her bathrobe off the chair and then tiptoes into the hallway. She doesn't want to wake Timmy or Kate; she doesn't want them to worry because they can hear their parents wandering around the house in the dead of night.

She listens for a moment outside Timmy's door, but it is completely silent inside. Then she starts down the hallway, irritated by thoughts of that idiot homeopath.

Had she really thought of Carissa that moment? Or was her annoyance a new addition a day and a half later, a fabrication of which she was completely unaware? Was it an invention to give her anger a channel through which to pass while talking to me the day after Christmas?

Honestly? I believe that she did think of Carissa. Given the way Richard had grown excited over the cure—given my own experience the days immediately after I swallowed my arsenic—I am sure homeopathy was a subject of frequent conversation in the Emmons household in December. Jennifer, I am convinced, had wondered often that month exactly what that homeopath had given her husband.

After all, soon after taking his remedy, his skin had cleared up completely, and the aches in his joints had diminished. Within a week of receiving his cure, Richard had decided to give up the inhalers and pills he took for his asthma.

Even on Christmas Eve, I can imagine Jennifer wondering if that had been the homeopath's idea, too: *It had to be. It just had to be.*

And so at the top of the stairs, she has a thought. Not quite a vision, certainly not a premonition. Clearly she has no idea what is before her. But she thinks to herself at the top of the stairs, I am going to end up driving Richard to the emergency room Christmas morning because some irresponsible homeopath has told him to go off his inhalers and his theophylline. Astonishing. Simply astonishing.

That's what she thinks.

It is as she is wrapping her hand around the knob to the kitchen door that she hears the thud on the other side. Instantly she knows what it is: a body falling to the floor. Richard. She whips the door open and sees first the refrigerator swinging shut in slow motion, and then her husband collapsed on the tile before it.

She told me she heard herself shrieking his name, then her daughter's name, and she disliked the sound of the howl that was in fact her voice.

"Kate! Get down here!" she screams as loud as she can as she crouches on the floor by her husband.

He is on his back, his eyes open. But he is no longer able to breathe, so now he can't speak. On some level, she is aware that he has something in his hands, but she is unable to focus upon it. All she can see is the way the muscles along the sides of his neck are billowing like sails as he struggles to breathe, and the desperate panic in his eyes—something like fear and fight at once.

"Kate!" she shrieks again. She wants her daughter to go to the bedroom and get the inhaler—though a part of her understands her husband has already tried this and it hasn't worked.

But…but…what else can she do?

She stumbles over Richard to get to the telephone, and when she has the receiver in her hands, she swears—"Goddamn it! Goddamn it!"—because their part of Vermont does not yet have 911 emergency service.

Had she therefore actually had to look up the number for the local rescue squad in the phone book? No, she recalled with me, it hadn't come to that: She'd remembered that the number of their first-responder neighbor was stuck to a label inside the receiver of the phone.

She punches in the seven digits, and she recognizes her friend David's voice instantly.

"Richard can't breathe," she says. "Get over here, please!"

"Jennifer? Is that you?"

"Yes! Help us!"

"I'm on my way," he says, and she hears him hang up just as Kate appears in the kitchen, and then Timmy behind her.

"Daddy!" her daughter screams, and she falls back against the doorway, her hands on her mouth.

"Get his inhaler!" Jennifer says, and for the first time since she has seen her husband collapsed on the kitchen floor, she hears more determination than panic in her voice: The rescue squad is coming. Kate is getting the inhaler. This will, in the end, be okay.

She kneels beside Richard, wishing to God she knew CPR, when he slams the back of his hand onto the floor so hard it sounds to her like a rifle shot. She sees his eyes roll back in his head, and then his lids fall shut.

"What's happening?" Timmy whimpers.

Already his lips have begun to swell, and the first hives have begun to form on his neck.

Though she doesn't know the details of CPR, she figures she understands the basics: You hold the nose and blow air into the mouth. And so she curls her body over Richard's and pinches his nose, and then takes a deep breath. Before she can exhale into his mouth, however, she feels his body spasm and— her face almost touching his—she smells the vomit a split second before she sees it, before his body throws up whatever remains of his Christmas Eve supper.

She remembered, she said, looking away, trying not to vomit herself, as Kate had returned with her father's inhaler.

But then she turns back and reaches into Richard's mouth with her fingers to make sure his throat is clear. When she sees that it is, she squeezes his inhaler inside his lips. Nothing happens, and she does it again. Still nothing. And so she starts trying to breathe for him once more, the smell of all that he's retched more apparent when she sits up and breathes in herself than when she exhales into his mouth. I can do this, she thinks. I haven't a choice...so I can do this.

She isn't sure how many times she has tried breathing her husband back to life—it might have been five times, it might have been ten—when she hears David pounding at their front door.

"Let him in," she tells Kate, but her daughter has already started for the door.

She sits back on her legs, catching her own breath. For a split second her eyes skip over the tile floor, and her mind finally registers what her husband was holding when he collapsed. Instantly she recognizes what it is, what is inside. It is a clear bag with a label, the kind that are sometimes closed with a twist-tie. The kind of thing she would get at the health-food store. But she can't believe what she sees inside it; it doesn't make any sense. Cashews.

Richard is allergic to cashews.

David—a huge man, she realizes, especially when you're kneeling on your kitchen floor—pounds over to her in his boots, and she scoots a step back so he can get to her husband.

"He can't breathe," she hears herself saying, but clearly he has figured this out. From his satchel he pulls a clear plastic mask and a bag linked by a tube, and places the mask over Richard's mouth. "Give me the phone," he says as he starts squeezing the bag.

Behind her she hears a car in the driveway, and then the front door opening once more. Someone else is arriving, another volunteer.

"I think he was eating these," she says to David. Her words, in her mind, sound more perplexed than urgent. *Cashews? What was he thinking?*

Then she hands him the clear little bag of nuts.

"He allergic to them?" David asks.

"Yes."

"He know that?"

She nods, thinking: Good God, of course he did!

Her daughter brings David the cordless phone, and he rests it on his shoulder after dialing. Someone at the other end answers instantly, and she hears words and expressions that she doesn't understood. Anaphylaxis. Agonal breathing. Epinephrine. Then she hears one that she does: cardiac arrest. It will happen any second now.

"I'm giving him epi, one to one thousand, sub-q," David says on the phone before putting the receiver down, rolling up the sleeve of Richard's pajamas, and giving her husband a shot.

She leans back against a cabinet. Within moments, it seems, her husband is surrounded by men and women in the khakis and the jeans they'd thrown on half-asleep. There is Stephen and Ruthie and Doug. They open a little suitcase with a machine inside and start pressing patches with wires to Richard's chest. The wires lead back into the box.

"I.V. Ringer's," David says to one of the other volunteers, then murmurs, apparently speaking now to her husband, "Hang in there. The ambulance is coming."

"How long?" she asks, referring to the ambulance. How long till it gets here?

"It usually takes at least seven or eight minutes before the damage is irreversible," Ruthie answers, and Jennifer realizes that Ruthie thinks she has meant something else.

Her children lean against her, Timmy practically burrowing into her nightgown. She wraps one of her arms around each of them, and watches her family's friends work on her husband. One of the volunteers—it happened so fast, she wasn't able to tell if it was Ruthie or Doug—had batted the bag of cashews across the floor when it got in the way. David, at some point, must have put it down.

Stephen picks it up, evidently deciding it must be important.

"Why was he eating them?" he asks her, standing.

"I don't know."

"But he knew he was allergic to them?"

"Yes! He has asthma, and he's allergic to them! He knows that!"

"Shit," she hears David hiss. "No pulse. Shit. Hit press-to-analyze."

"Hands off," Ruthie says. "Clear."

The EMTs sit back on their heels, and the room becomes quiet. Jennifer expects an electrical charge will rip through her husband any second now, and his body will bounce off the floor—they all expect it—but then a metallic voice from the little machine informs them, "No shock indicated."

"What does that mean?" Jennifer says. "What?" But none of them answer. Suddenly even Stephen is back on the floor with the volunteer rescue workers, helping Ruthie to insert a plastic tube into Richard's mouth, while David is back on the phone with…someone.

"He went bradycardic, and now he's gone flat-line! There's just no heartbeat!" David is saying, his voice loud with the desperation that often precedes defeat. Then: "We're working the airway, that's just what we're doing! But we're not moving any air!"

She watches them press on his chest with two hands at a time. They tilt his head back, they battle his ever-swelling tongue. They try tightening the seal on the mask on his face. Finally David drops the phone, nodding at no one, and shoots more epinephrine into Richard's system.

Outside, the night sky over their driveway is filled with the flashing red strobes atop two of the rescuers' parked cars. Jennifer can see the lights through the kitchen window.

She feels her daughter pressing her forehead against her chest, and Timmy's little fingers squeezing her side. *Cashews,* she cries in her mind even then, *cashews! What in the name of God was he thinking?*

✧

What indeed?

No one will ever know for sure. But there is, in my opinion, a good deal we can assume.

We can assume, for instance, that he was frightened when he awoke in the night and couldn't breathe, because he finally broke down and tried his inhaler. Six days away from his usual pharmacopoeia—almost, as a matter of fact, seven—and he had at last succumbed to his body's dependence upon it.

Unfortunately, it was already too late for that. He was already too far gone for albuterol, the drug in his reliever inhaler. He was probably, by then, too far gone for even his prednisone to have been of any use.

No, by then Richard was in need of emergency medical help; by then he was in need of a hospital.

Did he know this? Did he understand what he had done to himself? Maybe. And so, perhaps, he was desperate and panicked and scared. He could barely breathe, and he was thinking with that peculiar lack of judgment that seems to mark the middle of the night.

It is at night, after all, when without fail the strangest crimes in this world occur, and some of the biggest mistakes are made. I know. For years, I have helped clean up the mess that is left in their wake.

Whether Richard did what he did because of Carissa—because she, too, had made a mistake, evidenced a peculiar lack of judgment herself—is still debated with gravity and ardor in some circles in Vermont.

What was he thinking? Jennifer had told me she'd wondered. What?

I did not try and answer her question then; there had not been a need. After all, she had not expected an answer—and if she had, I most certainly would have lied. *I can't imagine, Jennifer. I just can't imagine.*

But if I had responded, and if for some inexplicable reason I'd told her what I honestly believed, I suppose I would have told her this: He was think-ing in some fashion about the Law of Similars. *Look at what an infinitesimal trace did for me*, his frenzied, oxygen-starved mind had concluded, *look at what it did for my skin. Maybe all I need now is a little bit more: one nut. That's really not very much, is it? It's not very much at all.*

It can't be enough to hurt me. Isn't that what Carissa had said at the health-food store?

He'd been clamoring for more medicine for almost two weeks, calling Carissa practically every other day. And consistently she had refused to give him another dose.

Well, now he had more. Right there in his hands. Same stuff, essentially, as his cure. Right?

Right?

And so he had put that one cashew into his mouth, and then he had bit into it.

And then his wife had found him on their kitchen floor.

✧

I could feel Margaret and Phil watching me. Waiting for me to crack. To rise in my chair before Margaret's desk, walk past Phil—leaning in the doorway like one of the rubber trees near the receptionist's desk that were always fighting like hell to get to the sun—and stroll with seeming casualness to the coffee machine. But I really didn't feel like a cup. I just didn't want one.

"Procuring another person to commit a felony is five years," I said to them. "Have you read the computer transcripts? They were serious, completely serious."

"They both pleaded innocent," Margaret said. "She looked it. He didn't."

I disagreed. In my mind, they'd both looked like war criminals at the arraignment: defensive, indignant, and angry at once. And guilty as hell. The pair were married, though not to each other. That was the problem. They were having an affair, and at some point had concocted an absolutely lunatic scheme to have the woman's husband kidnapped and beaten, in order to convince him to grant her a divorce in which she would get most of the couple's worldly possessions—including their cottage not far from Lake Champlain. Kidnappers, of course, don't advertise in the yellow pages, and so they had gone on-line to a variety of chat rooms on the Internet to try and find one.

"Frankly, five years is too good for that pair," I said. "I'm sorry, but there are some things you just don't do in this world. Like asking somebody on the Internet to kidnap someone and threaten him with a wood-splitting maul."

"They did that?" Phil asked. "A maul, really?"

"Sure did. And the two of them were on-line at the same time. Same chat room."

"It's in the information?"

"You bet."

Phil glanced at his watch and shook his head. "What about those thugs who beat up that little guy with the saxophone the other day? The street musician? Where are we with them?"

"Probably we'll settle on a misdemeanor: simple assault," Margaret said.

"Not aggravated?" Phil asked, disappointed.

She shook her head. "No. They were actually pretty banged up, too. He may not be able to play the saxophone very well, but he sure can swing it. And they were all in an alley by the parking garage, so we don't have any witnesses to the start of the fight. Just the end, when the officers arrived and broke it up."

Outside Margaret's window, massive waves of clouds the color of burned charcoal briquettes were rolling in from the north. Ashy gray. Layered like scallops on a curtain that stretched all the way into Canada. Beautiful, I thought. Just beautiful.

"Any idea why they were putting the hurt on the fellow?" I asked.

"He was butchering 'Love for Sale.'"

"He butchers everything," I said. "That's part of his charm."

"There really is no motive," Margaret insisted. "Just a little random street rage."

"I have a meeting, so I have to go," Phil said. "But please see if we can do better than a misdemeanor. I don't like living in a city where little street musicians get clobbered because they can't play the saxophone. Okay?"

Margaret and I nodded as one.

"Want me to get you a cup of coffee before I go?" Phil asked me, a vaguely malevolent smirk on his face. "I'm already up."

"No, I'm okay."

"Good. I'm glad to hear it. Surprised. But glad."

When Phil was gone, I stretched my legs toward Margaret's table of toys and murmured, "Unbelievable, isn't it? Can you imagine beating someone up because he can't handle Cole Porter?"

"Or using the Web to find a kidnapper?"

"Ah, the things we do for love."

"Think we'll find any other witnesses?" she asked.

"For the assault? No, I wouldn't get my hopes up."

I couldn't actually see the cold front moving, but I noticed when I looked away from the window and then glanced back that the shape of the mass would be different, and there'd be somewhat less blue in the sky. What a magnificent night it would be for a fire in the woodstove. Perfect, I thought. Just perfect.

"Leland?"

"Yes?"

"Are you okay?"

"Why?"

"I don't know. You sound almost…I don't know, serene."

"I'm fine."

"You're not on Prozac or something, are you?"

"Nope." I shrugged. "It's just a beautiful day in the neighborhood."

There was a time when the locals threw rocks at Samuel Hahnemann's windows. The homeopath had just left Leipzig for Köthen, a much smaller city with a less educated populace, and the people there decided he was some kind of evil wizard. A sorcerer the local physicians and apothecaries neither trusted nor liked.

That was in 1821. He was in his mid-sixties by then, and most of his provings were behind him, as well as a great deal of his writing. Not *The Chronic Diseases*, of course. He would write the first edition right there in Köthen. But if one of those rocks had crashed through the window of his study where he'd been scribbling and hit him squarely on the head, if somehow one of those stones had killed him, he would still have left behind early editions of his *Organon*, a *Materia Medica*, and a library of notebooks and test results. He would still have left behind a foundation for modern homeopathy. He would still have been the first real homeopath.

The first, too, ironically, to have slept with a patient. He and his second wife, Melanie, were the precedent for that also.

After all, Melanie had come to see him in Köthen as a patient. She'd been troubled by stomach pains, and left Paris—traveling across Europe dressed as a man—for a consultation with the much older physician.

He was seventy-nine when they met in 1834. She was somewhere in her mid-thirties. Unmarried.

Hahnemann had proposed to Melanie three days after they met. When you're seventy-nine, you don't dilly-dally. And Melanie had said yes almost as quickly: "No other man will ever lay a profane hand on me, no mouth other than yours will kiss my mouth." When Carissa showed me her books with Melanie's poems and letters, she told me that was her single favorite line. She said the Hahnemanns would have nine glorious years together, and Melanie would go on to become a groundbreaking homeopath herself.

It was due in part to Melanie that Carissa chose, in the end, not to have the tip of Hahnemann's tomb among those with small cameos in the lower corners of the view from Père-Lachaise. Melanie is buried along with Samuel in *le cimetière* now, but the massive vault is a homage solely to Samuel, and the great sepulcher exudes his arrogance. An obelisk towers above a bust of the man, surrounded by—astonishingly—one wall listing his books and another one listing his maxims.

Similia similibus curentur, for example. Let likes be treated by likes. The Law of Similars.

Or *Maladies Chroniques. The Chronic Diseases*—the monster opus he first published in 1828 and would update throughout the next decade.

Balzac and Proust and Richard Wright are buried nearby, and even they don't have the names of their books on their crypts.

And yet despite the fact that the remains of his wife exist as well under all that granite and stone, you won't find Melanie mentioned anywhere on the monument.

Not a word. Not even her name.

9

ARSENICUM ALBUM

WHITE ARSENIC

When the All-merciful one created iron, He granted to mankind, indeed, to fashion from it either the murderous dagger or the mild ploughshare, and either to kill or to nourish their breathren therewith. How much happier, however, would they be, did they employ His gifts only to benefit one another!

DR. SAMUEL HAHNEMANN,
The Chronic Diseases, 1839

Five days after taking my homeopathic arsenic, the taste was still a wonderful memory on my tongue: a flavor somewhere in the world of sugar cubes and mint chocolate pie.

It was a Saturday, and Abby and I wandered into the woods behind our house with a bow saw, and there Abby picked a dense, lush cat spruce that was just about the right size for the bay window. It was perhaps seven feet tall, and almost a perfect cone.

I dragged it back to our house through the three inches of snow that had fallen on Friday, a good half-mile—though it didn't feel that great a distance to me—and left it on our front porch to settle overnight. We planned to trim it after church the next day, though Abby did insist that we get down the ornaments from the attic right away so she could begin removing the sheets of tissue and newspaper that protected them.

Then I called Carissa for the second time that day. The first had been to invite her to come with us to choose a tree. She'd declined, but I was sure she was glad I had phoned. Especially when I told her how great I felt. How unbelievably great I felt. In the five days since I'd seen her, I hadn't sneezed or coughed or endured a single headache. And while my throat had indeed burned a bit that Monday night, the burning had been gone Tuesday morning.

And then Wednesday—a day when I would have to spend four-plus hours in court—I'd discovered to my horror that I'd forgotten a handkerchief when I was opening the door to Courtroom 3A…only to find I hadn't needed one. Didn't blow my nose a single time.

Just to see if I could do it, I'd then purposely sat in the swivel chair in the courtroom that didn't have my own special cinnamon bun stain. And it hadn't mattered. I'd asked for an in-patient evaluation of a psycho real-estate agent—he'd stopped a teenager with a Trans Am he insisted was always speeding past his house like a madman, tied the kid up, and brought him at gunpoint to the police station claiming citizen's arrest—and I had gotten it.

I'd also realized that I was no longer woozy. Ever. And Thursday morning when I was awakened by my alarm, I was shocked—pleased, of course, too, but first and foremost shocked—by the revelation that I'd slept through the night. Hadn't woken up once. The same thing had happened Friday morning. I realized I had slept soundly through the night.

"I probably shouldn't be telling you all this," I'd said on the phone the first time I called Carissa that Saturday.

"Why not? I'm thrilled to hear it."

"Because you'll think I don't need a booster."

"You *are* a junkie."

"I think my throat's getting sore," I said, pretending the pain was unbearable.

"Never lie to your homeopath, Leland."

"Bad karma?"

"Bad cure."

She couldn't join Abby and me in our hunt for a tree because she was going to be in her office, working on a paper she was supposed to deliver that week to a group of homeopaths in Massachusetts. And so when I phoned her later that day, I was calling her in her intoxicating little world in the Octagon. I used the phone in my kitchen so I, too, could be facing west: Together, sort of, we could watch the December sun sink.

"Find a tree?" she asked.

"A big, beautiful cat spruce. Just about two times Abby's height."

"Cat spruce?"

"A white spruce. Some people call them cat spruce because they smell a tad catlike once the season's over. But they're gray-green instead of a really deep green, and they always worked best with Elizabeth's ornaments. She was into blue and silver."

"Have you trimmed it?"

"Oh, no. Not till tomorrow. Want to join us?"

"Have you discussed this with Abby?"

"I'd warm her up. I wouldn't surprise her. For obvious reasons, she's a very adaptable kid."

"Leland, you know it's impossible. I'm going to have to take a pass. I'm sorry."

"Is this because of the paper you're writing? If that's all that's stopping you, we can trim the tree later this week—when you're back. You know, after you've dazzled the Mass homeys."

"I don't expect to dazzle anyone."

"You will."

"It's not going well."

"Then it's time to cut bait for the day. It's almost four. You're done."

"Probably."

"You should come have dinner with Abby and me. Join us for our special Saturday-night Disney film festival: Abby's favorite five minutes of every single video she owns. She's like a deejay."

"It's just not appropriate, Leland. You're a patient," she said, emphasizing *patient* like it was a new word in a foreign language I was struggling to understand.

"Then you should let me take you to dinner some night to thank you for the incredible work you've done. Just the two of us."

"Can't do it."

"Just can't go out on what the uninformed might mistake for a date?"

"Absolutely not."

"In that case, consider me cured. Emeritus. Better. *All* better."

Carissa continued to decline—that afternoon, and again when she returned Wednesday from Massachusetts—and so I decided I had only one alternative: I'd have to woo her.

✦

Saturday night when I was reading to Abby in bed, she asked, "What's *adaptable* mean?"

I put down the book about the little girl and the corn cakes and the wild animals in the woods, and leaned back against the headboard of her bed. I hadn't realized she was paying attention to my conversation with Carissa.

"Let's see, adaptable. Flexible. Able to do lots of different things, and able to do them well. Our truck, for example. I think that's adaptable. I drive you and me to day care and work in it, and it's very comfortable. But I can also use it to haul lots of stuff—like those long pieces of wood for the church railing last week. Does that make sense?"

Her eyes on the bunnies on the knees of her pajamas, she said, "Why did you tell someone I'm adaptable?"

"I did, didn't I?" I said. I hoped I sounded nonchalant.

She nodded without looking up.

"Well, I probably told someone you were adaptable because you are. Like me. We're both very good at taking care of ourselves. When Mommy died, for instance, we were adaptable. We were used to having a house full of three people, and suddenly there were just us two. But we adapted. We were flexible."

She looked up. "Who were you talking to?"

"A lady doctor."

"But you're not sick, right?"

"Oh, no. I'm fine. Very fine, as a matter of fact."

"Why were you talking to a lady doctor about me? Do I have to see her?"

"Lord, no. You, my dear, are as healthy as a...as I don't know what. But you're not sick. You're the only kid in the history of day care who doesn't live with a runny nose and a cough."

"That's your job," she said, teasing me with one of the expressions she heard me use often.

"Well, it was. Hopefully it isn't anymore."

"So why were you talking to her about me?"

"Mostly I was talking to her about me."

"How come? You said you're not sick."

I lifted her up under her arms and she squealed. "Put me down!" she shouted, pretending to sound indignant, and she curled her legs at her knees as I bounced her up and down on her pillow.

"You ask too many questions," I said, smiling, and then I cradled her in my arms as if she were still a little baby. She giggled, and pulled at the ties to the hood of the sweatshirt I was wearing.

"Someday let's make this a house of three people again," she said.

"Want a new mom, eh?" I asked without thinking, the sentence escaping my lips before I'd had a chance to edit the content in my head. For a brief moment I was angry with myself, because the sentence had more to do with my fantasies for a future with Carissa Lake than it did with the care and nurture of my four-year-old girl.

"A new mom?" she asked, dubious. "I meant a brother. I think I'd like to have a baby brother someday."

I sat her up on my lap. "A brother?"

"A *baby* brother. Like Jesse," she explained, referring to the toddler who'd recently started coming to Abby's day care.

"Someone to boss around?"

"Yeah!"

"We'll look into it," I said. "But it might take a while."

I watched her digest what I was saying, and I could tell she was interpreting it accurately. Translation? *You might be in high school before you get that sibling, kid, so don't hold your breath.* And she understood. That was the great thing about Abby. She really was very adaptable.

"Can we do more projects tomorrow?" she asked, moving on when it was clear the brother was out.

"Projects?"

"More Christmas decorations!"

"Oh, yes. Absolutely. I've already rounded up pinecones, and I think we have just enough red ribbon from the presents people gave us last year."

"And cotton?"

"We'll get some."

"And we'll put the ornaments on the tree?"

"Of course."

"And we'll go to the church for the Christmas tea?"

"You bet."

"And there'll be the mushy chocolates I like?"

"I'm sure."

She nodded, satisfied. Although she wasn't going to get that brother, she would get to play Martha Stewart for an afternoon.

✧

I hadn't tried wooing a woman in years. Maybe ever. After all, I hadn't exactly had to woo Elizabeth. We were both in our early twenties and had wound up in her bed together two nights after we'd met.

And in the years since she'd died, how many dates had I really gone on? Six? Eight? Certainly no more than ten. The result was six or eight or ten women with whom I was now a passing acquaintance or very casual friend. I never made enemies, and I always called them again when I'd said that I would. But it was hard to find time for that second date when I wasn't on fire for someone.

Carissa, however, was different. Moreover, I was different. I'm changed, I would think to myself as I drove to my office in the morning, sometimes actually waving at the gas station where I used to stop daily for coffee and cough drops. I'm a different guy, I'd say to myself as I toweled the sweat off my neck after another thirty minutes on the StairMaster at the health club during lunch. Pure and simple, I'd conclude as my ripe breakfast pear would melt in my mouth, I've been blessed with good health. Son of a gun. Me.

And so on Wednesday afternoon, immediately after Carissa had told me yet again that she couldn't possibly date me, I sent her a single red rose with a card. On Thursday I sent her a yellow rose. And when she arrived at her office on Friday, she found three white roses waiting for her at the door, one for each day of the weekend. It was hard not to phone her that Saturday or Sunday—I kept hoping she would call to thank me or, at the very least, tell me it was wrong to send my homey some posies—but I always managed to stop myself before I'd punched in the seventh digit of her number.

And while it seemed that she knew dramatically more about me than I did about her, she had revealed a few personal details I could use. She had said she dreamt sometimes of butterflies, so I bought her a butterfly-shaped Christmas ornament, the glass colored the orange and black of a monarch. When I recalled her saying she probably loved dates as much as I clearly despised them, I stopped by the health-food store where I knew she must shop, bought a bag of dates, and left them there with a note in the care of her niece. The note listed the nineteen ritualistic uses for the date that I'd been able to find on the Web. (My favorite? Some Berber tribesmen in the Atlas Mountains used them as ceremonial gifts for the parents of the women they wanted to wed.)

"Why don't you just leave the note and the dates at her office?" Whitney had asked. "She has a little wicker basket on her door."

"Because I want her to get them here," I'd answered, and Whitney had nodded knowingly. *I get it*, that nod had said.

I did utilize that little wicker basket, however: One day I left Carissa a colorful nylon loop for her eyeglasses, and on another I left her a pair of red wool socks with green reindeer and white snowflakes. For a moment the socks had seemed a little personal, but then I told myself I was the only person on the planet who grouped pretty wool socks with lingerie—it wasn't, after all, like I was giving her a pair of silk tap pants and a camisole, for God's sake—and so I offered her that gift as well.

And I knew Carissa had a cat, and her cat's happiness mattered to her greatly. Consequently, I left off a care package for both, a calico bag filled with catnip for the kitty and home-baked chocolate Christmas cookies for her that I had bought when I was taking Abby to meet Santa in Middlebury.

When she finally called, the Monday after I had begun my courtship in earnest, she begged me to stop and said she couldn't possibly accept the gifts I had given her. She said she would have to give them all back.

"Even the catnip?" I asked.

"Well, not the catnip. Sepia's spent the last couple days in kitty heaven."

"And the cookies?"

"Okay, not the cookies, either. But that eyeglass thing, and that Christmas ornament, and—"

"You can't give back the dates, Carissa. For all you know, I'm a Berber warrior with one very macho temper."

"The fact is, I know you're not."

"And the loop for your eyeglasses cost ninety-nine cents. Even if you give it back to me, I promise you I won't bother returning it to the store. Christmas is only a week away. Keep it."

"You really want me to?"

"Desperately."

She sighed, and the moment I heard the whisper of her breath, I knew she was, at least for the moment, wooed. I closed my eyes and pulled the mouthpiece away from my lips so she wouldn't hear my own little snuffle of rapture.

"You know if I agree to go out with you," she said, "you'll have to see a new homeopath."

"I'll be strong."

"I'll give you the name of a fellow in Burlington. He's excellent."

"Thank you."

"And I hope you know I don't feel good about this."

"I won't think less of you in the morning. I promise," I told her as I glanced at the calendar I kept on my desk. I saw Wednesday night was the yearly meditation on boredom that posed as a party at the mayor's office in City Hall, and Thursday and Friday nights I had important dates with my daughter: Thursday was the preschool's annual holiday play, and Friday we were shopping for Christmas presents for her cousins in New Hampshire. No matter. I would see Carissa tomorrow night. Tuesday. Tomorrow night I'd be on a date with my homey. Ex-homey. Erst-homey. Homey from heaven.

10

FROM PSORA

(OR PSORIASIS)

The good physician will be pleased when he can enliven and keep from ennui the mind of a patient.

DR. SAMUEL HAHNEMANN,
The Chronic Diseases, 1839

"Spend Christmas Eve with us, too," my sister, Diana, was saying. "Drive down here the day before. Abby can bunk with Lydia."

Even before Elizabeth had died, we'd always seemed to spend Christmas Day with my sister's family in Hanover. Thanksgiving was usually earmarked for Elizabeth's family, but Christmas seemed to be devoted to mine. I wasn't sure why, but I thought this had something to do with the teddy bears, and the huge numbers of them that had wound up with Diana—including the eight-foot display teddy our father's company had used for years in its trade show booth. Initially, Diana had been reduced to shrieking and sobs when she first saw it when she was nine: The poor child had wandered downstairs in our house in the middle of the night Christmas Eve and discovered what we would come to call Giganto Bear sitting upright in the doorway. Our father had thought it would make a fun Christmas surprise, and indeed it had. Sort of.

In any case, the teddies were now a symbol of Christmas for Diana, and that meant spending the holiday in New Hampshire.

"I can't imagine not being here Christmas Eve," I said, resting the cordless phone on my shoulder and spooning the last bite of breakfast melon into my mouth. I pressed the rind into the garbage and wandered into the living room to admire the tree Abby and I had decorated. About ninety-nine percent of the ornaments were on the branches Abby could reach, and so the spruce looked a bit like a mountain with a tree line: About three feet off the ground, the glass balls and cloth reindeer and silver tinsel started to diminish. By four feet the decorations went from sparse to nonexistent. My contributions, essentially, were the blue angel and the star that sat perched at the top of the tree.

"Abby expects Santa to find her here," I continued. "She expects to wake up in her very own house and find her presents under her very own tree."

"Santa somehow gets to those kids who are away from home all the time. Just tell her about the Christmas bookings at hotels in Hawaii."

"And one of Abby's friends is having a little party that night. They're all going to bake cookies for Santa. And you know how I love the Christmas Eve service here. You know how I love all the candles."

"We do have churches in Hanover, you know."

"Yeah, but you people are smarter than we are. You don't give the little kids candles."

"You really want to be there when the church goes up in flames. Is that it?"

"Have you ever watched their faces when they're raising and lowering their candles? They're so earnest about it. So serious. It's wonderful. They get the meaning of the ritual much better than we adults do."

"They're just little pyros. It's the only time they're given an adult-sanctioned chance to play with fire. Will Abby get her own candle this year?"

"Maybe. I think we're going to go to the eight-thirty service. It'll depend on how awake she is."

"So you'll drive down here Christmas morning?"

"You bet. Will you be done opening the loot Santa left by early afternoon?"

"God, yes. Will and Lydia will have ripped apart the mountain by seven A.M. By early afternoon, they'll have the list ready with everything Santa forgot—and the stores where Mom and Dad can find it."

"Then we'll leave here about eleven. We should be in Hanover by one."

"What will you do Christmas Eve?"

"You mean besides the candlelight service?"

"Besides that, yes."

"I'm having dinner with someone."

"Like a date?"

"Romantic dinner for two."

"Where?"

"Here."

"*Here*, like your house?"

"Like that. Yes."

"Is this a woman you've been seeing a long time? Is this some secret you've had all fall?"

"Oh, no. I would have told you. Tonight's our first date."

"But you're spending Christmas Eve together?"

"Well, it's not official. I haven't asked her," I said. I reached down for one of the silver and blue bells on the tree and turned it so that the swirls faced the center of the room.

"But you think she'll say yes."

"I do," I said, and I noticed the ornament sparkle as it reflected a fragment of light from the sun. "I'm absolutely sure of it."

✧

Do I know Richard Emmons because I know his cure? Sometimes I believe that I do. Biographers, after all, often begin their books knowing that little about their subjects. Besides, I know what Carissa was thinking when she administered Richard's remedy, and what Jennifer told me about the weeks before and after the tiny pellets of medicine rolled in the pink-and-white froth of his mouth.

And so it is not merely the blistering nodules on his hands I can see: I can see also the way he would self-consciously kiss his daughter or his son on the cheek before leaving for work, touching them by design with only his lips. An embrace is out of the question, because that would mean nearing their skin with his.

I can see him unwilling to run his fingers along his wife's thighs.

And, like many adults who are no longer young, I, too, have felt aches and pains in my joints. Richard's arrived in the fall of the year he would die, twinges and pricks that came on with cold weather. When he would stretch, the needles would ebb, but it would take time.

Besides, when we're asleep we don't stretch, and so he had yet one more reason that autumn to be awake in the night.

And, of course, there was the asthma. But it usually wasn't the asthma itself that frightened him, it was the chemicals he used to control it. It was the idea that his regimen already included a combination of drugs with incomprehensible names, and now his doctor was offering more. There was, I imagine, the fear that he would grow into an old man with a wallet card listing his meds, a cardboard *materia medica* of the capsules and pills dissolving every day in his stomach.

Often those cards are twenty names long. I fear them, too.

And so in his bed in the night, his world would be reduced to his infirmities. Arguably, they were neither debilitating nor incapacitating. Not in reality. But that changes nothing. In the night he'd still fret.

Yet Richard was, like all of us, more than the sum of his symptoms. There he is with his hands in his pockets, putting up a good front before the young art directors and copywriters who work for him at his ad agency. There he is in the spring, a patient Little League coach, managing somehow to teach eight-year-olds how to bunt. There he is driving home from Boston in a blizzard so bad the airports are closed, so he can see his daughter as Dorothy in a junior-high-school production of *The Wizard of Oz*.

And there he is surprising himself with a desire—a wish in some ways more pronounced than the hunger to look at his hands and not find them repellent, to breathe without medication, to grow old with something that resembles serenity—he'd shared with only his wife.

Richard Emmons really did wish that his kids could have a pet.

✧

"I don't want to know everything there is to know about homeopathy," I said to Carissa over dinner. "It's enough for me to know it works."

I'd chosen one of the restaurants in Burlington on the shore of Lake Champlain, and while it was too dark to see a bloody thing but an occasional light from the ferries crossing the water between New York and Vermont, I liked being close to the lake. I heard in my mind the word *aura* when I suggested the spot, wondering if I'd ever before thought of the word in my life, or whether that, too, was a bonus from arsenic: access to the vocabulary I had stored somewhere in my head that I never bothered to use.

We'd met at the restaurant so I wouldn't have to drive all the way back to Bartlett to get her—although I had indeed offered—and so for the first few minutes of dinner I found myself ruing the fact there was absolutely no chance we'd sleep together that night. After all, we wouldn't wind up back at her house together since I wouldn't be driving her home, nor would we wind up at mine because one of us had suggested in the warm little cocoon of an auto in winter that we give each other a tongue-bath.

At some point soon after our menus arrived, however, I stopped wondering where the dinner would go. It might have been the quiet Christmas music in the background, or the red candles on the table. It might have been the wine.

It might even have been the arsenic.

And so I shared with Carissa my enthusiasm for the remedy as we sipped herbal tea over dessert.

"I'm glad you feel so good," she said. "I'm surprised—not by the fact that your remedy seems to be working, but by your confidence in the protocol."

"Well, it did what it was supposed to do."

"Apparently."

"How did you become a homeopath?" I asked.

"I met one on an airplane when I was going to England. It was eight years ago now. He sat next to me."

"Were you already a psychologist?"

"I was still getting my hours for certification, but I'd finished school."

"Was he British?"

"The homeopath? No. He lived in London, but he was originally from New Delhi. He's Indian."

"And while you were chatting about medicine, you grew interested in homeopathy?"

"There was more to it than that. I was flying to London to see my best friend, my college roommate. She'd been spiraling downhill for months, and she'd just been diagnosed with schizophrenia. I wanted to see what was going on firsthand. And the fellow I met on the plane, the homeopath, actually ended up treating her. He took the time to visit her and see what he could do. We're still good friends."

"Did she see a traditional doctor, too?"

"He is a doctor. He's a psychiatrist."

I nodded. I was surprised, and I realized I shouldn't have been. Carissa had already told me that many homeopaths were medical doctors. "Did he treat her with purely homeopathic remedies?"

"No, it was a combination therapy. He and her doctors gave her some of the more usual medications for schizophrenia, too."

"But it was the homeopathy part that impressed you."

"It was."

"So you've only been doing this six or seven years, then?"

She leaned back in her chair and smiled. "Suddenly afraid you put your health in the hands of a novice?"

"No, not at all."

"I've been a full-time homeopath for just about six years."

"I gather you've treated Whitney."

"You and Whitney talk way too much."

"She's a big fan of yours."

"She's young."

"How's your friend now? The one with schizophrenia?"

"She's doing fine. Maybe you'll meet her someday."

The waiter returned to our table with the check, and while I was dropping my credit card onto the plastic after-dinner mints tray, I heard a sentence form in my head and was unable to stop it from escaping my lips: "Spend Christmas Eve with me."

Instantly the waiter retreated.

"Spend Christmas Eve with me," I said a second time, hoping when I said the words again I'd understand exactly what I meant. Was I asking her to visit me in the early evening for a chaste dinner while my daughter was off baking sugar cookies, was I merely asking her up to see the tree? Certainly that's what I'd had in mind when I told my sister my plans that morning.

Was I now, however, asking her to, literally, spend the night with me? Did I really just ask this woman to sleep with me? I wondered.

I realized I wasn't sure what I'd meant. Immediately, of course, I began hoping she'd come to the worst—no, not the worst, simply the most erotic—interpretation and answer yes. I hoped she'd assume I had just asked her into my bed. Or onto the couch by the tree. Or onto the thick rug on the floor by the woodstove.

She ran her fingertips along her collarbone and stared at the black window facing the lake, and then at me. There was a tiny hint of candle flame in her eyeglasses.

"Sure," she said, "that would be nice," her answer not offering me the slightest clue as to what she'd heard in my invitation. As with our dinner together that night, I'd just have to wait and see where Christmas Eve would go.

✧

I had not honestly expected we would make love Christmas Eve. I'd hoped we would, but I certainly hadn't expected it. Carissa had been unable to get her car started, however, and so after dropping my daughter off at her friend's house, I'd driven into Bartlett to get her. And when she'd climbed into the truck a little past five and shown me the wicker basket of food she'd assembled as a present, I'd decided there was a pretty good chance we'd wind up in my bedroom before Abby returned.

"One-stop shopping," she'd said when I told her she shouldn't have brought me a gift (though I had gotten her a book about dreams that had just been published, an absolute natural since it had the word *butterfly* in its title). "It's all from the health-food store. It seemed appropriate to shop there, given the way we met."

When we arrived at my house, she began pulling the items from the basket one by one, laying them side by side on the counter in the breakfast nook: There were truffles made with carob and honey, and cookies sweetened with fruit juice. There were dates rolled in coconut and dates that were plain, neither of which, Carissa told me, she expected me to eat. "I just didn't want to offend a Berber in his own home," she explained. And there were bags and bags of nuts, which she said she wouldn't have thought of bringing if she hadn't run into another patient of hers in the store, an asthmatic who was allergic to cashews.

But it was the whole-wheat English muffins, delivered daily to Bartlett from the natural-foods bakery in Burlington, and the box of breakfast tea that I found most arousing. English muffins weren't usually an aphrodisiac, but I remembered she'd said Tuesday night that she always had an English muffin for breakfast. And while I couldn't imagine that she thought we'd actually be having breakfast together Christmas Day—would there be a worse way to introduce Carissa into Abby's life?—the muffins and the tea were a signal, a gesture that was tender and amorous at once.

And so as she was showing me the remainder of the contents of the basket and explaining the significance of each—the echinacea was obvious, it was sort of like our song, but I wouldn't have understood that a garlic clove smelled a bit like arsenic if she hadn't told me—I kissed her, a brush across her lips barely more passionate than the chaste peck on the cheek I'd offered in the parking lot of the restaurant earlier that week.

"I just had to do that," I said, and she nodded, putting the garlic bulb she was holding on the kitchen counter and wrapping her fingers behind my neck and kissing me back. We kissed there in the kitchen, then on the couch in the living room in the dim light from the bulbs on the Christmas tree, and then on the floor before it. Before we'd opened a bottle of wine or I'd given her the book I had bought about dreams, while the Brie on the table near the wood-stove melted untouched, we undressed and I pulled the pillows from the couch and laid her upon them in the midst of the presents and the lowest branches of the white spruce. I insisted she keep on her panties—a ritual red, she murmured, to celebrate the season—so I could lick her through the silk and feel the material get wetter and wetter from my tongue and her lips. Sometimes when I'd pull away the elastic for brief moments, I'd hear in my head the sound of a click as I washed my tongue over her as fast as I could. Then I'd pull her panties back across her vagina and lap at the silk until I thought I'd explode if I didn't taste her—all of her, my tongue probing deeply inside her, along the thin strip of skin buffering vulva and anus, then between those cheeks that smelled slightly of bubble bath.

When she came, her thighs tightening in my arms as I held her, my chin and my neck wondrously—bountifully, beneficently—drenched, I looked up and saw a star. There it was, hanging from a branch by her face. Hanging beside the very branch on which her eyeglasses dangled like tortoiseshell tinsel. A modeling clay star. It was no longer bright, because my daughter had painted it in Sunday school a year earlier and the colors had begun to fade, but it still had a trace of its original canary luster. I hadn't really noticed it or thought about it when Abby and I had trimmed the tree, but there it was. An ornament, the first one my little girl had ever made. And it was right there beside Carissa's eyes, opening slowly now as she took a deep breath and sighed.

I am blessed, I thought. Really and truly blessed.

✧

It had practically killed me to wash Carissa off my face as we showered together before I left to get Abby alone, but when I hugged little Chloe's mom, I was glad that I had. The evening, after all, was a celebration of a pretty darn clean conception.

Carissa was waiting for us back at the house. If it seemed to me that Abby had consumed enough sugar to get through the eight-thirty service, then the three of us would go to church together, and from there we would drive Carissa home.

"A friend of mine dropped by," I told my daughter as I buckled her into the truck, hoping the remark sounded offhand. "Would you like to meet her?"

"Nah. I think I just want to go to church." She had a plate of the cookies she'd made balanced in her lap. Her plan was to leave out the gingerbread ones for Santa because she hated gingerbread, but Santa, apparently, loved it. She also had carrots and celery sticks for the reindeer.

"We will. But my friend's waiting at home. She wants to say hi. It'll just take a minute."

"It's a lady?"

"Oh, yes."

She looked straight ahead and I could tell she was mad. A year ago, when she was three and a half, she might have had a tantrum. Now, I imagined, she'd just grow silent. Make Carissa work extra hard.

Yet when we got home and I introduced her to that friend who just happened to be a lady, she rallied. For a moment she did what I called her "coquette thing," hiding half her face behind my hip, but showing the stranger a single eye and what might have been half a smile. She didn't ask any questions of Daddy's new friend, but she answered in reasonably polite little grunts all of the questions that were put to her, and even corrected Carissa on some of the finer points of cookie decorating.

"Who are those cookies for?" Carissa asked.

"Santa."

"They sure look good. And the carrots. Are they for his reindeer?"

"Uh-huh."

"I love the sparkles you put on that star."

"Those aren't sparkles. That's colored sugar. You can't eat sparkles, because sparkles are just for projects."

"Projects?"

"Arts and crafts," I said.

When the three of us went to church, I downplayed the idea that we would all sit together. I tried to present it as, more or less, a coincidence that Abby might happen to sit on my right and Carissa on my left.

But I knew my joy in the fact that Carissa was with us was evident when I introduced her to Paul Woodson in the narthex. Woodson was the church's ageless pastor, a fellow my parents' age whom I had come to view as a godfather of sorts ever since Elizabeth had died.

"We have a guest tonight," Paul said, speaking more to Abby and Carissa than me. "A minister from Korea."

"Terrific," I said.

Paul leaned over so he was closer to Abby. "I wanted you to know ahead of time, because he's going to teach you a little song with your name in it."

"My name?"

"Yup. You'll see."

Briefly, I tried to come up with a hymn with the word *Abby* or *Abigail* in it, but I realized quickly it was a lost cause, and found myself focusing instead on the lobe of Carissa's ear, and the channel I'd licked just beneath it along the back of her jaw.

Soon into the service, however, after the children had placed the doll-sized figures of donkeys and wise men and a virgin in the crèche by the tree, Paul had them surround him in a half-circle at the front of the church. There an elderly Korean joined the group, squatting before the children and telling them that he wanted to teach them a song that youngsters sang in his own land. The moment he said it was inspired by a verse in the 124th Psalm, I knew instantly where Abby's name would fit in:

"Our soul is escaped as a bird out of the snare of the fowlers; the snare is broken, and we are escaped. Our help is in the name of the Lord…"

I hadn't thought of the psalm in years, but I'd certainly become aware of it soon after moving to Bartlett. Paul had told me about the verse the first time Elizabeth and I had come to his church, and shown it to me in the Bible.

"A fowler's a kind of hunter," he'd said. "You must be a very good prosecutor."

When the children sang the chorus—*Our help is in the name of the Lord!*— I saw the back of Abby's head bobbing up and down to the strains of the song, and I felt the side of my hip pressing against Carissa's. I wasn't sure if I'd been that happy for a single moment since Elizabeth had died, and then I decided I hadn't. No way. Not a prayer.

And when Paul had the deacons pass out the candles and dim the lights a few moments later, and when the choir members started passing the flame to the congregation in preparation for "Silent Night," I thought I might cry.

"You okay?" Carissa whispered.

I nodded, unable to open my mouth. I felt her take my hand and squeeze it as we stood, and then give it back to me so I could help Abby with her candle. I listened to the congregation begin murmuring the words to the carol, singing each line a bit louder than the one before it. When Carissa sang, her voice was slightly higher than when she spoke, but it still radiated confidence and beauty and calm.

I watched the long rows of small candle flames slowly rise and fall, each pew packed as it was no other day or night of the year, and I saw my daughter gazing enrapt at her own teardrop-shaped bubble of incandescence. She was holding her candle with both hands.

When the hymn ended, Carissa and Abby blew out their candles almost as one. Abby looked up at me, smiling, and then I saw her face abruptly turn worried.

"Daddy? Are you crying?"

"I am," I said, aware that my face was indeed growing wet. "But it's because I'm happy."

"Happy," she repeated.

"Happy," I said. This is happiness, I thought, desperately in love with the woman and the little girl who surrounded me. This is what it feels like to be happy. Complete. To see a family intact.

I couldn't imagine a better present at Christmas.

11

NUMBER 1

The physician's highest calling, his only *calling, is to make sick people healthy.*

DR. SAMUEL HAHNEMANN,
Organon of Medicine, 1842

We are no longer a body with all that word means in the particulars of a unified whole. An indivisible system of organs and flesh, tissue and synapse and soul. We are parts. We are divisible.

Sometimes we say the brain is dead though the heart is alive: The heart is working, in other words, but no thanks to the brain. The brain is gone.

Well, not all of the brain. Even when someone is by all accounts brain-dead, there may still be an infinitesimal bit of cerebral matter continuing to signal the pituitary gland to create the hormones that help the kidneys produce urine.

But most of the brain has expired.

Somebody somewhere had to invent the concept of brain-dead. For millennia we based death on the heart. But then we discovered that hearts were more transferable than passports—they were recyclable cherry-shaped pumps that could be reconnected to a second set of hose lines—and so we broke the body into components. Take the heart though it's beating: He's brain-dead, that's what counts.

Someday we'll get to a point where we'll only need a part of the brain to be dead to begin the harvest.

His brain stem is working—the section that controls his heart rate, his blood pressure, the ways his eyes might be moving beneath his lids. But those parts of the brain that allow him to think, that make him sapient and feeling and present? Gone. No electrical activity whatsoever. He's as good as dead, I assure you. I mean, he's still alive. Technically. But he's no longer…there.

It was Jennifer's sister, Bonnie, who had asked whether Richard Emmons was an organ donor. And it was Bonnie who told me she had handled the inquiry badly.

"They'll want to know at some point, you know. I guess sometimes they learn these things from a driver's license or something. But of course he didn't have his wallet with him in the middle of the night," she told me she'd stammered when she saw the anger and astonishment that had transformed her sister's face after she had made the mistake of broaching the subject.

Jennifer had stared at her for a long time, her hand lingering on the spot on Richard's leg where his shin met his ankle, a sheet resting upon him like a tent that's collapsed.

Finally Jennifer had said, "He is."

"Of course it won't come to that," Bonnie remembered adding, but she had known her lie was hollow.

"We know it will," Jennifer had said, though she had responded in a whisper just in case Richard could hear.

"Look, I'm sorry."

"I understand."

"If they ask, should I tell them?"

"Tell them what?"

"Tell them he's a donor," Bonnie had said.

"Sure. But please remind them he's alive."

Bonnie had sighed and looked up toward Richard's face. Anything to avoid her sister's gaze. And though Richard had indeed looked alive at that moment, there was still that silver disk in his forehead, and it still disturbed her. Yes, it looked a bit like a watch battery, nothing more. But it nonetheless meant that someone had a drilled a hole into her brother-in-law's head, someone had bored a shaft into his skull.

"You know it's the right thing to do," she had said, her voice defensive.

"Without a doubt," Jennifer had agreed. "But we haven't come to that point yet. Now, have we?"

✧

It is inevitable: Sometimes when I recall my happiness that Christmas Eve and that Christmas Day—my happiness, even, upon waking up the day after Christmas—I think of Jennifer Emmons. I think of Richard.

I wonder if Jennifer groups those days before Richard awoke in the night and fumbled with a little bag of cashews, and then those after. For a long time, I certainly grouped my life into the period prior to Elizabeth's accident, and then the days since.

Now, it seems, I have three parts, with a car accident and a cashew forming the two great divides.

Sometimes I find myself imagining how the Emmons family spent their last moments before their lives were changed forever. I see them wrapping a few remaining presents Christmas Eve, I envision Jennifer filling her children's stockings. I line the four of them up together in a pew in the church for the last time, standing and singing at the seven o'clock service.

The service before the one Carissa and I would attend.

Then there they are once more, all of them, spending Christmas Day at the hospital ICU, while I am driving to and from central New Hampshire almost inconceivably happy.

I can remember thinking Christmas Day in the car that English muffins had never tasted so good. Abby and I had eaten Carissa's English muffins for breakfast Christmas morning, and all the way to and from my sister's in Hanover, their taste kept floating to the surface of my mind.

And then I'd conclude that while the muffins had been delicious, a little toasted bread dough and farina sure as hell couldn't compete with anything I'd tasted the night before. My God, I thought once as I approached the interstate exit, even Carissa's body lotion had tasted like heaven.

I would recall all the parts of her body I'd tongued, my mind making an inventory, and then quickly I'd stop myself: *She isn't a map; you're not counting the number of states you've visited!* But flashes would come back to me nevertheless, and the experience would grow real once again in my mouth and my nose. There was that aroma along her neck—just below her ear—that I associated with Elizabeth's garden and she had murmured was freesia. There was the scent of an apple, her shampoo, as I ran my tongue from the tips of that fine mane down her spine—literally, my tongue never leaving her skin—and there was the taste of vanilla body lotion mixed with perspiration, offering me for the first time an understanding of why cake recipes often called for a pinch of salt. And there were the heavenly smells of soap and musk when I'd finally pulled off her panties near the Christmas tree, but more than that there had been the astonishing texture of thick, sweet cream on my tongue.

Still, it was the English muffins, in my mind, that had become a symbol for everything—and not just the sex, though that had indeed been amazing. They'd become a symbol for the dinner we'd made together, embellishing the pasta I'd planned with the garlic and cashews she'd brought. A memory of those muffins would instantly conjure for me the candlelight church service we'd attended with Abby, my wondrous little girl at that moment asleep in the booster seat beside me. Napping after all the excitement that had come with the presents. We'd both been awake since six.

It had been the English muffins, after all, that had given credence to my fantasy that Carissa might be interested in more than just dinner, and it had been the muffins that had become an icon for what had been the single best evening I'd had in well over two years.

I remember deciding to call her from the interstate while Abby was dozing, and reaching carefully for the phone by the radio. I knew she was with her brother's family—with Whitney's dad's family—and so I knew I'd hear only her voice on the answering machine. No matter. I just wanted to leave her a message. I just wanted to tell her I was falling in love.

✧

By the time Abby and I had returned to East Bartlett Christmas night, it was close to ten o'clock. Together we stared for a moment at the layer of crinkled wrapping paper that coated the living-room floor like mulch, and then Abby picked out the toys and books and trolls that she wanted upstairs beside her in bed.

I was disappointed when there was no message from Carissa on my answering machine, but not overly concerned. I wondered if the old Leland would have convinced himself he'd scared her away with the message he'd left on her answering machine. Probably, I decided. And while for a brief moment I feared that the fact that such a ridiculous notion had even crossed my mind meant the arsenic was wearing off—or whatever it was that arsenic did—I couldn't imagine there was really any reason to worry. It was highly unlikely she liked me any less because I'd told her I loved her.

Of the half-dozen messages on the machine, most of which were from friends and cousins calling to wish Abby and me a Merry Christmas, only one might even necessitate a call back in the morning. Rod Morrow. I had known

Rod since high school, but it was clear Rod wasn't calling solely in his capacity as an old acquaintance. It sounded like Rod was calling in his role as a detective sergeant with the state police.

A fellow named Richard Emmons had almost killed himself Christmas Eve. Or something like that. It was still pretty unclear what had happened. Rod had been on duty Christmas Day when Emmons's wife had called, wanting them to arrest some witch doctor that very instant.

Rod said that based on the story the woman had told him, they weren't about to arrest anybody. At least not right away. He'd told her he wasn't even sure if a crime had been committed. But he had met her at the hospital that afternoon with the trooper who'd handled her call, and together they'd taken a formal statement.

"Anyway," Rod babbled into the machine, "I figured you should know. She's upset—not without cause—and I think she's going to call you folks directly. Besides, the guy lives in Bartlett, so I figured there was a chance you two might even be friends."

I was pretty sure I knew who Richard Emmons was—a businessman, I thought, who did something with advertising or marketing—but I wasn't positive. We certainly weren't friends.

Still, it was a terrible shame. The poor guy was up in Burlington in a coma.

✧

Most years, most of the world seemed closed to me the day after Christmas. In my mind, only supermarkets and shopping malls were open on the twenty-sixth. Not that year, not with Christmas falling on a Monday. The courts were open, and so was my office.

Of course, Abby's day care was closed—along with the public schools. It's inevitable, it's a law of nature: If something can happen to make a single parent's life harder, it will. And so I'd arranged to drop her off with Mildred in the morning, and then—because Mildred had plans in the afternoon—made arrangements for Greta's mom to pick Abby up at noon for a play date till dinner.

In any case, I was up as usual at five-thirty A.M. Tuesday morning, and I seemed to be moving with especial efficiency. I was showered and shaved and dressed in twenty minutes, and I'd finished my melon and juice by six o'clock.

I wondered if this, too, was a side effect of the arsenic: an ability to knot a necktie in seconds, or shave with uncanny speed. Maybe it was simply a result of having slept soundly. I had, as usual since I'd been given my arsenic, fallen into a deep sleep the moment my head hit the pillow.

I considered waking Abby to see if she wanted to play with me before we left the house for the day, but then I decided she probably needed sleep right now more than Dad. She had stayed up late two nights in a row and was undoubtedly exhausted.

And so I made myself a cup of herbal tea and sat down in the den with the computer. I logged on and took a quick peek at the on-line edition of *The New York Times* to make sure the world hadn't exploded while I'd slept, and then visited *USA Today* to see that paper's daily paragraph about Vermont on the "States" page. I was always fascinated by the single story from my state that someone had determined was big enough for inclusion in the section but still too small to warrant a news article. In the fall, I could always count on an entry about the colors of dying leaves, and between Christmas and New Year's—any day now—there was likely to be a forecast of how the Vermont ski areas would do that season, based on the number of visitors who were descending upon the slopes that holiday week.

Sometimes there were forty or fifty words about what was a huge story in Vermont ("WINDSOR—The gasoline additive discovered in the drinking water at Windsor-Stearns Hospital does not pose a safety threat, hospital officials insist."), and usually the paper noted each of the state's infrequent homicides: We had between ten and fifteen a year, and single homicides usually wound up in single-paragraph form in the roundup section, while domestic murder-suicides were usually given a small story of their very own.

Other than foliage, skiing, and murder, however, there was just no telling what about Vermont would wind up on that page. As I clicked through the menus to get to the section, I decided this morning probably wouldn't be the ski day. That would come later in the week.

When I reached the little green rectangle symbolizing Vermont, I abruptly fell back in my chair.

Son of a bitch! I thought as I stared at the name of the village next door in bold. Bartlett! In *USA Today!* I couldn't believe it: There was the teeny-tiny town on the Web. And in print. I sat forward and read:

BARTLETT — A 43-YEAR-OLD ADVERTISING EXECUTIVE AND FATHER OF TWO WENT INTO ANAPHYLACTIC SHOCK ON CHRIST-

MAS EVE AFTER EATING CASHEWS AND TODAY REMAINS IN A
COMA. NEIGHBORS SAY RICHARD EMMONS WAS AN ASTHMATIC
AND MAY HAVE KNOWN HE WAS ALLERGIC TO THE NUT.

I read the paragraph a second time. With the exception of notable celebrity suicides, *USA Today* never goes out of its way to advertise the fact that a person has killed himself. Or tried to kill himself. It's a courtesy, of sorts, for the family. Most newspapers do this.

But there are code words or signals reporters use, and as a state's attorney I'd read enough death notices in which I knew what had really occurred to be able to separate the suicides from the accidents and natural causes.

And though this Emmons story was short, it had the unambiguous signal of suicide written into it: The allegation from neighbors that he may have known he was allergic to cashews. The absence of the word *mistake*.

That poor, sad family, I thought. And on Christmas Eve.

I'd always heard that the December holidays could be particularly stressful for the lonely or the depressed, and I could certainly remember how difficult that first Christmas after Elizabeth died had been for me. But I still couldn't imagine being so despondent that you might try and kill yourself.

I tried to find a picture in my mind of Richard looking downcast and downhearted, but there wasn't one I could conjure. I barely knew what the guy looked like when he was happy. It was possible that as soon as I saw his wife I'd recognize her, and then realize I'd known the whole family all along. For all I knew, they went to the same church I did, and I'd seen the kids some Sunday morning when they'd come forward through the pews for the children's moment. Perhaps Abby and I had seen them a half-dozen times last summer, while buying soft ice cream at the Creemee stand in Bartlett.

I wondered if Rod Morrow would be working the day after Christmas, or whether I'd have to bother the detective at home. I couldn't wait to get the inside story on this one.

12

NUMBER 259

Considering the smallness of the dose, which in homeopathy is as necessary as it is effective, it is easy to understand that during treatment everything that could have any medicinal action must be removed from the diet and the daily regimen, so that the subtle dose is not overwhelmed and extinguished, not even disturbed, by any foreign medical influence.

DR. SAMUEL HAHNEMANN,
Organon of Medicine, 1842

By seven-fifteen in the morning, I figured, there was a pretty good chance that Carissa was awake. But I still couldn't bring myself to phone her. Not just yet, anyway. It was, after all, the day after Christmas. I decided I'd wait until at least seven twenty-five. Perhaps even seven-thirty. I would make calling her the very last thing I did before Abby and I left the house.

When I finally did dial her number, pleased with myself for hanging in there until seven twenty-eight, I was prepared to apologize if I'd woken her up by explaining—with absolute candor—that I *had* to hear her voice. I simply had to. And then I'd tell her how much I hoped I'd see her that night, how I hoped she'd come to my house and play with my daughter and me until my daughter went to sleep, and then play with just me.

That's what I'd say, I decided. I was ready.

I wasn't, however, prepared for her to answer her phone and sound like death. I discovered instantly that I wasn't ready at all for her hello to be the two-syllable monotone of someone—my mother, I remembered—who has just been told she has inoperable cancer.

"Carissa?" Asking her name was a reflex of sorts: I knew it was her, but her voice nevertheless sounded too beaten and sad for my homey.

"Leland. Hi."

"Merry day after Christmas."

"Oh, God. Thank you."

"Is everything okay?"

A sigh. Then: "No."

The old Leland would have begun to fear from the tone, *You are about to be dumped.* But it was clear that whatever was tormenting Carissa was about her. Not about *me.* Not about *us.* A big part of hypochondria and anxiety is narcissism, and there may be no better way to kill that awful piece of oneself than with a little arsenic. Just enough. A homeopathic hit.

"What happened?" I asked.

"I think one of my patients is going to die."

"My God, Carissa, I'm so sorry. Is this sudden?"

"Yeah. Oh, yeah."

"Is there anything I can do? Would you like me to come over?"

She was silent for a moment, and I couldn't tell if it was because she was tearing or deciding whether to accept my offer.

"Don't you have to go to work today?" she asked finally.

"I do, but I can be late. I don't have to be in court."

"Do you mind?"

"Coming over? No, of course not. I'm happy to. Can you tell me anything?"

"I really don't want to go into it on the phone...."

"Fine. I'm already dressed. I can be there in fifteen or twenty minutes—as soon as Abby's settled in with her baby-sitter."

"Thank you."

"Can I bring anything?"

"No. Just come."

My eye caught the blue and gold diamonds dancing across the screen saver on my computer. I wondered if it was the computer that made me recall Richard Emmons, or the fact that only a moment before I'd had to restrain myself from calling Rod Morrow about the asthmatic. It may even have been the reference to cashews in the *USA Today* paragraph about my neighbor: Hadn't I, too, eaten cashews Christmas Eve? Hadn't they been in Carissa's basket of goodies?

For all I knew, the connection came to me because of all three, because of the computer, the phone call, and the cashews combined. In any case, it didn't matter. Before I could decide whether this was a question I really should ask, the words were out there and impossible to take back.

"Does this have something to do with a fellow in town named Richard Emmons?" I asked.

I heard just the whisper of a moan, and I understood that I'd hit a nerve.

"Carissa, I'm leaving now. Okay?"

"Thank you," she said once again, no longer hiding the fact that she was crying.

Carissa sat at her kitchen table in a red flannel nightgown. Sometimes Sepia, her cat, would rub up against her legs, expecting, perhaps, that her owner would reach down and pet her. Perhaps pick her up and drop her into that soft, warm, red flannel lap.

"Have you slept at all?" I asked Carissa.

"A little bit. Sometimes I'd doze off in spite of everything. But it was never for very long."

Her house was on Mountain Terrace, one of the two residential streets north of the commons. I could tell instantly that it was one of the homes built shortly after the Civil War by the local coffin company for the families of the workers who toiled in the mill. Until the early twentieth century, the Bartlett Casket Company was producing more coffins than any other factory in the country, and at one point in the 1890s the selectmen had put a tremendous boulder beside the main road into the town reflecting a well-intentioned but somewhat artless attempt at civic pride. "Bartlett, Vermont," they had chiseled into the boulder, "Home of the long homes people remain in forever." The boulder was moved away soon after the coffin company closed in the early 1930s, but almost every merchant in town had at least one magnificent black-and-white print of the rock somewhere in his or her shop. Even the health-food store, no doubt, had one of those coffin rock prints. Next time I was there, I decided, I'd have to check.

"How did you hear about Richard?" I asked. "It couldn't possibly have been in yesterday's newspaper."

"No, I heard about it the way most people who live here in the village did. Through the grapevine. Through people talking."

Like many of the mill houses in the village, Carissa's had changed dramatically since a coffin builder had last lived in it. It looked to me as though different owners had affixed a family room of sorts to the first floor, and added a third bedroom upstairs. Someone had built a garage and constructed a glass sunroom facing west. And at some point someone—and I had no idea if the house had had two or three or even four owners between a Bartlett Casket employee and a homeopath—had decided to build a ramshackle passageway between the garage and the kitchen, so it was possible in the winter to walk from the house to the car without ever having to brave the worst that winter could offer.

In the process, the small house had gone from a tidy little box with a porch and a pitch to an unruly pile of packages thrown atop and beside one another without any conscious design. Lots of homes in Vermont were like that. And while virtually anyone could have been responsible for the exterior alterations, the interior was distinctly Carissa's. My homeopath, I was sure, could take credit for putting in the jet-black kitchen counters and having different constellations painted in yellow upon cabinets the color of the night sky at dusk. A blue that was almost sapphire. It was Carissa who'd decorated the kitchen with beautiful hand-painted bowls and replaced the conventional doorknobs with handles the shape of sickle moons.

"Who told you?" I asked.

"Travis Patterson. His brother David is on the rescue squad and only lives a house or two away from the Emmons family. Travis said his brother was the first one at their house Christmas Eve."

"And you saw Travis yesterday?"

She nodded. I'd noticed that she'd wrapped her arms around her chest the moment I'd arrived—easily fifteen minutes ago—and she hadn't uncrossed them since. With the exception of an occasional nod of her head, I wasn't sure she'd moved any part of her body.

"Walking home from my brother's," she added.

"Why did Travis tell you? Did he assume there was a connection between you and Richard?"

"No, no. No. He was just telling me because it's…it's news. And his brother had told him."

"How long have you been treating Richard?"

"Not long. You two probably became patients about the same time."

"Just after Thanksgiving?"

"I think so. I think if I looked back at my records—"

"You keep records?"

"Of course I keep records," she answered, sounding slightly hurt. "I took notes with you, didn't I?"

"I didn't mean anything by that, I'm sorry. It was just the lawyer in me." I realized that until I'd opened my mouth, she hadn't comprehended she was talking to an attorney. She had simply been talking to Leland. Her lover, her— please, I thought—boyfriend. She knew she was talking to a lawyer now, though. No doubt about that.

"Am I in trouble?" She hadn't looked at me as she'd spoken; she'd stared straight at the box of tissues on the table. "I mean, I know I'm in trouble emotionally. Or spiritually. But am I in…"

"Legal trouble?"

She nodded again.

"I don't know. I'd need to know what happened to get a sense of that," I said, trying to keep my voice calm. A fuzzy notion in the back of my head began to come into focus: I should leave. Right that second. I should tell Carissa to call a good attorney—a guy like Oren Candon, maybe, or Becky McNeil—and then not talk to anyone. Not a soul. Then I should stand up and say, *Don't tell me another word, don't tell me a single thing.* And then I should go. Just get the hell out. That was the appropriate thing to do. The reasonable thing to do. The ethical thing to do.

Yet it wasn't, I told myself, the moral thing to do. At least not necessarily. After all, she might need me.

And I'd only be obstructing justice if it turned out in the end that she had committed some kind of criminal offense. If whatever she'd done with Richard Emmons turned out to be a crime.

"Do you know him?" she asked.

"Richard? No, not really. I mean, I think I know who he is. But that's about it."

And it wasn't as if I could even bring myself to stand up and go in the first place. I put my hands on the arms of the chair to see what would occur—to see if they would press down on the wood and propel me to my feet—and not a thing happened. I was simply a guy sitting there with my hands on the arms of a ladder-back chair instead of in my lap. Maybe my hands would have sent me to my feet if Carissa had been only my homeopath, but she hadn't been *only* that for a week now. That day was the one-week anniversary of our very first date.

"I never thought he'd really buy the nuts and eat them," she said, her voice growing animated for the first time since I'd arrived. "I guess I knew he was very intense about homeopathy. And of course I knew how badly he wanted me to give him more of his remedy. But I would never have told him about cashews if I thought he might buy some."

No, I decided, I wasn't going to leave. It didn't matter that Phil would expect me to. Or that the other attorneys in the office would want me to. Or that certain investigators and police officers would view my behavior as somewhere between sleazy and illegal. None of that mattered that moment; I just didn't care.

"You suggested he eat the cashews?" I asked.

"Sort of."

"Sort of?"

"It was a joke."

"You knew he was allergic to them?"

"Yes."

"Like, I don't know, seriously allergic to them?"

She wiped her eyes with her fingers and then put on her eyeglasses. "I knew he was allergic to them," she said, staring right at me.

I nodded, aware that we were about to cross some sort of line. Was there a way to ask her my questions, I wondered, that would prevent her from incriminating herself? A way that would give her the chance to say whatever she wanted to say—release whatever was inside her that needed a vent—yet not put me in the position of knowing her absolute guilt or innocence for sure?

I reminded myself quickly that I shouldn't even be thinking about guilt or innocence. I didn't even know what she had done.

Or, more important, what people would *think* she had done.

"But you didn't actually buy him the cashews, right? It wasn't like that."

"Of course not. It wasn't like that at all." She blew her nose and stood up, and pulled a box of tea from a cabinet. "I used to smoke," she went on. "In college, I smoked like a chimney. A blast furnace. I wish I smoked now."

"No you don't."

"Trust me, I do. You ever smoke?"

If I were a criminal defense attorney, I knew, I'd be sure not to ask any questions that might give her the chance to implicate herself. After all, that was a big part of being a criminal attorney: You wanted to make absolutely sure that the murderer sitting beside you hadn't told you he'd done it. You just didn't want to know, you just didn't want to put yourself in the position of knowingly allowing someone to perjure himself when the case went to trial.

Unless, of course, you wanted to get disbarred. Or handed a suspension for misconduct. Then you might.

"No, I never smoked," I told her.

"Even with all that anxiety inside you?"

"Nails," I said. "Fingernails always seemed to suffice."

I watched her make tea, rallying a bit with each step: Filling the kettle with water. Turning on the burner. Removing the top from a teapot shaped like a cat. Filling a mesh tea ball with leaves and herbs and placing it in the pot. She leaned against the counter as if she expected to wait there while the water came to a boil, and I could almost see the color return to her cheeks. I wondered if it was because we were crossing that line together and she felt less alone. I hoped so.

"I stopped smoking when I first went to England," she said.

"When you were visiting your friend?"

"Yup."

What did she see when she saw me sitting at her kitchen table? Did she see simply her boyfriend the lawyer who understood the Byzantine workings of the law? The man who could help her understand if she was, as she had put it, in trouble?

Or did she see a state prosecutor? Did she even begin to comprehend the nightmarish conflict of interest that waited with us there in the kitchen for... for something to happen? For the water to boil. For the phone to ring. For the state police to call.

Or, perhaps, a reporter.

I glanced at my watch: It was eight-fifteen. Vermont was awake, starting to function. Soon the phone might really ring.

"Why did you quit? Was it the homeopath you met?"

"He might have been a small influence. I know he didn't approve of the habit."

"But there was more?"

"I didn't like British cigarettes. And I felt like an ugly American whenever I'd buy U.S. brands."

"Oh."

Carissa was smart, I decided, but Carissa lived in a different sort of world. A world where friends simply helped friends and you didn't sweat the details. On some level she probably sensed that what I was—what I did for a living— had some bearing on what I was thinking, but I don't believe the idea that I could be of use to her in some vaguely shadowy way had dawned on her.

"We never decided," she said after a long silence. "Am I in trouble?"

Outside her window was a bird feeder, and a pair of phoebes descended upon the wooden bar by the seeds.

"I have a message on my answering machine from Rod Morrow," I told her.

"Should I know that name?"

"He's a friend of mine from high school. Now he's a detective sergeant with the state police."

"So I am in trouble."

"Not necessarily. Like I said, it all depends on what happened."

"Do you want to hear?"

The spoken word has substance. You can't see it, but it's as real as the wind. As breath. A breeze between mouth and ear, a wave against tympanic membranes.

How many sentences had I said in my life—gentle wafts of words, little airstreams of syllables—that once spoken changed everything? Probably not more than half a dozen, but certainly they were the five or six most significant sentences I'd ever formed in my mind. Asking Elizabeth to marry me. Agreeing, almost on a lark, to interview for the opening in the State's Attorneys Office. Telling Whitney Lake I'd like her aunt's phone number.

I knew at that moment in Carissa's kitchen I was about to do it again. I was about to speak words that, for better or worse, could never be taken back.

"Yes, of course," I said as I stood and wrapped my arms around the small of her waist. "I want to know exactly what happened. Tell me everything you can remember."

✧

When Carissa went upstairs to get dressed a little later, I sat with her cat in my lap and tried to imagine how people would see what had occurred the day before last at the health-food store. A lot would depend upon whether homeopaths were regulated in Vermont. Or psychologists. After all, she was a psychologist, too. Still, no two attorneys would probably view what had happened in exactly the same way.

Some would simply decide Richard Emmons was an idiot who mistook an offhand remark—a joke, for crying out loud—for medical advice. They'd view Emmons as an adult who was fully capable of making his own choices, and it was his decision—and his decision alone—to buy nuts that he knew he was allergic to and then eat them. Even if he had bought them because Carissa had suggested the idea, he was completely free to ignore her advice. Just like someone with arthritis could choose to wear a copper bracelet around her wrist… or not. Or someone else could go to bed wearing cold wet socks under dry wool socks because a naturopath had recommended it as a way to relieve sinus pressure from a cold. Or not.

And if homeopaths weren't regulated, then she wasn't even a professional giving bad advice; she was merely a neighbor giving bad advice. A quack he ran into at the health-food store. Richard was free to disregard anything that she said.

Others, however, would see Carissa as a professional and Richard as her patient. Granted, in their eyes she might also be the sort of holistic shaman who shouldn't be allowed to dispense even garlic or honey, but she was still treating Richard. He was still her charge, and her advice therefore carried enormous weight: She had a duty to answer his questions responsibly. If she had given him the impression, no matter how inadvertently, that cashews wouldn't hurt him, his coma—his death by now, for all I knew—was her fault. If she'd said he should eat a nut that she knew he was allergic to, then she'd have to pay for this tragedy.

Oh, God, I thought, pay. Until that moment, I hadn't even considered the possibility of a civil suit, too. Clearly, however, this could be the bloody mother lode for some ambulance chaser.

And so exactly how Carissa had formed her opinion—the way that she'd said it—would be a factor in what everyone thought. What was it she believed that she'd said?

They're from the same plant family as your remedy.

And then he'd said he was allergic to cashews.

And she'd said she knew that. He'd told her.

Then they had talked about what was in his remedy, the one that he'd taken already. That thing called Rhus tox.

She'd explained to Richard it was poison ivy.

At first, it seemed, he hadn't believed her. Had he really and truly eaten poison ivy? he'd asked. He was allergic to poison ivy, too, and not like most people were. He was *really* allergic to it!

And she'd told him he had. Homeopathically, of course.

But nothing happened to me! he had said. Astonished. Impressed.

Of course not, she'd said.

And then he'd asked what she meant by her remark that poison ivy and cashews were in the same family.

She'd been in a hurry—shopping, after all, for her boyfriend, the prosecutor—but she recalled elaborating a bit. But just a bit. She'd said they were both in the Anacardiaceae family: Cashews and poison ivy, pistachio nuts and poison sumac. Mangoes. They all had resinous and sometimes poisonous juice, nuts or fleshy fruit, and small flowers.

Like cures like, remember? The Law of Similars?

And so he had asked what would have happened if she'd given him a small dose of cashews—and here, I decided, their exchange had the potential to get real muddy—and she'd answered, Nothing.

Or, as precisely as she could recall, *Probably nothing.*

She told me she had meant: It probably wouldn't cure you.

She had not meant: Probably nothing will happen to you.

But the thing was, if he had ingested cashews homeopathically—one part cashew, a million parts water—nothing would have happened, in all likelihood. After all, a dose that size probably would have been insufficient to cause an allergic reaction.

What Richard had heard in her response, however—those simple words "probably nothing"—could mean everything. Perhaps he'd assumed she'd meant nothing would happen if he ingested them normally, as whole nuts—though still, of course, in what was in his mind just a small dose.

He had, Carissa was quite sure, used those two words: Small. Dose.

But what really constituted a small dose in his opinion? Was it what Jennifer, a veterinarian, would consider a small dose? Or what his homeopath would regard as one?

Clearly they were very different. Jennifer told me she had once been treating a cat for diabetes and on the first day of therapy had given the animal the absolute minimal dose of insulin recommended: four units, or about an eighth of a syringe. And the cat's blood glucose level had plummeted from diabetic to normal to hypoglycemic within ninety minutes, faster than any of the vets in the practice had ever seen. Here they had barely begun to monitor the cat, and the animal was practically falling off a cliff to his death, and so an hour and a half after giving the cat insulin, they were actually giving him glucose to prevent fatal seizures.

Eventually the cat would be getting a mere one unit of insulin a day: One quarter of the recommended dosage. About a thirtieth of a syringe. And the cat had responded.

No, it was clear that no two individuals were likely to view a small dose in quite the same way.

And for some people, a thirtieth of a syringe of certain homeopathic substances, undiluted—a small dose to some, a huge one to others—could be fatal.

Nothing? Richard had asked her, trying to confirm what she'd said. Thinking, perhaps, that a cashew or two was a small dose.

Nothing, she thought she might have repeated, shrugging.

Really?

She'd wanted to finish filling her own basket, she'd been in a hurry. She wasn't exactly irritated with Richard, but he had been phoning her off and on for almost two weeks, insisting that she give him another dose of his remedy. Whatever it was. Just a little bit more.

And so she was growing tired of his questions. His persistence. His neediness.

His demand for more medicine.

Look, remember what I told you about Hahnemann and his provings? Well, pretend you're Hahnemann, and try some. Do the proving and record the results. We'll talk after Christmas.

And then she had rolled her eyes to make it clear she was kidding. She was being sarcastic. Cashews, after all, had already gone through a proving. They already were a remedy. An obscure one, certainly—Anacardium occidentale, a cure in some cases for brain fog and hallucinations—yet a remedy nonetheless.

But she hadn't said that. She had simply suggested the proving and moved on to the English muffins, while he had remained there by the nuts.

Exchange over.

Man's now in a coma.

Was there more to it than that? Possibly. For all I knew, it really was a suicide attempt. Here Carissa and I had been sitting around her kitchen table, stewing about the likelihood that Richard Emmons had misunderstood what she'd said and mistaken cashews for his homeopathic cure, when it was possible he'd understood all along that cashews might be fatal for him, and been inspired by their conversation to choose them as his way out of this world. Agonizing. But creative.

And the guy had asthma. I couldn't lose sight of that. Clearly that was a factor, too.

Any way I looked at it, I decided, I had only a small part of the story.

I put the cat down on the floor and went to the counter by Carissa's phone. People usually kept paper and pens by their phones. Indeed, right there beside the cordless receiver's cradle was a wicker basket of scrap paper—not unlike the basket outside her office door at the Octagon—and a promotional pen from some national homeopathic group. On a half sheet of paper I started writing a list of questions, scribbling the key words as they came to me. I had close to a dozen questions before the ideas even started to slow, and I realized I'd better phone my office to let them know I was alive and I'd be in later that morning. It was already past nine o'clock.

When Carissa returned, her hair was still wet from her shower, but she'd managed to pull on a pair of khakis and a blouse and run something glossy and cheerful over her lips.

"Any patients today?"

"Uh-huh. But not till eleven."

She dropped a handful of dry cat food into Sepia's bowl, and the animal raced out from under the kitchen table at the sound. She knelt by the cat, stroking the back of the animal's neck for a moment as she started to eat.

"I assume you have malpractice insurance," I said.

"I do. But as a psychologist."

"Not as a homeopath?"

"No. Few homeopaths do," she said, standing up. "They might as doctors,

they might as dentists. They might as psychologists. But not, usually, as homeopaths. In theory, there isn't any need: The remedies can't hurt you."

"You were treating Richard solely as a homeopath?"

"That's right. That's why he came to me, so that's how I treated him."

"Like me?"

"Like you."

"He came to you for asthma?"

She nodded. "That was his chief complaint."

"And Rhus tox is the cure for asthma?"

"No."

"No?"

She shrugged. "Why would you think that?"

"Oh, I don't know. Maybe because that's what ailed him."

"You came to me for a cold; that was your chief complaint. A runny nose.
A sore throat. Right?"

"Right."

"Well, if I'd decided that was indeed the problem, I wouldn't have prescribed arsenic."

"But it worked!"

"I understand. But if I'd wanted to simply treat your cold or your sore
throat, I'd have given you something like aconite—"

"Aconite?"

"Wolfsbane. Or maybe Pulsatilla—a windflower. I wasn't treating your
cold, Leland; I was treating your fear."

"What was the Rhus tox…treating?"

"Richard has a skin disorder that goes hand in hand with his asthma," she
said, opening a drawer in a cabinet beside the refrigerator. Then, as if I weren't
in the room beside her, she reached inside for a dish towel and resumed dry-
ing her hair as she spoke. "It's not a horrendous disorder, but he thinks it is.
In his mind, it's a profound disability—especially given the number of times
every single week when he meets people for the very first time. It shows up
mostly on his hands, and it makes him extremely self-conscious."

When she was finished, she shook her head the way I imagined Sepia
might if she'd just run inside from a cloudburst—vigorously, her hair a shampoo commercial in fast-forward—and then draped the towel over the sink.

"Does it itch?"

"Sure does."

"And the Rhus tox treated it?" I asked.

She nodded. "What he really wanted was his skin disease to go away. He might have been able to live with his asthma if he didn't have a kind of eczema that went with it. But Rhus tox wasn't simply the appropriate remedy because of Richard's skin complaints. It was also apt because of the joint pain he's had off and on this fall, and because of the type of person he is."

"What's he like?"

"I don't know, he's a patient. Our conversations are confidential."

"And I don't want to violate that. I just want to know what kind of person he is."

She took a deep breath and collapsed into a chair by the kitchen table. "He has his own little ad agency up in Burlington. I guess it's not so little—at least by Vermont standards. He probably has twenty or twenty-five employees."

"Any partners?"

"I don't think so."

"Clients?"

"The state lottery. A bank. A ski resort. A lot of business-to-business stuff."

"Tell me about him."

"Just how well do you think I know him?"

I shrugged. "I guess about as well as you'd know me if we hadn't gone out to dinner last week."

"Fine. Here's my sense of the man based on two appointments and some phone calls. He can be charming and funny and very fast on his feet. He can also be extremely self-absorbed."

"Thoughtless?"

"Not necessarily. Just self-absorbed. There's a difference. I think he's probably a very nice dad. A perfectly fine husband."

"Is he smart?"

"Certainly. He's smart and he's intense, and he's incredibly hard-working. Driven. He wants things now, and he's easily frustrated."

"And he was frustrated with his skin thing and his asthma."

"Yes."

"But not, I assume, suicidally frustrated."

"No."

"Did you give him anything separate for his asthma?"

"I know some homeopaths who'll administer a compound tincture or cure, but I'm not among them. I view myself as a pretty classical homeopath."

"So you only gave him the Rhus tox."

"Right."

"In the form of little pills? Like my arsenic?"

She nodded. "Four or five, I guess."

"And it worked?"

"It was working. His skin had cleared up completely."

"And his asthma?"

"It was under control."

I glanced at the questions I'd written on the scrap piece of paper and considered not asking them. They might make it sound as if I doubted her. But someone was going to ask them at some point soon, and she might as well hear them from me.

"I presume he's been seeing a regular doctor for his asthma."

"Yes. I don't remember the guy's name, but it's at my office."

"Asthma's one of those chronic things you keep under control with pills. At least that's what I've always thought."

"Pills and inhalers. Most asthmatics use a combination of controllers and relievers—bronchodilators and inhaled steroids. Some are old-fashioned pills, and some are delivered by those little pumps that spray the medicine right into the lungs."

"Prescription stuff?"

"Uh-huh. Proventil. Vanceril. Theophylline. And that bothered Richard. He feared he was putting a pharmacy into his bloodstream."

"Would that pharmacy affect the Rhus tox?"

"Certainly it could," she said.

"Dilute it?"

"We use the term *antidote*. Were his regular drugs a possible antidote to his homeopathic cure? Yes. In theory they might have affected it. But when I gave Richard his remedy, I did not tell him to give up his regular asthma medications. And when we spoke on the phone a few days later, his skin had improved."

"So his drugs weren't an issue."

"They were an issue in his mind—not mine. It was one of the first things we…"

"We what?" I asked when the pause had grown long.

"I just shouldn't be telling you this, Leland. He's my patient. We have a relationship founded on trust."

"You want to know whether you're in trouble, and I can't answer that if I don't know what happened."

"Will other people ask me these questions?"

"Probably."

"Will I have to answer them, too?"

"You'll have a lawyer."

"It's that bad...."

"I don't know."

She sighed. Then: "One of the first things he told me was that he wanted to control his asthma without drugs. But that's not unusual. Half the asthmatics I see want to give up their drugs."

"Why? Dependency?"

"Dependency's part of it. But have you ever read the warnings that come with most asthma medicines?"

"Nasty stuff?"

"Not really, but they sound nasty—inhaled steroids, theophylline—and that's the point. They sound scary."

"And homeopathy can help an asthmatic give them up?"

"Sometimes. I can think of two asthmatics off the top of my head who I helped wean from their drugs."

"What did you tell Richard?"

"I told him we'd see what happened."

"So you weren't concerned that his conventional medicines were preventing the Rhus tox from working?"

"It was something we talked about. If you must know, it's something we talked about a lot, because Richard kept bringing it up. But they didn't seem to be affecting his remedy."

I scanned my questions once more, and for a split second I had the sensation I was in Courtroom 3A. It was the way I was standing, the notes in my hand, the sense that my questioning was supposed to be going somewhere. Quickly I leaned against the sink—slouching intentionally—to help push the image from my mind.

"How did he seem the other night at the store?" I asked.

"He seemed fine."

"Healthy?"

"Yes."

"Then why did he feel a need for the cashews?"

"I don't understand what you mean."

"If he was fine…if he was…healthy, then why did he try to medicate himself with the cashews?"

She stared at me for a long moment, then reached behind her for the large shoulder bag hanging behind the kitchen door and pulled out her wooden hairbrush. I could see she wasn't happy with my question, but before I could open my mouth to apologize or explain, she said, "I'm a homeopath. I'm not a mind-reader."

"I understand."

She started brushing her hair almost angrily. "What are you suggesting?"

"I'm not suggesting a thing. I just want to know why he was trying to medicate himself if he wasn't sick."

"I didn't give him a complete physical in the health-food store Christmas Eve. But he didn't seem to be sick."

"There were no lesions on his hands?"

"I didn't notice any."

"And his breathing was okay?"

"Yes. Earlier in the week he'd said his chest felt a little tight, but he seemed perfectly fine that night."

"Was he short of breath?"

"No!"

"Don't be mad—"

"How can I not be mad? All of a sudden you're treating me like a criminal!"

"I'm trying to understand what this looks like to—"

"A state's attorney! That's what you're doing. You're interrogating me! Why don't you just arrest me? We'll go to Burlington together, and you can indict me or arraign me or whatever it is you do with people you're arresting!"

I looked at the birds on the feeder and tried to gather my thoughts. The last thing I wanted to do at that moment was fight with Carissa. She didn't need that. But as badly as I felt for her given all she'd been through, she wasn't the victim in this disaster. Not by a long shot. The victim was up at the hospital in Burlington at that moment, lying flat in a bed in a coma.

I wonder if the guy has disability insurance. I wonder if life insurance kicks in if you're in a coma.

"I'm sorry," I said, without looking away from the window. "I was just trying to get a sense of whether there might be criminal...whether there might be grounds to investigate what happened."

She tossed her hairbrush on the table, and the crack of wood on wood scared the cat. "And I didn't mean to snap at you. It's just..."

"It's just what?"

"Oh," she said, waving a hand in the air, "I could just throw up. That's what. I could just throw up."

Sepia jumped onto the dish rack beside the sink, and the birds on the other side of the window flew away. A thought crossed my mind: This is such a nice house. I hope she can keep it.

I sat down beside Carissa and began rubbing her back. I murmured over and over that this would all turn out fine in the end, eventually everything would be okay, while trying to decide whether I should have her call Oren Candon or Becky McNeil. They were both excellent lawyers, with outstanding records in civil trials.

And, as defense attorneys, they'd both beaten the State.

13

NUMBER 264

It is for [the true physician] a matter of conscience to be absolutely sure that the patient always receives the right medicine.

DR. SAMUEL HAHNEMANN,
Organon of Medicine, 1842

I felt a tad queasy as I drove to work, and I told myself it was my driving: I was so concerned about Carissa, I was handling the truck like a drunk. Swerving at the last minute to avoid a rural mailbox. Slamming on the brakes when I almost went into the rear of another pickup stopped at a light. Sliding into the wrong lane while taking a turn particularly badly.

What must it be like to live with the possibility that you put someone in a coma? I'd certainly seen the faces of remorse enough in my life: The real drunk (versus the merely preoccupied prosecutor the day after Christmas) who kills a five-year-old and cripples her mother while driving under the influence. The uncle who shoots his niece's boyfriend when he gets the mistaken idea that the young guy was abusing her.

But I'd never really experienced remorse myself, I decided. I understood regret; I'd certainly made my share of bad decisions in my life. And clearly I knew guilt, at least the sort of guilt I assumed most people experienced every day: Telling Abby I was too tired to read her one more book. Taking months to build the handicapped-access ramp at the church. Spending massive amounts of time on the Web looking up sites devoted solely to female ejaculation.

Guilt? Oh, yeah. Been there, done that.

Not so, I thought, with remorse.

I wished it was the Emmons woman's predicament that was making me queasy, but I was afraid it wasn't. A few times, I had to remind myself that she wasn't a terrible, evil person—a stalker bent senselessly upon the ruination of my girlfriend's life.

By the time I got to the office, it was almost eleven-thirty. Emmons's wife had to have called, I was sure of it. Often that morning when I'd been trapped in my truck behind lumbering milk tankers, I'd imagine her on the phone with Phil Hood.

No one in my office was aware that I was dating Carissa, which meant there was still a chance I could be the one to chat with the wife. Call her back if she'd phoned and no one had dealt with her. Take the call if for some reason she was only just now contacting the State's Attorneys Office.

Your husband knew he was allergic to cashews, Ms. Emmons? This is a real tragedy, and I'll be sure to review your statement very carefully. But I just don't see a criminal offense. Bye.

If she was adamant, I could tell her to call the Vermont Attorney General's Office.

Or, perhaps, I could tell her that I'd look into her charges. And then do nothing. Or everything. Or whatever in between was appropriate, with the singular goal of making sure that Carissa was never charged with a crime.

Which would mean making sure that no one ever discovered I was dating her.

Which was impossible.

Someone was going to find out I was seeing the woman. It was inevitable.

If this thing did explode, at some point I'd have to 'fess up. And if I did have to fess up, the sooner the better. Like that morning.

When I arrived, I asked Gerianne, our receptionist, what sort of Christmas she'd had, and then realized I was completely unable to focus on her response—despite the fact that I was dimly aware that she was telling me something about a toy fire truck, her six-year-old son, and a hook and ladder snapping shut on his finger.

"Any messages?" I asked, fearing for a brief moment she'd just told me her little boy had lost a pinkie while I wasn't listening.

"Oh, yeah," she said, and she handed me a typical pile of five or six little pink squares. I glanced at them quickly and saw none were from a woman named Emmons.

"Any unusual calls this morning?"

"Someone called in a bomb threat to Wal-Mart. Put a damper on the day-after-Christmas sale."

I nodded. "Anyone looking for me?"

"You shoot somebody?"

"No."

"Nobody's looking for you."

"Thank you."

She gave me a smile that looked plenty maternal, despite the fact that it was coming from a woman five or six years my junior. "Leland, it's okay to be a little late the day after Christmas. Trust me. Seems to me we shouldn't even be working today."

I tried to smile back. I hadn't realized I was acting so squirrelly.

I put my head into Phil's office before I'd even ventured into my own, unsure what I was planning to say. I like to believe that I was about to tell him about Carissa, but that's probably rubbish. I was relieved when I saw that Margaret Turnbull was there with him, because it meant I had an excuse not to say a word.

The two attorneys were sitting around the small round conference table opposite Phil's desk.

"Leland, good morning!" Phil said when he saw me, actually rising from his seat in a show of mock earnestness. "Merry day after Christmas. I'm so glad you decided to join us."

"Phil, Margaret. Good morning."

"Hi, Leland. A little too much Christmas cheer yesterday?" Margaret asked.

"Day-care problems," I told her.

"Nice Christmas?" Phil asked, and I realized instead of "day-care problems," I could have told Margaret, *Yeah. I was doing speedballs with my daughter,* and Phil still would have asked whether I'd had a nice Christmas. It wasn't that they weren't listening, and it wasn't that they didn't care. It was simply that I was so reliable in their minds, it hadn't fazed them a bit that I was late. Day-care problems? Happens all the time.

"Wonderful Christmas," I told Phil. "You?"

"Aces. Barbara made the most magnificent stuffed squash you've ever tasted—a Christmas dinner absolutely free of dairy and meat. And almost no fat."

"Yummy."

"I assume you feasted on the usual dead flesh of animals great and small?"

"Of course. But this year we decided we wouldn't even cook them. *And* we killed the critters ourselves on Christmas morn." I turned to Margaret, planning to change the subject by asking her how her Christmas with Dr. Strangelove had been, when I heard Gerianne paging me, telling me I had a call waiting.

"Be sure to connect with Justin when you're done," Phil told me, referring to one of the younger attorneys in the office.

"For sure. Anything unusual going on?"

"No, I think he simply has a couple questions. Why?"

"Just curious."

"Do you feel okay, Leland?" Margaret asked. "You look a little pale."

"It must be all that meat," I answered. "You know how unhealthy we carnivores are."

✧

"It's Rod Morrow," Gerianne told me on my speakerphone as I took off my coat and dropped my attaché onto the credenza behind my desk. I thanked her and picked up the line that was blinking. As we compared our holidays—and Rod really didn't sound as though he minded having to have worked a part of Christmas Day—I hoped my voice didn't sound as uneasy on the phone as it apparently sounded in person to Gerianne and Margaret.

"You get my message?" Rod asked me.

"I did. I wasn't sure if I was supposed to call you back. And then I figured it could wait till today."

"She call in yet?"

"The…Emmons woman?"

"That's the one."

"I don't know."

"I told her if it would make her feel any better, she should call your office."

"Very kind of you."

"You know them?"

"The Emmons family? No."

"She seems…"

"Angry?"

"No, not really. Scared. She seems sad and scared."

"Oh."

"She seems like this sweet lady who's just scared shitless for her husband and kids. Actually, she probably seemed a hell of a lot more reasonable than I would have if I had two children and some quasi-doctor had just put my husband in a coma."

"Did she know the doctor's name?"

"Carissa."

"Carissa," I repeated.

"Carissa Lake. She's a homeopath—whatever that means."

"Uh-huh."

"I think it's some kind of alternative medicine."

I said nothing, and he quickly filled in the silence: "The woman— Emmons's wife, not the quack who was treating him—is very concerned this Carissa Lake is going to kill someone someday. Assuming, of course, she hasn't already."

"Killed someone."

"Right."

"If Emmons had died, I think I'd have heard," I said. It wouldn't, technically, be the sort of unattended death that automatically involves the State's Attorneys Office, because the fellow would have died at the hospital. But it would have been a death triggered by an unforeseen event in his home. And that would have involved my office, and surely Gerianne or Margaret or Phil would have said something to me if a possible homicide or suicide had come in earlier that morning.

"I guess."

"What's the Emmons woman's name?"

"Jennifer."

"What exactly did she say happened?"

"Well, in the middle of the night Christmas Eve, her husband got out of bed. He's an asthmatic, and he was having trouble breathing. He went downstairs, opened the refrigerator, and ate cashews she didn't even know they had in the house. When she found him, he was already on the floor, and he couldn't breathe. See, he's allergic to them."

For the first time, the image of a family man—a father like me—collapsed on the kitchen tiles grew real in my mind. Then I imagined this Jennifer Emmons person crouched over him. "It must have been horrible for her," I said.

"I'm sure. And so she called the rescue squad, and now the guy's in a coma."

"Where did she say the homeopath fits in?"

"She thinks the woman advised her husband to eat the cashews, because he wouldn't have bought them on his own. And she thinks this voodoo doctor told her husband to go off his meds."

"He was off his meds?"

"Apparently. Now, this lady admits she doesn't know a damn thing about the law—she's a very reasonable woman, all things considered—but she can't believe it isn't illegal to be some kind of doctor and tell an asthmatic to stop taking his medicine and then eat foods he knows he's allergic to."

"She doesn't just see it as stupid advice?"

"No way."

I sighed. "I'm sure they've already done blood work at the hospital. I'm sure they know whether or not he was taking his asthma drugs."

"His wife will tell you he wasn't."

"But that doesn't mean the homeopath told him to give them up."

"His wife will tell—"

"Would you just let his wife tell me, then!"

Rod whistled. "What kind of coal did you get yesterday?"

"I just walked in the office, and I've got a stack of messages as fat as my briefcase. I'm sorry."

"Hey, just thought you'd want to know. He is sort of a neighbor, after all. Fact is, she is, too. The homeopath. I looked her up in the DMV computer, and there she was. She lives in the village itself, of course, unlike you and Abby up there in those hills. But this Carissa Lake is a Bartlett resident, too."

I glanced up, and Margaret was standing in my doorway with a yellow pad in her hands. She signaled that she wanted to chat when I was off the phone. "Thank you," I said to the detective, while holding up one finger for Margaret, trying to tell her I'd be done in a minute. Then, to be sure, I mouthed the words "One minute," and she nodded and disappeared down the hall.

"You're welcome, Mr. Grinch."

"I'm sorry I snapped at you."

"Noted."

"Do you have any idea how old her kids are?"

"One's a teen. And one's a little younger."

"Boys? Girls?"

"One of each."

I wondered if it would kill me to have a single cup of coffee. Suddenly, for the first time in days, I had a desire for even the sludge we called coffee in the State's Attorneys Office.

"I'll let you know if she calls, okay?" I told Rod.

"No obligation, we're investigating. I just called you 'cause I thought you might know her."

"Jennifer Emmons?"

"Of course! I thought you might know the whole Emmons family! Why in the name of God would I think you knew the homeopath? You're not into that kind of thing, are you?"

"Do I seem like the type?" I asked, realizing as I spoke that if I had waved Margaret into my office instead of away, I might have just told Rod the truth. Come clean right there on the phone. After all, it's no easy task to obstruct justice when there's a witness who happens to be a state's attorney.

It really is the little things in this world, isn't it? I thought. It's the little things that change everything. If Margaret had been sitting across my desk from me then, I might have been completely unable to withhold from Rod the fact that I was indeed into that sort of thing, and that I was actually getting to know the homeopath in question rather well.

"Are you kidding?" Rod told me. "I can sooner see you getting a recreational enema than wasting your time with some New Age quack."

"I'll take that as a compliment," I said.

"That's just how it was meant," he said, and then we both said good-bye. In the ensuing silence, I tried not to regret not asking Margaret to wait.

✧

It was possible, I decided around two-fifteen, that Jennifer Emmons was never going to call. Unlikely. But possible. After all, for one reason or another I'd spoken with a half-dozen of the attorneys in the office, and there had been absolutely no sign of her.

At least no sign that I'd seen: I reminded myself that there were four or five other lawyers wandering through the courthouse, and any one of them could have heard from Jennifer that morning.

It was right around then, I believe, that I first decided I really wanted more arsenic. That I really *needed* more arsenic.

Not like a junkie, of course, not the way an addict needs drugs. It wasn't like that, I told myself. Besides, the arsenic I craved wasn't really a drug anyway. In reality, it was just sugar. Right? It was a little sucrose pellet that belonged in a big bag of candy. Not a tiny pharmacological vial.

No, I simply needed arsenic the way I'd once needed cough drops. I needed those little white pills as a psychological crutch, and it had absolutely nothing to do with a physiological or chemical dependence.

Besides, wasn't homeopathic arsenic safer than cough drops?

Maybe. Probably. Certainly.

And it sure as hell worked better. Throughout that interminable summer and fall, lozenges had never done a damn thing for my sore throat, but that arsenic Carissa had given me had worked wonders on my anxieties and fears overnight.

For all I knew, I might never have found the energy and the courage to court Carissa Lake without arsenic. I might never have asked her to spend Christmas Eve at my house.

Without arsenic, I might never have beaten back the cold that had lived inside me for a full half a year, I might never have been able to stand in Courtroom 3A without my nose running. My throat burning. My pockets overflowing with handkerchiefs and Halls.

I might never have risked arguing a case from the seat without the cinnamon bun stain.

I began to wish I'd gotten more arsenic from Carissa when I was at her house that morning. Surely she kept some in the bathroom cabinet. Like Pepto-Bismol. And ipecac.

I considered calling her once again—I'd probably left a half-dozen messages on her answering machine at the Octagon and her home already—when Gerianne knocked on my half-open door.

"Are you doing anything right this second?" she asked.

"Of course," I said, hoping I didn't sound too defensive. My desk was a mess, but only because I hadn't finished a single thing I'd started in over two hours.

"I mean anything you can't drop. Or are you due in court in a minute?"

"No."

"Good. There's a woman in the reception area who had a two o'clock with Bob, and it's pretty clear Bob isn't going to be back for a while."

"Is he in court?"

"Yeah, and I just ran down the hall to see how it's going. There's no way he can leave. Would you mind seeing her?"

"I can't just jump into a case he's working on."

"It's not like that. It's a new thing. It's a woman who wants to talk to an attorney—any attorney—about her husband. I can't tell, but I think it's abuse. Domestic abuse."

"Fine. Send her back."

"Thank you, Leland. She really seems incredibly sweet. I don't know the details, but I think something horrible happened to her on Christmas Eve."

I nodded, hoping Gerianne could not see the blood literally draining from my face.

"Oh," I said. I knew I was supposed to say more, but I couldn't imagine what. I wondered if it was possible to have a stroke without pain, and if at some point in the last half-day I'd had a doozie and done in a sizable number of my once-healthy brain cells.

"I'll send her back."

"Yes. Why don't you do that. And why don't you see if she'd like something to drink."

✧

Jennifer Emmons's hair wasn't quite as long as I recalled from the few times I'd seen her in church, but it was the same brown-and-henna mix: streamers of orange and red, some more subtle than others, coursing through an otherwise calm river of bay. She usually sat with her husband and children in the pews far to the left, midway to the back. But it was definitely her. The Emmonses weren't members of the church, but they made it there a couple of Sundays every year.

And I must have seen her shopping for groceries in Bartlett any number of times, because I had a vision of her pushing a supermarket cart, and hoisting brown bags into the air and then into a car trunk. I could envision her on the cement sidewalk outside the store, wearing the sort of trim cardigan sweater and blue jeans she was wearing right now, perhaps even followed out the door by a boy. A boy bigger than my Abby...but still very little. Surely I'd seen such a thing.

I guessed she was a few years older than I was.

"You live in East Bartlett," she said, taking my hand before sitting across from me. Her mouth quivered just the tiniest bit, as if she might have smiled when she'd spoken if she weren't in the midst of a disaster. She looked like she hadn't slept in days, and I wondered if she'd been awake for close to thirty-six hours now—since her husband had collapsed in the middle of the night Christmas Eve.

"I do indeed."

"I've seen you around. I guess I just should have called you first."

I smiled.

"You've had tragedies of your own," she went on.

"I have."

"You have a little girl, right?"

"Abby," I answered, nodding. I was about to add Abby's age and then recount her latest malapropism: After viewing her aunt and uncle's new mini-van Christmas Day, she'd said she thought she'd prefer a Mickey van. But I feared if I went on about my daughter it would open the door to a friendship. A fellowship. A bond. It would make us more intimate. It might make me want to help her.

"Short for Abigail?"

"That's right."

When I didn't say more, she nodded, then looked at a small note in her hand. "Did Bob McFarland tell you why we were going to meet?"

"I haven't spoken to Bob. But the detective you saw yesterday told me a little bit on the phone."

She sipped the glass of water she'd brought with her into my office and sat forward in her chair. She seemed almost to be steadying herself against the front of my desk, holding on to the desktop with both hands once she'd put down her glass.

"In that case," she asked, "where should I start?"

"Start wherever you'd like."

"Okay," she said, and she began by telling me that her husband had not tried to kill himself. Some people seemed to think it might have been a suicide attempt, but that was the last thing in the world Richard would have done. He'd be furious if he knew what some people were suggesting. She then went on to explain her husband's irritation with his asthma and dermatitis, and his frustration with his disease—"Though it's under control so much of the time, I don't think of it as a disease"—and the way he'd started exercising and changed his diet. The way he'd removed the carpets from every room in their house, except the kids' bedrooms.

Apparently in the latter half of November, however, he'd nevertheless had an asthma attack—"We went to the emergency room, but in the greater scheme of things, it really wasn't that big a deal"—and that attack had been the last straw. That attack, she thought, was what had led him to the homeopath.

"Did it work at first? The homeopathy?" I asked.

"No!"

She told me how the eczema on Richard's hands and arms had cleared up, but sometimes it just cleared up on its own. It usually ran its course and then went away. Or it would respond to a salve called Eucerin. She certainly didn't believe it was some homeopathic magic bullet that had cured it this time.

"And his asthma?"

"His chest was a little tight that week. But he was doing okay until he stopped using his inhalers and taking his theophylline."

"Theophylline's an asthma drug?"

"Right."

"Why did he stop taking it?"

"This woman told him to."

"How do you know that?"

"Richard told me."

"Richard told you?"

"He told me she said they were affecting his homeopathic remedy—whatever it was she was giving him. She said they were working as an antidote."

I folded my hands across my lap, clasping my fingers together. I thought they might shake otherwise. "She used that word?"

"Antidote? She must have. It's the word Richard was always using."

"And so he stopped taking his drugs?"

"That's right. A week ago yesterday. After talking to her." She let go of my desk and reached into the handbag she'd dropped by her chair for a handkerchief. I saw her eyes were about to start tearing.

"And his rationale was—"

"*Her* rationale," she corrected me.

"*Her* rationale was that the remedy would not be completely effective as long as his body was full of his regular anti-asthma drugs."

"Exactly. His eczema had cleared up, but his breathing hadn't improved."

"They had this conversation on the phone?"

"I don't know. Maybe he went to her office. We live nearby. But it was last Monday, I do know that. And that was the last day he was using an inhaler or taking his pills."

"And then his breathing got worse?"

She dabbed her face with her handkerchief, a white cotton square with delicate blue flowers along the edges. "Not right away. For a couple days, it seemed, he was sort of on a plateau. It was around Thursday, I guess, that his breathing started to get bad. His wheezing sounded worse, that's for sure. And he said a couple of times that his chest really felt tight."

"When did he first get his remedy?"

"About two weeks ago. Obviously I can get the exact date for you."

I nodded. "Why don't you tell me what happened Christmas Eve."

"Should I begin with the cashews?"

"Sure. Begin with the cashews."

"You should know that she told Richard to eat them."

"She did...."

"There's a witness." She crumpled her handkerchief into a ball and looked at her note once again. "Her name is Patsy Collins. She works at the health-food store in town, and she was there when the woman told Richard to eat them. She heard it all."

"Older woman? Silver hair?"

"That's right. Do you know her?"

"Not really. But I've shopped there a couple of times."

"Well, she heard the whole conversation."

"Oh, good."

"I have her number for you."

"Thank you."

"And I also brought the name of my husband's allergist. He wants to see you press charges, too."

"He does," I said. I wasn't sure if it came out like a question or a confirmation. Mostly it just sounded in my head like a monotone.

"Here's his card," she went on, pulling a doctor's appointment card from a sweater pocket and passing it across my desk. "He thinks it must be criminal for this woman to tell my husband to stop using the medications that control his asthma, and then suggest he eat a food that's sure to cause an allergic reaction."

"You've spoken to him?"

"I have. And Patsy Collins."

"You've been busy."

"No, not really. But Richard just lies there in this bed. And I sit and I sit, and I know I'll go insane if I don't do something." She shook her head and shrugged. "Yesterday I called the state police. Today I called his doctor."

"And the health-food store..."

"No, I actually went there. I went there during lunchtime, after I'd gone home to get a change of clothes."

"What made you think to go there?"

She reached once again into her purse and pulled out a small plastic bag filled with cashews. "When I went home for my clothes, I remembered this. It had been on the floor beside Richard in the kitchen. It's what he was eating. Can I give it to you?"

"You mean, like, officially?"

"Yes."

"Certainly. I'll hang on to it." I put the Baggie in a corner of my desk and already saw it on an evidence cart in a courtroom, marked with a number by the State. "So...Christmas Eve. What exactly happened?"

She took a breath and started to speak, beginning with Richard's troubled breathing at dinner. It had gotten worse as the evening progressed, and she thought he was wheezing rather badly as they wrapped the last of their children's presents later that night. She'd practically begged him, she said, to use his inhaler, but again he'd refused. He didn't want to go back on the drugs, he'd insisted. About three-fifteen in the morning he'd woken up, and she'd asked him once more to use the inhaler. Finally he had. Grudgingly, she thought. But at least he had used it.

And it hadn't worked, at least not right away, and he'd gone downstairs.

"I was hoping he was going to go take a prednisone. Maybe get a drink of water."

"He wasn't?"

"No. He was getting the cashews. They were in the refrigerator. I didn't know that at the time, but that's where they were. I didn't even know he'd bought any."

Jennifer then managed to recount for me the sound of the thump she'd heard before she even got to the kitchen, and her discovery of her husband on the floor, gasping for air. Whenever she thought she might cry, she would stop speaking and allow herself a short, quiet moment.

When she was through, she said simply, "And now my husband's in a coma. A coma."

"Any change since Christmas Eve?"

She shook her head no and bit her lip.

"I can't tell you how sorry I am this happened to you. To him."

"Thank you."

"We'll look into it all, of course," I went on as gently as I could. "But I should tell you right now—so you don't get your hopes up too high—that it might not be a criminal affair. A lot will depend on whether homeopaths are regulated by the state."

"I understand."

"And—"

"And so I thought it might be helpful that the woman is also a psychologist."

"Uh-huh. Really?"

"And they are regulated by the state."

"You've already checked?"

"I have. I wanted to know as much about this woman as I possibly could."

"Well, okay. Thank you." I made a show of looking at the appointment calendar on my desk, hoping to signal that our meeting was over. When she didn't move, I asked, "Is there anything else you need? Is there anything else we can do?"

"Don't you want the woman's name?"

"Yes," I said, "why don't you tell me." And as she said the words Carissa Lake—spelling for me the homeopath's first name, then providing me with her home and office phone numbers—I couldn't imagine there was any way in the world I could help my healer. There was absolutely nothing to do but make sure she'd linked up with someone like Becky McNeil. And then, perhaps, say a prayer for the Emmons family.

✧

"That's the Eiffel Tower," Carissa was saying to Abby that night after we'd all arrived at my house, as she pointed at the picture in *Madeline's Rescue.* "It must be very far from Madeline's house in this drawing. It's actually very tall."

"Madeline doesn't have a mother, you know," Abby explained, a connection I understood instantly. It came up whenever we read a book in the Bemelmans series. "She died. At least I think she died. See, her mother didn't visit her in the hospital when she had her operation."

Carissa looked up at me while Abby was gazing at the picture in the storybook, and in the brief second we made eye contact, I nodded, hoping my small motion reassured her: *It's okay. We talk about this stuff all the time.*

"The operation's an appendectomy, isn't it?" she asked Abby.

"Uh-huh."

Though Abby was sitting on the den floor next to Carissa, my daughter was pressing her free hand on her hip exactly the way her mother once had—her palm upon the velour of the dress, her fingers pointing down her leg toward her knees.

Sometimes I would be surprised when I'd see Elizabeth in Abby. It wasn't that the little girl didn't look like her mother, because most certainly she did. They had the same brown eyes, and the same rosebud-shaped mouth. Actually, the only part of Abby that seemed to be mine was her hair: lion-colored, and of a texture so fine that even after two-plus years of trying, it was still impossible for me to get a barrette to stay in.

"And, let's see, on these pages you can see a big church called Notre Dame—"

"Quasimodo lives there! I have the movie! And his friends are these three talking gurgles."

"Gargoyles," I said.

"And this is the Hôtel des Invalides," Carissa continued, thumbing through the book for landmarks she knew. "And here's the merry-go-round in a big garden called the Tuileries. The horses are painted the most magical colors you've ever seen."

"Are the horses magic, too?"

"Sort of. They won't come to life or anything like that. But the world spins by when you're on them, and the music's lovely. When you ride them, it's as if you're in a very special and beautiful place."

Abby seemed to like Carissa, but I wondered if she was simply putting up a good front because she hadn't a choice. First this woman had joined us at the church Christmas Eve, and now, two days later, she was at our home reading to her before dinner. Abby was indeed adaptable, but she was also very smart: I figured she probably knew she could get this lady to read her a few extra books. Maybe she thought she could even convince Carissa to invent some new voices for the small world of Barbies she liked to build on the floor.

"And this is my favorite part of Paris. It's a cemetery called Père Lachaise. Madeline and all her friends are running through the tombstones looking for the dog that rescued Madeline."

"My mommy's buried in a cemetery. But it's not in Paris. It's right here in Vermont."

"I'll bet it's very pretty."

"I guess. It's different from this," she said, pointing at the picture in the book. "Nothing looks as big."

"There's something to be said for small, Miss Abby Fowler. Don't lose sight of that."

Abby twirled a tuft of her hair, unsure whether she agreed. When she was silent, Carissa went on, "The markers at Père Lachaise just happen to be very large. Some people would say too large. And there are lots and lots of them, and they're all very close together. The statues, too. See this one? It's a statue of a famous musician." She tapped the spot in the illustration where Bemelmans had drawn Chopin's headstone, and then quickly turned the page.

"These are called domes," she said, referring to a picture of Madeline and the girls near the Sacred Heart Basilica in Montmartre. "They're a part of the church on the highest hill in the city. When you stand on the hill, you can see almost all of Paris."

"Daddy, someday can we go to Paris? I want to see those domes and those statues. And that tower."

"Absolutely," I said. I wondered if showing Abby Paris via a Madeline book was helping Carissa to press Richard Emmons from her mind, or whether—perhaps like Abby—she was being polite. This little girl, after all, was the daughter of the man she was sleeping with. Slept with. Slept with one time. Either way, Carissa seemed to be content. And Abby was entranced.

"If you go, you have to let me come, too," Carissa said. "I love Paris."

"You can see a really big picture of Paris on the walls in Carissa's office," I told Abby.

"How big?"

"Floor to ceiling."

"Is Madeline in it?"

Carissa abruptly reached under the girl and picked her up, then dropped her into her lap. "Nope, she's not. Maybe someday you'll have to bring your crayons and markers and put her there."

"In the picture?"

"Sure."

"You'd let me draw on the wall?" Abby sounded at once incredulous and pleased.

"Well, it sounds like I need a Madeline."

"I'm not allowed to draw on the walls here, you know."

I climbed to my feet and began to roll up my sleeves. "I'm going to make dinner," I said. "I don't think I even want to know where this conversation is going."

✧

When Hahnemann began his provings two centuries ago, medicine had been in an especially grotesque phase. Doctors were still bleeding their patients with leeches. They were giving them tartar emetic to make sure they would vomit, they were filling their bodies with mercury. They were still drawing out what they called the bad humors.

And so even if you had little faith that a homeopathic remedy would heal you, at least you could be fairly certain it wasn't going to make you any worse.

Ask a homeopath if conventional medicine is like that today, and you will he reassured it is not. But you might also see her raise an eyebrow and remind you—her voice rich with sarcasm—that chemotherapy often adds three to six to nine months to a person's life. *And not all of that bonus time is spent vomiting into toilets and lobster pots, or fearing you're about to. Much of it is. But not all of it.*

And perhaps she'll bring up modern medicine's brief but tawdry infatuation with the artificial heart: No one lasted on one for very long, and the dying pioneers who had them implanted into their chests seemed particularly unhappy in the newspaper stories that dogged their last days.

Maybe she'll mention the fact that we can now remove the organs from a healthy baboon and place them inside an ailing human being. We can keep a person alive on a respirator. We can keep him alive in a coma.

The message underneath the rant? At least a homeopathic cure won't leave you nauseous or cause your hair to fall out in great handfuls; it won't leave you entombed in a machine that does for you what your lungs no longer can.

It won't put you in a coma.

Yet conventional doctors have always been wary of homeopathy, and—viewing the debate with the somewhat dispassionate perspective of a lawyer and not a physician—I don't believe their unwillingness to embrace it has been due solely to the sense a reasonable person might have that the very notion of homeopathy is nonsense. After all, the homeopaths were often successful in the great epidemics of the early and mid-nineteenth century after the heroic physicians had failed. It was *their* patients who were surviving influenza. Yellow fever. Cholera.

Not the sick who were being bled by freshwater species of worms.

In a nineteenth-century cholera epidemic in Cincinnati, homeopaths would claim they had cured over 97 percent of their patients—well over 950 people—printing the names and addresses of both the living and the dead in the newspaper.

Some mainstream physicians in that city would convert. Others would keep bleeding the dying. And some simply got mad.

In 1846 doctors banded together and formed the American Medical Association, and then added a membership clause that excluded homeopaths.

And when even that didn't work to dissuade people from the idea that they could get better without being cut apart or filled with toxic heavy metals, in 1910 the association received help from the Carnegie Foundation in what has come to be called the Flexner Report—educator Abraham Flexner's examination of the quality of medical teaching in this country. The paper suggested that all medical schools use science-based curricula that by necessity ruled out homeopathy, and recommended that every medical school in North America earn a similar license.

Before the report was published, there had been twenty-two homeopathic medical schools in the U.S. By 1940, every single one had been forced to close.

Yet even today, even though most of us don't know the difference between a homeopath and an herbalist, Americans still spend well over two hundred million dollars a year on homeopathic remedies.

This is not a great sum—it's less than half of what we spend annually on Listerine mouthwash—but homeopaths nevertheless view it as a sign that their profession is in the midst of a renaissance.

✧

This isn't eggnog, I thought as I sprinkled nutmeg atop two of the thick goblets Elizabeth had always used during the holidays. It's a big glass of rum.

In all fairness, I reminded myself, there was some eggnog from the supermarket in there, too. But not a whole lot. The drinks were pretty watery. Mostly they were rum.

"And so I only saw my eleven o'clock," Carissa was saying, referring to the one patient she had seen that day. "I canceled everyone else."

"And then went home?"

"And pulled the sheets over my head. Literally. I threw up first. And then I went to bed. The only person I talked to other than you was a mechanic from the garage. He walked over to look at my car."

"And?"

"It's running again. Sort of. I'm here, after all. But I have an appointment for a tune-up Friday morning."

She was sitting on one of the bar stools by the kitchen counter and resting her feet on the slats of another. She'd kicked off her shoes at some point when I'd been putting Abby to bed, and I couldn't help but notice her socks: a thin white cotton, covered with candy canes. I assumed they didn't go much higher than her ankles. Barely midcalf at the most. Maybe.

I'd tasted those calves.

Quickly I took a long swallow from my eggnog as I placed her drink on the counter before her.

"How are you feeling now?" I asked as I sat on the bar stool beside her. I realized I'd had my guard up ever since Jennifer Emmons left my office. I'd tried to convince myself that it was simply because I could now attach a face to the tragedy, I'd seen the woman struggling to be strong across a desk barely three feet wide. But I knew there was more to it than that. In the morning, I'd been absolutely convinced that Richard Emmons was a dope and Carissa had done nothing wrong. Now I wasn't so sure.

"Well, I feel okay physically. Sort of numb. A little foggy. But at least I don't feel like I'm going to vomit anymore."

"And emotionally?"

"Part of me thinks Richard must be insane to have taken me seriously—it was so clear I was pulling his leg. But another part of me feels horrible. Just horrible. I think I feel like I would if I'd just run over a child while backing my car out of my driveway."

"It's not like that," I said.

"I want to drive to the hospital. I want to hug that poor woman."

"You wouldn't really do that, would you? Of course you wouldn't. You won't."

"I know it wouldn't be smart. But the desire's still there."

"Have you called Becky McNeil?"

"I'm seeing her tomorrow."

"You'll like her."

"I gather you do."

I sipped my eggnog. "No, but that doesn't mean anything. I've just seen her win one too many hearings with child molesters."

"She's good."

"She is."

"Should I tell her about us?"

"Nope."

"Is that to protect you or me?"

"Both."

She nodded. "I got a call today from the state board. The psychology board."

"What did you say?"

"I didn't talk to them. I took your advice and didn't speak to anybody. But a fellow named Garrick Turnbull left a message on my answering machine."

"How did he sound?"

"He didn't sound nasty, if that's what you're thinking."

"Garrick never sounds nasty. Just condescending."

"You know him?"

I could see into the living room, and I noticed I'd plugged in the lights to the Christmas tree when we'd gotten home that night. It must have been a reflex, because I couldn't remember doing it. "He's married to an attorney in my office."

"He wants me to call him as soon as I can."

"Just be sure to talk to Becky first."

"Everyone seems to have heard."

"Any reporters call?"

"Not yet."

Was it only two days ago that I'd buried my head between her legs under that very tree? "Not everyone has heard, then," I said. "But they will soon. Jennifer must have simply run out of time yesterday and today. For all we know, she's calling the newspaper right now."

"I'm glad I'm here, then."

"Uh-huh." It was only two days ago that the world—at least my little part of it—had seemed an astonishingly beautiful and simple little place.

"Leland?"

"Yes?"

"You've been a little distant tonight."

"Have I?"

"You have."

"I'm sorry. I don't mean to be."

"Meeting Jennifer changed you," she said.

"It didn't change me. It just showed me the…the other side."

"I didn't mean to hurt him. You still believe that, don't you?"

"Good God, of course I do!"

"Do you still believe it's not my fault?"

I saw a part of myself reflected in her eyeglasses. The side of my face. The collar of my shirt. "Absolutely," I said.

"You're lying, I can tell. What did she say that makes you doubt me?"

I took a big swallow of eggnog and surprised myself by finishing the glass. I considered making myself another one right away.

"What did she say?" Carissa asked me again.

I sighed. "Well. She didn't really say anything. At least anything I didn't know. But she used the word *antidote*."

"And?" I saw nothing in her face to suggest she had a clue as to what I was thinking.

"She said you told Richard to stop taking his asthma drugs. She said you'd told him they'd act as an antidote to his homeopathic cure."

She ran a finger along the edge of her goblet. "I don't believe Jennifer was ever in the room with Richard and me. How would she know such a thing?"

"She used the word *antidote* this afternoon. That's my point. She got that from Richard, and he got it from you."

"Or from the paperback I lent him—same one I lent you. I have a half-dozen copies I circulate among my new patients."

"Jennifer was clear on this: Richard told her that you'd told him to stop taking his asthma medications. She even thinks she knows when you gave him this advice."

"And that was?"

"A week ago Monday. She doesn't know if it was on the phone or at your office. But she is sure the conversation occurred a week ago Monday."

"I didn't see Richard last Monday. The only time I've seen Richard in the last two weeks was when I ran into him at the health-food store."

"Well, that Monday…did you speak to him on the phone?"

"Maybe. I don't know."

"You don't know?"

"He called a lot."

Like you, I heard her add in my mind, but I told myself that was simply another residue from my pre-arsenic anxieties.

"But he might have called Monday?"

"It's possible. Hell, if she thinks he did, he probably did. It seemed like he was calling me every other day. I'm sure that was part of the reason why I was so short with him at the health-food store."

"Why was he calling so often?"

"He wanted to talk about his remedy. A day or two after taking his cure, his skin had cleared up and the pains in his joints had gone away. But his chest still felt tight, and he wanted to know why."

"What did you tell him?"

"I probably told him lots of things. He must have called four or five times in the two weeks after I gave him his remedy."

"Did you ever tell him that his conventional drugs were acting as an antidote?"

She rested her chin in her hands and looked down at the floor. "God, at some point I'm sure I did. I'm sure I told him his theophylline or his Vanceril was acting as an antidote. The fact is, they probably were. In one of those conversations we even scheduled an appointment for the first week in January to talk about it."

"It."

"His frustration. He was frustrated with me because I simply wouldn't give him more Rhus tox. He thought a second dose would do for his chest what the first dose had done for his skin and his joints. Or…"

"Or?"

"Or if he gave up his conventional drugs, the first dose would finally start working."

"And you said?"

She looked up. "I did not say he was right. Maybe he was. But I certainly would not tell an asthmatic whose chest is tight to stop taking his regular medication. I just wouldn't do it."

"Could he have misunderstood something you said?"

"Look, I'm trying not to get defensive about this, I really am. I feel bad enough as it is. But listen to the conversation we're having! I'm defending myself against things Jennifer's *claiming* I told her husband: I told Richard this. I told Richard that. Isn't there a word for this?"

"You mean hearsay?"

"Yes! Or ludicrous, maybe? I mean, I feel awful that Richard is in a coma, but I didn't put him there! Don't you doubt me, too!"

"I don't doubt you. But—"

"But, shit! Listen to you: You do! She's got you convinced I'm some irresponsible quack who made a sick man sicker!"

"She hasn't convinced me of anything. But she has convinced Richard's allergist, the state psychology board, and Patsy Collins—"

"Patsy?"

"Patsy."

"Oh, God. What did Patsy say?"

"I don't know, I haven't spoken to her. Jennifer just gave me Patsy's number and said I should call her. She said Patsy was in the store that night and heard you tell Richard to eat cashews."

"That's not what I said!"

On one of the shelves on the wall behind her—the shelves with the cookbooks Elizabeth and I had once used—sat the basket she'd brought me Christmas Eve. Some of the items we'd put in the refrigerator that very night, but others still sat in the wicker. The echinacea. The box of breakfast tea. The garlic. How could it all have gone belly up so fast? I wondered. Two fucking days! That's all it's been! Two fucking days!

"What you said matters less than what she heard," I said.

"What does that mean?"

"Her testimony wouldn't be hearsay."

"Testimony? You make this sound like we're going to be in court tomorrow!"

"Jennifer Emmons is an extremely resourceful woman. She's lined up a lot of people who will make absolutely sure the State does something. Doctors. The psychology board. She's got a witness to one of her allegations—the cashew part."

"Patsy's an acquaintance of mine!"

"That won't matter."

She put her drink down on the counter and said simply, "I'm going home. Good night."

"I don't want you to leave."

"Well, I don't want to stay."

I felt, I realized, a bit like I did when I was driving at night on a two-lane road in the middle of nowhere and the oncoming car wouldn't turn down its high beams: blinded and frustrated at once. "It's not that I doubt you," I said quickly. "I don't think that's it at all. It just came out that way."

"Then what is it?"

"I don't want to lose you. My God, Carissa, you can't know how happy you make me."

"You just think I'm inept—"

"I just don't think I can help you! This morning I thought maybe I could, but I was wrong. Jennifer Emmons already has a small army of people interested in making sure the State investigates this."

"And me."

I nodded. "It's inevitable."

She stood, pushing her hands against the countertop, and I knew she was going to step into her shoes and take her coat off the rack by the door. I was going to hear the keys jingle in her hand as her fingers searched for the one that would start the ignition.

"I just don't want you to go," I said again, and I heard in my head a little boy's whine.

"Well, I can't stay. Not after what you think I've done."

I watched her climb into her shoes, wondering why I wasn't standing up. I wondered if it was because I couldn't imagine how I could hold her if I did. Literally. What was I going to do, physically restrain her? Of course not. But a part of me wanted to rise up off the bar stool nevertheless, because a part of me couldn't believe I was letting this woman slip away. It didn't seem reasonable, it didn't seem fair or just or right. Not after all I'd endured. Not after all I had—suddenly, generously, unexpectedly—been given.

"You know what the damnedest thing is?" she asked as she stood by the door, her coat draped over her arm.

I shook my head. I was afraid if I opened my mouth to simply say "What?" my voice would crack.

"Even if there was a way you could help me, I don't think I would let you. I don't think I could. I'm the one who has to live with this."

For a long moment we looked at each other, and then she put on her coat and left, and I knew she'd be crying by the time she reached her car door. At first I thought she'd be crying only for Richard and Jennifer Emmons, for what she feared she had done, but then I decided she'd be crying for us, too.

For Leland and Carissa.

For our ending, for the sudden and unnatural finitude of our relationship—our friendship, our love.

For the fact that we were winding down before we'd ever really had the chance to get started.

And so I went to her. I caught her before she had reached the end of the bluestone walk that linked the front porch with the driveway, and together we cried in the cold. She didn't pull away, and I could smell the rum on her breath, and in the light from the porch I could see the almost impossibly slim lines in her eyes: small winding streams on a map. Had she been crying late that afternoon? Apparently. Her eyes were red and slightly swollen.

For a long moment we stayed like that, and then she murmured, "You must be freezing. Go inside."

"Is that a doctor's advice?"

"I'm not a doctor," she said, sniffing.

"I know."

"Go inside. Please."

"I will," I said, "but only if you'll come with me."

She choked back a sob, but those gently heaving shoulders—I could feel the firm hints of her bones, even through her parka—did not resist when I turned them back toward my house. And braced by the cold, I escorted her back inside with me.

Upstairs, my daughter slept. And for a long time we sat on the floor before the tree, neither of us saying a word, as I worked out in my mind exactly what I would have needed to prosecute this case if a summer cold had not lasted into the fall, and I had not met Carissa Lake. Once I knew, nothing seemed quite so hopeless, and I began to sketch aloud for her exactly what we would want to create in the morning, and exactly what we would want to destroy.

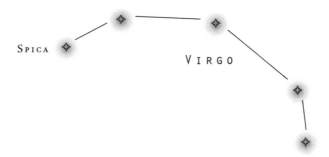

SPICA

VIRGO

3

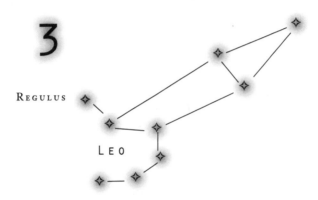

REGULUS

LEO

CANCER

14

S E P I A

This brownish black juice is found in a sac in the abdomen of the large sea animal, called cuttlefish. This the animal occasionally squirts out, to darken the water around it, probably in order to secure its prey, or to conceal itself from its enemies.

DR. SAMUEL HAHNEMANN,
The Chronic Diseases, 1839

It started to snow late morning, and I whispered to Carissa to stay on the couch. I spoke so softly into her ear that I could barely hear my own voice. I watched her pull the quilt up over her shoulders, nodding but not opening her eyes, and then I walked as quietly as I could to the chair before her computer upon which I'd draped my clothes.

Perhaps because the sky was so gray and the only light on in the room was her desk lamp, it felt nothing at all like midday. It felt like a Saturday afternoon at dusk, one of those cold winter days when Elizabeth and I would make love in the afternoon and then doze until dinner.

As I pulled my boxer shorts and my socks off the seat of the chair, I noticed for the first time the windmills on her wall, and I realized I was looking at the dramatic hills of Montmartre. *When this passes,* I thought as I began to get dressed, *we really will have to go to Paris together.*

I wished I hadn't thought that: *When this passes...*

When we'd made love—holding each other at first with somnambulant hunger, the two of us needy but unaware—the details of what we had done became fuzzy shapes in a fog. They grew distant. When we were through, I was mindful mostly of the idea that Carissa and I were lying naked like spoons, and we were together upon the very same couch on which I'd recounted my medical history the night we met.

Neither of us had said a word as we undressed, or as we slowly and deliberately had sex. Sometimes we just held each other as tightly as we could, unmoving, with me inside her.

Occasionally I'd look up at the constellations that dotted her ceiling, squinting at the nebular swirls of white to give them an aura.

I think we were both surprised by how sad the sex had made us feel. Afterward, Carissa was so still it was like she was napping beside me, her shoulder rising and falling in barely perceptible little sighs.

Only when I had climbed off the couch did the fuzziness in the mist grow clear. *When this passes…*

I glanced at the clock on her desk. Eleven forty-five. I'd dropped Abby off at day care a good half-hour early, arriving there by seven-fifteen. I'd read her two books with the speed of an auctioneer, and kissed her good-bye before seven-thirty. And then, just as Carissa and I had discussed in front of the Christmas tree the night before, I had gone straight to the Octagon to meet her at her office.

I tried not to think about what we had done before we made love, focusing instead on the twin towers of Notre Dame. And while I could push it from my mind for brief moments as I buttoned my suspenders into my suit pants, once I had knotted my tie and pulled on my jacket, it grew completely impossible.

Even her cat seemed to be passing judgment. Apparently, some days Carissa brought the animal with her to work, and today was one of those days. Sepia sat on the windowsill and watched me get dressed from a distance. She didn't lick herself or scratch herself or amuse herself with the cord for the blinds the way I imagined most cats would: Instead she just stared at me as if I were a small rodent or bird too poisonous to pursue, but interesting enough as entertainment.

I tied my shoes. I guessed we'd worked for about two and a half hours. That's how long it had taken. The length of a baseball game. A long movie. And then it was done.

Outside, a town snowplow rumbled down one of the streets around the green, and Sepia turned away from me toward the noise. I worried briefly about the roads: I am a good driver, but I know better than most how hazardous the act of driving can be.

That morning, of course, it was easy to find other worries. Witnesses, for instance. There were always witnesses, it seemed. At some point, someone would emerge from the woodwork with the news that Carissa Lake and Leland Fowler had had dinner together the week before Christmas.

Someone had seen us.

But, I would reassure myself, that would be fine because I would not hide that fact.

And there was Whitney. She knew as well as anyone how long the chief deputy state's attorney had been interested in her aunt. This, too, would come out—it was inevitable—and titillate the press a short while. But then it would fade into the irrelevant void of memory that swirls about us.

Irrelevant for most people. Not for Jennifer Emmons.

And, finally, there was the church. My church. Some people had certainly noticed that Leland and Abby Fowler had arrived at the candlelight service with a very attractive woman who had never before been inside the sanctuary. Some, no doubt, would recognize her as that homeopath, the one from the village. The one with the walls. Some would even know her name was Carissa Lake.

Without question, someone had seen me introducing her to the pastor.

But had anyone actually seen the two of us holding hands? Unlikely, I told myself. It was dark, and people were focused on their candles. They were focused upon each other, their children. The images that were conjured for each of them by the hymn.

For long moments that morning, I was able to convince myself that as long as I spoke with Phil Hood that afternoon, nothing any witness might say would present a problem. Phil would give me some grief about not coming forward the day before, and he would surely subject me to a lecture about talking to Jennifer: That, Phil would tell me, was an inexcusable lapse in judgment. He might even suggest to me in his *Fit for Life* tone of voice that I was allowing myself to be led around by my dick.

Well, yeah.

My only real worry, I decided, was that someone might make the connection that it had been my pretty good-sized four-by-four that had been parked near the Octagon in the village on the morning of the twenty-seventh.

Then things might go from embarrassing to problematic. *Problematic? Try cataclysmic.*

After all, I was going to claim I'd gone home after dropping off Abby at day care, and climbed back into my bed until midday. Resting. Trying to beat back the flu. That was why I was not struggling in to work until the middle of lunch.

I fastened the leather strap of my watch around my wrist. I had just enough time, I decided, to leave Carissa a note that I loved her, and kiss her once more. I'd already warned her that we'd have to avoid each other—no phone calls, no dates, no slumber parties at one or the other's house—for a while. At the very least, for a couple of weeks. Perhaps for substantially longer.

Then, for what I told myself was the last time, I picked up the vial of tiny pills I'd noticed near her computer soon after I'd arrived. Arsenic. Arsenicum album, technically.

Off and on that morning, whenever Carissa hadn't been looking, I'd found myself picking up the small tube, rolling it around the palm of my hand, and then dropping it back onto the desk. I wondered if Carissa would miss it if I took it, or whether she'd even notice the vial was gone. It was, after all, only sugar and water. It really didn't have any arsenic. Or value. Except for me.

For me, it had tremendous worth. It hadn't been so long since I'd discovered just what those little sugar pills could do. At the time, I couldn't have begun to explain how they worked. *Just sugar,* I might have said if someone had asked me how I'd gotten better so fast, *so it must have been a placebo effect. You know, my head did all the work.*

But I didn't really believe that: I knew even then there was something magic in the remedy, something tangible that could at once break up the porridgelike slough of anxieties in which I'd been mired for more than two years, and cure the cold that for me was not merely common, it was continuous and everlasting.

Yet I was absolutely convinced the remedy was harmless.

As harmless as Halls.

And I was entirely comfortable with this paradox—preternatural efficacy, completely benign.

Nevertheless, once more I placed the vial back upon Carissa's desk blotter. Maybe after I'd kissed her I'd go back for it. See if the tube wanted to jump into my suit pocket and leave with me.

When I emerged into the snow outside the Octagon a few moments later,

I was relieved to see my truck was coated with powder. It looked exactly like any one of the dozen pickups that dotted the main street of the village.

✧

"Someone gave you Barbies for Christmas?" I asked Margaret, more than a little surprised. I tried to figure out whether Dr. Barbie was wearing panties, or whether the white under the doll's incredibly tight dress was merely a part of the plastic figure's torso. But it was clear I was going to fail unless I rolled up the skirt, and if I tried that, I knew, Margaret would nail me for lewd and lascivious with a doll.

"Just that one," she said.

"I wish my doctor wore dresses this slinky."

"You have a female doctor? I'd never have thought that of you, Leland. Bravo."

"Well, I don't. But I might if female doctors started dressing like this."

She reached across the desk and took the doll away from me. "Sometimes I want to wash my toys in bleach after you've handled them."

"I have very clean hands."

"But just a filthy, filthy mind!"

"I only say the things most guys think."

"Then you're a very sick gender. All of you."

"Only at moments. I assure you, my mind doesn't work like this when I'm playing Barbies with Abby. Santa brought her a pair of the dolls, and not a single lurid thought passed through my brain when I was picking them out at the store."

"You know Barbie's very bad for little girls, don't you? Just a terrible influence. Even with her new shape. She—"

"If you and Garrick have kids someday and figure out how to tell them Barbie's forbidden, I'll listen. I promise."

She adjusted the stethoscope around Dr. Barbie's neck and sat her down beside the other toys on the credenza. "Did you hear I arraigned Jesus on Christmas Eve?"

"No, I missed that."

"Yup. It just isn't Christmas Eve if we don't bust the Messiah."

"And at least one sex offender."

"Isn't it awful?"

"What did he do? Jesus?"

She glanced at a note on her desk. "Disorderly conduct. Unlawful mischief. Simple assault."

"Jesus did that?"

"Yeah, he did. But this one spells the Christ part with a Y."

"Where was this?"

"A bar on College Street."

"Did the fellow look like Jesus?"

"Not a bad likeness, I guess. At least at first. Long brown beard. Kind of thin. But when you got up close, you saw he had lizard tattoos on the backs of his hands, and it was pretty clear they went way up his arms."

"You didn't check to be sure?"

"No, I did not check."

"Was there room at the inn?" I asked, referring to the state psychiatric hospital.

"Yup. For the moment, anyway, he's in Waterbury. On a happier note, did you and Abby have a nice Christmas?"

"We did. We were at my sister's in Hanover."

"Santa was good to Abby?"

"Santa was excellent to Abby."

"I was actually a little worried about the two of you. I was kind of afraid something had happened. You spent all yesterday afternoon holed up in your office."

"I was busy."

"On?"

"A variety of things."

"And then you didn't come in this morning...."

"I feel much better. Really."

"What did you think of Jennifer Emmons?"

"You know Jennifer?" I asked, instantly fearful that I'd sounded more scared than surprised. This wasn't supposed to happen. I'd planned on telling Phil first about Jennifer, and explaining to my boss before anyone else that I happened to be a casual acquaintance of the homeopath who'd treated her husband. But Phil had been on the phone, and so I'd wandered into Margaret's office to see how she was doing while my boss finished his call.

"No. But she spoke to Garrick yesterday morning, after connecting with someone in the Attorney General's Office in Montpelier. The fact that the homeopath's a psychologist will probably be our saving grace."

"Jennifer Emmons is nothing if not resourceful."

Margaret raised her eyebrows. "Are you being sarcastic? Is she going to be an irritant or something?"

I shook my head. "No, not at all. She's a…she's probably a perfectly wonderful person. I didn't mean anything by that remark. I really didn't."

"It's just that it's all so murky. Is that it?"

"Yeah, that's it. It's…"

"Murky."

I smiled, hoping I looked sympathetic—agreeable—as I felt inside the front pocket of my suit jacket. There beside my keys was the vial of tiny pills I'd taken off Carissa's desk before I left. I'd need another one for sure before I saw Phil.

"I just don't understand why you saw her in the first place," Phil said after I told him. "Why didn't you come get me?"

For the first time in my life, I actually thought I saw lines in a person's brow. Furrows. Honest-to-God furrows. And while I hoped they were there simply because Phil was angry, I knew in reality they were there because he was disappointed. I had let him down, and now he was hurt. I could see it in his posture: He was actually slumped in the chair behind his desk.

"I know I should have," I answered. "But I didn't realize where the conversation was heading until we were pretty far down that path. And by that time, I thought it would have been just plain…just plain cruel to tell the poor woman that she had to stop talking, because she'd need a different attorney."

"Was she that upset?"

"Wouldn't you be?"

It seemed to be snowing harder than when I'd left Bartlett just before lunch. I couldn't even see the lake outside Phil's window, much less the mountains across the water in New York. My drive home that night would be a disaster if it kept up. An absolute disaster. Defroster on high, unable to use my high beams with the air filled with white. If I was lucky, I'd wind up behind the snowplow.

"This just isn't like you."

"I know."

"I just can't imagine what you were thinking."

"It's hard to imagine," I said. "I'm sorry."

He sighed and shook his head. "I guess it's not really the short-term I'm concerned about. I think I can probably handle this with—it's Jennifer, right?"

"Right."

"She might be pissed—God, she'd have every right to be. You understand that, don't you?"

"I do."

"But then again, she might not be. Who knows? Especially when I explain to her your reason for not mentioning you know this homeopath. And I think I'll tell her I'll handle the case myself."

"That's a good idea." In the back of my mouth, I felt the last of the arsenic dissolving. I wondered if the pill just got smaller and smaller, or whether snowflake-sized granules of powder broke off and existed in my mouth for brief seconds before disappearing.

"And I don't give a damn about the newspaper. They'll only care if Jennifer cares. And even then it might be one story and an editorial."

"And that's only if Jennifer's angry," I said. I wondered just how angry Carissa would be if she knew I'd taken a vial of arsenic, and a part of me thought she'd be furious. No one, after all, likes a filcher. And no healer wants a patient self-medicating.

But I also told myself there was a chance she'd see the whole thing as silly. *You took a little vial of sugar pills? Leland, why didn't you just ask?*

Either way, however, even if she smiled and called me silly, I was confident she would insist I return the tube. And that idea gnawed at me, because it seemed to suggest the remedy was more risky than I realized, and I shouldn't be quite so cavalier with my cure.

"Anything in the paper today?" Phil asked.

"A small story in the local section. It says we're investigating. No mention of the homeopath by name."

"Really?"

"Nope."

Perhaps she wouldn't even miss the arsenic, perhaps she wouldn't even notice the vial was gone. She had at least five or six more tubes in the cabinet, and she had other things on her mind than one little vial of sucrose. And the stuff couldn't have been expensive: Wasn't it mostly sugar? Wasn't it almost entirely sugar? It better be, I thought.

"Jennifer must have given them the woman's name," he said.

"She must have. But the reporter probably couldn't reach her"—though not, I knew, for lack of effort. The reporter had left three messages on her answering machine at the Octagon last night, and another two at her home.

"So how well do you know this woman? Honestly?"

I shrugged, using the pause to view once more the file card in my head with the outline of my story. A few bullets. Easy. "I've seen her twice in my life. We went on a date the week before Christmas, and then we ran into each other in the parking lot of my church Christmas Eve and sat together during the service."

"One date? Last week?"

"That's it."

"Are you still seeing her? Do you plan to see her again?"

"I doubt it. It didn't really work out."

"After one date…" Phil murmured slowly, and I realized I was hearing his incredulous courtroom voice—a tone I had seen him use to great effect with lying defendants and perjuring witnesses alike. But I was the one on the stand now, I was the one being cross-examined, and I wondered if I'd already fallen so far in Phil's esteem that he no longer trusted me.

"You've been married a long time," I reminded him. "You've forgotten: Sometimes it only takes a single date to see there's no chemistry."

"And there was none in your case?"

"Not really," I said. At some point, when this nightmare was behind us and Carissa and I had resumed seeing each other, Phil might remember I'd said that. But there wouldn't be a whole lot he could do.

"So you've only seen her twice in your entire life."

"That's right."

He sat up in his seat, pushing more with his feet than his hands, and then reached inside a desk drawer for a yellow pad. "I'm assuming, in that case, that someone fixed you up," he said, and he began taking notes.

"Her niece."

"Name?"

"Whitney."

"Whitney what?"

"I don't know. I guess Lake. She's Carissa's brother's daughter. I don't really know her."

"Do you always go on blind dates initiated by people you barely know?" he asked as he scribbled.

"Not always."

"Tell me about this Whitney Lake."

I told him about the health-food store, and my conversations with the younger woman about herbal remedies and rice and tea. I explained that she'd given me Carissa's number on a piece of paper she'd torn from a brown paper bag.

"Whitney thought you two should go on a date?"

"Something like that."

"So you called Carissa..."

"I did. And we met at the Buttery for dinner."

"The Buttery is very nice."

"It is."

"How did you leave it? After your...date?"

"We left it very open-ended. I said I'd enjoyed meeting her, and maybe our paths would cross again someday."

"You said that to someone after a first date? Pretty curt, don't you think?"

"We had nothing in common. Absolutely nothing. It was clear to us both before our entrees had arrived that we'd both made a howling mistake. She felt exactly the same way I did."

"Yet you sat together at the church Christmas Eve?"

"We did, and I'm sure half the congregation probably thinks we're an item. But we're not. We just ran into each other in the parking lot before the service began, and it would have been rude not to sit with her. It was awkward, but there was nothing I could do."

"What about Abby?"

"I introduced them. It wasn't a big deal. Abby was much more interested in the chance to hold a lit candle."

Phil looked up from his notepad and stared at me. I hoped I hadn't been touching my nose as I'd answered his questions, a sure signal in his mind that a person was lying. And I'd tried not to fidget, another indication that someone was uncomfortable. Phil looked for both in depositions and trials.

"Tell me about Carissa Lake," he said.

I wrapped my fingers together in my lap and planted the soles of my wingtips into the carpet. *I am a shrub. I don't move. But I'm a happy shrub. I smile as I speak.* That morning I'd made a list in my mind of all the points I'd want to convey to Phil Hood, and the order in which I'd present them. I'd begin with Carissa's competency and her reasonableness, my sense that she was a careful, cautious, and thoughtful healer. Then, once I'd established her profi-

ciency, I could elaborate on the reasons why I hadn't pursued a serious relationship with her: the notion that she was too, well, New Age for me. Too
Birkenstock. Too granola.

"My sense is she's no shaman or quack," I heard myself saying to Phil.
"My sense is she's extremely competent. I got the impression at dinner that she
has a lot of training—schooling—and she's incredibly knowledgeable."

"This appraisal is based on your extensive understanding of homeopathy?"

"It's based on the sensible way that she spoke."

"Do you know anything about homeopathy, Leland?"

"Just what she told me at dinner that night. Do you?"

"A bit."

"Does it work?"

For a long moment Phil and I watched each other, unmoving. I hadn't
meant to challenge him, but I had. In his mind, I'd just questioned his asser-
tion that he knew a bit about homeopathy. Moreover, I'd asked a question
from the witness stand, and there was no quicker way to piss off a lawyer than
to become a recalcitrant or disobedient witness.

"Let's postpone our discussion of the pros and cons of alternative medicine for another time, shall we?" Phil suggested. "We both have a great many
things to accomplish today. At least I do."

"Look, Phil, I know I fucked up yesterday, and I'm sorry. I'm really and
truly sorry. But do I deserve that tone?"

"You tell me."

"No. You're interrogating me. You're treating me like a criminal. You're
acting like you don't trust me."

He tossed his pen onto the pad on his desk. "I trust your ethics. Completely. I'm not sure I trust your judgment."

"What does that mean?"

"Something's going on in your head. Or in your pants."

"Oh, for God's sake, Phil, give me a break. I hardly know the woman.
We've seen each other twice in our whole lives."

"And both in the last week or so."

"It happens. Bartlett's a small town. Vermont's a small state."

"I understand that, I do. But I also know how this will look to some people. And so I want to know every single thing you know. Comprende?"

"Absolutely. But you're still making me feel like—"

"I don't care how I'm making you feel. I'm disappointed in you, Leland."

"I know...."

"And here's another thing: I do not want you to see this homeopath again while she's under investigation. Understand? I don't want you to go to the Buttery together, or attend church together. I don't want you two to wind up in the damn grocery store together. Or that health-food store. Or wherever the fuck it is you hang out in Bartlett or East Bartlett. Are we clear?"

I had a powerful desire to scratch my nose, but I kept my fingers linked in my lap. I nodded. A part of me was surprised at the depth of Phil's anger, but another part of me saw it as about what I'd expected. Not necessarily what I deserved—*Lord, Phil, if you only knew. I deserve far worse....*—but certainly about what I'd expected. And while it hadn't been pleasant, it hadn't been unendurable, either.

The hardest part, really, might be living for a few weeks or months without Carissa.

When this passes...

"Leland?"

"Yes?"

"Are we clear?"

"You bet," I said, finally allowing myself to unclasp my fingers. I bounced the palm of my hand on my suit jacket pocket, the shape of the vial behind the wool a small totem of hope: *This, too, shall pass....*

15

NUMBER 281

*If... traces of the previous disease symptoms are still mani-
festing at the end of this period without medicine, they are
remains of the original disease, which has not yet been completely extinguished: treatment must be resumed with
higher degrees of dynamization.*

DR. SAMUEL HAHNEMANN,
Organon of Medicine, 1842

I knew I had seen the roads worse.
I'd driven on pavement I couldn't find because the plows couldn't keep up
with the snow, and it was only the muscle memory in my hands—*Straight here
past the Fullers' barn, a slight right beyond the manure bank*—that had gotten me
home. And I'd probably spent the equivalent of whole days of my life navigating highways in the midst of the worst that winter could offer: an inch or two
of ice cube–colored slush on the asphalt and more in the air, so that neither
tires nor wipers worked the way they were meant to.

The roads that night weren't nearly that bad. They weren't good, because
a steady snow was falling and there was a layer of powder on the pavement.
But it was pretty dry snow, and there wasn't a whole lot of it. Yet I'd already
slipped into a pair of skids, one of which should have sent me into the ditch
beside Lewis Creek. I had no idea why I wasn't standing in the snow in my
wingtips that very moment, thumbing for help by the side of the road.

I tried to focus on my driving, convinced it was negligence that was getting me into trouble. My mind was wandering too far from the snow and the

road and the speedometer: I'd found myself going forty-five at one point, which was just plain dumb in a truck in a storm. But my day kept coming back to me, and not merely my conversations with Margaret and Phil about Jennifer Emmons.

I kept thinking of that fellow—now in the Chittenden Community Correctional Center—who'd cracked open his landlord's skull with a wrought iron skillet. I had assumed at first that they had fought over the rent or the apartment conditions, but they hadn't: The landlord had been sleeping with his tenant's girlfriend. The assailant would be arraigned in the morning. The landlord would be in the hospital through New Year's. And no one knew where the girlfriend was, though her parents told us she had called from Montreal and was perfectly fine.

When I stood before the judge that afternoon, I'd planned to ask that bail be set at twenty thousand dollars. Yet when I opened my mouth to speak, out had come the number five thousand. I surprised both myself and the p.d. I probably surprised the judge. The skillet swinger was no more likely to be able to post five than he was five hundred thousand dollars, but it was still a sum that suggested—at least to me—an exceptional beneficence.

I recalled in detail the time I'd spent in court watching two twenty-one-year-olds get suspended sentences and probation for stealing adult videos and beer from a general store. The pair had claimed that they planned to return the videos after watching them, but the store's owner had a list of missing films going back to Labor Day, most of which were found in the dark little garage-apartment one of the defendants rented nearby.

"Exactly how many times did you plan on watching them? Until your VCR broke?" Judge Townsend had asked, before deciding to be kind and spare the pair even a night or two behind bars.

And was it only fifteen minutes later, I wondered, that I'd asked that very same judge to give a computer executive with three kids thirty days in jail for his third DWI…but had suggested that all but two be suspended? It was. And I'd been pleased when the judge agreed. I'd been downright relieved.

Looking back, I wasn't sure why. Normally I would never have suggested such a thing, and I would have been livid if a judge had made such an offer. I would have been furious. The guy was an irresponsible drunk, kids or no kids, high-power job or not.

But, at that moment, I'd been satisfied. Just like when those petty larcenists were told they wouldn't be going to jail for a night. They'd seemed contrite. And embarrassed. And in the afternoon that had seemed to me to be enough.

I pumped the brakes as I started down the last hill before Bartlett and then shifted into second gear. I'd been going forty-two when I felt the truck hurtling forward into the slope.

I wondered if I was going soft. I wondered if I'd turned some corner in my life and I no longer felt the need to be a hard-ass. After all, those twenty-one-year-olds had been sneaking into a general store in the night for months now, pilfering videos and beer. Normally, at the very least, I would have wanted them to endure a few days in the county correctional center—not escape with probation.

But people make mistakes, I'd told myself. *We all make mistakes.*

There was no reason to believe the snow had slowed or the roads had improved, but I decided both had to be true. On some level, I knew I was deluding myself—if anything, the snow was falling harder and the wind was picking up. But I planned to stop at the Texaco on the village green before getting Abby: The gas station had an exterior pay phone along a side wall, and I could use it to phone Carissa. Not only did I want to know how her meeting had gone with Becky McNeil, I had an almost palpable longing to hear the sound of her voice.

That husky and low and deeply confident voice.

Once-confident. Now wounded.

From that pay phone I could call Carissa, and the exchange could never be traced back to me.

Unless, of course, someone happened to see me using the phone. But no one would, I imagined, because I was virtually the only idiot who was still out on the road.

Moreover, I was sure that Carissa needed to hear from me, too. If she was feeling what I was, then she was feeling guilty and scared, and she was in desperate need of reassurance. She needed to hear, at least one more time, that we had done the right thing when we doctored her notes.

As we worked in her office that morning, I had told her repeatedly that Richard had brought this tragedy upon himself, and she wasn't to blame. At first the words had seemed somewhat hollow to me—I wasn't sure I believed them myself—but the more I said them aloud, the more truthful they sounded. Carissa simply wasn't the type who would tell someone to go off his meds. She wasn't that irresponsible. She simply wasn't the sort who would tell someone she knew was allergic to cashews to risk death with a couple of nuts.

At least a half-dozen times I'd insisted that she was simply protecting herself from a possibly horrible miscarriage of justice.

Granted, we were obstructing justice to do that. But I didn't tell her that part. At least not with those words. Once she asked me if what we were doing was illegal, and while I mumbled it was, I tried to imply that it was a minor sort of crime. Not exactly a misdemeanor. But it wasn't, well, homicide. It wasn't as if we were sending letter bombs through the U.S. mail.

And the likelihood we'd ever be caught was…negligible. It had to be. After all, how would anyone know unless one of us came forward? Certainly I'd noticed that Carissa's penmanship was slightly different in the notes she'd supposedly scribbled with Richard Emmons than in the volumes she'd amassed with her other patients: Try as she might, she couldn't make the writing on the new pages look quite as natural and spontaneous. But I couldn't imagine it would ever get to the point where Phil would bring in a handwriting expert to compare the Emmons files with those of her other patients. He would have to suspect there had been tampering to do such a thing. And surely he wouldn't think that.

We'd gotten the hard part over with first: re-creating her nineteen pages of notations and summaries from Richard Emmons's two visits. While I was sitting beside her or pacing her office—avoiding her windows with a paranoia that seemed frighteningly reasonable to me at nine-fifteen that morning— Carissa rewrote every single page, peppering the document with the key points that I said would protect her most in an investigation.

It wasn't that Carissa's real notes were particularly incriminating, though those references she'd made to the drugs and foods in Emmons's life that might serve as "antidotes" to the cure certainly made the state's attorney in me grow interested. But there was also nothing in them that would protect her. Properly enhanced, however, they might. Properly enhanced, they might prevent both a criminal investigation and a civil suit.

And so I made sure the notes showed clearly that Richard had asked if he could stop taking his inhalers and pills. And then the notes showed equally clearly that Carissa had said no. Absolutely not. She scribbled that she'd told him to not even consider such a thing.

And she'd said it again when she gave him his remedy.

Then, just to be sure there could be no doubt in anyone's mind that Carissa would never have recommended he give up his medications, I suggested that the pair had had a similar exchange the Monday he phoned her. And she had taken a few notes during the call, because she had been in the midst of reviewing patient files when he happened to phone.

"Make Richard adamant," I told Carissa. "And make yourself equally adamant. I think you told him it would be irresponsible and dangerous and stupid."

"The thing is, I probably did say something just like that," she murmured, and I nodded.

"Good," I said.

And I had her layer in what would look like some remarks about cashews and poison ivy and Rhus tox in the second of their two meetings. In her fake— *No, not fake. Embellished*—notes, she made it clear to her patient that while these plants were all from the same family, he should never consume a cashew. Never. Not with his allergy. Not with his asthma. He just shouldn't do it, it was just that simple.

In the distance, I saw lights in the oncoming lane. For a second I was sure the other vehicle was going to swerve into mine, since I was just beyond the turn I should have made to get Abby, a right onto the street on which sixteen-year-old Mildred Reinhart lived with her family. So I was sure to have an accident.

Just where were you going, Leland? Phil would ask. Or Margaret. Or Rod Morrow, perhaps. Didn't matter. They'd all want to know.

The gas station.

But you had almost three-quarters of a tank. And you were almost a half-hour late for your daughter.

Oh.

Fortunately, the oncoming car didn't slide over the double yellow line buried somewhere underneath the thin layer of snow, and I kept my truck safely in my own lane. We were just two vehicles passing in the night. Harmless, completely harmless. It was simply that I'd gone five or six miles without seeing another car, and for a moment I'd panicked. I'd frightened myself. And so I did exactly what I had done all day whenever I felt a slight twinge of alarm: I popped another one of those teeny-tiny little pills with corpuscular traces of arsenic.

Ironically, in the end, I think it was exactly those jitters that gave me the courage to pull into the gas station on the green. After all, if I was this fidgety and unstrung, how must Carissa be feeling? Far worse, no doubt. No doubt at all. And so I had to call her. Tell her how much I loved her, and that we had most assuredly done the right thing.

Most assuredly.

After we'd finished revising her notes from her meetings with Richard, fabricating entire new sections, we took care of the easy part. The fast part. The part that probably took about eight minutes. We burned the pages of notes she'd scribbled about Leland Fowler. All fifteen of them. We burned them bit by bit in her aromatherapy diffuser, a shallow clay vase filled with lavender oil, with a small burner just below it. It was in the flame in that burner that we torched my homeopathic history. Little by little, the record just disappeared. And it went up in lavender-scented smoke without my stealing a glimpse. Not one peek. It was hard, but Carissa had insisted. Not a single glance, she said, not one single glance.

Then we destroyed the pages in her date book where my name had appeared. Just ripped them out. If anyone ever asked—*And why would they? Just why would they?*—she'd simply say that she'd used them as scrap paper for grocery lists. Or Christmas shopping lists. That was all. Two missing pages in December? No biggie, no biggie at all.

I parked as far from the station's streetlight as I could, and I parked so that only the front of my truck faced the commons. If, by some chance, someone from Bartlett who knew my truck should drive by, they'd be less likely to recognize the vehicle this way.

I figured Carissa was at home, and so I tried there first. When her answering machine clicked in, I listened to her entire recorded message before hanging up. For a moment, I actually considered trying to let her know it was me—*Carissa, it's me! Pick up!*—in the event that she was simply screening her calls and standing beside the machine that very moment.

But in the end I didn't dare say a word. I simply hung up and stamped my feet against the cold creeping up my shins through thin socks and pants legs, and wished that Carissa and I had thought to devise some sort of phone code. *Three rings and a hang-up means it's me. Three rings, then two rings, maybe. Something like that.*

Next I tried the Octagon, though I didn't have much hope she'd be there. She wasn't. Or, at least, she wasn't answering the phone.

No, I decided, she wasn't there. She was home. Probably. I began to wonder what would happen—what *really* would happen—if I simply stopped by her house. What, in reality, would be the big deal if I dropped by for a brief hug on my way to get Abby? It wasn't as if the state police had a stakeout across the street; it wasn't as if she was under surveillance.

Maybe I'd even borrow a towel from her and dry off the snow that was piling atop my head and shoulders like frozen moguls of dandruff.

Who'd know? Who'd really know?

I couldn't name names, but I knew in my heart that someone would know. People are everywhere. Even in snowstorms. If I stopped by her house, I deserved to be making license plates at the correctional center in Windham, it was just that simple.

And so I resolved, finally, to just go and get my daughter. Abby wouldn't exactly be worried about me, but she understood enough about time to know I was late.

As I brushed the hillocks of snow off my overcoat and climbed back into the truck, a little shiver coursed through me: What if Carissa had gone to the hospital to see Richard Emmons? Highly unlikely…but she'd said at least twice the night before and once in the morning that she knew she'd feel better if she could just say something to his wife. Maybe stroke Richard's arm.

"He's in intensive care. They might not even allow you to touch him," I recalled saying, wishing my response had been a tad more sympathetic.

Carissa also felt an acute need to embrace Jennifer, to wrap the poor woman up in a generous, unreserved, peace-love-and-tie-dye sort of hug. She wanted to say she was sorry: not sorry because she had done something wrong, but sorry, pure and simple, that it had happened.

Did I want to go to the hospital, too? I did, though I should also confess that in those first two days after Christmas it took very little restraint not to visit either Richard or his wife. But I did feel for them: Here was a sweet, loving, capable woman—*Good God, was she capable!*—who through no fault of her own was faced with the daunting task of raising two kids on her own and coping with a husband in a coma.

And, apparently, Richard was not in the sort of coma from which people awoke. At least not very often. He might, Phil had told me at the end of the day; there was at least a chance because Richard's brain was still alive. But the level of insult to the brain cells had been profound: somewhere between seven and nine minutes without oxygen. Maybe even longer. Consequently, it was likely that Richard would simply remain in a coma for weeks or months, and then die.

"It's a bad coma," Phil had said with characteristic piety. "This isn't one of those good ones we read about in the tabloids, where a fellow wakes up one day and smiles at his wife like he just took a nap."

I had nodded. It was worse than being a widow. Being a widow was what she had to look forward to, for God's sake!

A piece of ice was frozen solid to the wiper blade on the driver's side of the windshield, leaving a milky smudge in my line of vision every time the blade clicked before me like a metronome. If I wanted to see the road—which would certainly increase the likelihood that I'd get to Mildred's and then home in one piece—I decided I'd better climb back out of the truck before leaving the gas station and clean off the wiper. Once more I pulled the collar of my overcoat around my neck and jumped back into the storm.

"Leland? That you?"

I turned, hoping I hadn't really heard my name.

"Leland, what are you doing out on a night like this? By now you should be home eating dinner with that little girl of yours."

Approaching me was Paul Woodson, the pastor of the small church in East Bartlett. My church. My daughter's and my church. Paul was crossing the strip of snow-covered asphalt separating the pumps from the station and the pay phone, navigating the slick surface with far more confidence than I imagined I would when I was somewhere past sixty.

"I could ask you the same thing, Paul," I said, trying to smile.

The minister took off one of his thick ski gloves, extending his hand to me and clapping me on the back with the other. "I was visiting Ray at the nursing home in Middlebury," he said, referring to the congregation's oldest member. "There was some talk this afternoon that he might have to go to the hospital."

"It sounds serious. What happened?"

Paul smiled and shrugged. "When you're ninety-three, everything's serious. A cold is serious."

"Is that what it was? A cold?"

Paul pulled his glove back on as he spoke, and then wrapped an exposed earlobe underneath the wool of his cap. "Pneumonia, probably," he answered.

"I'm sorry."

"Old man's friend, you know. But I'm not writing Ray's eulogy just yet. He's still got kick in him. Refused to go to the hospital for what he called a little winter hack, so he's still in his bed at the home. His son put a terrific little Christmas tree in his room and covered it with ornaments the great-grandchildren made—all seven thousand of them."

"Very nice."

"On your way to get Abby?"

"I am."

Paul motioned to the truck beside us and said, "Doesn't technology drive you wild sometimes? Here you spend all that money on a car phone, and when you need it most—like in the middle of a snowstorm—it doesn't work. You have to pull over and use a regular pay phone like it's 1971."

"It's true."

"Snow or hills?"

I thought for a moment, trying to follow the minister's train of thought. When I realized I didn't have the slightest idea what he was talking about, I repeated, "Snow or hills?"

"I was just wondering: Think it was the weather or some mountain that forced you to pull over? I've always heard how car phones don't work in Vermont because the state's so hilly. Think that's why you had to stop? Or was it the snow maybe?"

"Maybe both."

Paul nodded. "Can I buy you a cup of coffee for the road? Our six or seven miles up to East Bartlett is going to seem like a hundred, and this place actually brews a surprisingly drinkable pot of coffee."

"I shouldn't."

"Oh, come on, it's on me. You look a little peaked. A little pale."

"Just frozen."

"More the reason you should come in for a minute."

"I'd love to, but I'm already running late. Mildred and Abby must be wondering where I am. But thank you."

Paul clapped me once more on the back. "You're very welcome. Are we still on for Friday night? Nora plans to cook up a storm."

"We are," I said. I had completely forgotten that Abby and I were having dinner there in a couple of days.

"Good, good. We'll see you then."

"You bet."

"Drive safely."

"I will," I said, and I watched the minister duck into the gas station and beeline for the coffeepot on the warmer across from the register. Then I ripped off the icicle that clung to my wiper blade like a frozen leech and heaved it against the brick wall of the station.

✧

"At Kelly's today, I named my new Barbies Elizabeth and Carissa," Abby said. Kelly was the woman who ran Abby's day care.

I nodded, hoping my face betrayed nothing. I watched as my daughter looked down at the pile of books on one of her pillows, ostensibly preoccupied with choosing the next story she would want me to read.

"Was that a good idea?" she went on when I was silent.

"Elizabeth is a beautiful name. So is Carissa."

She had insisted on wearing her cotton summer pajamas because they were covered with flowers, and so I had insisted that she wear her bathrobe as well until she climbed under the covers for the night.

"They went on a picnic," she said as she handed me the next book to read. "Elizabeth was the boss. She was in charge. She picked out where they went, and she made all the food."

"Your mother loved picnics," I said, and I wondered if in some small, accessible part of her brain Abby remembered the picnic the three of us had taken less than a month before the accident. I'd carried her in a backpack, and we'd hiked to the top of Snake Mountain, a scant ninety-minute walk with even twenty-plus pounds of toddler upon my back. Perhaps because Elizabeth and I had been told before starting that the mountain was a mere thirteen hundred feet—a foothill, really, a glorified bluff—we'd never expected the vista to the west that greeted us at the summit. The Champlain Valley farmlands spread out in the perfect squares I'd seen before only from an airplane, with Lake Champlain rippling just beyond. And across the water were the Adirondacks, much higher than the serpentine Snake, but so close, it seemed, they were peers.

Once there had been a small hotel at the edge of the cliff, but it burned down a century ago. The stone foundation remained, however, and for a moment Elizabeth and I thought the spot would be a fine place to unpack the picnic and settle down for lunch. I had actually emancipated my daughter from the backpack, and Elizabeth had already begun removing the sandwiches and cookies and Abby's blue juice box from her knapsack, when we realized just how steep the nearby ledge was, and how easy it would be to slip over the side. A person wouldn't fall anywhere near thirteen hundred feet, but it would nevertheless be a pretty rocky tumble before finally landing—with a more than ample complement of bruises and broken bones—in the midst of the trees that seemed to grow almost parallel to the ground from the cliff walls.

Quickly I had taken Abby's hand and we retreated to a clearing a few hundred yards away from the peak.

"Barbie Elizabeth loves picnics, too, you know," Abby said.

"I'm glad."

I'd thought of that final family picnic together often the summer Elizabeth died, and, occasionally, in the two summers since. It had been one of those fantasy days that was absolutely wondrous at the time, but managed, somehow, to grow even better with age.

"Does Carissa—real Carissa—like picnics?" Abby asked.

"I don't know. Why don't you ask her someday?" I smiled, if only to repress the whine that sometimes overwhelmed me: After all I had lost and all I'd endured, was it asking too much to be picnic-happy again?

Happy the way I'd been with Elizabeth?

When I'd been one-third of a family? One-half of a couple?

I looked at my daughter, aware that she was saying something to me.

"I'm sorry, sweetheart," I said, "I think I was in a fog."

"Pensive?" she asked, a word I'd recently taught her when she'd thought I was mad. *No*, I'd explained, *just pensive.*

"Yes. Pensive."

"Can we read this one?" she said, handing me another book.

"Of course we can," I said as she climbed into my lap. I wrapped my arms around her, pressing her tight against my chest. "Forgive me when I'm pensive," I said. "I love you."

"I know."

"I love you like crazy."

"I know."

I sighed, and tried to press my guilt from my mind. *Forgive yourself. You're entitled to be tired.*

"Daddy?"

"Yes, sweetheart?" *You're entitled to be selfish. You're entitled to try and snag a bit of happiness with Carissa Lake. You're entitled—*

"Have you known Carissa a long time?"

"No. Not long at all. We only met a few weeks before Christmas. How come?"

"Kelly asked."

I felt a rush of dizziness surround me like a cloud, and then the peripheries of my vision grew dim. I leaned back against the wall by Abby's bed and willed myself not to faint. In my head I heard the two words of my daughter's small sentence once more, *Kelly asked*, and it sounded now like she'd been speaking underwater. In slow motion. In a nightmare voice.

"Why?" I mumbled.

"I don't know."

"Were you talking about Carissa with Kelly?"

"No. I was just playing Barbies," she said, and then I realized instantly what had happened. Kelly had heard little Abby Fowler calling one of her new Christmas dolls Elizabeth and the other one Carissa, and understood at once that the child's dad was now dating that homeopath. The one with the stars on her ceiling. The one with the weird painting on the wall. The one who—and Kelly might or might not have heard this part, it depended entirely upon whether she'd heard the latest gossip that day—might or might not have put Richard Emmons in a coma.

"Was that okay?" she asked, and I could see she could tell she'd upset me. She looked almost alarmed.

"Oh, it's fine." I saw I was shaking, and locked my hands together so Abby couldn't see the spasms in my fingers, and then pulled her against me once more. "You use any names you want with your Barbies," I said. "You call them anything your beautiful heart desires."

✧

I recalled praying alone at night in the church at least a dozen times when my mother was dying of cancer and Elizabeth's accident was still years away. I'd fall to my knees before the altar and pray, "Lord, please give my mother a miracle. Do for her, please, what we can't."

Whenever I prayed alone, I knelt. On Sundays, the congregation always prayed standing up or sitting down, and I missed the submissiveness that I felt on my knees. The sense of absolute deference. Humility. Obedience.

Before I climbed into bed that night, I fell to the floor and prayed, "Lord, please forgive me if what I have done is wrong." Almost instantly I opened my eyes and shook my head. Even in prayer I was hedging. And so I started again, this time trying to be clear that I knew I had made a mistake: "Lord, please forgive me. Please forgive Carissa. And please, somehow, heal Richard Emmons."

That, I decided, was what I really wanted: I prayed that God would open Richard's eyes and the fellow would abruptly sit up in his hospital bed. I prayed that Richard would get better. I prayed, almost as I'd prayed for my mother, that the Lord would do for the man in the coma what mere mortals could not.

Outside I heard the wind gusting against the sides of the house, the sound a low rumble against the clapboard walls of my home. I stood up, listened to make sure the gale had not frightened my daughter, and then turned out the light in my room.

✧

Once, I kept a square tube of Halls in the nightstand beside my bed, and now it was a vial of arsenic.

In the night I awoke and I reached for the container, and I shook a tablet into my hand. Then I sucked on the minuscule pill, and within moments I had fallen back into a deep and dreamless sleep.

16

ARSENICUM ALBUM

WHITE ARSENIC

When I have done with the wiseacre, who ridicules the small doses of Homeopathy as a nonentity, as effecting nothing, and who never consults experience, I hear on the other side the hypocritical stickler for caution...inveigh against the danger of even the small doses used in homeopathic practice.

DR. SAMUEL HAHNEMANN,
The Chronic Diseases, 1839

In the morning, before waking my daughter, I checked my computer to see if there was an E-mail from Carissa. I'd fantasized briefly there would be—I knew she was on the Internet, too— but I also feared I'd have a heart attack in my chair if this particular fantasy came true. Though Carissa and I had not specifically discussed E-mail, I assumed she was smart enough to avoid it. These days, it was almost easier to build a case with E-mail than with phone records, because the actual contents of an E-mail message remained in existence for months on a main server's computer: Not only did you have proof of contact, you had the details of the exchange.

And so I was relieved when I saw that the only message I had was a post-Christmas greeting from my friend the medical examiner.

But still I was desperate to know how Carissa was doing. I shut down my computer and went to the kitchen for a banana, and stared longingly at the coffee machine as I passed it. I hadn't had coffee in weeks, and though I'd had powerful cravings, it didn't make sense to me that I'd be having one now: I'd certainly given myself a pretty solid arsenic booster in the last eighteen hours.

Or maybe I hadn't. Maybe taking them one or two at a time was worthless, and any relief I'd felt had just been that placebo effect. Maybe I needed to take them four or five—*Or was it five or six?*—at a time, the way I had when Carissa administered the remedy almost a month ago in her office.

I finished my banana, washed the mushy fruit off my hands, and went back upstairs to see if Abby was starting to wake up. I thought I might also glance through the little book on homeopathy Carissa had lent me. Maybe the book would offer a clue about dosage.

✧

I did not actually vomit. I had been sure that I would, but I didn't, and eventually the nausea subsided. I stood up and leaned against the side of the truck, aware that the sand and salt from the road that stuck to the pickup would wind up all over the back of my navy blue overcoat, but I didn't care: At least I no longer felt sick.

I took a breath and looked around. This had been a thousand times worse than the car sickness I'd felt two days ago while driving to work. This time, indeed, I'd had to pull over. I'd had to swing my truck to the side of the road— oblivious to where I was stopping—and practically jump from the driver's seat to the pavement. I'd had to scurry around to the far side of the vehicle, where I'd leaned over and stared into a drift of brown snow the plows had created the night before, prepared to puke for the first time in years.

And then the sensation had passed. It had taken a moment. But it had passed.

I saw I had stopped by a Morgan horse farm just north of Hinesburg. If one had to pull over and vomit, it wasn't a bad spot. There were no houses nearby, though I could see the peaks of the horse barns in the distance through the rows of leafless trees. With their foliage gone but their branches glazed over with ice, those trees—mostly maple and birch and ash—looked for a moment like elegant black and crystal sculptures. Each was a willowy raven-dark frame, layered with a luminous sky-blown glass.

I stood for a few more minutes, breathing in the crisp air, and then walked in a few yards from the road to press a clean handful of snow to my mouth.

I could use some sun, I decided, staring up at the overcast skies. I returned to the road and started the truck, and then pulled a glove off with my teeth and felt my forehead. It didn't feel like I had a fever, but then I'd just spent five or ten minutes doubled over a snowbank in fifteen-degree weather. Of course it felt cool.

I wanted to attribute my queasiness to a virus or bug. Perhaps even the flu. Even the flu would be better than guilt heaves. But aside from that brief bout with nausea, I hadn't felt sick. I wasn't coming down with something, much as I might wish that I were.

No, it was clear to me that I'd almost retched up a banana, a muffin, and whatever remained of herb tea over guilt. Anxiety. Fear. And it wasn't simply what I had done that was making me worry, it was the fact that I had brought Carissa along with me.

Or, to be precise, down with me.

Moreover, I'd begun to realize I'd been kidding myself when I'd thought our story wouldn't unravel. What if I was wrong and someone had seen me holding hands with Carissa at the church Christmas Eve? It was certainly a packed sanctuary; it was certainly possible someone had taken his eyes off a candle for a brief moment.

Or what if that Patsy person at the health-food store was aware that Carissa had been shopping for Leland Fowler—chief deputy state's attorney—that very night? What if Whitney had already said something to Patsy about her aunt's new beau before Carissa could get to her? Or what if Whitney was simply incapable of keeping a secret?

The possibilities were endless: What if one of Carissa's neighbors had noticed my truck at the homeopath's house the morning after Christmas? Or near the Octagon the day after that? What if someone official—someone in my own office, perhaps, or someone with the state police—decided to speak with local day-care owner Kelly McDonough, and Kelly mentioned the names little Abby had given her new Christmas Barbies?

What if someone checked the phone records and saw the toll calls I'd made to Carissa from my office, or the cell phone call I'd made Christmas Day?

I felt a strange shudder in my chest—not exactly a pain, but not a pleasant sensation, either—and I realized my heart was starting to race. It wasn't a heart attack: There were no shooting pains down my left arm, and the flutter behind my ribs certainly wasn't the agony that I'd always heard would come with a heart attack. But my heart was definitely…palpitating. That was the word. I was giving myself heart palpitations.

I was pretty sure one little arsenic pill would restore my confidence and calm me down—they'd certainly gotten me through the last day—but I wanted to postpone taking another pellet for as long as possible. I'd discovered that morning when I'd gone upstairs to skim the homeopathy book that I'd already gone through at least a quarter of a tube. The vial had been half-full when I'd taken it, and now there was only a quarter remaining. Yet it wasn't how much I'd taken that mattered to me, it was how much I had left. I knew I might have to make what was there last a very long time. Days, certainly. Maybe weeks. Perhaps even a month or more.

And that would mean rationing the twenty-five or thirty pills that remained.

Unfortunately, the book hadn't said anything helpful about arsenic and dosage. The book was an introduction to homeopathy for laypeople, not a guide to treatment. I found one reference to arsenic application, but it was simply presented as an example so a patient could understand the way a homeopath might prescribe a cure: "One dose of Arsenicum album 200c, to relieve anxiety with restlessness."

Nevertheless, I'd immediately looked at the tube on my nightstand to see if there was a reference to the potency of the arsenic I'd swiped. There wasn't. At least there wasn't one I could read: Carissa had pressed a small sticker with the date she'd received the pills over a part of the manufacturer's label, and she'd placed it right on top of the potency and warning. When I tried to peel the sticker away, I merely ripped the label. There was just no way I was going to be able to determine whether each pill was six or sixty or—for all I knew—two hundred c.

Whatever that meant. I realized I didn't even know what a c was.

The one thing the book had done was reassure me that I wasn't going to make myself sick with the arsenic. I'd reread the whole section on "potentization" and "successive dilution," and come away with the faith that my remedy had been diluted and shaken so many times that in reality I was ingesting virtually no arsenic. Zip. Zero. Nada.

Well, almost zip. In theory, there might be a trace left. But not enough to make me sick.

Still, I was actually relieved it was only arsenic. I was glad Carissa hadn't cured me with something from one of those other vials I'd spied in a little corner on the bottom shelf of her cabinet: Tuberculinum. Vipera. Syphilinum.

I don't even want to know where they get Syphilinum, I had thought.

As I pulled into the parking garage by the courthouse, it dawned on me that I hadn't thought once about work during my drive in. Real work, anyway. I hadn't thought about the depositions, arraignments, and felony status conferences that would pepper my day. This was rare. And I hadn't even noticed the gas station where as recently as a month ago I would stop daily for my cough drops and coffee.

Maybe the arsenic I'd taken before leaving home was finally kicking in. Maybe I really had nothing to worry about.

✧

I imagine these are the thoughts Jennifer Emmons dreaded but had frequently in the days after Christmas: She could always return to work full-time at the animal hospital. Technically, they didn't need another full-time vet. But how could they deny her the job now? Her husband was in a coma!

Of course they would give her more work. And benefits.

And she didn't need to worry about Kate after school; Kate was way too old to be latchkey. But Timmy? The one day a week she was not home for him now, Thursday, he usually played at his friend Isaac's house. Or at J.J.'s. Or Brad's.

The boy would do fine when she went back to work; the local parents would be sure to help out.

And there was insurance, of course. Richard's life insurance. She couldn't imagine the policy wouldn't take effect if her husband was in a coma, but she made a mental note to call their agent. You never knew.

Perhaps she had even reached into her purse for a pen to make an actual note.

She and the kids would stay in their house, they definitely would not move. This was the only home Timmy had ever known, and the one Kate had lived in since she was three. She would make sure her children had that stability: Same bedrooms, same schools, same friends. Same views from their windows, same spots for a toy chest, a bureau, a bookcase, a bed.

That's what I had done, after all, when Elizabeth died. I'd tried to keep things as stable as possible for my Abby.

And, for two and a half years, I had succeeded.

✧

"You know her!" Margaret was saying when I returned from court late that morning, intercepting me as I passed her office on the way to mine. I couldn't decide if she was raising her voice because she was angry or shocked or because she thought she had to shout to be heard as I raced by in the hallway. "Why didn't you tell me?" she went on, following me into my office, and I wondered if she was actually hurt.

"Yes, I know her," I said.

"Why didn't you tell me?"

"I wanted to tell Phil first."

She leaned against the radiator, and her face grew soft. "This doesn't look good, does it? But you realize that, don't you?"

I nodded. "That's why I thought I should tell Phil first. It may not look good...but it isn't bad. That's the thing."

"You're not in trouble, are you?" she asked, and her concern surprised and depressed me at once. Sometimes I lost sight of the fact that we were friends. "You know you could tell me? Right?"

"Everything's fine, Margaret. Really. Fine."

She fiddled for a moment with one of the dials on the thermostat, turning it abstractedly. "She's going to give a statement to the police today," she said finally.

I focused on the arms of my chair as I sat down, trying to ignore the sudden wobbliness in my knees, and the little surge of nausea that rippled over my stomach. This is just what we expected would happen, I reminded myself. Just what we'd planned. A statement. Carissa would inform her attorney that she wanted to clear her name, and insist on giving a statement.

"Phil tell you?"

"Uh-huh."

"He's not going to tell me anything about this, is he?"

"Doubt it."

But while it may have been exactly what we had planned, it was still happening awfully quickly. There was no way I'd thought Becky McNeil would move this fast. Unless, of course, Carissa wasn't with Becky. Maybe she hadn't liked Becky, and she'd wound up with someone like Oren Candon instead.

"Is she with Becky McNeil?" I asked, aware that a sizable part of the woman's name had remained caught in my throat.

"How did you know that?"

I started to answer, but I discovered my mouth had gone dry. Bone dry. I had to have water. "They're both women," I croaked.

"Have you talked to her?"

"Who?"

"Leland, I'm your friend. Tell me."

"Who? Carissa or Becky?"

"Well, I meant to Carissa. But have you talked to Becky?"

I coughed into my hand to try clearing my throat, then answered, "I haven't talked to Carissa. And I don't think I've spoken to Becky since we argued about Charles Aiken before Thanksgiving."

"Assault and robbery?"

"And I caved to simple assault," I said, trying to find even a tiny oasis of saliva in my mouth with my tongue.

"Seriously: How did you know she hooked up with Becky?"

I shrugged my shoulders. "I told you, it was just a guess. They're both strong women. It seemed natural they'd wind up together."

"That's all?"

"That's all," I said. "Now, I need some water. Feel free to wait here if you want to continue this conversation."

"She's in the paper today, you know. Your friend."

"Quoted?"

"Nope. Unavailable for comment. But Garrick is."

"Quoted…"

"Right."

"Do you have a copy?" I tried to sound casual, as if I was interested only because my friend's husband and an acquaintance both happened to appear in the same story. Nothing more.

"There's one in reception."

I nodded and walked past her into the hallway, and took a long drink at the water fountain. A few minutes later, when she was behind closed doors with a twelve-year-old and a social worker, I went straight to Gerianne for the newspaper the office kept in the waiting room.

Other than a criminal prosecutor, no one likes a creative murder weapon more than a journalist. A few years earlier when one Vermonter had murdered another with a ski pole, it was impossible to read a newspaper article that didn't refer to the homicide as the "Ski Pole Slaying," and one even created a small graphic of crossed ski poles to accompany the stories that followed the investigation and trial.

And though no one thought Richard's plight had anything at all to do with murder, I saw the press would have a field day with the singularly unusual cause of his coma, and with the opportunities for alliteration his situation offered a headline writer. The banner above the article Margaret had mentioned read, CHRISTMAS EVE COMA CAUSED BY CASHEWS.

Emmons's story had not yet been reduced to the "cashew coma," but it was only a matter of time.

And while there was nothing in the article itself that was particularly surprising, I was alarmed by the byline. Actually, it wasn't even the byline: It was the three words underneath the byline. *The Associated Press.* The article had been written by Deborah Fairchild, the AP writer in Montpelier. The story had gone out on the wires.

I sat down in my office and read it a second time.

BURLINGTON, VT—INVESTIGATORS ARE CONTINUING TO EXPLORE THE LIFE-THREATENING DECISION OF A BARTLETT, VERMONT, MAN CHRISTMAS EVE TO EAT A NUT THAT HE MAY HAVE KNOWN HE WAS ALLERGIC TO.

RICHARD EMMONS, 43, REMAINS IN A COMA AT BURLINGTON'S FLETCHER ALLEN HOSPITAL AFTER EATING A CASHEW.

AUTHORITIES ARE FOCUSING ON THE POSSIBILITY THAT EMMONS MAY HAVE BEEN A VICTIM OF A MISGUIDED ATTEMPT TO HEAL HIS OWN ASTHMA.

"WE'RE EXPLORING A VARIETY OF REASONS FOR MR. EMMONS'S BEHAVIOR CHRISTMAS EVE," SAID CHITTENDEN COUNTY STATE'S ATTORNEY PHILIP HOOD. "RIGHT NOW WE HAVE NO EVIDENCE THAT A CRIME HAS BEEN COMMITTED OR ANY LAWS HAVE BEEN BROKEN."

AT 3 A.M. CHRISTMAS MORNING, JENNIFER EMMONS, 41, FOUND HER HUSBAND ON THE KITCHEN FLOOR OF THEIR BARTLETT HOME, UNABLE TO BREATHE AFTER EATING CASHEWS. RICHARD EMMONS APPARENTLY KNEW HE WAS ALLERGIC TO THE

NUTS AND MAY HAVE BEEN AWARE THAT HE WAS RISKING ANA-PHYLACTIC SHOCK AND DEATH BY EATING THEM.

HE HAS BEEN IN A COMA SINCE HE WAS RUSHED TO THE HOSPITAL BY AMBULANCE EARLY CHRISTMAS MORNING.

AT THE TIME, EMMONS WAS BEING TREATED FOR HIS ASTHMA BY BARTLETT HOMEOPATH AND PSYCHOLOGIST CARISSA LAKE, IN ADDITION TO SEEING A CONVENTIONAL PHYSICIAN AND ALLERGIST.

SOURCES CLOSE TO THE INVESTIGATION BELIEVE THAT EMMONS MAY HAVE BEEN TOLD THAT CASHEWS WERE A HOMEO-PATHIC CURE FOR ASTHMA.

ACCORDING TO BURLINGTON HOMEOPATH JEROME WALSH, M.D., HOMEOPATHY IS A 200-YEAR-OLD MEDICAL SYSTEM FOUNDED ON THE EXACT OPPOSITE PREMISE OF CONVENTIONAL MEDICINE. WALSH, WHO IS A LICENSED PHYSICIAN, SAYS HE USES HOMEOPATHY AS A PART OF HIS PRACTICE, AS WELL AS HERBS AND CONVENTIONAL DRUGS.

"WHEREAS MODERN MEDICINE FOCUSES UPON REMEDIES THAT COUNTERACT A SYMPTOM, HOMEOPATHY OPERATES ON THE PRINCIPLE THAT 'LIKE CURES LIKE,'" WALSH SAID.

A HOMEOPATH WILL THEREFORE TREAT A PATIENT WITH A SUBSTANCE THAT WOULD ACTUALLY CAUSE A "SYMPTOM" IN A HEALTHY PERSON.

THE SUBSTANCE, OFTEN MADE FROM A COMMON PLANT OR MINERAL, IS APPLIED IN INFINITESIMAL DOSES. HOMEOPATHS LIKE WALSH, HOWEVER, BELIEVE THERE'S JUST ENOUGH THERE TO HELP THE BODY TO HEAL ITSELF.

THE INVESTIGATION IS COMPLICATED BY THE FACT THAT VERMONT DOES NOT REGULATE, CERTIFY, OR LICENSE HO-MEOPATHS.

"HOMEOPATHIC REMEDIES AREN'T MEDICINE," EXPLAINED ROSEMARY HAIG, A DIRECTOR OF PROFESSIONAL REGULATION WITH THE VERMONT SECRETARY OF STATE'S OFFICE.

PSYCHOLOGISTS ARE REGULATED, HOWEVER, AND IT IS HERE WHERE A CRIMINAL INVESTIGATION MAY WIND UP FOCUSED.

"IF A HOMEOPATH TELLS SOMEONE TO EAT A CASHEW EVEN THOUGH SHE KNOWS IT WILL MAKE HIM SICK, AND THAT PERSON

DOES, IT MAY NOT BE A CRIME," SAID GARRICK TURNBULL, A
PSYCHOLOGIST AND THE DIRECTOR OF THE VERMONT BOARD OF
PSYCHOLOGICAL EXAMINERS. "BUT IF A PSYCHOLOGIST SAYS TO
A PATIENT TO EAT THAT CASHEW, THERE MAY BE A CLEAR
BREACH OF DUTY. POSSIBLY CRIMINAL NEGLIGENCE."

EMMONS HAS NOW BEEN IN A COMA FOR THREE DAYS.

DR. JAN DUBUISSON, ONE OF THE NEUROLOGISTS TREATING
HIM, SAID THE LONGER HE REMAINS IN A COMA, THE LESS
LIKELY IT BECOMES HE'LL EVER AWAKE.

LAKE DID NOT RETURN CALLS TO HER HOME OR OFFICE.

The story could have been a lot worse, I decided. The AP had been careful not to libel Carissa.

And I wasn't in it. Jennifer hadn't told a reporter that the first person she spoke with in the State's Attorneys Office was some sleazy lawyer who allowed her to babble for half an hour without mentioning that he knew Carissa Lake.

After all, surely AP reporter Deborah Fairchild would have called me if she had. And Fairchild hadn't phoned.

No, the only thing that should concern me, I decided, was the statement Carissa was going to give to the police later that day. And even that shouldn't concern me. It was just that it was all happening so fast. It was just that I hadn't spoken to Carissa since I'd left her office on Wednesday. It was just that I no longer knew what the fuck was going on.

I wondered if it was worth trying to connect with Carissa through Whitney. See how she was doing.

No, I shouldn't do that. I couldn't do that.

And so I wouldn't.

But, of course, I did. Whitney was at lunch when I called, but the young man who answered the phone volunteered the information that she'd be back about one and done for the day about five. He never even asked who I was. Naturally, I was waiting outside for her when she emerged from the shop for the night.

When she saw me, she pulled her scarf up further around her neck and pulled her wool hat down to her eyes. Already it was covering her ears. Her long coat looked a bit like a giant cape of Mexican or Central American origin: There was a giant bird on the back that seemed to belong on the front of a Cancún travel brochure.

"You shouldn't be here," she said.

"I know."

"My aunt said you two need to keep your distance."

"She tell you why?"

"Not really. She said it wouldn't look good with her being investigated and all. But I know there's more to it than that. Like, I'm not supposed to tell anyone she had a really nice time at your place Christmas Eve. Or she was up there again the other night."

"How does that make you feel?"

She started to walk down the residential street around the corner from the health-food store, and it was clear I was supposed to walk with her. "Slimy," she said. "And I'll feel even worse if I have to lie to somebody."

"Like an investigator?"

"Is that who's going to interrogate me?"

"No one is going to *interrogate* you. Maybe someone will *interview* you. But I promise, there won't be any gorillas with cigarettes, or any harsh lights in your face."

"I mean, what if someone sees us right now?" she went on. "Isn't even *that* a problem?"

"It's five degrees outside. Have you seen anyone but us on the street?"

"Any minute now, Reed Pecor will be out walking his dog. Or Ginny Mayo with hers. They always walk them right before dinner."

"Let's talk fast, then."

"We'll have to talk real fast. I live at the end of the block."

"Fine."

The sidewalk had small ridges of rock-hard ice, and I found myself moving gingerly in wingtips, the stupidest shoe a man can wear in the winter. I noticed Whitney was wearing big heavy boots over those small feet that I imagined always naked in sandals.

"So you're mad at us because we've made you feel slimy," I said.

"Us? I'm not pissed at Carissa. I'm pissed at you!"

"Me?"

"Duh. I don't know what you two did, but I'm sure you're behind it."

"Now, why is that?"

"I know my aunt!"

"Does your aunt feel slimy, too?"

"God, of course! Come on! I don't know exactly what's going on, I don't know what you did. But whatever it was, it was exactly the wrong thing to do. I have never in my life seen Carissa the way she was today."

A little geyser of defensiveness spouted inside me. There were a variety of reasons why Carissa might have seemed out of sorts that day, including her own conversation with Richard Emmons Christmas Eve. But I kept that thought to myself.

"She was depressed?" I asked.

"Like catatonic."

"She say anything?"

"Not really. She stopped in to get some stuff a little while ago. And she must have spent ten minutes just staring at bulgur."

"Could her depression have something to do with her statement this afternoon?"

"What do you mean, 'her statement'?"

"She met with the police. She and her lawyer. Didn't she?"

"I'd think you'd know."

"I don't. I only said about five words today to the attorney who's handling the case."

"Well, her meeting went fine. At least I think it did. She was a zombie this morning, and that was before she'd said word one to you lawyers."

"You saw her this morning, too?"

"She had breakfast with my mom and dad."

I nodded. Of course Carissa's family would rally around her right now. Of course they would circle the wagons.

Whitney motioned with her face toward a gray clapboard Victorian on the corner. "This is where I get off," she said. "That's my family's house."

"Is there anything I can do for your aunt?"

"Doubt it."

"Would you give her a message for me?"

"Why don't you just go and throw some pebbles against her window?" I remained silent, and her anger abated a bit—just enough that she rolled her eyes and asked, "All right: What?"

"Tell her, please, that I'm thinking of her. Every minute."

She tilted her head and raised a single eyebrow. "Now, that," she said, "is one very sickening thought."

I had just about run out of patience with Whitney and her barely post-adolescent self-righteousness. But the last thing I wanted to do at the moment was alienate her any more than I already had, and so I tucked away my court-room scowl—a combination of contempt and disgust—and said in the most sincere voice I could muster, "I have no idea what you mean by that. Care to translate?"

She took a deep breath, shuddering, it seemed, somewhere underneath that wool coat. Or cape. Or shawl. Then she turned away from me and started up the steps of her home. I thought she was done, and I was about to walk back up the street to get Abby when I saw her look back at me from the porch. Her eyes were tearing and I hoped it was due to the cold, but something told me it wasn't. Holding the glass storm door open in one hand, the fingers of her other one wrapped around the brass knob of the main door, she hissed, "My aunt didn't do anything wrong, but you made her think she did! Don't you get it? You're the one who's making her feel like a criminal!"

And then she was inside the house and the doors—both glass and wood—were shut tight against the cold and the night and the prosecutor in the street.

✧

Had I not gone straight home after getting my daughter, I might have run into Carissa in Bartlett. She went to the Octagon that night, where she dozed and read and for a time surfed the Web. She was searching for examples of home-opathic malpractice. She was trying to find homeopaths who'd been charged with manslaughter or criminal negligence.

She was doing, essentially, the sort of thing the lawyers around her might be doing very soon. And while she did not find everything a lawyer in my office would have discovered because she did not know exactly where to look, she found enough. Once when she felt a spiky pain in her lower back, she looked down and saw that she had curled her legs up against her chest and was sitting in her seat like an egg.

At one site, she read about a California homeopath who was being sued by the family of a young man who'd died of AIDS. When the chemical regimen that had kept the virus in check for five years started to fail, he turned to homeopathy to bolster his vital force. He stopped taking the drugs that had kept him alive half a decade, replacing them first with Gelsemium, or the Car-olina jasmine: a beautiful climbing flower with yellow petals and long green leaves that remind me of phlox. Then, when that didn't work, he tried aconite, a European plant known also as wolfsbane because its juice is so deadly that hunters once dipped the tips of their arrows into it before hunting wolves. *Aconite*, the word, is actually derived from the Latin word meaning dart.

Then he died.

In their suit, the family was alleging that the homeopath had encouraged his patient to stop trying to manage the disease with the accepted, customary treatments.

On another site, she discovered a baby who had died of a ruptured appendix. The infant's parents had assumed her howling was due simply to colic, and treated her with Chamomilla—the homeopathic version of an herb that in one form or another has been a medicinal standby for centuries. By the time the parents concluded the crying was due to something more acute than colic and taken their baby to the pediatrician, it was too late.

She found a psychiatrist who'd treated a patient's depression with Ignatia and then had to cope with the fact that the patient would take his own life. She discovered a naturopath who'd offered an elderly cold sufferer Pulsatilla, only to learn later that the cold had become pneumonia and the patient had died alone in her bedroom.

Arguably, homeopathy was blameless in every single death. The remedies themselves did no one any harm.

But isn't that usually the case with conventional medicine, too? At least *modern* conventional medicine?

Most of the time, it isn't that a physician has given a patient a medicine that has made him sicker. Usually, the physician has simply failed to see something someone else will believe he should have seen. Or done something someone else will believe he should have done. Or done that something differently.

Most of the time, medicine itself is blameless. It's the doctor who has made a mistake.

And while Carissa reminded herself that physicians were sued for their mistakes—real or imagined—all the time, the realization did not make her feel any better. Nor did the fact that physicians had patients die all the time.

That night in her mind there was really only one reality: She had told Richard Emmons that his conventional drugs might be acting as an antidote to his cure. And she had told him to eat a cashew.

Granted, she did not believe she had ever said he should give up the drugs he'd been taking for years. Nor did she believe she could have sounded serious when she'd said in the store that he should pretend he was Hahnemann and try a nut they both knew he was allergic to.

But she kept thinking of something I'd told her the day after Christmas: It's not so much what you say that matters, it's what people hear.

And as much as a part of her wanted to despise Richard Emmons for his obstinacy and his persistence, for his idiocy and his determination—for what he had done to his wife and his children and now to her—she kept coming back to the things she had said to him, and the last of her confidence waned. The despair conceived inside her Christmas Day promptly hatched, and the void in her soul was replaced almost wholly by doubt.

Imagine a vase that is watertight but cracked. Now imagine it poured full with regret.

She grew less and less interested in whether she'd be prosecuted or sued; she cared less and less about the law.

She cared less and less about how I'd tried to help her.

I, after all, had been working on the supposition that if I didn't protect her, she might lose everything in her life that mattered.

Neither of us understood at the time that she already had.

I can see her alone in her room that night, gazing up at the stars on her ceiling. Staring at the windmills and church spires on her walls. Sainte-Chapelle. Notre Dame. The great gold dome of the Invalides.

Perhaps she pretended she saw Madeline, the figure drawn by the hand of a little girl.

Perhaps she looked out the window and saw the moon over Bartlett.

Perhaps not. Perhaps she just sat in her chair and shook.

17

NUMBER 96

Not even the most extreme hypochondriacs will entirely fabricate their complaints and symptoms.

DR. SAMUEL HAHNEMANN,
Organon of Medicine, 1842

I was getting paranoid. I'd found my exchange with Whitney so upsetting that I'd almost run back to her house and pounded on the door, and demanded that she come outside and let me defend myself. And while on one level I understood she was merely a kid who was spending her last few weeks home from college on a higher moral plateau than the rest of us mortals, it still gave me yet one more thing to worry about: Exactly what did that young woman believe I had done? Just how loose was that cannon she was calling her mouth?

Clearly I wasn't cut out for a life of crime. It was making me nauseous and giving me the trots. It was making my hands and feet tingle. All the time. Tingle.

I felt a pressure building up in my bowels and walked with haste to the bathroom, stopping only briefly as I passed by the hall closet: My arsenic was still in my overcoat pocket, and I recalled the little book on homeopathy saying something about arsenic being a good remedy for the runs. And so I shook another two pills into the palm of my hand on my way to the bathroom and dropped them under my tongue.

Tomorrow, I decided, I'd try and connect with Carissa. Definitely. I had to know if she was aware of her niece's anger with me, and whether she understood what was really behind it. Maybe she could nip it in the bud.

Abby woke up early Friday morning, and then woke me up, too. She carried Candy Land into my bedroom, plopped the game board upon my bed, and handed me the green gingerbread man.

"I'm littlest, so I go first," she said.

We played the game for half an hour, and for thirty minutes I don't think I thought about Carissa Lake's statement or Whitney Lake's accusation, or the fact that Jennifer Emmons was about to start raising two children on her own.

I don't believe I thought of Richard Emmons on his back in a coma, shrinking a bit each day because he was living on glucose and vitamin water.

I was not exactly happy. But I was still dazed with sleep and I was with my little girl, and so I was content.

✧

Later that morning, I found myself wondering who would benefit that day from my uncharacteristic mercy. It was the very last workday of the year. I glanced at the date book on my desk as soon as I'd hung up my coat and opened the venetian blinds in my office—it was sunny, and I wanted all the daylight and cheer I could secure—and saw the usual litany of wife beaters, larcenists, drunk drivers, and drug dealers. As far as I knew, however, none of them was a full-fledged justice obstructor. Or whatever the hell the noun was.

I looked at my ten o'clock, still almost ninety minutes away. It was a thirty-one-year-old guy named Paquette with no apparent source of legitimate income. He'd been charged with two counts of delivering marijuana, each one a felony. But each bag he'd been delivering was a whopping five ounces, and the guy had no priors. So I could envision exactly what would transpire in Courtroom 3A later that morning: The two charges would be amended from delivery to possession, and would therefore become mere misdemeanors. Paquette would be sentenced to six months for each count, with both terms suspended. He'd walk out the door with a year of probation.

Normally, I knew, I wouldn't cave to possession. Not with two counts and ten ounces. But I was positive I would today.

"Your Honor," I imagined myself saying, "at least Mr. Paquette did not fabricate evidence to preclude a possible criminal charge, and destroy the evidence of his own involvement with a woman being investigated for criminal negligence."

I sat back in my chair and decided I was going to have a cup of coffee. I was going to stand up, walk to the coffee machine I hadn't touched in a month, and make a full pot—twelve killer cups—of joe. Fuck the fact that I already had a case of the trots. And I was a little bit nauseous. And I had the weirdest tingling in my fingers and toes.

I wanted a cup. I needed a cup. And it was important that I was alert. If I had any chance of getting through the last workday of the year, it was important that I was...together.

I stood up, felt the small prickles I'd come to know well run across the soles of my feet, and immediately sat back down. I didn't need coffee. I needed arsenic. That's what I needed. I pulled the tube from my pocket, tapped the pills that remained into a small anthill in the palm of my hand, and with the tip of my tongue speared the pair that had bounced to one end of my lifeline.

And then, just to be sure, decided to seize another two.

Just before nine, Phil Hood came into my office without his jacket and closed the door. "So you honestly saw this homeopath a total of two times," he said. He looked tired and sad. He was leaning against the back of the door, his hands behind him.

"Good morning, Phil."

My boss nodded. "It isn't good, Leland."

"It's sunny."

"Two times?"

"Two times."

He sat down across from me, and I thought the lines in his face looked deeper in the morning sun.

"Why do you ask, Phil?"

"I don't know."

"You don't know...."

"No."

"Did she give a statement?"

"She did," he said, and he looked away from me, out the window at Burlington. "At Becky McNeil's office. A mere three blocks away. A delightful little walk most days of the year."

"You waited in the next room?"

"I did."

"You almost never bother with statements."

"I wanted to make sure the right questions were asked. And given the… the runaround Jennifer Emmons got from you, I thought it was the politic thing to do."

"A public-affairs gesture?"

He turned to me, and I realized instantly that I'd just said exactly the wrong thing. The weariness that masked his face had been transformed by my four words into disgust. "A human gesture," Phil answered, and his lips went thin.

"I see," I said. I hoped I sounded as chastised as I felt.

"You really don't drink coffee anymore, do you?"

I shook my head. "Oh, but I still hanker for some."

"I'll bet you do." Phil crossed a leg in his lap and wrapped his hands around his knee. "Ever hanker for a homeopath?"

I took a breath and tried to decide whether I should sound indignant or merely perplexed. The words that came out, I thought as I said them, were somewhere in between: "Is this badgering? Or does this line of questioning have a purpose?"

"I honestly don't know," Phil said.

"Because two days ago, you made it clear to me you didn't want me anywhere near Carissa Lake or this case. And now you've come into my office and all you want to do is talk about her. Have I missed a step?"

"Know what?"

"No. What?"

"I'm not sure there is a case."

"Really?"

"Surprised?"

I shrugged, hoping I looked unconcerned.

"I was," Phil said.

"Surprised…"

"You bet. I think that's why it doesn't seem like a very good morning to me. There's a very nice man in a coma at the hospital and a very nice woman who's going to have to raise a couple of kids on her own. And there's a homeopath who I am absolutely convinced is responsible, but who we can't touch."

I rubbed the bridge of my nose. Better now than when I was actually speaking. Then Phil would assume anything I was saying was a lie—which, of course, it probably would be.

"Every week there's a case like that in this office," I said finally. "Every week we come across someone we know is guilty as hell—and who, for one reason or another, we'll never, ever prosecute. Why does this one disturb you so much?"

He raised his eyebrows. "Because this one has the taint of our office."

"Taint? Taint? Give me a break, Phil. I went out to dinner with the woman one time."

Outside my shut office door I heard laughter. I wondered how long I'd have to endure Phil mano a mano before I could escape into the hall for a drink of water. Or a run to the toilet. I didn't dare, I decided, cut short our conversation.

"One time," he murmured.

"Yes. One time."

"It's just…No, it isn't *just* anything. It's everything. It's everything your friend said in her statement. It's everything she had ready for the detectives at Becky's office."

"Not my friend. That's not fair."

"Forgive me. Your acquaintance."

"Thank you."

"She brought her notes with her. *Lots* of notes."

"I'd expect that."

"Of course you would. Would you expect them to be perfect?"

"Perfect?"

"Perfect. At least from the perspective of a woman who doesn't want to be charged with a criminal offense. Or face a civil suit that would make her gray before her time, and not leave her a dime for a rinse."

"You've already gone through them?"

"Carefully."

"And?"

"And it was like she knew exactly what we'd be looking for, and what she'd need for an airtight defense. There's Richard Emmons asking Carissa Lake if he can stop taking his asthma drugs. And there's Carissa Lake saying no. 'Told him not to consider it.' No, wait, it was better than that: 'Told him not to consider such a thing. Told him to stay with his inhalers and pills.' Isn't that terrific? *Told him not to consider such a thing.*" His voice had gone almost liq-uidy-sweet.

"Terrific," I said.

"The notes show the two of them had a similar exchange when she actu-ally gave him his homeopathic medicine. And then, when he called her a week or so later, they show her telling him that going off his regular drugs would be dangerous and stupid and…and irresponsible."

"Most doctors keep pretty good records."

"I guess."

"Anything about cashews?" I decided I would probably have asked that question even if I'd known nothing about what was actually in those nineteen pages of notes.

"Ah, the cashews. The notes are quite clear about the cashews, Leland. About cashews and poison ivy. Seems they're in the same plant family."

"I didn't know that."

"Yes, indeed. And Carissa Lake told her patient that he should never, ever eat cashews. Not with his allergy. Not with his asthma."

I wondered briefly if Carissa and I had overdone it, if we'd gone too far in the Octagon Wednesday morning. But we'd had to go far, that was the point: We had to be absolutely sure we'd built such a strong defense that the State wouldn't bother to prosecute. Of course Phil Hood was going to be angry. That was to be expected. It was the suspicion—the mistrust and the cyni-cism—that surprised me.

"Have you broken the news to Jennifer Emmons?"

"What news is that?" He looked directly at me for the first time in minutes.

"The news that we're not going to prosecute."

"No."

"Telling her will be hard. You have my sympathies."

"Does she, too?"

"She?"

"Jennifer Emmons. Does she also have your sympathies?"

"She does. Of course."

"I'm glad. Because you know what? While the odds are slim to none that we'll ever build a case, I'm not prepared to close the investigation just yet."

I felt something ripple across my stomach. "No?"

He stood and glanced once more at the city from my window, squinting for a moment against the sun, and then went to the door. With his fingers on the knob he said, "Nope. Want to know why?"

I wasn't at all sure that I did. In fact, I was pretty sure that I didn't. I knew that whatever Phil had to say would make me sick. "Sure. Tell me why."

"Her car wouldn't start. I left Becky's a couple minutes before she did, but I had to stop at that little gourmet shop on Bank Street. We're having a few people over for dinner New Year's Eve, and Barbara asked me to pick up some wild rice. Well, when I came out, who should I see but your friend—excuse me, your acquaintance—standing beside her slick little Audi with the hood up. She was parked at one of the meters beside the diner, and a young fellow was about to jump her car. 'No problem,' she said to me, smiling. 'This happened Christmas Eve, too.'"

Was I sweating? I doubted it. But I did feel sickly and nauseous and warm.

"'Before or after church?' I asked, just being polite. And Leland? That smile on her face evaporated, it just disappeared. 'Before,' she mumbled, and I nodded—there wasn't a damn thing I could say; we both knew I didn't dare ask her another question without Becky present. And so I just said good night and went to the parking garage to get my own car.

"But all the way home, I kept thinking to myself: That lady must have had one hell of a strong desire to go to Leland's church Christmas Eve. After all, she'd had to find someone willing to jump-start her car. But that kind of interest seemed a little unlikely, since she'd never, ever been there before. So then I thought, What if someone picked her up and drove her there? That's possible. Right?"

"Right."

"Of course, then you'd expect her to have sat with them. And not with you."

"I don't recall seeing her car Christmas Eve."

"No. I don't think it was there. I think Carissa was telling the truth about that. I think she really is having trouble with her battery. Or her alternator, maybe." He pulled open the door. "See why I'm not quite ready to close the investigation?"

"I do."

He looked into the hallway, and I thought he was going to leave. But then almost abruptly he asked, "How are you feeling?"

"I've felt better. But I'm okay."

"You don't look okay. Take advantage of the three-day weekend. Get some rest. Sometimes…" His voice trailed off uncharacteristically.

"Sometimes what?" I asked.

"Look, I know we don't talk about Elizabeth very often these days, but don't think I don't think about her. And you. Everyone in this office remembers what you went through. Everyone respects how you've handled yourself since the accident. How you've lived your life."

"I appreciate that."

"But your…misfortune," he said, choosing his words with great care, "awesome as it was, is still no excuse to start cutting corners. Especially now. Especially after keeping body and soul together for so damn long."

"I'm fine, Phil."

"I'm worried about you, Leland. That's all," he said, and then he was gone. And I ran my handkerchief over my forehead.

In my mind, I saw somebody's fingers closing Richard Emmons's eyes for him, the fingers a part of an arm that was draped in loose hospital scrubs. I saw Jennifer in a chair beside the bed, whispering a sentence now and then, her lips close to her husband's ear. I saw children, a teenage girl and a younger boy, staring out the window at the sky.

I had no delusions that a visit to the ICU would offer atonement.

But something—no, some *things*—were beginning to bubble beneath the surface of my world. I could feel it. Something in Phil's head. In Whitney's. No doubt in Carissa's, too. Soon one of those somethings was bound to erupt, and the mess was going to be monstrous.

And so I decided I would visit the man in the coma. I would go that very day, and I would witness, if only through glass, the way Richard's whole world had shrunk to a bed and some tubes and his wife's fingertips on his shin.

18

NUMBER 276

Excessively large doses of an accurately selected homeopathic medicine, especially if frequently repeated, are, as a rule, very destructive. Not infrequently, they endanger the patient's life or make his disease almost incurable.

DR. SAMUEL HAHNEMANN,
Organon of Medicine, 1842

I was back from my ten o'clock by ten-twenty, having agreed that justice would be served if Teddy Paquette endured a year on probation for two counts of possessing marijuana. I told myself that the little hustler had learned his lesson, but I didn't really believe it. I just didn't hear a whole lot of contrition in his voice when he told the judge he understood well he had made some mistakes.

And he certainly wasn't the physical wreck I was; he certainly didn't *look* like he felt any guilt. My body, on the other hand, had become a mass of tingles and bowel spasms, my stomach a fishbowl on the seat of a speedboat.

When I returned to my office I placed my last two tabs of arsenic in separate envelopes and then licked and sealed them. One I would open when I got to the hospital that afternoon, and the other I'd have before bed. Tomorrow, I was positive, I would see Carissa. And while we were together, I'd be sure, somehow, to get more.

✧

"Do you remember the name of the woman you first met at the health-food store?" Phil asked me near the water fountain just before lunch.

"No," I lied.

"It's Patsy. Patsy Collins. Just think of how much it sounds like that old country western star, and you'll never forget it again."

"Thank you."

"Happy to help," Phil said. "She seems like a very nice woman—also all too happy to help."

When I neared Margaret's office early that afternoon, I heard her talking on the phone. Something—a word, a phrase, perhaps the anxiety in her voice—led me to believe she was talking about me. And so I paused just before the doorway, just beyond her vision if she should happen to look up from her desk.

Quickly I realized the concern in her tone was indeed for me, but at that moment she was actually talking about Carissa Lake.

"I know Phil would like to subpoena her notes, medical records—I think he'd cart away half her office if he could get a court order," Margaret was saying, and I could tell she was sharing the news with her husband.

"Oh, he definitely thinks Leland's involved," she said a moment later. "He just hopes the involvement isn't criminal. You know how fond he is of Leland. He really cares for him."

I turned around and went straight back to my office. I didn't want her to worry that I'd overheard what she'd said.

✧

In my truck in the parking garage at Fletcher Allen Hospital, I ripped open one of the envelopes with arsenic, and I heard myself sigh when I slipped it under my tongue. I leaned back against the seat and closed my eyes, bracing myself for a vision—raw, real, unabridged—of Richard Emmons. Maybe Jennifer, too.

No, not maybe. If I got Richard, I got Jennifer. I'd been afraid to call ahead, fearing that she wouldn't want me to come because I hadn't told her I knew that homeopath, and so I had no idea if she was actually at the hospital that moment. But I assumed she was.

I wondered if another reason I hadn't called ahead was because deep inside

I was hoping there'd be no family members present in the ICU, and the nurses would keep me away. Far away: no family, no visitors. I'd never have to see the man in the coma, yet I could tell myself that I'd made a good-faith effort.

But I didn't really think that was the case, either. I honestly wanted to see Richard. I honestly wanted to be a presence for Jennifer.

I'd always been pretty good with the dying, including, of course, my own parents. But I wasn't half-bad with elderly neighbors and distant uncles, either, or with the few acquaintances my own age who'd died young. Leukemia. AIDS. Lou Gehrig's disease. With them, I had discovered that I was fully capable of sitting passively in a chair by a bed, listening to the raspy breathing and the incomprehensible murmurs—witnessing the twitches and spasms and seizures—that marked a body in shutdown. Some people found it difficult to brush the back of the hand of a man in a deep morphine sleep, but I wasn't among them. A hypochondriac, I'd realized, actually had a very great deal to offer the authentically sick: a profound empathy combined with genuine vitality.

I climbed from the truck, adjusted my suit jacket under my overcoat, and started across the cement of the parking garage. The sun was about to set, and the garage had the feel of night. I wondered if Jennifer, too, sat alone in her car in this lot, trying to find the grit to go in.

Madame Melanie Hahnemann, Samuel Hahnemann's much younger wife, was tried in Paris for practicing medicine without a license, and she was found guilty.

Her mistake? She'd gotten too brazen with her business cards. And she'd placed an announcement in the newspaper, advertising her practice.

Samuel had been dead for about three and a half years at the time, and some people said his widow was being prosecuted because she was a woman. But certainly she was being prosecuted as well because she was a homeopath.

Even then—1847—orthodox medicine was apprehensive when it came to alternatives. Even in Paris, where the Hahnemanns had settled within a year of their meeting in Kothen.

Yet it was clear the court didn't see Melanie as a villain. They were merely enforcing the exact letter of the law. She wasn't a doctor, but she had patients. Her only accreditation was from an American academy, and it had been granted simply because Samuel had written the school's founder, insisting that his wife was a brilliant healer and deserved recognition. As a courtesy to Hahnemann, they'd sent Melanie a diploma.

And while the French medical authorities might have recognized the diploma had she submitted it to them for consideration, she'd never bothered. After all, she explained during the trial, she was a woman. Though there was a female obstetrician in Paris, obstetrics and medicine were then viewed as wholly separate universes: There were certainly no female medical doctors at the time in the City of Light.

There were no medical schools in Europe that even admitted women.

Melanie's sentence? She was asked to pay a fine of one hundred francs. About what she was paying for her annual newspaper subscription. Or what she charged a patient at a first consultation.

And she was asked to stop practicing medicine.

Apparently she paid the fine in full.

And then continued her practice.

She was simply more discreet than before the trial.

But, much to her patients' relief, she continued to heal them, treating them without poisonous doses of mercury, or strychnine, or opium. Without subjecting them to venesection.

She merely stopped passing out business cards.

✧

Jennifer Emmons smiled when she saw me in the windowless waiting room outside the ICU, and for a second I was surprised. I hadn't expected a smile. But there it was, that small but sincere, close-lipped little grin I had gotten before from the partners and children of the not-quite-dead: the smile of thanks. Thank you for coming. Thank you for remembering us. Him. Me. Thank you for not making me do this alone.

I surprised myself by giving her what I'd come to call my friend-of-the-family hug—arms around the shoulders instead of the lower back, a scapula pat to signal separation—and she surprised me by staying there a second longer than most people, her arms against my chest in a variation of what my friend the M.E. described as the pugilist's pose: her fingers balled into fists, her elbows bent and pressed flat against her ribs. It was one of the basic postures of death.

"How nice of you to come," she said when we finally parted, her voice soft and hoarse.

The television on the wall behind her was tuned to the Weather Channel, although the sound was all the way off. A pair of elderly women in slacks and scarves had been playing gin rummy on a couch when I'd arrived, occasionally looking up at the screen. I'd offered to turn up the volume for them—I was standing, after all, and they were sitting—but they'd passed. Then a nurse had come in and told one of the women that her brother was cleaned up and they could resume their visit.

"I wanted to come sooner," I said. "But I let the...the awkwardness get in the way."

"You shouldn't have felt awkward. Vermont's a small state."

"Still..."

"We all know people. You know Carissa Lake, so what? I must have three or four friends who know Carissa Lake."

"They're not prosecutors."

"No. But you won't be prosecuting her, either now, will you?"

"Nope."

I noticed most of the doctors and nurses who passed between the ICU and the waiting room were wearing surgical scrubs.

"Probably nobody will be," she continued, just the tiniest hint of frustration in her voice. "Phil Hood told me it isn't likely you'll ever file a criminal charge."

"The case is still open. It's only been three or four days. An information—an indictment—often takes months."

"I don't expect anything. There isn't even much chance of a civil suit, I'm told. My Richard just...he just did this to himself. Made a mistake. I wanted to blame that woman because I wanted to blame somebody—God, wouldn't you?—but it doesn't seem like she did anything wrong."

On the radar map on the TV screen, a swirl of clouds was stretching in a wide band through Minnesota, the Dakotas, and most of Iowa. It looked like we'd be getting more snow in Vermont in another day or two.

"It must all seem pretty complicated," I murmured.

"It did. It doesn't anymore. At first, we all thought for sure she was responsible. I did. Richard's allergist did. The state psych board did," she said, and then gave me that thin little smile once again.

"What do you do, Jennifer?"

"I'm a veterinarian. But I went part-time after our second child was born. Timmy. So now I only work Thursdays and Saturdays."

"In Bartlett?"

"Uh-huh," she said, adding, "I guess I'll be going back full-time as soon as I can."

"How is he?"

She puffed out her cheeks for a brief second. "He flexed his arm this morning when they knuckled his chest."

"That sounds like progress."

"It is. It means he's dying."

I nodded, and tried hard not to blink or look away. "I'm sorry," I said.

"Me, too."

"And they know this...for sure?"

"They do."

"Because he moved..."

"He's posturing. Isn't that a great word?" she said sarcastically. "It sounds like he's putting on airs."

"It's a terrible word," I agreed.

"Yup. The decorticate posture. Poke him or prick him or knuckle his chest, and his arm flexes." She flexed her own arm. "Like a spring. It means the brain is malfunctioning. It means he's probably lost his cerebral cortex."

"I am so sorry," I said again. "I'm so very sorry."

"I talk to the doctors and nurses, and I know they're doing all they can. But it doesn't do any good."

I thought of all the things the doctors had done for Elizabeth in the four hours she'd lived, unconscious, after the accident, and what I gathered had been the Herculean efforts of two volunteer EMTs just to keep her alive long enough to die in an operating room. Doctors had sewn her spleen and re-inflated the lung that had collapsed. They'd set her broken arm. They'd given her blood, at least seven pints I believed, and then a powerful cardiac potion to help her heart pump blood to her brain.

I realized I didn't know which lung had collapsed.

"Do you want to see him?" Jennifer was asking.

"May I?"

She nodded, and motioned toward the shut double doors with an imposing list of visitor regulations.

✧

Although my father had died in a nursing home, my wife and my mother had died in this hospital. Neither, however, had ever spent a day or a night in either of the two adult ICUs. Elizabeth had never even made it to post-op.

But my mother's death, at least, had lasted so long that I'd been able to behold all kinds of long-term interventions: Heart monitors and bladder catheters. Bags of blood and nutrition dripped into her veins through the sorts of tubes I saw every spring linking maple trees in the woods. A big hole with a plug in her chest to pump in the food when it became impossible for her to swallow because the esophageal radiation had so badly burned her throat.

The difference that struck me most between the ICU and the regular hospital rooms in which my mother had wasted away—a feature even more evident than the rustling from the respirators, a sound like the wind—was that the walls facing the massive nursing station were made largely of glass. There wasn't a lot of privacy in those high-tech little chambers, but if you were sick enough to be there, it probably didn't matter.

"Now, I know you two never met," Jennifer said when we finally stopped, and I realized that if she were to move her body a bit to the left or the right, I would glimpse Richard in his room. I noticed a lump under the sheets that I assumed was the fellow's feet, and I could see the bed rails were up. "But... well, he looks different than he used to."

"I understand."

"He looks older."

"Thank you."

When she entered the room, I saw Richard for the first time. Only his feet and his shins were under the sheet; the rest of his body was covered solely by a short hospital gown and a filigree of fat and thin tubing. And he did indeed look old, as if his body were collapsing in upon itself: He could have been the father of the Richard Emmons I had glimpsed in church a couple of times, a wrinkled and shrunken and pale version of the fellow I'd seen in the sanctuary.

On his forehead was a flat silver circle.

"Richard, I've brought a visitor," she said, and she leaned over the thick respirator tubes covering his mouth to get close to his ear. "Leland Fowler. He lives up in East Bartlett."

"Hi, Richard," I said, hoping my voice sounded friendly and warm. I glanced around the room: Although I'd expected a fair amount of hardware, I was still unprepared for the mass of hoses and wiring and monitors. I could only guess what most of the screens were tracking and what most of the tubes were draining. All I could tell for sure was that one large box—a ventilator, I assumed—was breathing for Richard, and that the screen on the wall mount over the bed was shadowing his heart rate and rhythm.

"Leland's a lawyer," Jennifer said. "He's Bob Fowler's son."

"He knew my father?"

"Not well. But Richard's ad agency did a little work for Green Mountain Grizzlies a few years ago."

"I see," I said, nodding.

"Some brochures, a catalog. The annual poster."

"I'm sure my dad was a very difficult client. He really loved his bears."

"Oh, Richard's had worse."

"Thank you."

"How's your little one? Abigail?"

"She's fine."

"Bonnie will be bringing my kids by a little later," she said, and then lowered her voice: "Bonnie's my sister. I don't know how I could have gotten through this without her."

"Do you and Richard have big families?"

"No, small. Tiny. I have Bonnie, that's all. And Richard's an only child."

"What about your parents?"

"My mother's alive, but my father passed away."

"Richard's?"

"Both of his parents are gone."

"Who's taking care of the kids right now?"

"Kate's thirteen, so she doesn't need much supervision. And it's been mostly my mother or Bonnie looking after Timmy. He's eight. It'll get a little easier for the kids next week when school starts again."

"I'm sure," I said. I wondered how much time Richard had left. I wondered if next week those kids would be at their father's funeral.

"Your room got a lot of sun today," Jennifer said to her husband, including him once more in the conversation. "It was nice and bright around noon."

I half-expected the body in the bed to respond. I wondered if Jennifer still fantasized about such things.

"Don't you think you can already feel the days getting longer?" she asked, and it took me a second to realize she was now speaking to me.

"I do."

"God, winter. It can be endless." She shook her head and then leaned into her husband and murmured, "Richard, I'm going to walk Leland back outside. I'll be right back."

I went up to the bed for the first time and ran my fingers along Richard's pale, thin arm. "I'll see you again, Richard," I heard myself saying. "In the meantime, I'll be praying for you."

✧

We stood together for a moment in the hallway beside the ICU waiting room, separated by double doors from the glass chambers the hospital had built for the likely to die.

"Do you know your way back to the elevator?" she asked me.

"I do. It's a labyrinth, but I figured it out."

"Thank you for coming."

"It's nothing. You know that. It's just…it's nothing."

"No, it was really sweet of you to visit. Will you do something else for us?"

"Of course."

"Pray. You said you would. But really do it. Okay?"

"Okay."

"But don't pray for any miracles."

"No?"

"No," she said, bowing her head and shaking it, and then falling forward into my chest. "There won't be any miracles, so don't pray for one. You'll only be disappointed."

I rubbed her back with both hands. "I'll pray for whatever you want."

"Then pray he isn't in pain," she said, a slight tremor in her voice. "They tell me he isn't, but please: Pray he isn't in pain."

19

NUMBER 225

There are of course a few psychic diseases that have not merely degenerated from physical ones; instead, with only slight physical illness, they arise and proceed from the psyche, from persistent grief.

DR. SAMUEL HAHNEMANN,
Organon of Medicine, 1842

Abby and I were having dinner at Paul and Nora Woodson's Friday night, so before leaving Burlington I bought some gourmet coffee and chocolate truffles in a store in a strip mall near the hospital. Then when I realized how close I was to the mammoth two-story bookstore that had just gone in beside the little mall, I decided I'd take a quick peek at the books in the health section. I wasn't sure if I'd find anything about arsenic poisoning, but the fact that my feet were continuing to tingle and I'd had to rush to the men's room before leaving the hospital—the Pepto-Bismol wasn't doing a damn thing—had me worried.

Intellectually, I knew I couldn't possibly be poisoning myself with homeopathic arsenic, but I figured I'd check the symptoms of an arsenic overdose just in case, so I could rule it out and find another life-threatening, ICU-triggering ailment to worry about instead.

✧

"I think I'll bring some underpants for Merlin and Addison," Abby was saying, referring to the Woodsons' two cats. Earlier in the fall, Nora Woodson had informed Abby that when she'd been a girl just a bit older than Abby, she had put underpants and a small T-shirt on her cat. For months now, Abby had been contemplating the idea of dressing up the pastor's wife's cats, and she figured tonight was her big chance.

"Bring the ones with the trolls on the front," I said, clicking the word *Search* on my computer screen in the den.

"But they don't fit me anymore!"

"Exactly." Within seconds, a list of more than forty-seven thousand sites appeared, all of which had either the word *arsenic* or the word *poisoning* somewhere in them. The bookstore may not have had a treatise devoted to arsenic or arsenic poisoning, but the Internet was a virtual library on the subject.

"Can I bring a shirt, too?"

"Sure."

Next I typed in the word *arsenic* alone, hoping the Internet search engine would offer a less impressive but more manageable number of entries.

"I better bring two shirts and two pairs of underpants."

Eleven thousand–plus possibilities came up. Smaller. But still astonishing.

"Okay."

"Can I bring a suitcase?"

I turned to her. "We're only going to be there a couple hours, sweetheart. We're just going for dinner."

"I know. But I have to bring the clothes for the cats. And then I have to bring some Barbies and some books and some stuff for me."

I nodded. The Woodsons' children were grown, and there weren't a whole lot of toys left in the parsonage. "Sure. You go pack. But we need to leave in about fifteen minutes. Okay?"

"Gotcha!" she shouted, and raced up the stairs to her bedroom.

For a moment I glanced at the entries on the screen before me, but there were still way too many, and so I decided to winnow the search one more time. I linked the words *arsenic* and *poisoning* with the word *AND* in capital letters, signaling the search engine that I wanted only those sites that had *both* items somewhere within them. The result was a mere 978 entries—mere, of course, only when I thought back on the numbers I'd seen a moment before. It still wasn't a bad total. In fact, it seemed pretty damn impressive: everything I could ever want to know about arsenic, right there at my fingertips.

The source of the sites, as always on the Web, was a mélange spanning the sublime and the ridiculous. An occupational safety organization in Australia followed a group of high-school kids in Kansas who'd just performed *Arsenic and Old Lace*. A university professor presented his theories about Napoleon's death, and then a country inn used its home page to advertise an upcoming Murder Mystery Weekend for Lovers. There were entries from journals devoted to timber treating, hepatology, the preservation of animal skins, and nineteenth-century embalming. I learned about the 1991 investigation into President Zachary Taylor's death—they'd actually exhumed whatever remained of the fellow from the ground, and quantified the amount of arsenic in his nails and his hair—and the problems of groundwater contamination in neighborhoods near century-old cemeteries.

It was a full and rich exploration. And if Abby and I weren't due at the Woodsons' in a little while, I thought, I might be happy hanging out with these links for hours. But since we had to leave soon, I started scrolling through the computer sites in search of a basic primer on arsenic poisoning: its symptoms and, I hoped, its antidotes. Quickly I found what I thought I was looking for, the Treatment of Arsine Toxicosis, at a site run by the Iowa Agricultural Information Retrieval System.

It took no more than ten or fifteen seconds for the entire site to download into my computer—no filthy, time-consuming graphics here, I thought—and I started to read. And then I tried to be calm, but it wasn't easy. I could hear the sound of my breathing through my nose, whistles of air that went up and down, and every time I exhaled I could feel the warm wind on the backs of my fingers and hands, still poised atop my keyboard.

The good news was that I didn't have any lesions on my skin. At least any that I'd noticed. And I didn't think the reflexes in my extremities were impaired, but in all honesty I wasn't sure I knew how to test such a thing. Still, I seemed perfectly able to slam on the brakes in the truck, and that had to count for something.

I had virtually no opportunity to savor the good news, however, because underneath skin lesions and impaired reflexes was a litany of symptoms that I did have. Anxiety. Diarrhea. Tingling along the soles of my feet, numbness across the palms of my hands. Vomiting.

No, I haven't vomited, I reminded myself, I've simply felt nauseous! And there's a big difference!

The last paragraph of the page offered the mesmerizingly unhelpful—and inappropriately unscientific, I decided—information that arsenic had been used for centuries to poison people (including popes and politicians) because the symptoms resembled those of so many other illnesses, and the toxin was almost impossible to detect in a corpse. It wasn't until the late 1800s that forensic medicine had figured out how to grind up livers and test them for heavy metals.

I clicked on the link in blue titled *Treatment* and swore out loud as I read, "The quantity of arsenic that must be absorbed by the body to cause poisoning is relatively small: Don't expect high levels in urinary excretion in even severe cases."

Not even an exclamation point, I noticed. It seemed to me that when someone was writing about severe arsenic poisoning, one should use an exclamation point.

And the cure? Fresh air, if it was acute. Intravenous fluids, to keep the urine as dilute as possible. Perhaps sodium bicarbonate to keep the urine alkaline.

Be sure, meanwhile, to watch for renal failure.

Other treatments? Hemodialysis, whatever that was. And a drug called dimercaprol, though it only worked a small percentage of the time.

I pulled my hands from the keyboard and rested them in my lap. I tried to remind myself that nothing on the Internet was gospel, that the Web was—in addition to everything else—the world's greatest source of misinformation. How could it not be when any eleven-year-old who was proud of his little paper on Quito could post it on the Net as a resource on Ecuador?

Still, this looked bad. I didn't imagine I was as frightened as I'd be if a plane I was aboard was about to auger into a mountain near Denver, but this sure as hell didn't look good. I wondered if I should go to the hospital. By now Abby had her suitcase all packed with her toys, and could entertain herself on the floor of the E.R. while the doctors took care of her dad.

Unfortunately, I didn't have the slightest idea what I'd say to those doctors. Would they think to check for arsenic poisoning if I didn't tell them I was pretty damn sure that was the problem? Probably not. This wasn't the Middle Ages, after all, and I wasn't a pope.

And I certainly couldn't tell them what had really occurred. At least I didn't think I could. I tried making up a story that would get me to arsenic poisoning, but there just didn't seem to be any route there but the truth.

So you see, I swiped a bottle of her arsenic while we were doctoring her notes so she wouldn't be charged with a crime or lose her whole world in a civil suit. And I figured the stuff was completely harmless—well, I guess I knew it wasn't completely harmless, because it sure as shit gave me a rush the first time I took it, but I guess I assumed it wasn't toxic. Just a really good drug—but not exactly a drug, of course. I'm not like the little shits I prosecute, you know: creepy little turds like Teddy Paquette. I'm not like him. Oh, no.

I wished I were friends with a doctor. Really good friends. Close enough that my friend the physician would swipe a hemodialysis machine for me. Or that dimercaprol stuff. But I wasn't. The only doctors I knew were the doctors who actually treated me, or the doctors I'd met as a prosecutor: the physicians who'd testify on behalf of the State, explaining what the wounds meant in the photos of battered women, beaten children, bruised and hammered junkies and dealers and whores.

Probably my only real friend who'd gone to medical school was the State Medical Examiner, Steve Wagner, and Steve made it clear whenever we talked about good health and well-being that he spent most of his time with bodies sadly lacking in vitality. "I don't even play a doctor on TV," he'd said once when I asked his advice.

Besides, I didn't want to bother Steve at his home on a Friday night. Usually I only did that when someone had died, and I sure as hell hoped we weren't about to reach that point.

No, the closest thing I had to a good friend who happened to be a healer was my homeopath. Former homeopath. Current co-conspirator. I had no idea if she'd have any suggestions or antidotes, but here was clearly one more reason why I had to see her: Perhaps she could undo what I had done.

✧

It was really only a week of my life. Six days, arguably.

I suppose I should be grateful. I've prosecuted criminals whose sprees lasted far longer. I've certainly prosecuted criminals whose crimes were far worse.

Afterward, for a time I played a game in my mind that was briefly made famous by a substance abuse counselor from Oklahoma. The game, "What if, then what?," makes some people feel better. It opens some people's eyes to life's possibilities. Usually I'd play it when I was alone in my truck, or when I was alone in my bed and unable to sleep. For me, it would go something like this:

What if I'd told Carissa the night after Christmas when she'd come to my house that I absolutely could not help her? Then what?

Then she would have left.

And we would not have doctored her notes.

And she would not have felt even worse than she did. She would not have felt like a criminal.

And I would not have swiped a vial of arsenic.

And she would have gotten a good lawyer.

And, after an investigation, the case would—at the very least—have gone to a grand jury.

And the grand jury might or might not have recommended prosecution.

And, either way, there would have been a civil suit.

And either Carissa would have settled. Or not.

And so there might have been as many as two trials. Or as few as none.

And Richard Emmons would still have been posturing in his bed in the ICU in those days before New Year's.

Would I have lost Carissa?

I could never decide. But when I think back on that Tuesday night in my house, I see Carissa standing to leave not because I will not help her, but because she fears that I doubt her. The difference is a chasm.

And so if I would have lost Carissa, I would have lost her for other reasons. Because she could not invest emotional capital in a new relationship when the State was about to begin prosecuting her. Because one of her patients had misunderstood what she had said and was now in a coma. Because, perhaps, she simply didn't love me, and we were no longer linked by a crime.

Sometimes I would tell myself that I did what I did—the notes, the arsenic, the lies—because my wife had died. Because my wife had died and I was raising a little girl on my own. Because, after two and a half years, I was simply exhausted.

But this is a pretty tawdry justification, a pretty slippery bit of rationalization. It excuses nothing.

And so the game never once made me feel better.

✧

Nora Woodson answered the front door and gave Abby and me each a huge hug. Nora was somewhere in her mid-sixties, but I thought she still had more energy than I'd ever had in my life. She was the choir director, she ran the church women's circle, and she volunteered three or four days

a month in Burlington, helping the state resettle the steady stream of Bos-
nian and Croatian refugees who made their way first to the United States and
then to Vermont. Sometimes the deep lines in her face made her look even
older than sixty-five or sixty-six, but the wrinkles hadn't diminished her stam-
ina. She was relentless, a deceptively tiny woman with eyeglasses that covered
half her face and a fine soprano voice that was only now starting to show its
age.

Once Abby had climbed out of her coat and her boots, she started unpack-
ing her tiny red suitcase. She showed Nora the T-shirts and troll underpants
she had brought, and Nora pointed upstairs.

"They're asleep on our bed," she said, referring to the cats. "First bedroom on the left."

Abby looked at me to make sure it was okay to disappear, and then ran up
the steps with her handful of clothes.

"Leland, you look like you've got quite a…I don't know, something,"
Nora said to me when Abby was out of sight. "I'd say a cold, but you don't look
coldy."

I smiled and shrugged. "Maybe I have a bug. But I feel pretty good," I lied.

"I got my flu shot in the fall. So do your worst."

I handed her the coffee and chocolates as she led me into the living room,
and there I saw Paul, as well as my friends Howard and Anne Lansing. The
group was standing before the woodstove.

"I hear I just missed you at the hospital," Paul said.

"You were there?" I wasn't sure why, but the fact that Paul had just been
there unnerved me. It shouldn't have. Paul was, after all, a minister, and hospital visits were a part of the job description. Still, it seemed to be further
proof that events were linked in ways I did not comprehend, that people knew
far more than I realized.

"I was. Maybe if you'd gotten there a little later or I'd gotten there a little sooner, we might have bumped into each other in the ICU."

"Could have happened," I murmured.

"I didn't know you knew them," Anne said to me.

I tried to smile. Howard and Anne were both schoolteachers. They had
two boys in elementary school, one who I thought might be as old as ten.
"Only a bit," I said.

"Oh, I get it, you were there professionally. You're going to prosecute,"
Howard said. "There's a case against our local homeopath."

"Now, that would be tricky. Aren't you and Carissa friends?" Paul asked me, and then took a sip from the mug of hot cider in his hands.

"I know her," I said.

"If I remember correctly, you introduced us Christmas Eve," he said.

"I did."

"So your visit wasn't professional," Howard observed.

I shook my head. "Nope. Just moral support."

"What can I get you?" Nora asked me, and I wanted to answer a tranquilizer. But I restrained myself and asked for hot cider instead.

"And a glass of water," I added, figuring I should be doing all I could to keep my urine dilute.

"We don't know Carissa very well, but we like her brother and sister-in-law. And we think the world of her niece," Anne said.

"Whitney?"

"Whitney," she repeated. "Until she went off to college, she was our number-one baby-sitter. The boys love her."

"Colgate, right?"

"Yup. She was going to sit with them tonight, as a matter of fact, but then had to cancel."

"She hadn't planned on going back to school for another two weeks," Howard explained, "but apparently she changed her mind. She's going back tomorrow instead."

"Really?"

"Yup. Her aunt's driving her."

"Carissa?"

"Uh-huh. Whitney says they're leaving at the crack of dawn."

"Tomorrow? Carissa's leaving tomorrow?"

"Carissa and *Whitney*," he answered, emphasizing the younger woman's name.

"Oh," I said, aware that the sound had come out like an agonized grunt. Like I'd just been hit hard in the stomach. All I'd meant to say was, *Oh, how nice*, but somehow I'd never gotten as far as the second part. I was starting to feel sick once again, and it was coming on fast: a nor'easter blowing hard and swift into my stomach, the storm triggered by the realization that Carissa was going to flee. I was sure of it. This was not just arsenic-inspired paranoia, a poison-induced panic: This was the sort of incomprehensible but often life-saving intuition that's triggered by adrenaline, hormones, and fear.

Carissa was going to leave. She was going to drop off Whitney in upstate New York and then continue on to Toronto. Or Ottawa. And then get on an airplane and fly...

Anywhere.

Paris, maybe. Perhaps someplace she had found where there was no reciprocity with the U.S. No extradition.

"Leland?"

The timing was perfect. Colgate was far enough away that everyone would expect her to spend the night in New York and drive home the day after that. No one would expect her home until Sunday night. And so no one would expect to see her until Monday morning. New Year's Day.

By then she could have been flying for thirty-six hours. Since Saturday night. And one can fly far in a day and a half.

Quickly I sat down on the arm of the couch. This time I'm really going to puke, I thought. I'm about to be sick all over Paul and Nora's beautiful living-room furniture.

"Leland, you're getting pale! Do you want some water?" It was Howard's voice, and I knew the man was right beside me, leaning over me, but the fellow still sounded like he was talking to me through a pillow. I stared down at the carpet—Was that an Oriental rug I was about to ruin?—and tried to breathe in deeply and slowly.

"Get him some water," Anne said.

I put my head between my knees and reached for my feet. There was that tingling. There were those splinters.

"I'm fine," I mumbled. "I'm fine."

Somewhere nearby were a woman's feet in blue pumps, and I could sense Howard backing away. Then before me were a woman's shins and her dress, and I saw Nora putting my mug down on the coffee table and kneeling beside me.

"Leland, do you want us to call a doctor?" she asked, her lips almost in my ear.

"No, Nora, please don't. I just need a minute," I said quietly.

"Do you want to go upstairs and lie down? We'll entertain Abby."

I did, but I wasn't sure my feet would function. The tingling seemed so bad, it was like both of my feet had fallen asleep. And so I shook my head and tried to focus upon nothing but the argyle swirls on my socks.

"He really didn't look well when he arrived," Nora was saying to someone, and I imagined Paul nodding and adding, *He hasn't looked well for days. You should have seen him the other night by the pay phone in town. In the storm. Looked awful. Just awful!*

"Flu?" Paul asked his wife.

"Maybe," she said, and I saw her legs disappear as she stood, taking a step back to give me some air.

"It's going around. Apparently, half the doctors and nurses up at the hospital have it."

Oh, but I've been taking echinacea, I wanted to say. *As a matter of fact, I've been taking echinacea with goldenseal. And I've been in the care of a homeopath. A wonderful homeopath. You all know her. So how could I possibly have come down with the flu?*

"I'm sure school will be half-empty next week," Howard said.

"I was up visiting Eleanor Atkins this morning, and she's not doing well at all. Her spirits are failing, too."

"She must be eighty-five, eighty-six years old?"

"About that."

I breathed in through my nose, a stream of calm, steady breaths, and with as much relief as I'd ever felt in my life understood the nausea was starting to subside. I looked up and saw Anne smiling down at me with pity and love in her eyes—What a teacher she must be!—and Howard sipping his coffee cup of hot cider.

"How are you doing?" Anne asked.

"Better."

"I think the color's coming back to your cheeks," she said, and I tried to offer back a small smile.

Nora scurried over to me. "Are you sure you wouldn't like to go upstairs for a few minutes?"

"I think I'm going to be okay."

"You're positive?"

"I'm positive. Maybe it was something I ate at lunch."

"Well, my feelings won't be hurt if you don't touch a thing tonight."

I stretched my legs, hoping the tingling had disappeared enough that I could stand, and stifled a yawn. I had no idea what nausea and yawning had to do with each other, but I'd noticed in the last few days that they seemed to be somehow related.

"I don't think it's possible to sit down at your table and not eat everything," I said. "But I'll be careful. I won't overdo it."

"Let's make it an early evening, and get you and Abby home soon," Nora said. "I think dinner's ready and I can start serving. Paul, can you help me?"

"Let me lend a hand, too," Anne said, and suddenly, I realized, I was left alone with Howard.

"That was quite a scare you gave us," he said.

"Sorry about that."

"Don't be sorry. It happens."

"It does."

"I guess you didn't know she was leaving." Howard's face was a blank, completely unreadable.

"Guess not."

He wasn't smiling or frowning; there certainly wasn't a hint of judgment. But it was a signal between us that he knew. Everyone knew. Not everything, not by a long shot. But something.

"How long have you known her?" he asked.

"Not long."

"You two have plans for tomorrow?"

"Not really," I said, rising slowly from the arm of the couch. "Well. I should probably go find my daughter."

He nodded. Poor Leland, I imagined him thinking. Wrong woman. Wrong time.

20

NUMBER 93

Anything shameful that has precipitated the disease...the physician should try to uncover.

D R . S A M U E L H A H N E M A N N ,
O r g a n o n o f M e d i c i n e , 1 8 4 2

I decided during dinner that I would go and see her that night. Anne was playing on the floor with my daughter, and Nora was bringing out coffee and pie, and the plan grew real in my mind: I would stay at the Woodsons' until Abby had fallen into a deep sleep, and then I would bundle her up and carry her to the truck, and together we would drive into the village. Abby, I knew, would sleep through it all.

It was almost nine-thirty before Abby curled up on Paul and Nora's living-room couch and nodded off, and so it was well past ten before I went to the truck to turn on the heater. It was ten-thirty before I had said my good-byes and sat Abby upon my lap—a rag doll without a spine that bobbed, eyes closed, as I pulled the sleeves of her coat over her arms and slipped her feet into her snow boots—and thanked Nora and Paul one last time.

Somehow, it was nearing eleven o'clock by the time I lifted my sleeping daughter from her booster seat and carried her to Carissa's front door.

Though it was late, I'd parked my truck at the rear of her driveway, part-way into a snowdrift that marked the beginning of her backyard: You could see the truck from the street if you bothered to look, but you'd have to crane your head and stare.

When I got to the front door, I paused for a moment before ringing the bell. I had expected she'd still be awake, packing, but there were no lights on. My plan did not include waking her up.

No matter, not now. And so I rang the bell and waited, and then rang it once more. I was beginning to fear that she had somehow convinced Whitney to leave that very night, when she pulled open the door.

It had only been two and a half days since I last saw her, but she looked as if she'd been battling illness for months. For a moment I thought it was merely the fact that I had woken her: Her hair had been puffed out by her pillows as she'd slept, and she had wrapped a tired-looking shawl around her nightgown. But there was more to it than that. There were dark bags under her eyes, and that round, girlish face had grown thin. She looked pale.

She motioned me inside without flipping on the hall light, and then lifted my little girl from my arms.

"God, she's out like a light," she whispered as she carried her into the living room and unzipped her coat. For a moment I watched from the hallway, trying to decide whether I should take off my boots. I wondered if I gazed into the kitchen or the dining room—my eyes straining in the dark—whether I would see suitcases.

When she returned to the hallway, she took my hands in hers and told me they were ice-cold. "Have you ever tried gloves?" she asked.

"They're in the truck. I thought the truck was warm."

Her face was a drowsy mask. I kissed her lightly on the lips, and she pulled me to the stairs. As we sat down she said, "You need to take better care of yourself."

"I know."

"You have Abby to think of."

"And you," I said.

She was sitting a step below me, and she rested her head on my leg. I realized I still had my overcoat on.

"I'm glad you're here," she murmured.

"Me, too."

"Someone will see your truck, you know."

"I'm parked in the back."

"Still…"

"I know."

"I'll be gone tomorrow," she said.

"I heard."

"How?"

"I saw Howard and Anne Lansing tonight. It was a little dinner party. Whitney was supposed to baby-sit for them."

"I'm not coming back until Sunday," she said.

When she was gone, I knew, I would try not to think of her. But I would. I would think of her all the time. The more, in fact, that I tried not to think about her, the more I would find reasons to recall what her body lotion had smelled like. Or the way she would toy with her eyeglasses. Or sit in her chair with her feet curled beneath her.

And then, suddenly, I'd stop. There would be times when I'd recall her, moments when she would return to me. There would be images and events that would bring her back as an almost tangible presence. But I would stop consciously reminiscing. Obsessing.

This was, after all, exactly what had happened after Elizabeth died. At some point after the first anniversary of the accident, I began going whole mornings or afternoons without once recalling the woman I know for a fact I had loved. It is possible that if I had not had photos of her by my bed, I might have gone a whole day now and then.

"Really? Sunday?"

"It's a long drive," she said.

"But you're getting an early start."

"Still. It's a haul."

I wanted to tell her not to go, but I wanted to make sure I could say it without desperation or panic in my voice. I wanted to be sure my voice wouldn't break.

"This is awful sudden," I said simply.

"It is. I don't honestly know whether it was my idea or Whitney's. We were talking about when she should leave, and one of us just decided that we might as well go now."

All this time her head was against my leg. I stroked her hair and asked, "Will you really be back on Sunday?"

She was quiet, and I saw her shoulders rise in either a sigh or a shrug. I couldn't tell.

"Promise me you will," I said.

"No."

The syllable was long but airy. In my head I heard myself whisper, *Please*.

"Where will you go?" I asked.

"You know I'm going to Colgate. Hamilton, New York."

"And then?" I ran the tips of my fingers in circles along her temple, occasionally sliding them gently behind her ear. When she didn't answer, I asked again.

"I don't know," she murmured.

"Home to Bartlett," I said.

She rested one of her hands on my knee and allowed herself a tiny purr. "That sounds nice," she said, as if she were imagining fresh strawberries in December: impossible, but nice to conceive.

"I went to the hospital today. I saw Richard."

"Tell me about it," she said.

And so I told her about my visit, and that I thought the worst would soon be over for Jennifer. Her husband would die, and she would begin to heal. I told Carissa that Jennifer seemed to have a wonderful family and that the children would be fine.

"And Jennifer?"

One moment she was cupping my knee in her hand, and the next I could scarcely feel her fingers at all. "Jennifer will be okay. She will. And she no longer blames you, you know. Not at all."

"She's being kind."

"She's being realistic. Honest. She understands it wasn't your fault."

"I don't believe that."

"That Jennifer doesn't blame you?"

"That it wasn't my fault...."

"No, Carissa, it wasn't. It just wasn't. If you feel that way, it's because of me. It's because I had us doctor the notes, it's because—"

"Us?" she said, sitting up and pulling away from me. "You didn't tell him to eat cashews! You didn't give him the idea that his drugs were an antidote to his cure!"

"No. But I—"

"Leland. No. Please stop." She stood up and shuffled toward the living room, and gazed in at my daughter on the couch. She watched her for a long moment and then returned to the hallway. She pulled her shawl tightly around her and leaned against the front door.

"I'd tell your lawyer friends in your office everything if you didn't have Abby," she said. "I really would. I'd tell them everything."

"Would that make you feel better?"

"Except for what would happen to Abby? I think so. This afternoon I thought I might allow myself one more lie: I'd tell them about the notes, and what I said in the store. But I wouldn't tell them you had anything to do with it. I'd say doctoring the notes was all my idea, and I did it all by myself. But that would still put you in a horrible place."

"I'd come forward."

"I know that. You're not the type who could watch me go it alone."

"No. I couldn't."

She smiled at me and shook her head. "What will you do tomorrow? After I've gone?"

"Oh, maybe I'll look at a map on the computer. Maybe I'll follow your trip. I'll tell myself you'll be back on Sunday, because that's what you've told everyone else. Maybe on New Year's Day, Abby and I will get in the truck and we'll drive into the village. I'll insist we drive down your street, so I can be reassured by the sight of your car."

"And if it's not there?"

I stood up and went to her, and pulled her against me. We rocked each other, and I imagined I was on a small boat: The waves were comforting and small, and we were together.

"Can you spend the night?" she asked, her voice so quiet that for a second I didn't understand what she'd said.

"I can."

"Abby will be okay in a bed she doesn't know?"

"I'll be sure to get up before her."

Outside a dog barked, and I wondered if at that very moment someone was walking down Carissa's street and noting a strange truck in her driveway.

No, not strange. That's a truck like Leland Fowler's. Maybe it is Leland Fowler's.

"I should tell you," I said, "that I'm sick."

"Really?"

"I mean, it's not contagious. But I did something Wednesday morning when we were together. It was stupid, but I did it."

"Go on."

"I found a vial of arsenic on your desk. And I took it."

"Do you mean you took it home? Or do you mean you ingested it?"

"The latter."

"How much?"

"All of it. Every single pill."

"A full bottle?"

"About half."

"Why?"

I shrugged, and for a moment I had a vision of one of my daughter's friends, a five-year-old boy I'd once caught peeing into her sandbox. "Why did you do that?" I'd asked him then, and he, too, had shrugged.

"It made sense when I did it," I began, and then I tried explaining what her remedy had done for me at first, and how I had felt. I told her how sure I had been that the remedy was harmless, how I'd managed to convince myself that each pill was as safe as a cough drop. I confessed that I'd been taking them one and two and even three at a time since Wednesday morning, viewing them in my head as a sort of homey-tranquilizer.

When I was done, she asked simply, "How do you feel?"

"Right this minute? Okay. A little weak, but okay. But I've had a very strange tingling in my fingers and hands, and my stomach's been a little off."

"Diarrhea?"

"A bit."

"Well. This might be one for the lecture circuit."

"Am I…sick?"

She pushed off my chest and looked at me. "It was homeopathic arsenic. Health-food store arsenic. Five dollars a vial. You're going to live."

"Have I poisoned myself?"

"A conventional doctor would tell you no. He'd tell you it's all in your head."

"Mind-body hokum?"

She nodded. "Or perhaps a virus. He might believe you'd caught a virus—coincidentally."

"What do you think?"

"I think you shouldn't be swiping arsenic."

"Can you help me?" I asked, and she patted my shoulders through my coat.

"No one can help you, Leland. You're hopeless. Absolutely and completely hopeless."

❖

She did help me, of course. She made me drink glasses and glasses of water with lime juice in it, and then she gave me the homeopathic cure called Carbo vegetabilis: wood charcoal. Arsenic and charcoal, Hahnemann had observed, are antidotes of each other.

And then I took a shower and cleaned myself up while Carissa got Abby settled in the bedroom next to hers.

The next morning I was up at five-thirty, and Abby and I were gone fifteen minutes later. The two of us had breakfast together at the diner in town: Though it wasn't supposed to open until six A.M., the cook had mercy on the father and daughter who showed up at the front glass door a few minutes early.

"Can we have a sleepover at her house again someday?" Abby asked as the waitress, a woman old enough to be Abby's grandmother, brought us our pancakes.

"Did you have a slumber party at a friend's house?" the waitress asked her, smiling at the image, perhaps, of two little girls in a bed full of teddy bears.

"No, it was at my daddy's friend's house," Abby explained, and I looked out the window at the streetlights.

A few minutes after that, we went home.

By mid-morning, the sugar from the maple syrup had worked its way through Abby's system, and we each decided we'd take a nap until lunch. We'd been up early.

By then, I guessed, Carissa and Whitney had almost reached Albany. Perhaps they were already heading west on I-90.

I think, looking back, that I had come a long way since the night before at the Woodsons'. I think I'd managed to convince myself that Carissa really was planning to return.

21

NUMBER 17

It is possible to create a very grave disease by acting on the vital principle through the power of imagination and to cure it in the same way.

DR. SAMUEL HAHNEMANN,
Organon of Medicine, 1842

Early Sunday afternoon, Abby sat forward on the living-room floor and picked a Candy Land card from the pile.

"I hope I get a person," she said, and she allowed herself a small squeal when she saw she had chosen Queen Frostine, the confectionery monarch. This bit of good fortune was going to place her at least fifteen spaces ahead of me.

I gazed at the Christmas tree behind her. I hadn't remembered to water it in days, but it still looked pretty good. Granted, it was drenched in afternoon sun. But it was still hanging on to its needles as if it were standing in the woods in the middle of April, its roots sopping up the last of the snow while its branches stretched high into that long-awaited spring sky.

We put the pillows from the couch right there, I remembered as I looked at the spot on the rug where Carissa and I had made love Christmas Eve. *There's the branch where she hung her eyeglasses. And there's the star Abby made. The Sunday-school star. Her first. And here's where I tossed Carissa's panties when I finally pulled them over her hips and down those long and wondrous legs.*

"Your turn, Daddy."

"It looks like I have a lot of catching up to do," I said.

"You sure do," she giggled.

I sipped my coffee, inhaling the aroma deep through my nose as I brought the mug to my lips. It was high-test, dark brown pond water that tasted delicious. It was, I realized, the first coffee I'd had in close to a month.

"Well, that doesn't do me much good, does it?" I said when I saw my card was going to move me forward exactly one space, and I tossed it onto the game board in mock aggravation.

"I think I'm going to win," Abby said.

"I think you are."

I stretched my legs and wiggled my toes in my socks. Still no tingles. And none in the palms of my hands. They'd been gone now more than a day.

"Two reds," she said, and moved even closer to reaching the Kandy King in the Candy Castle.

I glanced at my watch: It was close to one o'clock. Any moment now, Abby's friend Greta and Greta's mom would be stopping by to pick Abby up. The two girls were going to another little friend's birthday party at the sort of indoor family entertainment center in which the acoustics and the video games and the token-fed race cars all conspire to trample the hair cells in the human ear, and guarantee a noise-induced hearing loss by the first grade.

While she was at the party, I planned on visiting Richard and Jennifer Emmons at the hospital. On my way home, I'd drive by Carissa's house. With any luck, I'd see her car was back in the driveway.

I reached for a card and showed it to Abby. She practically howled with laughter when she saw it was Plumpy the Troll and I would have to return almost all the way back to square one.

✧

It was after two by the time I got to the hospital, and the winter sun was already falling toward the Adirondacks. As I walked from the parking garage to the main entrance, I experienced what any other day I might have called a mere shift in the weather. A storm was coming. Or a warm front and a thaw. But not that moment. That moment when I felt the world around me fill with moist and mild eddies of air, I didn't think weather. I thought Richard. I took as deep a breath as I could—*Be happy in heaven…*—and imagined Jennifer was beside her husband when the whoosh of air that was Richard began its ascent from its shell.

I hoped I wasn't wrong about Jennifer. For a moment I feared she might have stepped away to get a bite to eat. Maybe she was downstairs in the hospital cafeteria when Richard had died, and he'd passed away with only an ICU resident or nurse for company. It was possible.

But I decided it wasn't likely. Jennifer was diligent about her vigil. She would be there when he died.

Moreover, people, whenever they could, died with a decency that was angelic. They waited. Even Elizabeth had managed to hang on until I'd been notified of the accident—no easy task since I'd been at a deposition across the lake in Plattsburgh—and had returned across the water to Burlington. I hadn't been in the room with her when she'd died, of course, since she'd died on an operating room table. But I had been at the hospital. This hospital. I'd sat for over ninety minutes in a chair with an orange Naugahyde seat, standing every so often to make a phone call:

"Hi, Kelly? It's Leland. Elizabeth won't be getting Abby today, and I think I'm going to be a bit late...."

No, if Jennifer had for some reason stepped away, then Richard was still hanging by a thread somewhere inside a torso and limbs that by Friday had forgotten how to respond to a knuckle or prod.

When I reached the entrance, I stepped through the automatic doors and into the hospital lobby. I passed the reception desk and the gift shop, the rest rooms and the long corridors to the mysterious places I hoped I'd never visit. I passed the cafeteria, and I was relieved that Jennifer was not there among the clusters of squat tables.

When I got to the elevator bank I was the only one waiting, and I rode the elevator to the fourth floor alone.

I saw instantly that I'd been right: The swirl I'd felt outside had been Richard. I couldn't see Richard himself, but I could tell by the crowd in the room, and by the fact that the nurses were keeping their distance behind the counter that formed the ICU's station.

"You were here Friday afternoon, weren't you?" asked one of the nurses, a fellow with an immaculate blond mustache and tiny glasses that didn't hide the inky circles under his eyes.

"I guess you were, too," I said.

"You related?" he asked, and motioned toward the cubicle in which Richard's family had gathered. Jennifer was sitting up on the bed, her hands in fists against her mouth, a tissue balled up in one. A girl barely a teen and a boy even younger stood with their backs against the wall with the window facing north. Two other adults were clinging to each other like a couple: No doubt the woman was Bonnie, Jennifer's sister, and the fellow was her brother-in-law.

Only the teen girl—Kate, I believed, was her name—was crying. Her shoulders were bobbing against the glass.

"No. Not related."

"Friend?"

"Neighbor."

"The family's been great. I see a lot of families just go fucking nuts when they have to go through this— Forgive me, I was supposed to be off today, and it's been a long shift."

"Jennifer's very strong."

I gazed at the cubicles on either side of Richard's, and at the rows of glass rooms that extended in a line along the wall. The very old in them probably would die. But what of the ones Richard's age? Were they likely to get better, move to an HMO-sanctioned hospital double, and then go home? Or were the odds against them, too, once they wound up in here? Unlike the surgical ICU one floor below, the people here had not just endured major surgery—coronary bypasses and organ transplants, colostomies and hip replacements; they'd come here because their bodies were tanking and there wasn't a damn thing surgery could do. It was stopgap medicine: Intensive, most certainly, but it wasn't the knife that had brought them together. Rather, it was the litany of ways the body can fail on its own, or be felled by the world through which it moves: Cancer in some cases. Car accidents in others. Cashews in at least one.

"You want me to give her a signal you're here?" the nurse asked me.

"Thank you, but you don't have to. I'll wander over in a couple of minutes," I said.

"Sure."

"Richard never had a chance, did he?"

The nurse was picking up a clipboard, and he bounced it softly along the counter while he thought about his response.

"He did, maybe," he said finally. "Slim, of course. But maybe if there'd been a way to prevent herniation…"

"Herniation?"

"Swelling. The brain doesn't have a lot of room to move when it starts to swell."

I nodded. I tried to push from my own mind an image of the brain trying to press through the cracks in the skull, failing, and then oozing like Jell-O through the base.

"So, you live near them?" the fellow asked.

"I do."

"I like Bartlett. East Bartlett, actually. You know, up in the hills? I really don't get to the village much. But I love to go cross-country skiing up in those hills."

"That's where I live—East Bartlett. Up in those hills."

I saw Jennifer glance at the nursing station. Wide blue eyes with a good dose of red. Clearly she was surprised to see me, and for a long moment we stared at each other.

We're two people from the mountains who didn't really know each other back in Bartlett, I thought. But here in this foreign country? This depressing world of ventilators and monitors and tubes, which isn't at all like back home? How wonderful it is to see a friend's face! To run into each other...here!

I started toward the room and saw everyone else in the cubicle note my imminent presence at once. None of them had the slightest clue who I was, and only Kate—though sniffling and wiping her eyes with the sleeve of her sweater—seemed to have observed that her mother knew this strange man in the navy blue overcoat. And so she went to Jennifer, pushing her way between her aunt and her uncle, and then stood beside her mother on the side of the thin bed closest to the door.

"I'm sorry," I murmured when I was inside the glass sarcophagus with them, and Jennifer surprised me by nodding and standing, and wrapping her arms around my back as I embraced her. No pugilist's pose this time: no fingers in fists, no arms curled in defense. Her fingers on my spine gave me the chills, despite the buffer of a wool coat, a sweater, and a turtleneck shirt.

"Thank you," she said, and I knew exactly what she meant.

"Shhhhh," I whispered as softly as I could, rocking her just the tiniest bit. "Shhhhh."

I looked over her shoulder at Richard and found myself marveling at how much he had changed since Friday. He was no longer merely a small, sleeping man with a silver circle embedded into his forehead. His skin had gone from pale to the gray of cigarette ash, and his face had fallen slack. I knew from my own parents' deaths that the transformation had occurred almost instantly, with silent but seismic force: One minute he was dozing, the next he was dead.

I decided he had probably been handsome before this happened, and he might be again if they would only remove that metal disk and replace the hair that had been shaved from the sides of his skull.

Surely they'd make him handsome, more or less, for the funeral.

When we pulled apart, Jennifer turned to her family and addressed her children by name. "Kate, Timmy: This is Leland Fowler. He's a member of the church we go to sometimes, and he's a lawyer for—what is your title? I just realized, I don't even know...."

"Chief deputy state's attorney for Chittenden County. I'm a prosecutor," I said, trying to direct my answer to everyone in the room.

The children looked at me suspiciously, but it was clear instantly that Bonnie and her husband were pleased I was there. In their eyes, I realized, I was suddenly both an emissary from the local country parish and the legal equivalent of the cavalry.

Bonnie's husband extended his hand to me across the bed—over Richard's bare knees—and said, "Hank Marshall. This is my wife, Bonnie."

I noticed as I shook Hank's hand that a respirator mask no longer covered Richard's mouth and nose, and the machine had been shut off. I wondered when Jennifer had given them permission to pull the plug. Had it been as recently as when I was playing Candy Land with Abby? When I was driving here in my truck? It had probably been before that. She'd had plenty of time over the last two or three days to decide what to do when this eventuality came.

I watched her sit back down on the bed beside her husband and take one of his hands in hers. She stroked his palm with her fingers and stared into his face.

"You want some more time alone with him, Jen?" Bonnie asked quietly.

Jennifer looked up at the people around the bed and then focused on her sister. Her lips were curled into her teeth, and she nodded.

✧

I chatted with Hank and Bonnie Marshall for a few minutes in the waiting room and learned the details of Richard's last hours. He had passed away no more than fifteen minutes before I arrived, but he had been brain-dead since early morning. Jennifer had not seemed surprised when she was told, and she'd remained calm for the children.

Someone had left the double doors into the ICU open, and I could see a corner of the nurses' station. When I saw the nurse with the massive circles under his eyes glancing toward Richard's room, it dawned on me that Jennifer might emerge at any moment. After all, she'd been saying good-bye to Richard for days now, and perhaps needed only a few minutes more once the body had grown cold.

What had I said, I wondered, to the surgeon who told me that Elizabeth had died? And then I remembered: The surgeon didn't say a thing. Technically he didn't say a word. The fellow just pushed through the double doors into the room where I was sitting and shook his head. *No, she didn't make it,* he meant. *She didn't make it, she's gone.*

And I nodded. I might even have mumbled, "Thank you. Thank you for trying."

If I said anything, that's what I said.

Soon after that, I walked into a world that was alien and eccentric and impossibly hard.

And then I met Carissa, and for a few days—no, a month; I couldn't lose sight of the pleasure I'd gotten from merely being her patient—it had once more grown familiar. Sunny. Easy.

Jennifer, I realized, was about to wander like a sleepwalker into my world. The world of the widowed with children. She would emerge from Richard's room, and everything would be quiet. There might be a faint ringing in her ears. A gauzy veil before her eyes. A curtain. A fog.

But at first the world would indeed seem oddly serene. Almost tranquil.

Later that afternoon I would have a cup of coffee with Jennifer in the cafeteria downstairs. Her sister and brother-in-law had taken the children somewhere, as if they thought Jennifer and I should be alone. The couple had still not disabused themselves of the notion that I was some kind of legal white knight.

There Jennifer told me fresh stories about Richard, and his history with his homeopath.

Over the next three days I would see her twice more, including the time we would spend together after Richard's funeral, and she would continue to tell me about her husband's asthma and his eczema and his growing discomfort with drugs. I, in turn, would tell her what the world was like when you were widowed and young.

It's clear she thought we would be friends in that new world.

It's less clear what I thought.

But I think I believed I was helping her.

22

HAHNEMANN'S PREFACE TO THE FIRST EDITION

If I did not know for what purpose I was put here on earth—to become better myself as far as possible and to make better everything around me, that is within my power to improve—I should have to consider myself as lacking very much.

DR. SAMUEL HAHNEMANN,
The Chronic Diseases, 1839

Carissa's car wasn't there when I drove by her home late Sunday afternoon, nor was it there Monday morning.

I wondered Monday evening whether anyone else knew she was gone.

"Did Mommy know Carissa?" Abby asked me that night over dinner, and I told her she hadn't.

"Oh," Abby said.

"Why?"

"I was just wondering," she said, and then informed me that for a while she would like to be called Abigail instead of Abby. She wanted to see how it felt to have a more grown-up-sounding name.

✧

Vermont may have a streak of cussedness in its soul, a bit of the curmudgeon in its spirit. But it can also be very humane.

You may lose your house if a civil judgment against you is enforced, but you will not be left destitute. Among the items that Vermont statute ensures a debtor may retain are:

- A wedding ring
- A cooking stove
- A sewing machine
- Ten cords of firewood
- A cow
- Two goats
- Ten sheep
- Ten chickens
- Enough feed to keep the animals through one winter
- Ten swarms of bees
- One yoke of oxen or steers
- Two chains, two halters, a pair of harnesses
- A plow and a yoke.

There is yet more. Alimony and Social Security benefits, for example, are protected. So is a percentage from the sale of the crops you've grown on your farm.

The statute is designed to ensure that after bankruptcy and loss, a debtor will still have sufficient property remaining to make a "fresh start."

By Tuesday morning, most people knew that Carissa had left. I detoured by her house on my way to work, but her car wasn't there. There had been a dusting of snow on Monday, however, and there were tire tracks in the powder in her driveway.

Driven more by curiosity than hope, I lined up those tracks with the wheels of my own truck and saw they were roughly as wide. They hadn't been made by Carissa's little Audi. They'd been made by someone who drove a pickup. Perhaps Carissa's brother—Whitney's dad.

And when I returned from court around eleven-thirty, Margaret told me that Phil had been on the phone that morning with Becky McNeil and Jennifer Emmons. I wondered if Becky and Phil were striking a deal, and I would miss Richard's funeral on Wednesday because it would conflict with my own arraignment.

But my name never even came up in Becky and Phil's discussion. Or in the conversation Phil had with Jennifer. I know, because I asked Jennifer and Becky the next day.

Instead, the widow and the lawyers were discussing the power of attorney Carissa had left behind with her lawyer. With Becky. Carissa wanted most of her assets—including her home and all that was there—liquidated, and the ensuing capital turned over to Jennifer Emmons. In return, she merely wanted Jennifer to accept the bounty, such as it was, and agree not to pursue any claims against her.

I am sure it was Becky who insisted upon that last part.

There were other, small details: Carissa hadn't any oxen or bees, but there were some investments and a bank account that she was hoping to keep. Not a lot. But enough to help her resume her life somewhere.

And she'd left behind a letter that Becky was to mail to her patients, informing them that she had closed her practice, but homeopaths in Montpelier and Burlington had offered to expand theirs to include them.

The funeral was held midday at my little church in East Bartlett. Phil and I drove there together, and the only time we spoke of Carissa or Richard or Jennifer Emmons was when Phil told me he had no intention of spending any more taxpayer dollars on the likes of that homeopath. She was gone, and Jennifer seemed satisfied with the settlement that had been proposed.

I introduced Phil to Paul Woodson in exactly the same spot in the narthex where I had introduced Paul to Carissa Lake.

After the funeral, I spoke with Becky, and she claimed that she hadn't a clue as to where Carissa had gone. But she told me she was pleased that Jennifer had agreed to the deal.

She also indicated that we had one small piece of business to transact: Carissa wanted Abby and me to take custody of her cat. Sepia. At the moment, Becky said, the cat was in the foster care of Whitney's parents.

That night when Abby and I picked up the animal, Whitney's mother told me she, too, had no idea where her sister-in-law was, and she insisted that her family hadn't heard from her. She asked me not to contact her daughter about Carissa, because Whitney was devastated by her aunt's disappearance.

And she said she wouldn't even venture a guess as to whether Carissa ever planned to return.

✧

For most of January and February, I checked the mail with more interest than ever before in my life, and I was calling my answering machine from work two and three times a day to see if there was a message from Carissa. There never was.

Some nights, I surfed the Internet for hours, trying to find a reference to her, or perhaps an E-mail address. I never found either.

At some point as the days began growing noticeably longer, rumors about my involvement with Carissa began to spread. As with all gossip, I doubt there was one single source, and when I thought back on December, it seemed there were whole battalions of people who could have seen Carissa and me together. Or heard my little girl mention her name.

Without ill intent, any one of those people could have started the rumors.

Sometimes those tales took on a particularly dark cast. One virtual conspiracy theory had me suppressing a criminal investigation into Richard's death. Another portrayed Carissa as a predatory lunatic bent upon her patient's destruction: She'd wanted Richard to die, and had prescribed cashews on purpose.

Sometimes the rumors were very close to the truth. One local newspaper columnist implied that I'd tampered with Carissa Lake's patient records, and that's why there'd been no action by the State's Attorneys Office. The column was barely this side of libel, and there were people around me who suggested I respond. I never did.

Eventually, Jennifer and I lost touch with each other, but there was more to it than merely benign neglect or the ordinary busyness of our lives: I heard from a variety of sources that she was saddened by the way she'd concluded I'd used her—especially that Tuesday after Christmas, when she'd first come to my office and I'd allowed her to tell me all that she knew.

Later, I heard, she'd grown mad.

Off and on that winter, my sister, Diana, tried to console me. The rumors reached her all the way in Hanover, New Hampshire, and she and her husband and the kids came for a visit one Friday and Saturday in February. Someone had told her about the walls and the ceiling in Carissa Lake's office, and she teased me that weekend that I should have steered clear of a woman with such taste.

And every few days Abby—now Abigail—would ask me whether Carissa was home yet. She still wanted, she said, to draw pictures of Madeline on the homeopath's walls.

✧

I went to Paris at the end of March. I'm not sure I expected I'd find Carissa, especially given the fact that the only French I could speak was what I had learned from a sixty-minute self-help audiotape. But certainly that was my hope.

I chose the last week of March for my hunt because the Hanover schools were closed then for spring break, and my daughter could stay with Diana, and her cousins would be home to entertain her—and she, of course, them.

My sister and brother-in-law disapproved of my trip, but mostly because they viewed it as a quixotic waste of vacation. They weren't really concerned that I'd find my homeopath.

But I brought with me a pretty good photograph I'd convinced Whitney to mail me from Colgate, as well as a photo from the newspaper. And I doubted the phone books in the City of Light would be particularly hard to use, especially if you were merely looking for a *homéopathie*.

I had never been to Paris before, but the city seemed immaculately well laid out on the maps I studied before leaving. I expected I'd visit the pharmacies in at least two arrondissements each day, and spend from five to seven P.M. on the phone with homeopathic physicians. Someone, I was sure, had met the new kid in town.

I had no idea what name that new kid would be using. But I knew I would miss *Carissa* if she had discarded it.

✧

The real problem proved to be call-backs: I'd leave messages for physicians late in the afternoon, and they'd call me back the next day while I was walking the streets with my photos. I'd return to the hotel and find I had missed a half-dozen calls.

And so on day four I started visiting doctors' offices, too. Often, they were across the street from the homeopathic pharmacies. Or above them. But it still meant that over the course of the day I'd be unable to cover completely even one accessible little neighborhood like the Marais.

Sometimes, when the homeopaths or the M.D.s could speak English, I would tell them that Carissa was my sister and she was estranged from her parents, but now her parents had died and she was a very wealthy woman.

Sometimes I said I was a lawyer and I had wonderful news for her of a personal nature, but I needed to find her to tell her.

And sometimes I simply told them the truth.

On day six, I finally visited Père Lachaise and walked among the stone tombs. Briefly I considered hiking to the top of the hillside necropolis, but it looked like a pretty good haul on the cemetery map, and I hadn't the time. Besides, I reminded myself, I already knew the view. So I merely wandered for half an hour among the crypts and sepulchers that lined the side near the metro stop. Seurat. Bizet. Jim Morrison. I saw the massive and wholly dispiriting Monument aux Morts—a long, wide statue of the dead, naked and sobbing, being led through the entryway to an afterworld that horrifies them—and then I turned back and returned to the Boulevard de Menilmontant.

There was a neon cross nearby with the words *homéopathie* and *herboristerie* upon it, and for a moment I was sure someone there would know Carissa. Briefly I imagined I'd be laughing at myself in a very few minutes, because it had taken me six days to finally get around to the neighborhood near Père Lachaise: *Of course, Carissa settled here. Of course! Wasn't it obvious?*

But the pharmacists there knew nothing about a new American homeopath, and the physicians with whom they worked hadn't heard of any recent arrivals from the U.S.

On my next to last day in Paris, I ran out of business cards. I'd brought about a hundred with me, and scribbled my home phone number and E-mail address on the back of each one. Someday Carissa might meet one of those homeopaths, and just maybe that homeopath would call me or send me an E-mail with the news. Maybe that homeopath would tell Carissa I was looking for her.

At the end of eight days, I came home. Because of those business cards, I was able to convince myself that the trip had not been a complete waste of time.

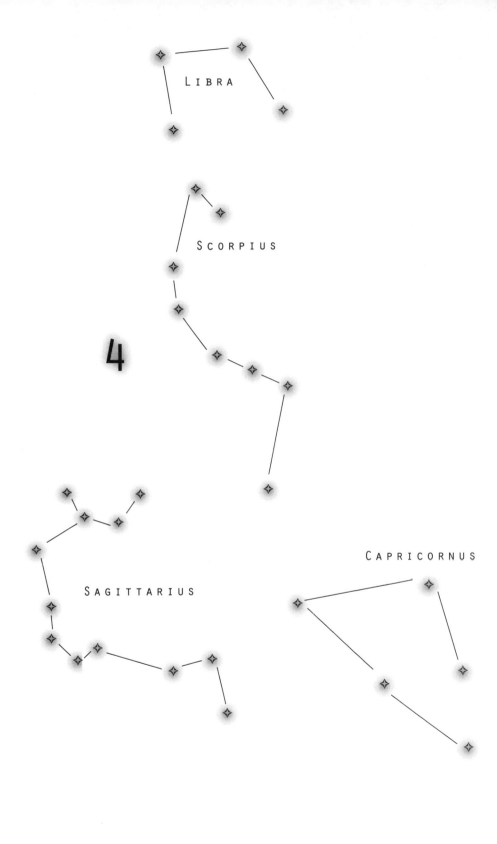

LIBRA

SCORPIUS

4

SAGITTARIUS

CAPRICORNUS

23

PHOSPHORUS

Dreams vivid, can be partly recalled.

DR. SAMUEL HAHNEMANN,
The Chronic Diseases, 1839

Some people do not believe that I know how to grieve. Probably they're right. I've never been very good at sobbing or howling or simply retreating, wordless and inert, into a shell.

But I am capable of mourning. I've been doing it for years now, and it's become second nature to me. I mourn, therefore I am.

I mourn for Elizabeth and the life that I know we once had. The specifics have grown foggy now, but not the sense that I was happy.

And I mourn for Carissa, and the what-ifs that surround the astonishingly brief time that we shared.

Recently I concocted a new and particularly punishing version of "What if, then what?"

What if I had not been so bold as to invite Carissa to my house Christmas Eve? Then what?

Then she wouldn't have been shopping for me at the health-food store.

And she would not have run into Richard.

And the subject of cashews and Rhus tox would never have come up.

And Richard might still be alive.

And Carissa might be practicing in Bartlett. Happy.

Me, too.

Though I am not, in all fairness, unhappy.

When people see Abigail and me chatting as she waits for the school bus at the end of our driveway, they see a father and daughter—he with a mug of steaming hot coffee in his hand, she with a navy blue knapsack overflowing with loose-leaf binders and Magic Markers and the software she can't wait to share with her friends—and they often see the two of us laughing. We do laugh often.

She has dance class on Monday nights, and she plays soccer two afternoons a week in the fall. When people see me watching her, they see a father as content as he is proud.

When people see my picture in the newspaper—and now that Phil has retired and I have his job, I am there often—they see a fellow nearing forty who seems awfully successful. Those rumors about me that circulated in the months after Richard died? They came and they went. Like all rumors. Rumors will always be less substantial than love, and there are a great many people in this world who love me very much.

I have now received four letters from Carissa. They are long letters she writes over days, but she only mails them when she is away from her home. Wherever that is. But I believe it is somewhere in Europe, because two of the letters were mailed from Italy, and one was postmarked in Germany. One was sent from London, where she was visiting her best friend from college.

I, of course, am unable to write back. There is never a return address.

But here is what I know of her: If my barometer for sentience is mourning, then her measure is remorse. Rightly or wrongly, she will always blame herself for Richard's death, and her letters are filled with her recollections of her last Christmas Eve in Vermont. That night, for her, has become protean: One moment she is standing at the health-food store with Richard Emmons, and the next she is lying on the floor with Leland Fowler. There she is singing, standing in a pew beside Leland and his little girl, while small flames quiver atop their three candles.

Carissa has indeed resumed practicing homeopathy, though she has not revealed where.

And she says that she thinks of me far more often than she writes.

When I line up her four letters chronologically, I convince myself that she is starting to recover.

Whitney, who has seen her aunt once, concurs. When she graduated from Colgate, they spent a week together in Paris. They stayed in a little hotel in Montparnasse, and Whitney said no one in the neighborhood seemed to know or to recognize Carissa. No one in Paris seemed to view her as anything other than the older of two American tourists.

The hotel reservation was under Carissa's name.

Whitney says she doesn't believe her aunt will ever return home, but I disagree. The fact that she writes encourages me.

And even if she never comes back to Bartlett, I believe she will come back to me. Or she will let me come to her. But she will emerge. I am confident she will emerge, and as she once—no, twice—healed me, she will let me heal her. And this time my head will be as sound as my heart, my judgment unclouded by loss.

And I will succeed.

In the meantime, I raise my daughter. I go to work. And though some days it is very hard, I try not to live for the future. And I try not to dream of the past.

ACKNOWLEDGMENTS

I could not have written *The Law of Similars* were it not for the generosity of several extraordinary people: Lauren Bowerman, State's Attorney for Chittenden County, Vermont; Edward Kent, M.D., allergy and asthma specialist; Elizabeth Macfarlane, C.C.H.; and Shaye Areheart and Dina Siciliano at Harmony Books. They gave me the great gifts of their wisdom and their time.

I used a number of books while writing this novel, some of which I found indispensable. Stephen Cummings and Dana Ullman's *Everybody's Guide to Homeopathic Medicines* and Richard Grossinger's *Homeopathy: An Introduction for Skeptics and Beginners* were consistently reliable resources. Rima Handley's thoughtful and moving history of the Hahnemanns, *A Homeopathic Love Story: The Story of Samuel and Melanie Hahnemann*, provided valuable biographic information.

The quotations from Samuel Hahnemann's *Organon of Medicine* come from the translation by Dr. Jost Kunzli, Alain Naude, and Peter Pendleton; the excerpts from *The Chronic Diseases* come from L. H. Tafel's translation.

I imposed upon a great many friends and experts to read all or part of the novel in manuscript form, including: Alicia Daniel, a naturalist and botanist with the University of Vermont; attorney Susan Gilfillan; Stephen Kiernan; Ellen Levine; Dan Manz, director of Vermont's Emergency Medical Services Division; Wayne Misselbeck, M.D.; Ken Neisser; Mike Noble, a public relations specialist with Fletcher Allen Health Care; Bill Pendlebury, M.D.; Reverend Randy Rice; and Bill Warnock, N.D.

Finally, my deepest thanks go, once again, to my wife, Victoria, a reader whose patience is endless and whose love is immense.

ABOUT THE AUTHOR

C hris Bohjalian is the author of five previous novels, including *Midwives* (which won a New England Booksellers Association "Discovery Award" in 1997 and was chosen by *Publishers Weekly* as one of the "Best Books" of the year), *Water Witches*, and *Past the Bleachers*. He lives in Lincoln, Vermont, with his wife, photographer Victoria Blewer, and their daughter, Grace.